THE
ONLY CLUE

by

Pamela Beason

Author of

THE ONLY WITNESS

Published by WildWing Press, 3301 Brandywine Ct, Bellingham, WA 98226

Printed in the United States of America

DEDICATION

This book is dedicated to all those humans who love animals.

ACKNOWLEDGEMENTS

Thank you to my wonderful critique partner Christine Myers and readers Marion Spicher, Pat Gragg, and Kirk Smith, who all helped make this a better book.

Chapter 1

Neema cowered in the corner of the pen, her back turned to the mass of people gathering behind her. She clutched eight-month-old Kanoni to her chest.

Dr. Grace McKenna totally sympathized with her gorilla. She didn't want to face the crowd, either. This was the fourth tour in as many hours. With Neema's pregnancy and Kanoni's birth, Grace had managed to put off the event for almost eighteen months, but finally the governing board at the local college had laid down an ultimatum. Her grant was still at risk, but if she refused to hold a public display, there would definitely be no more funding for her gorilla language project.

To make matters worse, Grace's associate Josh LaDyne had rushed off to Philadelphia after his father had a heart attack. She was stuck with managing the entire day. Neither she nor her apes were used to the din of calypso music blaring from the popcorn seller's cart and the shouts of excited children. Her head throbbed, Neema was headed toward a temper tantrum, and there were still a couple of hours to go.

She slipped in between the gorillas and the fence. Neema, her gaze full of reproach, hunched protectively over Kanoni, who nursed at her mother's breast with round worried eyes.

Grace placed her hands gently on the sides of Neema's massive head and pressed her forehead to the gorilla's. A low mournful sound rumbled from Neema's chest.

"I know." She kept her tone soft and low. "I know you don't want to be here. You're safe. Kanoni is safe. Just a little bit longer, and it will be over. Please stay calm. Please behave."

She leaned back and peered into Neema's cocoa-colored eyes. "Okay?" Grace made the hand signs as she spoke. "You promise to be a good gorilla, yes?"

Abruptly swinging her head upward, Neema planted a rubbery kiss on Grace's cheek. Grace smiled and quickly brushed her hand over Kanoni's head. She patted Neema on the shoulder, and then stepped away from them. As she neared the door, her gaze was stabbed with a piercing glint of sunlight from the lens of a television camera. Several student reporters and camera operators were attending her open house this afternoon, hoping their work would be chosen to air on the college's local public access station, which broadcast student-produced programs twenty-four hours a day.

Grace let herself out of the cage and turned to face the crowd pressing against the wire mesh.

"I can't see the gorillas!"

"Make him turn around!"

Grace scanned the gathering, looking for anyone who was acting strangely or was obviously sick. Her biggest worry was that a visitor would feed a gorilla a poisoned treat. Next, that an infected human would transmit a fatal disease to her apes. And third, that this event would be a disaster and the college board would cancel her funding. Their budget vote was only a week away.

"Are those monkeys real?"

"Mommyyy! Make the 'rillas talk!"

Forcing her face into a smile, she held up her hands. "Quiet, please! The gorillas aren't used to so many people."

"Hey, gorilla!" A little boy laced his fingers through the temporary fencing and shook it, clanking the steel mesh against the support poles. "Hey!"

Grace leaned toward him. "Shhh! No shouting! And no yanking on the fence."

His mother glared. Grace tried for a less strident tone as she asked the child, "What's your name?"

The boy frowned and stuck his thumb in his mouth.

"Landon," the mother said.

"Well, Landon, it's like this. Neema and Kanoni want to be your friends, but when you yell at them, they think you are mean and scary."

The boy's expression slipped into a mischievous grin. Uh-oh. The kid liked the idea of being mean and scary.

"Landon." Detective Matthew Finn materialized from the crowd's midst. He squatted down and thrust his badge toward the child. "I'm a policeman. Do you know what policemen do?"

Landon's mouth hung open as he silently regarded the dark-haired man with the shiny gold badge. He slowly shook his head.

"When people make trouble, it's my job to take them to jail. Have you seen anyone here making trouble?" Matt looked around as if trying to spot a criminal in the crowd.

Landon quickly shook his head.

"Well, help me keep an eye out, okay?" Matt held up a hand for a high-five. After the little boy smacked his hand against his, Matt stood up.

Grace gestured a quick thank you sign to him, and he nodded back before vanishing back into the crowd. She said to the audience, "Let's be very quiet and see if Neema wants to visit with us."

Looking down the fence line, she spotted the camera operator again, as well as two familiar heads of strawberry blond hair. Eighteen-year-old Brittany Morgan knelt on one knee, her arms around her toddler daughter Ivy, who stared raptly through the fence at the gorillas. Grace smiled at the friendly faces.

"Neema," Grace said softly, "Some friends came to visit you. Look! It's Brittany. And Ivy."

Tiny black fingers appeared on top of Neema's broad shoulder. Then Kanoni's head emerged, her soft black baby hair standing up in wild disarray as usual. The infant gorilla's eyes were liquid mahogany brown, huge and curious.

The crowd murmured a collective "Awww."

"'Noni!" Ivy chirped. The toddler's fingers were clutched tightly to the chain links. Her red curls bobbed as she bounced on her toes. "'Noni!"

Brittany stood up. Focusing on the gorillas, she gestured in sign language as she spoke. "Neema, Kanoni, come see us."

Neema glanced over her shoulder, suspicion darkening her eyes. Kanoni wriggled out of her arms and scampered across the grass to see Ivy. As they watched the interaction of baby human and baby gorilla, the crowd cooed and murmured. But when Neema turned and swung forward on her knuckles to follow Kanoni, several visitors gasped. Those closest to the fence took a step back.

Strangers were never quite prepared for the size of an adult gorilla, even a relatively small female like Neema. When the mother gorilla sat down a few feet behind Kanoni, the crowd visibly relaxed.

"Come here!" Landon yelled.

Unfortunately, Matt was no longer present to chastise the boy. His mother laid a warning hand on his shoulder.

"When are they gonna talk?" A freckled girl slumped against the fence.

Neema jerked her head sideways to glare at the noisy children. Then she slapped at one ear and shook both hands in the air, touched her mouth and slammed her hand down through the air.

Grace again held her hands up. "Please keep your voices soft," she said. "Neema *is* talking. She uses a version of American Sign Language. She just signed *loud, bad.*" Grace signed the two words for the group. Inside the enclosure, Neema repeated the signs, indicating her agreement.

"Did you see that?" A young woman in the front row elbowed a friend. "Sweet!"

"Neema uses about five hundred signs, and she understands many more spoken words," Grace explained. "Neema recognizes Brittany as a friend, because Brittany works here as a volunteer."

Neema made a quick cradling motion interspersed with other gestures.

"Neema says *baby Ivy here; baby Kanoni here*. Ivy is the only other baby that Kanoni has ever seen."

"Here's another one." A man held a squirming infant out toward the wire mesh.

Grace signed and pointed to the infant. "Neema, Kanoni, come see this baby."

Neema glanced at Kanoni, who now clung to the fence, her long black-haired arms stretched above Ivy's, her finger-like toes thrust through the mesh on either side of the toddler. The baby gorilla's eyes were locked onto her friend's blue-eyed gaze as if girl and gorilla were communicating telepathically.

Deciding that Kanoni was safe for the moment, Neema scooted toward Grace. The throng of visitors shifted backward another step. Even the infant's father withdrew the baby a few inches. Neema sat in front of the squirming bundle. Then she rose onto her knuckles and pressed her enormous face to the fence in the baby's direction, flaring her nostrils. Murmurs ran through the crowd. Finally, Neema rocked back onto her rump and began to sign.

"Small baby there," Grace interpreted.

Neema pinched the fingers of her right hand briefly against her flat black nose.

The infant's father asked, "Does that mean what I think it does?"

"Stink," Grace confirmed.

The father pulled the infant close to his face, sniffed at the diaper, and then held the baby out to the woman beside him. "Your turn."

The crowd chuckled. The mother gave her husband a disparaging look, then took the baby and walked away toward the parking lot.

Grace let her gaze stray to the camera for a few seconds. She hoped that exchange would make the local newscast this evening. It was a wonderful example of Neema's communication skills.

One woman waved a hand in the air. When Grace nodded at her, she asked, "How does Neema refer to Brittany and Ivy? Does she spell out names in sign language?"

Grace smiled. "Neema can't spell. Gorilla fingers are not as dexterous as ours, and I'm not sure letters would make sense to her. Neema uses signs to refer to everyone. She signs 'cheek'"—Grace demonstrated the sign for them—"to refer to Ivy."

"How peculiar," a man remarked. "Why 'cheek'?"

Grace called the red-haired toddler. "Ivy, where's your smile?"

Ivy grinned, displaying deep dimples in both plump cheeks. The adults laughed. Ivy squealed, pleased with the attention.

"Neema is signing *smile-cheek*." Grace pointed as the gorilla gestured toward her own thick black lips and hairy jaw line. "She calls Brittany *red tail*, for obvious reasons."

Brittany obligingly shook her head, swishing her ponytail.

Kanoni, excited now, raced to Neema, briefly swung on her mother's arm, and then scampered back to Ivy.

"What sign does Neema use for Kanoni?" a man asked.

"Neema calls her daughter *Little Bird*." Grace demonstrated the gestures. "We believe she named her that because of the chirping noises a newborn gorilla makes. For our own benefit, we humans translated 'bird' into Swahili—Kanoni. Neema's name is Swahili for 'divine grace.'"

"Don't you have three gorillas?" Landon's mother asked.

Grace pointed to a distant pen built around what had previously been an old horse barn. The enclosure was more than two stories tall, fenced on sides and top like an aviary. An extensive net of ropes stretched from hooks in the fencing, forming play platforms at various levels. In the highest corner was a snarl of blankets.

"That lump you see at the top of the netting there is Gumu, Kanoni's father. Gumu is twice as big as Neema, but he's more afraid of strangers. That's because when Gumu was a baby, he saw poachers in Africa shoot his whole gorilla family."

"How awful."

"That's horrible."

Multiple heads shook. Parents glanced at their children with concern. She'd probably hear next week from the college board about how inappropriate this depressing topic was for a public event. She was willing to take the flack. People needed to know about bad things happening in the world. How could anyone hope to change anything for the better otherwise?

"I want to play with Gumu," Landon said.

"That wouldn't be a good idea," Grace told the little boy. "Gumu could hurt you."

"But I would be his friend," Landon argued. "He wouldn't hurt me."

"Sometimes it's hard to be friends with Gumu," Grace told him. "He gets upset when he's scared. And he's super strong. He might not mean to, but Gumu could kill you."

The mother laid a protective hand on Landon's shoulder, and Grace instantly regretted using the word "kill." Damn, the camera was still recording. She hastily explained to the crowd, "Gorillas are several times stronger than people. And sometimes they bite, especially if they're scared."

"Neema, can you show us your teeth?" She signed the question as she spoke.

When the gorilla's gaze connected with hers, Grace felt a flash of anxiety. Neema's expression was distinctly annoyed. Grace had removed everything from the temporary pen, but under duress, Neema was capable of manufacturing her own ammunition and lobbying feces at the target of her anger.

Praying that Neema would not act out, Grace turned back to the visitors. "Showing teeth is not a natural thing for a gorilla to do," she told them. "What we humans would call a smile indicates fear or aggression to gorillas. But I've had Neema since she was a baby, and I trained her to show her teeth so I could brush them."

She asked the gorilla once more, "Where are your teeth?"

Neema flashed a quick grin, displaying sharp, fang-like canine teeth.

"Good Lord," Landon's mother exclaimed.

"Most gorilla teeth are a lot like ours, but gorillas have bigger, longer canines," Grace said. "Male gorilla canines are particularly impressive—Gumu's are several inches long."

Neema knuckle-walked to Kanoni, scooped her up, and retreated to the far corner of the pen, turning her back on the crowd. The gorilla was at her limit of tolerance for the day.

On the other side of the fence, Ivy fussed at the loss of her simian playmate. Brittany swung her daughter into her arms. "Dr. McKenna, could you show us the gorillas' paintings?"

Bless you. "Of course. Please come this way." She led the group toward the small gallery of bright acrylic abstracts.

Walking backward to address the following crowd, she told them, "Neema and Gumu have many fans in the art community. Sales of their paintings help fund our work here."

She wondered now if those sales could completely fund the project if the college voted not to renew her grant. Neema and Gumu enjoyed painting. Could she have them paint more? Was Kanoni old enough to participate, or would the baby gorilla drink the paint?

Near the barn, against the background of calypso music, she heard the plastic clack of a portable toilet door. That annoying sound had been repeated dozens of times this afternoon. She couldn't wait to get rid of the noisy odiferous boxes tomorrow.

In the temporary plywood gallery they'd constructed for this event, the questions continued, seemingly endless. *Did the gorillas have favorite colors?* Yes. Gumu's was fuschia and Neema's was purple. *Did they finger-paint or use brushes?* They used various brushes and sometimes sticks—gorillas loved tools of all sorts. *Did they have favorite subjects?* They painted a lot of flowers, and the gorillas often ate the bouquets afterward. The last comment provoked a ripple of laughter from the gathering.

The volunteer at the cash drawer sold several posters of gorilla art and two framed prints. Although the noise and crush of bodies were intense, the visitors all seemed friendly, and she was grateful to Matt for weeding out potential troublemakers at the gate. Their relationship was still in the developmental stage, so she'd been surprised and pleased when he volunteered to handle security for her open house event.

Either Matt had done a stellar job, or maybe the community of Evansburg had finally accepted the idea of signing gorillas living in their midst. Still, five hours of open house seemed like an eternity. Grace envied Gumu, resting in solitude high above the throng of humans.

"The last visitor just drove out," Matt reported on Grace's cell phone an hour later.

"Hallelujah! I'm putting Neema and Kanoni to bed. C'mon up and have a beer."

With the music and the crowd gone, the compound now seemed wonderfully serene. Neema knuckle-walked across the grass between Grace and Jonathan Zyrnek, her most trusted employee. Kanoni rode her mother's back like a jockey, clutching Neema's coarse shoulder fur.

"Tired?" Grace slid her hands against her own chest to make the sign.

Neema ignored her, paying abnormal attention to where she placed her hands and feet on the ground.

Ah, the cold shoulder treatment. Definitely preferable to gorilla revenge. Grace tried again, sliding a curled hand down the front of her shirt. "Hungry?"

Neema shot a quick glance at the tub of food that Grace carried, and then faced straight ahead toward the barn enclosure, pretending disinterest.

"I have cauliflower. Cabbage. Peaches."

Neema paused to sit back on her haunches. Kanoni peeked over her mother's shoulder. *Strawberries*, Neema signed, then *yogurt*. Two of her favorite foods.

Grace smiled. "I might have some of those in here."

They stopped in front of the padlocked gate. As Jonathan fished a key from his pocket, Kanoni grabbed the rim of Grace's food tub and pulled, trying to see the contents. Grace pried it back from her baby fingers.

Candy, Neema signed. *Tree candy Neema good.*

"Don't push your luck," Grace told her. The gate swung open and they all stepped inside. "Maybe you can have a lollipop tomorrow, if you're good again." She laid out the items on the food shelf, pulling the lids off the cartons. "Yogurt! Strawberries!"

Neema swung Kanoni to the ground and grabbed a handful of strawberries, shoving them into her mouth.

Gumu's nest of blankets remained curiously still.

Grace shielded her eyes with a hand against the low sun. "Gumu! You're missing strawberries."

"He's still pouting," Jonathan remarked. "He's been up there all day. You know what a wimp he is with strangers. He'll come down and eat as soon as we all clear out."

Jonathan was probably right. When he spotted strangers, the silverback's first tendency was to hide. Gumu's agitation turned to violence only when they came too close.

The corner of a blanket shifted slightly. Then there was another ripple along the fabric bundle. Gumu was a hulking 340 pounds of muscle, but he could be a scaredy-cat when it came to people. According to the rescue organization he'd come from, he had not only seen hunters kill his mother and other family members, but he'd also been present when they hacked them into pieces for bush meat. Any creature with an ounce of intelligence would find it hard to recover from that. He was probably peering out from under those blankets, biding his time until he was absolutely sure all the strangers were gone and it was safe to climb down.

Matt Finn approached the fence with a weary expression. Dust from the gravel road streaked his dark pants and shirt, and he carried several small picket signs in his right hand. Beside him was a young rent-a-cop with pimples on his brow and a sand-colored buzz cut. Grace didn't know the younger man's first name; Finn referred him to only as Scoletti or "the rookie." Together, Finn and Scoletti had spent the last five hours strolling through the compound, keeping an eye on visitors and volunteers alike.

Finn peered through the wire mesh. "Everything in order?"

"Just finishing up." Grace picked up the empty food tub, checked the gorillas' water bucket—nearly full—and then let herself out the gate. Jonathan followed and clicked the padlock shut.

"Zyrnek." Finn nodded at the volunteer.

Jonathan was equally curt. "Detective Finn. Most people call me Jon now. Or Z."

"Z?" Scoletti asked.

Finn raised an eyebrow. "Since when?"

"That's what Neema calls me. I have a T-shirt like that." He made a quick motion, carving a letter Z into the air. "It gets weird, having a Josh and a Jon working around here. And since my dad got out and is living with me, it's confusing to have two Zyrneks around, too."

"Got out?" Finn asked pointedly. His gaze shifted from Jon Zyrnek to Grace's face, checking to see if she got his drift.

Jon crossed his arms and stared Finn down. "Dad was released from Monroe twelve weeks ago. He works at the auto salvage yard. He's staying at my place until he gets a few paychecks in the bank."

"What was he in for?"

Jon squirmed for a second, but finally muttered, "Robbery. Fraud."

Scoletti looked from Finn to Jon and back again, no doubt wondering what to make of this conversation.

Grace sighed. Jonathan Zyrnek had been with her over a year now, but Finn still didn't trust him. The kid started working at her compound as a community service sentence after his conviction for an eco-terrorism stunt. He was still a member of the Animal Rights Union.

While Finn knew only Jon's record, Grace knew Jon. With a father in prison and a mother in and out of rehab, Jonathan Zyrnek had spent most of his teen years in foster care. The young man had a big heart and a quick mind. A natural leader, he organized her staff and volunteers and doled out work assignments. Best of all, Gumu trusted Jon almost as much as he trusted Josh LaDyne, and her big male gorilla tolerated very few humans.

LaDyne was in the throes of finishing his Ph.D. dissertation and would leave the project within months. Although Jon was not an academic who could design tests and document her research like LaDyne, she hoped Jon would take LaDyne's place as backup gorilla keeper.

Jon turned his back on Finn to tell her, "Sierra and I are on duty tonight."

"Thanks, Z." She gave his arm an affectionate squeeze.

Jon's companions in ARU crime, Caryn Brown and Sierra Sakson, worked for her, too. She depended heavily on the ARU trio. All three were fluent in American Sign Language. They helped with training as well as basic care of the gorillas. They also claimed to have some sort of commando training. Grace didn't ask for details; she was just happy they considered it their duty to guard her compound.

All three had stayed with the gorilla language project after their court-mandated sentences were up. Now, thanks to the financial support of the local college and sales of the gorillas' artwork, Grace was able to pay the three an hourly pittance, far less than they deserved.

Finn held out the signs to Scoletti.

"What are those?" Grace asked.

"Only two troublemakers." Matt turned the small hand-painted signs so she could read them as he handed them off to the rookie.

Apes Cant Think or Talk. Only humans have souls.

I am NOT a monkey's uncle.

So maybe the atmosphere at the gate had not been as peaceful as it had been inside.

Matt dismissed Scoletti. "Good job. See you at the station."

The rookie bumped knuckles with him before walking back toward the front lot where his car was parked.

Sierra and Caryn and a small cluster of volunteers were slumped against the picnic table across the yard, waiting for a final word from her. Grace strolled toward them. "Thank you for a great job today, everyone. I hope you can all stay to celebrate."

Their expressions perked up. She looked over Jon's shoulder to focus on Finn and invite him, too. He jerked a thumb toward his chest and mouthed *My place. Steak.* He mimicked drinking a glass of wine. *Hot tub.* His intense gaze suggested even more.

From the enclosure, Neema grunted softly, calling Gumu. Kanoni chirped in response.

Grace focused on her staff again. "Crew, there's a keg of beer in the staff trailer. Pizzas, too. Have a party. You earned it. I'll see you in the morning."

She had planned to stay with her volunteers, but Matt's invitation sounded like heaven. Adult talk, or even better, no talk at all. And no gorillas.

Chapter 2

Happy quiet. Neema listened to the birds. She liked to watch the little ones that flew in and hopped around. She liked to hear them sing. She hated big black birds. Grace had a name sound for them: crows. They stole her food. Their noises were loud and ugly. Crow shouts.

She put another strawberry in her mouth. *Good sweet cold.* Her favorite red food. She picked up another. Kanoni grabbed for it. Neema grunted and flashed her teeth. Kanoni let go. Crouching over the pile of fruit, the baby picked up a strawberry with her lips, and then moved it around inside her mouth with a question on her face.

Good, Neema signed.

Snow walked over to the strawberries and sniffed, moving his whiskers. *No cat food,* Neema signed. *Gorilla food Neema.* Kanoni stretched her hand out to grab the long white tail. Snow ran into the barn.

Neema grunted for Gumu. *Come tickle Neema. Chase.* Laughs came from the trailer where Z and the others stayed. Then music started again. She hooted louder for Gumu. No Gumu sound came back. She sniffed. Only dirty smells from toilet boxes.

Neema pushed a chunk of cauliflower into her mouth, then swept Kanoni into her arms. Clutching the baby to her chest with one arm, she pulled herself into the webbing and climbed to Gumu's nest. She poked his blankets with a finger. Kanoni sucked a corner of a blanket into her mouth.

The blankets felt apart.

No Gumu there. Only his nest.

From this high place, Neema saw a tiny piece of red-orange sun, almost gone. White dust over the road. Grace gone in gun man's car. Almost dark.

Z laughed from the trailer across the yard. Then Caryn did, too. Funny jokes? She wanted Grace to come back, tickle her, make her laugh. *Tickle Neema*, she signed to Kanoni. The baby stared, her eyes big. Neema pushed out her lips and dug her fingers into the baby's stomach. Kanoni hooted and rolled over backwards, then scampered down the netting, wanting a game of chase.

Was Gumu hiding in the barn? Was he sleeping in *her* nest, using *her* blankets? Did he have strawberries? Did he have candy? She climbed down the rope webbing, landed on the ground with a thud. She hurried into the dimness of the barn. Kanoni followed.

Dark inside. She knuckled her way over toys and blankets. The tire swings were empty. No Gumu in her blankets. Snow and Nest cats curled up there, washing each other's faces with pink tongues. Grunting, she signed *gorilla nest mine*, but they were not watching.

No Gumu in the corners. No Gumu on the tree trunks. On the floor was a big wet spot. Neema caught Kanoni as she scampered by. Creeping closer to the big dark wet, holding Kanoni tight, she looked at the spot out of the corner of her eye. Red wet. She leaned close. Meat smell. She touched her fingers to the red and tasted the wet. Meat wet. Red meat smell. *Bad, hurt*, she signed.

Where was Gumu? Kanoni slipped from her arms into the wet red. Raising her baby arms, she slapped them on the red dirt and rolled across the wet.

The red smelled like meat. Gumu was gone. *Bad*, Neema signed. *Bad. Bad. Bad.*

When Spencer was meat, he was gone. Was Gumu meat? Was Gumu gone for always?

She backed away from the meat smell and turned toward the back of the barn. Light. The wall was open, just a crack. It never was open before. She walked to the crack, looked through the open. Cars were there. She put a hand on the wall and pushed. It slid away. She could get out, away from the meat smell.

Was Gumu out? She hooted for Gumu. Kanoni's hand brushed her leg as she tried to slip past. Neema caught her by a foot. The baby screeched.

Neema squeezed through the opening. Out. She sat in the dust between the cars and pulled Kanoni into her lap. More bad meat smell. More car smells.

Gumu? She hooted. Kanoni copied her cry. A crow shouted back.

Meat. Bad black bird noise. No Gumu. This was bad. *Bad.* This was *danger.*

Chapter 3

Early morning sunlight poured through Finn's bedroom window, illuminating the intriguing sight of Grace McKenna sleeping beside him. He'd like to paint her just as she looked now. Her eyelids were pale lavender fringed by black lashes, the delicate skin there fading to rose and then to ivory under ebony eyebrows. Her face was tranquil, her lips parted slightly. Her dark hair fanned out over the pillow like a halo radiating from the moon on a frosty night. Spoiling this vision, however, was an orange cat that had snuggled into that luscious hair. Kee, one of the tabbies he'd inherited from his traitorous ex-wife Wendy. Finn briefly considered poking the cat, but Kee was unpredictable. He might unsheathe his claws and use Grace's head as a launch pad.

Cargo, the black behemoth of a dog also left behind by Wendy, sauntered into the room, toenails clicking against the hardwood floor. The Newfie-Chow mix rested his heavy skull on Finn's hip, fixing his eyes—one brown and one blue—on Finn's face. The dog sighed melodramatically to show he was waiting for Finn to fill his food bowl. The muggy wave of dog breath wafted across the bed. Kee opened one sea green eye. Half a second later, Grace opened her eyes, too. When she jabbed a finger into the warm fur above her head, Kee merely stretched to show his disdain, and then jumped off the bed. Grace had a magic touch with all his animals.

She slid toward him, finger-combing her hair away from her face.

He murmured, "Hello, beautiful."

Her brow abruptly furrowed. "Shit!"

"That wasn't quite the response I was hoping for."

She gestured at the bedside clock behind him as she

climbed out of bed. "Sorry, Matt, it's just that I should already be back at the compound. Where—?"

Then, spying her clothes heaped on the chair against the wall, she began to pull them on. Cargo trotted over to help and they engaged in a brief tug of war with her brassiere until Grace told the dog to stop.

Finn groaned. "It's not even seven-thirty. My shift doesn't start until three this afternoon."

"Josh is out of town. I have to do the morning feedings and lesson setups."

Sighing, Finn climbed out of bed and pulled on his own clothes. Cargo bounced to his side of the bed, grabbed the leg of his trousers and pulled, growling fiercely.

Grace extracted her long hair from the neck of her T-shirt. "You don't have to get up, too."

He flicked Cargo on the nose. The dog spat out his pants, sat back on his haunches and barked. Grace laughed.

His home life was a circus. How the hell was he supposed to romance a woman? He pulled his slobber-stained khakis over his jockey shorts and reminded Grace, "We drove here in my car."

"Oh, yeah. Sorry. And thank you." Snapping her jeans, she gave him a chagrined smile. "Forgive me for eating and running?"

"What? No mention of *dessert*?" He raised an eyebrow. This was only the third time she'd stayed over. He was delighted to wake up with her. But did she feel the same?

Grace stepped toward him, gave him a hug and a quick kiss. "*Dessert* was wonderful, too, Matt. But I really have to get back to the gorillas."

Why was his life ruled by animals? Two cats and a dog at home were bad enough. How had he fallen for a woman who kept gorillas? "Coffee before apes?"

"One cup."

They padded barefoot toward the kitchen, passing his home office, which he used mostly as a painting studio. The eastern light from the windows illuminated the back side of the watercolor he was working on, giving the field of red poppies a luminous glow.

Grace paused in the doorway to view the painting. "Oh, Matt. That's lovely."

He was ridiculously pleased. He had the brilliant reds and oranges down, but he needed to add the blue shadows. And the flesh tones to fill out the figure of the woman wandering through the meadow. "It needs a few more layers."

She leaned against him, teasing. "Is the woman me?"

He'd roughed in the figure with only a suggestion of blue jeans and yellow peasant blouse and long black hair streaming in the breeze. "I like to think so."

"Me, too." She splayed her fingers against his chest as she gazed at him, smiling. "Maybe tonight I can get Jon to gorilla-sit again."

He'd planned on painting the woman from the back, moving away, but maybe he'd change it so she was walking toward the viewer. "I'm on duty until midnight, but I'd love to meet you afterwards. We could share dessert again." He leaned forward to press his lips to Grace's.

Then Cargo nearly knocked them down in his rush to pass down the narrow hallway, eager to beat them to the kibble cupboard.

Clouds scudded across the sky from the west as they drove, obliterating the bright dawn, and a rising breeze gusted through the tall evergreens bordering Grace's compound as they drove in. From the courtyard, she could see neither gorillas nor humans.

"Looks like the gorillas are sleeping late," Grace said.

Finn's stomach chose that moment to growl.

Grace grinned and looked at his belt buckle. "After I feed them, how about I cook you an omelet?"

He rubbed his belly, embarrassed. "Sounds wonderful."

He trailed behind her as she hurried toward the mobile home she called the study trailer, where she worked with the gorillas and recorded their lessons. Finn leaned against the counter as she unlocked the chain on the refrigerator door and pulled out items. She quickly tossed together an array of whole fruit and vegetables and then used a giant knife to hack a loaf of heavy mixed-grain bread into chunks.

From what he'd witnessed so far, gorillas ate everything short of cheeseburgers. He was glad it wasn't his job to feed an ape. She loaded the hodge-podge into a plastic dish tub, which he carried as they walked toward the enclosure. Grace's two cats—a white one and a calico—materialized from wherever cats hid out. Just like his, these two did their feline utmost to trip him, twining around his feet, mewing hopefully.

"You're next," Grace told them. "Gorillas first."

"I thought Snow and Nest were the gorillas' pets." Finn still couldn't wrap his brain around the concept of one animal having another as a pet.

"They are."

"Then why aren't they the gorillas' responsibilities? Why don't you make the gorillas feed them?"

She laughed. "Because I don't trust gorillas with can openers? Because they'd eat the cat food themselves?"

Good points.

A door banged on the staff trailer across the yard. Jonathan Zyrnek stumbled out, raking his long dishwater-blond hair with his fingers. Looked like the kid had slept in his rumpled jeans and T-shirt. He wore tennis shoes without socks. He caught the door and carefully fastened it shut against the wind, then trotted down the steps toward them.

"Busted," he groaned, reaching to take the food tub from Finn. "Here, let me do that."

The cats promptly transferred their affections from Finn to him. "Sorry I'm late getting up," he apologized, ending with a yawn.

Grace shot the kid a dismayed look. "I'm surprised the gorillas aren't raising the roof."

"Me, too." He yawned again. "The barn was quiet all night long. Neema only hooted for a little while after she saw you leave."

Grace stiffened, and Finn wanted to smack the kid for laying a guilt trip on her. "Are you sure the barn was quiet? Maybe you couldn't hear the gorillas over your music," he suggested.

Zyrnek scowled at him. "Our music wasn't loud."

The kid turned to Grace. A long strand of hair blew across his face. He shoved it back behind his ear. "Gumu must have been stressed out. He left his nest blankets up in the net. He and Neema are probably huddled together inside. Maybe they don't want to come out because of the portable johns."

"Maybe," Grace agreed. When Finn raised a skeptical eyebrow, she explained, "Apes tend to get upset when unfamiliar objects suddenly appear in their environment. And they have sensitive noses."

Finn thought about how his cat Kee peed on his jockey shorts if he left them on the floor. And Cargo—the mutt ecstatically immersed himself in dirty laundry whenever he got the chance; the filthier the better. He didn't want to imagine what gorillas would do with portable toilets if they had access to them.

Pulling out a key on a retractable tether from her belt, Grace unlocked the padlock securing the gate. "Wait here."

Taking the tub of food from Zyrnek, she walked into the enclosure. The cats scampered in on her heels, and she pulled the gate closed behind them. "Breakfast, Neema! Gumu!"

Finn was surprised that three gorillas didn't race out of the barn. Even the cats seemed perplexed. They strolled to the entrance and stared in, switching their tails. Grace disappeared inside the building. "Neema? Gumu?"

Then he heard her shriek.

His heart lurched. Zyrnek beat him to the handle, jerking open the gate with his left hand as he grabbed a capture stick from its holder outside with his right. Finn unsnapped the safety strap on his holster and curled his fingers around the grip of his pistol as he jogged in behind the kid.

It took a second for his eyes to adjust to the dim light. He hadn't been inside the building since Grace and LaDyne had transformed it from a horse barn into a gorilla house. The interior was now a cross between a jungle and a playground. The diagonal trunks of several large trees were wedged at various angles between the walls. Swings and nets hung from the ceiling. Large square shelves jutted from the walls like bracket fungus. Dust motes danced in the weak sunlight filtering in from high windows, skating from side to side as puffs of wind blew in. At floor level, the interior was shadowy. Finn stumbled over broken branches and stuffed toys. Masses of greenery seemed to be scattered randomly around the floor.

"What the hell?" Zyrnek slammed to a stop in the middle of the space, throwing out an arm and accidentally setting in motion a tire swing that almost clobbered Finn in the forehead. Finn ducked and trotted to the rear of the building, where Grace was silhouetted against the sun.

She stood spread-eagled, one hand clutching the door frame, the other the sliding barn door, as she stared out into a dusty lot that held only her van. Her knuckles were as white as her face.

Finn touched her arm. "Grace?"

Letting go of the door frame, she turned toward him. "They're gone, Matt. Neema. Gumu. Kanoni. Gone!"

"They escaped?" That *was* bad news. The two cats joined them in the doorway. "I didn't know there was a door back here."

"We keep it padlocked from the outside. They couldn't have escaped on their own."

That was even worse news.

The calico cat scampered through the opening into the sunlight. Grace edged a foot through the door.

Finn pulled her back. "Evidence," he explained.

He leaned out through the opening as far as he could without touching anything, saw a sliding bolt and a hasp for a padlock. "No lock," he reported.

He stepped back to examine the inside of the wall. Scuff marks marred the rough wood surface along the lower portion. Significant? He glanced around. Probably not. Scrapes and stains adorned the siding everywhere, from the floor to almost six feet off the ground. Looked like the gorillas took turns tossing each other against the walls. "Could they get out on their own?"

"You should probably come see this." Jon Zyrnek's voice was gravelly. He stood in the middle of the cluttered floor, staring at the sawdust floor in front of his shoes. The white cat sauntered over to rub against his blue-jeaned leg, then jerked a paw up from the ground and frantically washed it.

They joined Zyrnek. A large dark stain spread darkly across the ground in front of their feet. Finn put his arm around Grace's rigid shoulders, but she slipped out from under his embrace to unlock a cover on the wall, then flipped a switch. An overhead light flashed on.

The wet patch on the sawdust floor was a dark rust color on the edges, a bright red in the center. The stain was roughly oval and at least three feet across.

Finn had never seen a bigger puddle of blood.

Chapter 4

Grace couldn't stop staring at the blood stain. Superimposed over the blood, her brain conjured up a gorilla corpse stiffened in rigor mortis.

She groaned. "No! Not again."

Matt's hand brushed her shoulder, but she shrugged it off, staggered stiff-legged to the low shelf that bordered the wall, and collapsed onto it with a thud that radiated up her backbone. Leaning forward, she lowered her aching head between her knees. *Wake up, wake up, wake up! Please God, let this be a nightmare.*

She felt his weight settle beside her. He pulled one hand away from her head and caressed it gently between his. "It'll be okay, Grace," he said softly.

She jerked her head up. "How could this ever be okay, Matt? You know about Spencer."

He nodded. "Your gorilla that died."

His words made it sound like a natural death. "Who was *murdered*!" she corrected, her voice shrill in the muffled stillness of the barn.

"We don't know yet that any gorilla was murdered here," he told her. "Someone broke in, and then—"

"Gumu confronted them," she ended the sentence for him. "He's afraid of people, but he would rush to defend his territory and his family. And then—blam!" She waved her hand angrily in the direction of the blood pool.

Jon's gaze was fixed on the stain at his feet. He pulled the long hair around his shoulders as if he intended to yank out huge tufts. "It's my fault. I should have walked all the way around the barn last night."

Grace looked up. "Do you usually do that?"

"No," he admitted sadly.

"Neither do I. So don't go blaming yourself." She put her face in her hands. "I didn't even look in the barn last night when I put Neema and Kanoni back. I didn't even make sure Gumu was actually sleeping in his nest." How could she have been so careless? She should have known better, with all those strangers milling around.

"I don't think this is enough blood for three gorillas," Jon murmured. "Maybe the gorillas escaped, at least some of them."

She could feel Matt studying him, and she knew what he was thinking. Jon Zyrnek had "liberated" animals before. He had easy access to the gorillas, and he spent his days in the company of his ARU comrades Caryn and Sierra.

Sure enough, Matt stood up and strode over to Jon. "What do you know about this?"

Jon blinked a couple of times. Then anger replaced his worried look. "I know exactly as much as you do."

"Maybe you and Caryn and Sierra only intended to set them free," Matt accused. "You probably weren't expecting a fight. You didn't mean to hurt any of the gorillas."

"Matt!" She jumped up to intercede.

Jon stiffened, fisting both hands. "I'd never hurt a gorilla. These gorillas are my life." The overhead light glinted off tears pooling in his eyes as he turned to her. "You know that, right?"

"I do, Z." She nodded. She put one hand on Jon's forearm and the other on Matt's. "He's not involved, Matt."

"I love these gorillas," Jon insisted.

Matt pointed to the open front door. "Wait outside. I'll be out to talk to you in a while."

Jon faced her. "I'll go search the woods. They could be out there."

She let go of his arm. "Good idea."

"Don't go far, and don't talk to anyone," Matt warned.

His eyebrows knit into a frown, Jon picked up Snow and hoisted the cat to his shoulder, then retreated through the shadows toward the yard.

Matt's attitude was maddening. He always had to believe he was smarter; couldn't stop being the jaded detective. Why couldn't he accept her judgment about the ARU kids? She worked with them daily. He didn't.

"Stop it," she told him. "Jon would not do this." Biting her lower lip and twisting her hands together, she looked around the barn, unsure of what to do next. She wanted to believe all the gorillas had escaped, but she couldn't erase the vision of Spencer's body from her brain.

"Is it possible there was a gorilla fight and they somehow pried open the door?" Matt asked.

"How could they open the door? The padlock was on the outside," she reminded him. "There's not even a handle on this side. And they'd never hurt each other enough to—" Her gaze shifted back to the blood.

"And this couldn't be like last time? Nobody forgot to lock that door?" he asked.

Her gaze met his. Why did he have to remind her of that mistake? She knew nobody had been negligent this time. "We don't use that door, so there's no reason to unlock it. It hasn't been unlocked since we remodeled in here."

"So there's no doubt that someone broke in. I'll get an evidence tech here ASAP." He pulled out his cell phone and scrolled through his contact list.

A new source of panic suddenly flared in her mind. She yanked his wrist. "Don't!"

He dropped the phone.

"Grace, what the heck?" He fished the phone out of the sawdust and wiped it against his pant leg. "The sooner we get a team on this, the sooner we'll find the gorillas."

She twisted a strand of her hair around her fingers as she explained, "The council."

Her words landed with a thud in the still air, and Finn instantly knew what Grace meant. After Neema and Gumu escaped from her compound last year, the county had passed a resolution against exotic pets. Only one vote had forced the county council to grandfather in her right to keep her gorillas in a "secure research facility." If word of this second incident got out, the county could yank her permit within days.

"And the college," Grace added. "They're voting next week about whether to continue my funding."

"Shit." Finn rubbed one hand against the back of his neck. He spat curses at the ground as he paced along the wall, scuffing sawdust into his shoes. "Shit, shit, shit!"

As soon as his report hit the police call log, this story would be all over the local news. It would migrate outward like a toxic waste spill. Finn could hear it now. *A pool of blood! Missing gorillas!* This was exactly the sort of news TV stations nationwide clamored for, an attention grabbing story they could twist in a dozen different ways.

"The whole county will freak," Grace murmured. Tears were pooling in her eyes. "They'll break out the guns again. If they're out in the woods, Gumu and Neema will be in even more danger then."

She was right. But three unpredictable apes were missing. The blood indicated major violence of some kind. A wounded gorilla could be a threat to public safety, especially if that gorilla was Gumu.

She read his mind. "They wouldn't hurt anyone, Matt. Not unless it was self-defense."

Finn gently touched Grace's shoulder. "I'm a cop," he reminded her. "I have responsibilities. The break-in is a crime. And the blood..." He couldn't figure out any good way to end that sentence.

She didn't respond.

"Grace, sweetheart. We need to think this through." The words sounded condescending, even to him. He tried again. "Don't you want the gorillas back? The faster we start—"

A tear streaked down her face as she interrupted, "Of course I want my gorillas back!" She swiped angrily at her face. "That's the whole point. If word gets out, I'll *never* get them back."

"This is a crime scene, Grace. Whoever did this"—he waved his hand vaguely to include the open door and the blood stain—"whatever *this* is, might be getting farther away each minute we stand here debating."

Grace locked both hands around his upper arm. "Just hold off on reporting this, just until we can get a handle on what happened? Just until we can tell a cohesive story? Just until *I* can tell the story? You don't even have to be involved."

"I'm already involved."

Another tear trickled down her face.

Tears. He never knew how to react when a woman cried. Wendy had turned on the waterworks every time they'd argued. Tears were a weapon in her arsenal. But Grace hated drama. She hated to break down. He'd only seen her cry a few times last year when her gorillas were in danger. He patted himself down, found a handkerchief in his front pocket and held it out.

Taking it, she mopped at her face. She didn't look as if she'd welcome a hug right now.

He had a duty to report crimes. Three missing gorillas were not in the same category as a wandering dog or cat, or even a stolen horse or cow. And with Jon Zyrnek involved, there was no way this was going to stay quiet, especially if ARU was behind it. The kid could be calling the local news right now.

He took a deep breath. Start at the beginning; the break-in. "What are the reasons someone would break in here?" He held out a finger. "One, someone wanted to set the gorillas free."

"It's not ARU." Grace bunched the handkerchief in her fist. "Jon and Caryn and Sierra would never let them."

"Or that's what they want you to believe." Those kids were a secretive bunch, and their records proved they had no qualms about breaking laws.

She locked eyes with him. "The ARU kids are *not* involved, Matt."

"I worry about them working here."

"You shouldn't."

"They're reckless, Grace."

She bristled, crossing her arms. "I'd call them dedicated. Fearless. Loyal."

He decided to let that go. For now. He thrust out a second finger. "Reason two. Someone wanted to kill the gorillas."

For an instant Grace looked as if he'd slapped her. Then her eyes narrowed. "Frank Keyes! He could have been at the open house. It's been years. Maybe I wouldn't recognize him now."

Finn knew that Keyes was the zealot who had killed Spencer with a cup of cyanide-laced Kool-aid.

"Last time we checked, Keyes was still in Tacoma." He pulled out his cell phone.

She put a hand on his arm. "Please don't say anything about this." She tilted her head in the direction of the blood stain.

"Okay." He called the station.

"Why are you looking for Frank Keyes?" Miki was a nineteen-year-old technician, a glorified go-fer, but she liked to think of herself as an up-and-coming detective.

"Dr. McKenna says she may have seen him yesterday, and a no-contact order is a condition of his parole. Get Tacoma PD to check on him." After pressing END, he stared at the phone, wondering what he should do next.

"Reason number three," Grace held up three fingers. "Someone wanted to kidnap the gorillas."

All animals were classified as property, so the crime would be theft, not kidnapping. "Why would someone want to steal a gorilla?"

"Gorillas are endangered. It's almost impossible to get one legally," she said bitterly. "Zoos want them. Collectors want them for pets."

"Pets?" he echoed lamely. That was hard for Finn to imagine. Then again, he'd read stories about wackos keeping tigers and cobras in their apartments.

"Gorillas are worth tens of thousands of dollars. I had to pay twelve thousand for Neema and eight for Gumu last year, and those prices were cheap because of the media pressure."

Money was always a good motive. "Who knows how much they're worth?"

She twisted his handkerchief in her hands. "Everyone who works with exotic animals."

Which turned his thoughts back to her staff. Especially to the ARU triplets. And most particularly to the one young man living with a criminal. The timing was too convenient. The more he thought about it, the more likely it seemed. The Zyrneks were in on this.

"Grace, what about Jon Zyrnek's father? He got out of prison a few weeks ago, and he knows all about the gorillas. This might have been his idea."

Her brow furrowed. "I met Tony Zyrnek yesterday. He's really interested in our project, and he's so proud of Jon. He seemed nice."

Finn kept his expression neutral. Most felons seemed nice when they were after something. That something was usually money or booze or drugs, but in this case, it might have been gorillas.

"No." She shook her head. "This is the work of Keyes or a stranger who wanted to capture or kill—" Her voice broke on the last word and she clapped a hand over her mouth to stifle a sob.

He wrapped his arm around her. "What do you want to do, Grace?"

She rubbed her eyes and took a few shaky breaths, composing herself. "You could start the investigation on your own, couldn't you?"

All detectives took crime scene classes; even patrolmen were educated in the basics these days. And like most officers, he carried rudimentary supplies to gather evidence that might disappear before the techs arrived. "It's been a long time since I processed a scene by myself. Any evidence I collect could easily be called into question in court, given our relationship," he reminded her.

She stepped out from under his arm. "But maybe we could find my gorillas before anyone realizes they're missing. Please, Matt," she begged. "You know I could lose everything if this goes public."

It was true. Gumu and Neema and Kanoni were *her* gorillas. And if Grace lost the gorillas for good, she'd have no reason to stay in Evansburg. He might lose *her* for good. He brushed a finger across her wet cheek. "You really think the public is not in danger?"

"If they're in the woods, they'll probably stay in the woods. Nothing happened last year," she reminded him. "If they're not outside..."—her voice cracked, and she swallowed before continuing—"if someone has them, then only the gorillas are in danger, aren't they?"

Her eyes pleaded with him.

He gave in. "We'll try it your way. But just for a day or two."

She nodded. "Just for a day or two."

"I'll get my camera and my kit." He fumbled in his jacket pocket for his car keys. He'd have to be damn careful. This was going to come back and bite him in the ass, he knew it.

A half hour later, he clicked the lock on his measuring tape and positioned it over the widest area of the blood stain. The camera's flash brought out the crimson in the center of the dark blotch, and he was briefly, irrelevantly reminded of the poppy field in his painting at home. Alizarin crimson, with a dash of indigo to dull the brightness.

Except for the occasional groan of siding when the wind gusted, it was quiet inside the barn. He could barely hear Jon Zyrnek shouting as he wandered through the thick forest that surrounded Grace's compound. "Gumu! Neema! Yogurt!"

The last word surprised him. Yogurt must be the gorilla equivalent of "Come here."

Using his pocketknife, he scraped a sample from the dampest section of the pool into an evidence bag. The stain extended the length of the blade—three inches deep into the sawdust. Could any creature survive that much blood loss?

How could he categorize these samples at the station? He couldn't ask for processing on a random sample. He'd need a case, or at least an incident report of some kind.

Grace stood a few feet away, quietly sniffling. "I have blood work on both Neema and Gumu, so we could match if you can get a lab report. I know I should pay for that, but there's just no money. We were making a fair amount from the paintings, but now—"

She didn't need to say it. No gorillas, no paintings. An absurd thought popped into his head. Could he fake a few gorilla paintings? Both Neema and Gumu painted in a loose abstract style; at best their works could be called impressions of flowers or landscapes. Surely he could copy... He stopped himself there. Crazy idea. He was already walking a dangerous path by not reporting this crime, and now he was considering fraud?

"If you can get a report, then we can see which gorilla—" Grace's voice broke. She left the sentence unfinished.

Was she envisioning the same gorilla corpse he saw in his imagination? A huge black furry body tossed out in a ditch alongside a road, or maybe crammed into a commercial garbage dumpster. He had to ask. "Could this be personal, Grace?"

"Personal?"

"Do you know anyone who would like to see you lose everything?"

She reflected on the question for a few seconds. "Just Keyes, at least that I know of. But some people despise scientists who show the world how similar apes are to humans. Remember those signs from yesterday."

She twisted the handkerchief in her hands. "I don't want to know which gorilla the blood came from, but I need to. I have to." She clamped a hand over her mouth to stifle a sob.

"The department works on livestock rustling cases. We match blood to animals all the time."

He'd solved one such case just last year, although unfortunately not before the hogs had been turned into hams and pork chops. "I'll think of a way to pass these samples off in that category."

But everyone at the station would want to know which

rancher was missing what animal. Nothing stayed secret for long in Evansburg.

"That won't work," she said, mirroring his thoughts. She folded and refolded his handkerchief, thinking. "This needs to be connected with a stranger, maybe someone at the open house."

Finn snapped his fingers, warming to the idea. "A stranger brought a dog, a valuable one, and it's missing. He found this bloodstain—well, not this one." He pointed to the large blood puddle. "A small one, in your front parking lot. He wants to know whether someone ran over his dog."

"Ran over? That's horrible." She made a face, but then said, "That could work. And nobody in town is going to care much about the claim of someone just passing through."

Like Finn, Grace was a newcomer to the area. It could take a couple of generations to be truly accepted here.

Finn focused on the scene again. Divots in the sawdust floor may or may not have been footprints. Parallel marks streaked through the sawdust from the blood pool toward the door as if a body had been dragged across the floor. The track marks disappeared in the gravel of the parking area.

Switching his camera to video mode, he pivoted in a slow circle, recording the whole interior of the building. Toys of all sizes, tire swings, shelves, tree trunks. Leaves of every description and clumps of pine needles and whole branches were tucked into every crevice and scattered across the floor. He couldn't decipher what might pertain to a crime and what were signs of normal gorilla behavior. There was no way to tell how many people had broken in, and no way to tell what happened after that.

Turning to Grace, he asked, "Is anything missing?"

"Three gorillas." She smiled wanly, her eyes glimmering with tears.

"Besides that. Or is there anything here that usually isn't?" Sometimes perps inadvertently left objects behind.

She walked slowly around the interior of the building, scrutinizing every inch. "I don't see anything. All this greenery is nesting material and food. We use it to create a more natural environment for the gorillas."

To Finn, it was just one giant mess. Which was, in his experience, the normal state the gorillas lived in.

He couldn't discern any shoe prints in the lumpy sawdust inside the building or in the gravel beyond the open door, but he took several photos anyway before he stepped out. Only Grace's van was parked in the small lot. Sounding closer now, Jon Zyrnek's calls emanated from the forest to the east of Grace's property. "Neema! Strawberries! Gumu! Neema!"

Dark clouds scudded by overhead to stack up against the mountains to the west. He needed to find and document any evidence that might be washed away by rain.

Loose gravel was not a good medium for capturing tread marks. He took photos of the few impressions he found, including his measuring tape in each image for scale. "I'll need photos of all the cars that normally park back here to compare with these. Close-ups of their tire treads. License plate numbers, too."

"I'll get those for you."

He was glad she didn't ask why he needed license plate numbers. He'd use them to check on ownership, see if others among her staff had relationships with criminals.

Grace crouched to focus on a spot on the ground.

He joined her. "Got something?"

Her hand hovered over a patch of dusty gravel. "It's just that"—she pointed to a faint rounded depression—"and those"—she moved her finger toward a few smudges to the right of the first—"look a little like gorilla toes."

Finn suspected that was hope speaking. He didn't see anything that looked remotely like a foot or toe print. Then he remembered that Neema's feet were more like hands, with the big toe angled sideways like a thumb, the toes curved over like fingers. Maybe those *were* gorilla footprints.

Grace shifted her gaze farther ahead. "And these"—moving her hand from side to side, she pointed to a couple of smudges that could have been anything—"could be knuckles."

Zyrnek appeared, walking around from the side of the barn. He'd combed his hair into a ponytail and fastened it with a rubber band. He gave Finn a sarcastic salute. "I've been waiting as ordered, sir. FYI: It's been a couple of hours."

To Grace, he said, "I'm sorry. I didn't see any signs of gorillas in the woods."

She nodded, disappointed.

"I didn't go too far," Zyrnek added. "And if they're running away, they could be moving fast."

Was the kid trying to give her hope, or stalling for time to move the gorillas farther away? A few fat raindrops spattered dark splotches on their clothing. Finn looked up at the darkening skies, which could open up any second.

"I'll go search too, in a few minutes. Z, did you ever bring Neema or Gumu back here?" Grace wiped at the wet spots on her shoulders as if she could brush them away.

Zyrnek looked surprised. "Yeah, sure, lots of times. Like when we loaded her into the van or something."

Grace's expression crumpled into despair. "Yes. Of course. So these prints are meaningless."

Zyrnek studied her. "You okay, Boss?"

"How could I be?" Her voice trembled.

"I sorta need to know...what's the plan? What do I tell the rest of the staff?"

Her face went stiff. "Jesus! What *am* I going to tell the staff? They can't know either." She bunched the front of her shirt in a fist and threw a look of panic in Finn's direction. "I've got to cancel all their shifts."

He could see that it was going to be a challenge to keep three missing gorillas a secret.

She suggested uncertainly, "Maybe one of the gorillas is sick?"

"Why would that make them stay away?" Finn asked.

"I have the flu," Zyrnek volunteered.

"Oh, no." Grace studied the kid's face. "When did you start feeling sick?"

Zyrnek's expression was pained. "Not *really*. But if I have the flu, then the staff all got exposed yesterday and they could pass it to the gorillas, or the gorillas could pass it to them. So I'm in quarantine in the staff trailer and the rest of them need to stay away until the incubation period has passed."

She relaxed. "That's an excellent plan. Thanks."

Zyrnek wiped a raindrop from his forehead. He shifted his gaze to Finn. "Anything I can help *you* with?"

Finn was not about to share any information with the kid. Zyrnek was already too savvy about skirting the law. "Can't think of anything. If you can keep this off the radar, then we've got it covered for now."

The youth narrowed his eyes. "Right." He turned his back to Finn. "I'll go call everyone now, Grace."

"Be careful what you tell them," Finn warned.

The kid snapped off another sideways salute as he walked away. If Grace hadn't been there, Zyrnek would probably have extended his middle finger. He seemed too quick on his feet. Had he been thinking about this very scenario awhile? Finn would have to interview all the staff to get a fix on who was where last night. And do it all somehow without letting them know about the missing gorillas, he reminded himself. Why had he agreed to this ridiculous scheme?

The wind gusted harder through the trees. They were about to retire to the barn when the rumble of a diesel engine caught their attention, and both he and Grace turned to peer down the back driveway. A flatbed truck pulled out of the trees into the gravel lot. The sign on the cab read *Samuels Sanitation Services*. The driver's window slid down and the ruddy bald-headed man spoke to Finn. "Sorry I'm late to pick up the shitcans."

Grace walked around the cab. "I forgot you were coming this morning."

"Sorry, ma'am. I didn't see you there." The driver's round face turned a deeper shade of red, and he slapped the gloves across his other hand. "Okay if I back up into position?" With a sideways twist of his head, he indicated the space to the side of the barn.

Grace glanced at Finn.

"Sure." He'd captured all the photos he needed for now.

The driver positioned the truck and slid out of the cab. *Nate* was embroidered in white over the right side pocket of his blue coveralls. He held a pair of heavy duty orange rubber gloves in one hand. A sullen-looking teenage boy slumped in the passenger seat.

"You drove up this same road and parked in this lot yesterday?" Finn asked.

"Yessir. We delivered around eight a.m., just as requested."

The road was a back way into Grace's compound, accessed through the woods, barricaded with a locked gate and normally used only by her staff.

"There wasn't a lock on the gate?" Finn asked.

Nate held a hand over his eyes to shield them from the rain. "Yessir. Hanging on the gate looking like it was closed, but open, just like that young feller told me he'd leave it. Did he say his name was Zeke?"

"Did you lock it when you left?"

"Yeah, I'm pretty sure we did."

"Was the gate unlocked this morning?" Finn asked.

"Yep. Figured that was so I could come through again." Nate swallowed and glanced toward Grace. "I didn't do anything wrong, did I?"

She shook her head.

He pulled on his gloves. "Anyhow, sorry I'm late. This wind is bringing branches down all over the place, and my worker from yesterday didn't show this morning." He rapped on the front of the truck. "C'mon, son. The sooner you get moving, the sooner we'll be out of the rain."

The teen slid from the passenger door, carefully tucking his IPod into his coveralls. Earbuds plugged both ears. Turning toward Grace, the driver rolled his eyes. "We'll be outa here in a jiffy, ma'am. Thanks for hiring Samuels Sanitation Service." He nodded in her direction and then pulled a lever. A hydraulic Tommy Lift platform ratcheted down from the rear of the truck.

As Nate and son gathered the johns, Finn and Grace turned back to hastily complete their examination of the barn's exterior. The padlock was nowhere to be found. Grace said she was the only one with a key, and it was on the ring attached to her belt. Finn hunched over his kit, trying to keep it dry as he dusted the latch and peeled off several partials. "I'll need the prints of everyone who might have touched this."

"You can take mine today. I'll find a way to ask Josh when he gets back. And you already have most of the staff's prints."

"True." Prints from the three ARU defendants were on file, and so were Brittany Morgan's. All four had court records.

Grace spent most of her time with criminals, even if they were minor ones. Now, with this cover-up of real crime and invention of a fictional one, he was in danger of joining their ranks.

Chapter 5

Grace pulled on a waterproof jacket and insisted on searching the surrounding woods despite the wind, while Finn finally sat down to talk to Jon Zyrnek. The passing time chafed at him. If he'd called in the case right away, a tech could have gathered evidence while he interviewed the staff. If the gorillas had escaped, they could be dozens of miles away by now. If they'd been stolen, that distance could be hundreds of miles.

When he entered the staff trailer, Zyrnek was sitting at a tiny kitchenette table with a cell phone to his ear. He pulled it away, punched a button, and then stuck the phone into his pocket.

Finn asked, "Who were you talking to just now?"

Zyrnek made a face, pulled his phone back out, punched a couple of buttons and then thrust it under Finn's nose. "Caryn Brown. She was on the duty roster for tomorrow."

Finn leaned back a couple of inches so he could focus on the call log on the minuscule screen. CarynB was the first name on the list. Zyrnek jerked the phone away before he could read the rest. Finn made a mental note to check the kid's cell phone records.

He had never been inside this trailer. Grace had purchased it last fall when she'd finally received some money for staff help. Like the other portable structures in the compound, it was very basic. The door opened onto a compact living area with a threadbare carpet, a thrift store couch, and two canvas sling chairs. To the left was a kitchen/dining area furnished with a small dinette set, separated from the living room by a counter/breakfast bar with three stools tucked beneath it. To the right, down a short hallway, Finn could see the single bedroom and the ends of stacked bunk beds. He was surprised how neat the place was. With the rain pattering on the roof, it was almost cozy. In the kitchen, a cardboard box held beer cans and soda bottles—recycling. Grease-stained pizza boxes were crumpled into a wastebasket, the sight reminding him that he'd had no breakfast, and now he'd missed lunch, too.

He pulled out a chair and sat. Scooting toward the table, he extracted the notepad and pen he always kept in his shirt pocket. "Tell me about yesterday."

"Uh...it was a busy day."

Smart aleck. "Start at the beginning, from when you got up."

Zyrnek launched into a detailed explanation of what he'd done all day long, starting with helping the porta-potty guys set up the toilets. Grace joined them the midst of his description. She hung her dripping jacket on a peg near the door and slid into a chair. Her shirt cuffs and hair were soaked and her expression was grim. She shook her head to indicate that she'd found nothing in the forest.

"You fixed the lock on the gate so the sanitation guys could get in?" Finn asked Zyrnek.

"Uh...yeah." The youth glanced at Grace. "I figured we'd be busy and it would be a hassle to wait for someone to walk down the road and let them in. The delivery guys were supposed to secure the padlock when they left."

"Did they?"

Zyrnek's gaze bounced sideways to Grace and then back again. "I didn't check."

The kid was obviously feeling guilty about that. And maybe about other things, too. "Did you open it for them this morning?" Finn asked.

"No."

"According to the driver, the gate was open."

Zyrnek had the decency to look upset. "Well, fuck!" He turned to Grace. "Sorry, Boss, but it had to be one of the others as they were leaving last night."

Finn kept his gaze on Zyrnek. "We'll ask all the staff about locking the gate. Did you notice any unusual activity yesterday? Anyone acting suspicious?"

The kid smoothed a strand of hair back from his forehead. "Everything was unusual. It's not like we have crowds of strangers crawling over this place every day."

They batted the talk back and forth for a few minutes more, but if Zyrnek had seen anything important, he either didn't remember it or said he didn't.

"Did your father come to the open house yesterday?"

"Yeah, he came during his lunch hour." Zyrnek grew defensive. "He wanted to see where I worked. He wasn't 'acting suspicious' in any way. I showed him around, we shot the breeze for a few minutes, then he left in his pickup."

Zyrnek Senior had recently gotten out of prison. His son worked with valuable gorillas. Now those gorillas were missing. Coincidence? Finn suspected that one or both Zyrneks were involved somehow. But as yet he had no evidence to back up his suspicions, so he merely said, "I want to talk to Tony. And to any other visitors we can find."

Grace nodded. "I'll make a list of the ones I remember."

Zyrnek picked up his phone.

Finn asked him, "Who are you calling?"

"My dad. To let him know you want to talk to him."

Finn clamped a hand around Zyrnek's wrist. "Don't." He didn't want the felon to have time to concoct a story or talk a friend into an alibi.

The kid grimaced and laid the phone back down on the table. "Of course. You want to ambush him."

Ignoring that, Finn turned to Grace. "I want to talk to the rest of your staff, too."

She said, "I want to be there. I'll have questions you won't think of."

Since this wasn't an official police case, he'd have to fit those interviews around his work schedule. "Let me set up the appointments. I'll let you know, okay?"

She started to protest, but then her shoulders slumped and she rubbed a hand across her forehead. "I was about to say it's not easy for me to get away. But it's not like I have a lot else to do now, is it?"

"Hang in there, Grace." Finn checked his watch and slid his chair back. "My shift starts in forty minutes. Gotta go put the gears in motion."

Placing a hand on her shoulder, he leaned forward and brushed Grace's cheek with his lips. "Tell him"—he tilted his head toward Zyrnek—"about our mythical dog."

Two hours later, Finn tried to act nonchalant as he wrapped up his fake dog mystery story with the sergeant. "Dr. McKenna swears the blood stain belongs to one of her gorillas that got injured a few days ago."

Behind his desk, Sergeant Greer leaned back in his chair, which creaked under his substantial weight. The fluorescent lights gleamed off his bald scalp. "I forgot that you're still hooking up with Gorilla Lady."

Finn bristled. "Her name is Dr. Grace McKenna, and her research has put Evansburg on the map."

"Can't deny that." Greer sat upright, snapping his chair back into its former position. "We used to be known for our historic churches and fine beef. Now we're Apeville. And you are without a doubt the finest ape detective in the state."

Finn thought he was past most of his challenges as a newcomer, proving himself with a one hundred percent resolution rate on his cases. But he'd given up on trying to befriend Greer.

Finn pressed on. "So, although I'm not sure that this is a bona fide claim of an injured or kidnapped dog, we need to get this blood tested to prove one way or the other." He waved the baggie of blood-soaked sawdust, feeling like a bad actor in an amateur play. "I need a case number for the lab."

Greer leaned forward and clasped his hands on his desk. His fingers were long and thick. Everything about him was super-sized. Finn was glad the guy was sitting down during this conversation.

"Why didn't the owner call in the crime?" Greer asked.

"He showed up at Dr. McKenna's this morning. I was there when he drove in, so I took the information from him."

The sergeant scowled. "Nobody else saw this champion stud dog? Seems fishy to me."

Finn exhaled dramatically to demonstrate his shared frustration. "I'm with you there. The guy is one of those high maintenance types from Los Angeles. You know how they love to sue if things don't go their way. Not just Dr. McKenna. He'd probably include the department if it looks like we didn't do our job. I figure we need to go through the motions."

He was proud of himself for tacking on the L.A. detail. Around Evansburg, Californians got blamed for pretty much everything.

"Huh." The sergeant crossed his arms and stared at the ceiling again, debating.

"Did I mention the guy's an attorney?" Finn asked. Might as well pile it on.

"Fantastic. Just what we need." Greer yanked a blank form from a stack, copied the number into a notebook, and then slid the form across his desk. "Deal with the idiot, Finn. I don't ever want to see him in here."

"Ah, c'mon, Sarge, you never know when you'll need a California lawyer."

"I'd rather get hemorrhoids."

"I'll need to spend time interviewing staff and volunteers who were at the open house yesterday," Finn told him. "Guests, too, if I can find 'em. See if they saw anything."

The sergeant waved him away. "Knock yourself out. But remember, any real case that comes up takes precedence."

"Got it." Finn took the form to his desk and set about filling in all the fictitious information. Then he had Miki run the sample and a copy of the form over to the lab. With luck, he'd have the results in a couple of days.

With better luck, he and Grace would find the gorillas before then.

Grace wanted to believe all three apes had escaped into the

woods, but the large blood pool and the drag marks in the barn made that seem improbable. Several dirtballs were going to be involved in this, whatever *this* was. And he was willing to bet that one or two of the dirtballs would be named Zyrnek.

After spending half an hour reviewing a check-kiting case that he was scheduled to testify on the next day, Finn looked up Anthony Zyrnek's history. The guy had definitely gone off the deep end fourteen years ago. A fraud charge for selling fake sports merchandise, followed by a count of armed robbery while awaiting trial on the fraud case, with the added bonus of felony evasion when the cops answered the robbery alarm. Three counts of major stupid in rapid succession.

He called the auto salvage yard where Tony Zyrnek worked. A recorded message informed him that the place was closed. Zyrnek was likely to be home. Finn grabbed his keys. The sooner he caught up with Zyrnek Senior, the better.

The address belonged to an ancient rusting doublewide with moss spreading up its sides, set back among the trees in a mobile home park. A fallen branch half-obscured the sign at the entrance: Brigadoon. The name was appropriate; the place seemed to have been forgotten by the modern world. A better name for it would have been Brigadoom; it looked like a retirement village for losers.

An old white pickup with a dented red passenger door and a crumpled brown hood occupied the gravel parking strip, which was also littered with clumps of fir and pine cones from nearby trees. A yellow pickup canopy leaned against the doublewide a few yards away, rainwater dripping from its edges.

The deluge had stopped for the moment, so Finn left his jacket in the car while he copied down the pickup's license plate and snapped a couple of photos from different angles. The lights of a television flickered behind the closed curtains inside the mobile home. Finn walked up the two cement block steps to knock on the metal door, which swung open before the third rap.

"Yeah?" Tony Zyrnek's short black hair was peppered with gray and sleeked back. Finn saw a resemblance to Jonathan, although this man had darker coloring and was a few inches taller and more muscular than his son. His thick mustache was sharply delineated and his hair neatly combed, in contrast with Jon's shoulder-length hair and wispy beard. Instead of the stained sweatshirt and sagging jeans Finn had come to expect from ex-cons, Zyrnek Senior wore a plaid cowboy shirt and jeans with pressed creases down the front. His feet were clad only in socks. Finn didn't remember seeing him at Grace's event, but he'd switched off with Scoletti at the gate, and there was nothing about this man's appearance that would particularly stand out in a crowd.

Finn showed his badge. The ex-con squinted at it, then at him. "You're not here about Jon, are you? Is he okay?" The guy had a slight southern drawl.

"Your son is fine," Finn assured him.

"Oh, thank God." Zyrnek's shoulders relaxed. "He called and said he wasn't feeling well and was staying at his workplace overnight, but you never know."

"He lies to you a lot?"

"What?" Zyrnek gave him a perturbed look. "No. I meant your coming here scared me."

"I'm here about something else. You were at the open house yesterday, correct?"

"Yeah. It was cool to see those gorillas. C'mon in."

The door opened directly into the living area, which held a small couch, an armchair, and a coffee table. A plate of what looked like goulash steamed on top of the table, an open bottle of beer and a folded paper towel beside it. The tops of a pair of cowboy boots peeked out from beneath the table. Next to the wall, the television was on. Zyrnek was watching *Jeopardy* as he ate.

The scent of tomatoes, garlic, and oregano filled the air. Finn swallowed the saliva pooling in his mouth as he explained about the missing dog. "I'm interviewing all the guests I can find to see if they saw anything."

Zyrnek gestured toward the chair. His right hand was swathed tightly in bandages. "Have a seat, Detective."

A loud thump sounded from the roof of the mobile home. They both looked up at the ceiling.

"Pine cone," Zyrnek said. "I thought we were done with that for a while. Squirrely winds we had earlier, huh?"

Clearly Zyrnek was into small talk. Finn said, "I hear it happens sometimes in the spring."

"Did you hear a plane crashed over at the Moses Lake airport? Wind shear or crosswind or something. Nobody died, though."

"Is that right? They must have been hit harder than we were." Moses Lake was more than seventy miles away. He knew there was a small airport there for cargo jets and personal planes.

Zyrnek nodded. "Want a beer or a soda?"

"No, thanks." Finn sat down.

"Let me get you something to eat." Zyrnek padded into the tiny kitchen.

"No, thanks," Finn said again, keeping a wary eye on Zyrnek over the counter that separated kitchen from living room.

The man returned with a food-laden plate in one hand, and a fork, paper towel, and open beer in the other. He set everything down on the table in front of Finn's knees. Damn, it smelled delicious.

"Might as well." Zyrnek sat down on the couch, picked up his fork, and pointed the tines at the plate he'd just delivered. "Chili mac. I cooked for two tonight, but Jon won't be back." He forked a bite of casserole into his mouth.

What the hell. Aside from a candy bar from the vending machine at the station, it was the first food he'd had all day. Finn picked up the plate and tried a forkful. Spicier than he expected, but flavorful. He took a swallow of the cold beer. Amber ale. Not bad.

"The only native marsupial of North America," read the *Jeopardy* host on the television.

Tony Zyrnek responded, "What is an opossum?"

Which turned out to be the correct answer. Registering Finn's startled expression, Zyrnek grinned. "What?"

Finn was surprised that Tony Zyrnek called the creature an opossum instead of just a 'possum like most people did. And he knew an opossum was a marsupial, which was news to Finn. There must be a lot of time in prison to memorize trivia like that.

Finn shoveled another bite into his mouth, then balanced his plate on his knees as he pulled out his notepad and pen. Fishing a remote from between the sofa cushions, Zyrnek muted the television.

"Do you remember what time you arrived at the open house?" Finn asked.

Zyrnek chewed for a second, considering. "Just a few minutes after noon. When did the dog go missing?"

Finn flipped a couple of pages, checking his nonexistent notes. "The owner said it was between noon and two." He forked up some more of the chili mac, took another swallow of beer.

"I did see a fuzzy white dog in a car in the lot, yapping and slobbering on the windows," Zyrnek volunteered. "Some kind of terrier mix. What breed are you looking for?"

"Weimaraner." Finn picked the first name that came to mind. His ex, Wendy, had a book of William Wegman photos of those dogs. "A silver gray one."

Zyrnek swallowed his last mouthful, wiped his mouth with the paper towel. "Aren't all Weimaraners gray?"

"Maybe." Finn fought to keep his expression impassive. Now he had to remember to tell Grace the dog was a silver gray Weimaraner before she invented an apricot poodle or something. This fictional dog was going to be a hassle.

He chewed, gathering his thoughts. "Can you tell me what you did while you were there at the open house event? Did you notice anyone behaving suspiciously?"

Tony moved his tongue around his mouth for a minute. Then he described how he stood in front of the cage with Neema and the baby gorilla and listened to Grace and watched them sign back and forth. Finn used the time to eat the rest of his food and finish his beer.

"Then I moved on with everyone else to the art booth they had set up. Do you know those gorillas paint?" Zyrnek asked.

"Yes." Finn set his empty plate and bottle on the table.

"Amazing, isn't it?" Zyrnek idly scratched his jaw. "There *was* one guy who asked if the gorillas liked special colors or subjects—is that suspicious?"

"Probably not." Finn said. Why would Zyrnek consider that an odd question? Fuchsia for Gumu and purple for Neema, he knew. Flowers. Landscapes. There could be a slight chance it had been Keyes, though. "What did he look like?"

Zyrnek shook his head. "Can't remember. Average joe, I guess. Didn't have a dog with him at the time." Then he added, "Did you know gorillas share ninety-eight percent of our DNA?"

Was the guy some sort of walking encyclopedia of animals? "Uh, no. Ninety-eight percent?" That was a little disturbing.

Zyrnek leaned back against the sofa cushion. "Well, don't feel bad. I wouldn't know that either except my son works with the scientist at that place. And he talks to the gorillas in sign language, too."

"I know."

Zyrnek pointed a fork at him. "*You're* the detective Dr. McKenna's involved with, aren't you? Jon told me about you."

"Yeah." Finn hated the way everyone knew everyone in this small town. "Did Jon take you on a special tour of the gorilla compound?"

Tony Zyrnek described walking around the barn and seeing the trailers where Jon slept and worked with the apes. "Didn't get to go in the barn, though," he volunteered. "Jon said the big gorilla was sleeping up in the net and he'd get upset if a stranger came into his territory."

Why had the man specifically mentioned the inside of the barn? Was this a case of protesting too much?

"What happened to your hand?" Finn pointed at the bandages.

Zyrnek held his injured hand out between them. "An engine slipped off the hoist and like an idiot, I tried to catch it. Got kinda mangled, but I'm lucky—no broken bones. Want to see?"

Finn shook his head. If Zyrnek was willing to show him, the wound wouldn't be a gorilla bite.

A phone on the kitchen counter rang. Zyrnek excused himself to get up and answer it. After a few seconds, he murmured, "I'm busy right now; call again later." He set the phone back in the base.

"Was that important?" Finn asked. "It would have been okay to talk."

Zyrnek slid into his seat. "Just a personal thing. I'll handle it later."

Finn made a mental note to check Zyrnek's landline records, and then tried to think of what to ask next.

Zyrnek filled in the conversational void. "I didn't see any dogs except that one in the parking lot. I saw a calico cat walk out of the barn, though, which surprised me. I would think a little kitty like that would be scared to death of a gorilla."

"There are two cats. Apparently the gorillas consider them their pets."

"Really?" Zyrnek shot a sideways look at Finn as if he thought the detective was pulling his leg.

"Neema, the female gorilla, even named them. The calico's named Nest, and the white one is Snow."

"No shit?" Zyrnek leaned forward, interested. "Why Nest?"

Finn had asked Grace exactly the same question. "The cat looked like a nest made of different colored blankets."

Zyrnek slapped his thigh and shook his head. "Well, I'll be damned. I'll have to ask Jon about that. I always liked cats. A friend of mine had an ocelot once. Man, I wish I'd seen it. You got cats?"

"Two," Finn said. "And a big dog."

"I knew it!" Zyrnek slapped his leg again. "You're a fellow animal lover."

Finn snorted. The conversation was getting off-track. To bring it back, he asked, "What did you do after you left the open house?"

Zyrnek's eyes twinkled as he used his thumb and forefinger

to smooth down his moustache. "You're asking just in case I ran across this Weimaraner later in the day?"

Smug, Finn thought. The guy was on parole; the cops could question him at any time about anything, and he knew it. He waited.

"Nope," Zyrnek finally responded. "No Weimaraner. After the open house I went back to work at the auto salvage. I only had my lunch hour free. You can ask my boss."

"I will." Finn closed his notebook, stuck it in his shirt pocket, then stood up.

Zyrnek walked him the few steps to the door.

Before stepping out, Finn narrowed his eyes at the ex-con. "I know about your record," he told him.

"'Course you do," Zyrnek responded cheerfully. "So you understand I don't know many folks around here. I'm heading off to the roadhouse in a minute to see if I can round up a pool game. Want to come?"

"I'm on duty until after midnight."

"Oh, of course. Some other time, then. Hey, you and I and Jon should all go out for a beer one of these days. Talk about animals."

Finn snorted and thumped down the steps to his car. No question, Tony Zyrnek was smart and charming. No wonder Grace had thought he was nice. He was a classic charismatic con man. And all too interested in the gorillas. Zyrnek's face and hands were mostly unmarked, so he couldn't have struggled much with a gorilla. But he might have been the leader of a group of thieves.

Finn barely made it into the driver's seat before the rain started to splat against the windshield again. He dialed Grace to see if she could join him to interview her staff members, Caryn Brown and Sierra Sakson. His call went to voicemail, but Grace called fifteen minutes later as he was driving back to the station.

"I was in the woods. No cell coverage," she explained in a dull voice. "No luck, either."

"Sorry to hear that."

"Do you think you could get a dog? You know, a canine unit that can track?"

"What would I tell them?"

There was a long pause on her end. "You can't make something up?"

It was bad enough *he* was running around talking up this nonexistent Weimaraner. Now she was asking him to lie to more cops so he could get more law enforcement resources? He needed to keep this job. "Everything goes on the record in police work, Grace."

"I get it." Then there was a strangled sound, like she was cutting off a sob. "I do. I'm sorry I asked."

"It's okay." He felt like he should say something else, but he had no idea what. He didn't want to tell her he was investigating the Zyrneks until he found something incriminating. The call waiting signal bleeped over his car receiver, rescuing him. The station.

"We'll have to do that interview tomorrow. I gotta take this," he told her, found the cell phone on the seat beside him, and hit the Flash button to switch over.

"Burglary," Greer announced. "This is the third incident. Looks like we got ourselves some pros."

"I heard about the first two." The detective going off duty from the early shift—Perry Dawes, in this case—filled in the one coming on in person, if time permitted.

"Good, you're up to speed. Rodrigo's on evidence right now; he'll meet you at the address." He rattled off a house number about six miles away.

"On my way." It was a relief to focus on a case that had nothing to do with secret missing gorillas or mythical dogs.

The burglary victims were Daryl and Bonnie Dupree, a retired couple. Their house was one of hundreds of the same ranch style, vinyl-sided homes of the Vista Village development across from a large farm and orchard. To the left of the Dupree house was a vacant lot, to the right a nearly identical house.

The only distinguishing aspect of the Duprees' home was a large RV parked off to the side of the two-car garage. It was a windy, mostly treeless area. The only charm was the view of the nearby mountains.

On seeing Finn, Daryl cocked his head. "I remember you from the TV last year. You're that gorilla guy, aren't you?"

Finn sighed. Why did everyone remember the gorilla connection and not the fact that he'd solved a kidnapping case? He guessed he should be grateful that the locals no longer referred to him as the detective whose wife ran off with the professor.

After a quick group examination of the smashed window in the back door, Rodrigo set about taking photos and lifting prints while Finn interviewed the Duprees at their kitchen table.

"Any idea who might have done this?" Finn asked.

They both shook their heads, then Daryl used his fingers to tick off the reasons they couldn't think of a likely suspect. One, they weren't rich by any means; two, they hadn't hired any temporary help recently; three, none of the neighbors seemed suspicious; and four, the migrant worker housing across the road was currently vacant.

"I don't know how the burglars guessed we weren't home," Daryl groused.

"We're *always* here, except for a handful of days when we go off to visit friends," Bonnie added. "We didn't even tell anyone, since we took the dogs with us."

"You normally park your RV out front?" Finn asked.

"Except for when we take it camping," Bonnie said.

Finn let the implication soak in.

Daryl got the point first. "Well, if I don't feel dumber than dirt." He passed a hand over his bald crown. "Guess I'll park the rig out back from now on or rent a space somewhere."

The Duprees were organized, giving him a neatly printed list of the stolen items. Chainsaw, miter saw, cordless drill, two gold class rings, half a bottle of old Oxycontin tablets (left over from Bonnie's knee surgery), a Colt pistol, and a Remington shotgun.

Finn gritted his teeth at the last two items. "Were the firearms locked up?"

Bonnie's expression slipped from angelic grandma toward peeved schoolmarm. "There's no point in having guns if you can't get at them quick, right? The pistol was hidden under some magazines in my bedside drawer, and the shotgun was under the bed on Daryl's side."

Rodrigo appeared in the kitchen doorway, fingerprint kit in hand. "Next?"

The homeowners stood. "Come on." Daryl pointed down the hall. "Maybe you can get prints from the jewelry case or the bed table."

As he waved Finn and Rodrigo past him into the bedroom, Daryl commented, "Should have taken the guns with us, I guess."

"At least we still have the Glock." Bonnie turned to Finn. "It was with us in the camper."

Two more weapons added to the street, one to go. "Keep an eye on that Glock," he recommended. "Burglars who score guns often come back looking for more."

The lights were still on in the house next door, so after dismissing Rodrigo, Finn knocked and chatted briefly with the neighbor. The rain, thankfully, had stopped for the moment, and although the moon and stars were still obscured, the evening seemed a little less dismal. Or at least less damp.

"I didn't see or hear anything unusual," the man told him. "Only thing going on was a little activity over there on Saturday evening." He briefly tilted his head to indicate the migrant worker housing across the road.

"And what activity was that?" Finn asked.

"I came out to have a smoke out on the porch because I had a carpet cleaner finishing up inside. Usually we just get one car parked over there—kids making out, but this time I saw two cars. Then, after a few minutes a white van swung in there and a couple guys got out and got into the cars and then they all took off." He lifted a shoulder. "I figured it was kind of a weird place to do a park and ride shuffle, but whatever."

"Can you describe the vehicles?"

"Can't say I paid too much attention. The van was white, one of those utility kind with no windows in back, and the other two were old and kinda dark colored. The two cars took off up the road." He pointed toward the mountains. "And the van took off toward the highway."

"When was this?"

"The carpet cleaner left around a quarter past six. He was loading up when I saw everyone drive off. But they never came back here, at least as far as I know. Do you think those cars are important?"

"Probably not." Finn handed him a business card. "But let me know if you see them again, okay?"

"Jeez, that's a shame, the Duprees getting ripped off like that. I'll spread the word around the neighborhood to be on the lookout."

Finn drove across the road to the migrant worker camp and walked around, shining his flashlight into the buildings. They were basic shacks, outfitted with plywood bunk bed platforms, tacky tables, and rusty folding chairs. Nothing more. Only the central building, which had water and electrical lines leading into it, was locked. He didn't see anything that seemed related to burglary.

It took him until nearly one a.m. to write up the report and do other paperwork at the station before he could call it quits for the day. He slid into his car and then called Grace. No answer. "Guess our rendezvous is postponed," he said to her voicemail. "Rain check?"

Of course there was no response, and after a couple of seconds he said, "I'll talk to you tomorrow. Together, we're going to figure this out, Grace."

In his home mailbox, among the usual bills and ads, Finn found an envelope from his ex-wife. He tossed the mail onto the table as he waded through the typical assault from his hungry dog and cats.

He fed Cargo and Lok and Kee, then took out a bottle of beer and sat down at the table. The return address on the envelope was Gwen Mankin Black in Spokane. Now his ex was going by Gwen instead of Wendy?

What the heck did she want this time? She had forfeited her share of his measly salary when she married her boy toy a year ago. She left Finn the animals and the house, and he'd be damned if he was going to share any of it with her.

After he'd popped the top from the beer and taken a sip, he opened the envelope. Inside was a card with a photo of Wendy holding a red, wrinkled newborn. *ANNOUNCING Aidan Alexander Black.*

He set the card on its edge, leaning it against the growing stack of junk mail to recycle. The baby boy had dark hair and eyes, like Wendy. At least he didn't look like Gordon Black, the guy she'd run off with.

Finn was now pretty sure she'd orchestrated their move from Chicago to Evansburg to get closer to her old flame. A better place to raise a family, she'd said; close to her parents. He'd given up his job and his condo with a view of the lake. And then she'd taken off only a few months after they'd moved here.

She had a lot of nerve, sending him a birth announcement for the kid that should have been his. And she didn't even live in Evansburg anymore but had moved to Spokane, so the baby wouldn't have his grandparents in his daily life after all.

His ex and her new baby boy stared at him. Wendy had established a whole new identity for herself.

"You may have Aidan in your life, *Gwen,*" he snarled at the photo, "But I have gorillas. Not many people can top that."

Of course, it was debatable how many people would *want* gorillas in their lives. And right now it was debatable whether there would be gorillas in his future.

* * * * *

Just after midnight, Jon and Grace split up to do a last tour through the dark forest that bounded her research compound. The beam of his flashlight soon faded through the trees, but she heard him shouting for Neema and Gumu as he moved northward while she moved south, turning now and then to flash her headlamp in all directions. It was difficult to tell if the rain had stopped. Branches overhead steadily dripped cold water down her neck.

The big male gorilla was unlikely to come to the sound of his name. But if Neema was out there listening, she might. "Neema!" she shouted. "Neema! I have a lollipop for you."

Neema called the suckers on a stick *tree candy*; they were her favorite treat. If Neema could hear her, if Neema was capable of moving, the promise of a lollipop might bring her. Grace stopped walking and held her breath, listening to the dark woods. All she heard were drips splattering the shoulders of her jacket and plopping onto the ground all around her.

Was she deluding herself? Was it wishful thinking that the gorillas might have escaped? Gumu was defensive with strangers and terrifyingly strong. If a man had tried to tackle him, Gumu could very well have prevailed and then led his family to safety. He was a huge animal, too. If the blood in the barn was Gumu's, it might not represent a lethal loss for an ape his size, but if the blood belonged to Neema, or Kanoni... No, she couldn't let her mind go down that black tunnel. "Neema! Kanoni! Lollipop!"

After ninety minutes, she returned to the compound exhausted, hungry, and depressed. After sunset, the temperature dipped here in the foothills of the Cascades. Gorillas were as susceptible to colds and pneumonia as humans. Maybe even more so. Especially gorillas who were used to sleeping indoors.

She pulled on a dry sweatshirt, and then busied herself cutting vegetables and fruit into a tub. She was laying them out on the food shelf alongside the barn when Jon reappeared from the woods, chafing his bare arms against the chill. His lips were tightly pressed into a straight line, and he shook his head. "No sign of them. Think it's a wild goose chase?"

"It's too soon to think that." She'd rather envision the gorillas in the woods than imprisoned. Or worse. The image of Spencer's contorted body flashed across her brain. She tried to push that scene out of her mind, but succeeded in replacing the horrific memory with an even worse possibility: Neema bleeding to death from a stab wound, Kanoni crying helplessly by her side. She pinched herself through the sweatshirt sleeve to bring her thoughts back to reality. "I'll leave the gate and the barn door open in case they come back."

Jon ran dirty fingers through his long hair as he peered through the gate out into the grassy courtyard. "You're not afraid of attracting bears?"

"Raccoons, probably. Maybe an opossum." She'd seen both of those in the yard at one time or another. "Bears?"

"You should check the news once in awhile, boss. This whole area's under a bear watch."

"Really?" She hadn't seen the news for several days. But she hadn't seen a bear, either. "Guess I'll take the chance."

She picked up the empty tub and started for the yard.

"Grace?"

She turned. Jon stared at the ground and scuffed a toe in the dirt. He looked like an overgrown three-year-old trying not to cry. "I really thought the gorillas were okay last night."

She walked back to him, touched her fingers to his shoulder. "I know you did. I thought they were okay, too. It's not your fault. Get some sleep. If they're not back tonight, we'll start looking again in the morning." She looked at her watch. "Later *this* morning, I mean."

When she returned to her personal trailer, Grace checked her phone. She knew Matt meant his voicemail to be reassuring, but instead, it annoyed her. Of course their rendezvous was off. How could he even think that it was a possibility when her gorillas were missing? Still, she liked that word *together*, although she wasn't sure what it meant to him right now. She texted him, saying she had searched the woods but found nothing and wanted to compare notes tomorrow. Then she nuked a bowl of soup and ate it in front of her television set, where she learned what Jon had been talking about.

On their round-the-clock local station, a woman holding a toddler was saying, "I heard a racket outside and there was a big black bear on the deck. It ate my dog's food. Then it ripped down my bird feeder."

The boy beside her smiled big for the camera and chirped, "It was real scary!"

The scene moved to the newscaster at a studio desk. "Homeowners are spotting more black bears in their yards this spring than ever before. Experts cite our late spring snowfalls and cooler than usual weather. Many of the plants the bears feed on are not yet abundant, and so hungry bears are wandering into urban areas. The state department of Fish and Wildlife urges residents to store garbage cans and food for pets and livestock inside buildings."

The picture changed to show a Fish and Wildlife employee in the woods standing alongside a culvert trap. "Efforts are underway to trap and remove problem bears as soon as possible. Property owners are reminded that it is *not* bear hunting season. We encourage citizens to use proven best practices with all wild animals. Lock up your garbage; lock up your pet food. If you see a bear, please call us so we can protect both you and the bear."

None of her gorillas had ever seen a bear, and it was a pretty good bet that no northwest bear had ever seen a gorilla. If confronted, Gumu would launch into a threat display, thumping his chest and rushing the bear. Neema would probably run. How would a hungry black bear respond?

Snow, the cat that Neema claimed as her own, climbed into Grace's lap and curled her paws under her body. Grace scratched her under the chin. The cat closed her green eyes and purred. Tonight the sound did little to soothe Grace's jangling nerves.

Should she have sounded the alarm immediately and set off the search for the gorillas? Matt thought so. But the county council would come crashing down on her like a spring mudslide, accusing her of endangering the community. They'd close down her research facility. The college would cancel her funding. With no budget and no place to go, she might lose the gorillas.

She bit her lip. Maybe she'd already lost them. Maybe she'd signed their death warrants by not calling the authorities.

Last time Neema and Gumu had escaped, they'd roamed the forest for four days before she'd tracked them down. No matter what Matt said, she'd give herself at least four days to locate them. Ninety-six hours. Setting the cat aside on the couch, she got up to mark the calendar. She made a big X through today's date. And then she saw a note she'd scribbled the square four days down on a Thursday: *County Agricultural Inspector.*

That was another condition of her county permit; that her facility be inspected once a year "to determine the health and safe living conditions of her livestock." And of course the college had scheduled their board meeting so they could factor the inspector's report into their decision.

What if the gorillas weren't back in four days? If she asked for a postponement, the inspector would want to know why. Feeling even more desperate, she turned off the television, and went outside to call the gorillas one more time. The only response from the woods was the haunting cry of a great horned owl.

Chapter 6

Meat. Danger. Run. With Kanoni on her back, Neema ran through dark night and then day, moving far from the meat smell. Now it was dark again. She stopped beside a stream, bending down to drink the cold water. Kanoni copied, slurping loudly and splashing with her hands.

Neema was hungry. She wanted yogurt; she wanted red fruit; she wanted cabbage. A long green yellow worm crawled across the ground. She put it in her mouth and chewed. She pulled some leaves from a bush and ate them. A plant with long green branches tasted better, so she ate most of it.

She sat between the roots of a big tree and pulled Kanoni to her breast to nurse. She was tired. She had been in the trees before, but always with Gumu or Grace. *Gorilla big here, gorilla baby*, she signed to herself.

Kanoni pulled away to watch her hands move. She whimpered and stretched her arm up to pat Neema's lips with her small cool fingers. *Dark here*, Neema signed. *Sad*. She wanted Gumu. Grace. Food. Blankets. Her white white soft cat. Gumu's orange white black warm cat.

Gumu! She hooted. Bird noises. Was Gumu meat for always? She stared into the dark trees around her. Where was safe? She pulled pine cones and twigs up around her legs and curled up against the tree with Kanoni in her arms. Small animals moved in the trees and on the ground. Neema grunted to let them know she was bigger. She curled over her baby and waited for the sun.

Birds came with the sun. Crows made noise in the trees. One landed near. Kanoni chased it while it hopped, then ran back when the bird flapped away. Sitting in front of Neema, Kanoni signed *Go*.

Bird go, Neema signed, then *hungry.* She and Gumu found apples in the trees before. She liked apples. Pushing Kanoni onto her back, Neema walked through the trees, sniffing for apples.

Ahead, she smelled food. *Sweet. Good.* And something dirty, like mouse turned meat. She followed the smell to a metal tunnel. Food was inside. Kanoni slid from Neema's back onto the grass. *Food,* Neema signed. Kanoni stared and sat playing with her toes, afraid of the strange tunnel. *Food,* Neema signed again.

She climbed in. It was a small round room, barely big enough for a gorilla. A fish hung on a wire. Dirty mouse meat smell. She turned away from it. The bread smelled better, but it was hard, wrapped in a net, tied to the window wire. Honey was in the pail. Neema picked that up, pulled against the rope tied to the handle.

With a screech, a door behind her slammed down. Neema dropped the pail and rushed back, huffing. She slammed a hand against the heavy metal grid. The door made a loud noise, but it didn't move.

Outside, Kanoni crouched half-hidden under a bush. The whites of her eyes showed. She whimpered. Neema stood on her hind legs and put her fingers through the wire squares. She pulled. The wire bent a little, but the door didn't open. She tried using her feet. More bending, but not open.

Kanoni came out of the bush and tried to pull, too, her baby mouth wide with fright. The door between them did not move.

Chapter 7

"Please describe all the vehicles you can remember in the staff parking lot," Finn asked Sierra Sakson.

His brain felt fuzzy. He'd had only five hours sleep, and judging by the purple shadows under Grace's eyes, she hadn't been to bed at all. They'd compared notes over coffee. He told her about Tony Zyrnek's pickup.

"Thousands of people have vehicles that gorillas could fit into," she'd retorted. "How about my van? Someone might have borrowed it while I was at your house."

Grace was right. He should inspect her van, too. But she agreed that locating a vehicle with traces of blood and gorilla fur might be the quickest way to find whoever had broken into the barn.

Sierra, a twenty-one-year-old college student, was one of Grace's most trusted staff members. Her roommate and fellow Animal Rights Union activist, Caryn Brown, perched beside her on the faded black futon couch in their apartment. The decor was garage sale chic. Finn and Grace sat on old-fashioned red canvas director's chairs, separated from the students by a couple of cheap round metal and glass tables of the type normally seen on patios. Movie posters in red, white, and black covered most of the wall space.

Both college students seemed to have added several piercings to eyebrows and ears since he had met them last year in court. Finn couldn't stop staring at the ruby-colored stud in Sierra's left nostril. Was it held on by a backing like a pierced earring? Did she have to stick her finger up her nose to fasten it? Did it get gunked up when she had a cold?

Sierra ran her fingers through her burgundy-streaked black hair and wrinkled her nose, twitching the ruby stud. "What would cars back there have to do with a missing dog?" she asked Grace.

"We just wondered if a stranger could have slipped in that way," Grace told her. "Was the gate locked when you drove in?"

The two young women shared a look. Caryn screwed up her lips for a minute as if considering, then said, "No, Z unlocked it for the porta-potty truck. We left it that way."

Anyone could have driven in after the staff arrived. Finn studied both young women carefully. Their faces and arms were unmarked, so they probably had not done battle with a gorilla. But that didn't mean they hadn't been involved; ARU was a big network and they might have directed an operation. He asked, "Has ARU pulled off any stunts lately?"

All three women scowled at him.

"We're not answering that," Caryn snapped. She picked up a bright blue pillow and hugged it defensively in front of her.

"As for cars in the lot..." Sierra raised her eyes to the ceiling, thinking. "My VW bug, of course, and Grace's old van. Some of the other volunteers came in a minivan. Hey, is your friend Scotty involved with anyone?"

Scotty? "You mean Officer Scoletti?"

"Probably." Sierra gave him a coy look. "Blond brush cut? Freckles? Cute, in a farm boy sort of way. Does he have a girlfriend?"

Finn didn't know. "I doubt it," he said.

"What's his first name?"

He was embarrassed now. "I think it's Rookie."

"Really?" Caryn said, running her chartreuse-colored nails through her white-blond pixie cut. "That's kind of cool. With a Y or an I?"

Grace gave him a dirty look. Finn cleared his throat. "Back to the cars, please, ladies."

Sierra volunteered, "Z drove a pickup that morning."

Finn perked up. Only Grace's van had been parked in the lot when they'd discovered the gorillas missing, and supposedly Z had been there all night.

"He usually rides his bike, but his dad loans him the truck if he wants to haul something," Caryn said.

"Jon volunteered to pick up the signs for the open house," Grace told Finn.

He turned to Caryn, his pen poised in the air. "Can you describe this pickup?"

The student absently fingered one of her eyebrow rings. "All I remember is that it looked like a patchwork quilt, all different colors. His dad puts pieces together—recycling, you know. But the important thing is, they run."

"Open-bed pickup?" Finn asked.

"It had a camper cover on the back," Caryn said.

Just as he suspected, Tony Zyrnek was involved in this, or at least his pickup was. He shot Grace a look out of the corner of his eye, but she was studiously ignoring him.

Sierra continued, "They might be gas-guzzlers, but reusing them keeps all that metal and plastic out of the dumps. And do you have a clue what sort of carbon load it takes to build a new car? Gotta consider the whole equation, you know."

Finn didn't really want to know what would be involved in that equation. He ripped a blank piece of paper out of his notebook, slapped it down on top of the left patio table. "Could you sketch where all the cars were parked?"

Sierra grabbed a pencil from the top of a crate doing duty as an end table. Then she slid off the futon seat to sit on the floor in front of the paper. "You want this to show the parking lot before or after the open house? 'Cause Z's dad took the pickup with him when he left. I went out to the bug to get a bo—" Sierra's gaze abruptly dropped to the tabletop before flashing back up to Grace. "Well, I went out there to get something, I forget now exactly what it was—after you guys left. So I was in the parking lot then, and the pickup was gone."

Bong? Bottle? Finn tried to complete Sierra's sentence. It probably didn't matter. "Before," he told her. "And mark the location of the pickup."

Finn tried to tamp down his surge of excitement so it wouldn't show on his face. The vanishing truck added weight to his theory that at least one Zyrnek was behind this. It was going to be hard for Grace to ignore.

They worked their way through the rest of the questions. No, the volunteers hadn't checked on Gumu because he was sleeping up in the net; yes, they had a good time at the party; no, they hadn't heard anything from the gorillas after Neema's initial hooting. Well yeah, there had been music and there had been some drinking and pot smoking. But nothing major.

"We were all responsible," Sierra assured Grace. That sounded to Finn like something a wayward teen would say to a parent.

"Zyrnek was at the party all evening?" Finn asked.

"You mean Z?"

"Yes," Finn said impatiently, "Jon Zyrnek."

"Yeah." Sierra exchanged another look with her roommate as if to confirm. "At least, I think so. It got kinda hot in the trailer and we all went out on the porch to cool off once in a while, but everybody was around until after midnight."

"Except Brittany—she wasn't there at all. She had to stay home with Ivy." Caryn sounded like she felt sorry for the teen mom. Then she met Finn's eyes with a smoldering gaze. "I can see what you're thinking. But I don't know why Z's dad would steal a dog."

"Unless it was being abused," Sierra suggested. "Then I'd steal it myself."

"I'd help you." Caryn pushed the blue pillow behind her.

Finn stifled an urge to roll his eyes. The county still crawled with the white rats the ARU trio had liberated from a research lab a year ago. "Ever considered stealing the gorillas?"

As if they'd rehearsed the move, both Sierra and Caryn leaned back on the couch and crossed their arms defensively.

Grace frowned. "Matt!"

"Hell no," Caryn spat.

Sierra added, "We never steal animals. We only set them free. But gorillas can't survive on their own around here, so we'd never do that." She narrowed her eyes. "Why are you asking about the gorillas?"

He'd slipped up. "You just said you'd consider stealing a dog…" He let the rest of the sentence trail off.

Caryn pointedly turned away from him. "Grace, that con artist is just trying to get money out of you. That dog probably doesn't even exist."

Finn was afraid to meet Grace's gaze for fear they'd both give away the truth of Caryn's statement.

The drawing Sierra handed him showed the pickup had been parked in the space in back of the barn door, the most convenient location for loading a gorilla or three. It also seemed convenient that Jon had forgotten to mention the arrangement for the pickup that morning. And Tony Zyrnek had gone out of his way to say he hadn't been inside the barn, while conveniently forgetting to tell Finn that he'd gone to the lot behind the barn and taken his pickup out the back way?

Finn stood up, calling an end to the meeting. "Thanks for your time."

"When should we come back to work?" Sierra asked Grace.

"I'll have to let you know." She pulled on her jacket. "We have to make sure the incubation period has passed."

"But how about you?" Caryn asked. "Aren't you worried about giving the gorillas the flu?"

Grace looked momentarily flustered, but recovered quickly. "I got the shot; I'm still immune."

As soon as the apartment door had closed behind them, Grace locked eyes with him. "I forgot about the pickup and the signs, too, Matt. It's not Jon."

"Did I say it was?"

She aimed an index finger at his forehead. "I can hear the gears grinding away in there."

"Grace, you need to consider all the possibilities." He beeped his car with the remote. "Jon is understandably loyal to his father."

"The timing doesn't make sense. You heard them. The pickup left mid-afternoon, when Tony Zyrnek did. Neema was with me until you and I left after five p.m. And then Jon was at the staff party all evening."

He searched her face. "Jon could have gone outside just long enough to tranquilize the gorillas and let his old man into the barn through the back door."

"But the gorillas know Jon, and the blood..." She pressed her lips together, not wanting to finish the end of the sentence.

"Maybe Tony Zyrnek got there first and things didn't go as smoothly as they thought it would. And he probably didn't come alone." It would be hard for even two grown men to move one unconscious gorilla, let alone three gorillas.

Grace shook her head. "You have no idea how upset Jon is right now. He feels so guilty that the gorillas disappeared while he was on duty."

Finn put a hand on her shoulder. "I know you want to believe Jon's innocent. And I hope he is. But consider the possibility, Grace, that Jon might know something about his father's involvement. He might feel guilty about that." He opened his car door. "Meet you at the Morgan house." They left in their separate vehicles.

"I'm feeling better, Dad," Jon Zyrnek told his father. "And Grace is taking good care of me. But I don't want to expose you, so I'm gonna stay here a little longer, okay?"

"You sure that's all? You sound depressed."

It sounded like his father had his head under the hood of a car. In the background he could hear the sound of an engine turning over and over without catching.

"I'm okay." He hated lying to his father, especially since they were still getting to know each other. It was absurd to think his father had anything to do with the gorillas disappearing. Wasn't it? His dad had taken the pickup and left long before anything had happened to the gorillas. Jon had personally walked him to the back lot and given him the keys.

"Hang on a sec." There was a clunk, and then his father said, "Try it now," to someone. A couple more grinding noises, and then he heard the engine fire up. There was another clunk and then less engine noise, so his father must have shut the hood or walked away.

"Dad, did you notice anything weird in the back parking lot on Saturday?"

"This about that Weimaraner? That detective seems to think I had something to do with that dog."

"I know you didn't." Jon was tempted to add *because the damn dog doesn't even exist*. "But there was some damage to the back side of the barn, and I told Grace I'd ask you about it." More lies.

"Now she thinks I rammed the pickup into the barn?"

"No, Dad, she doesn't," Jon hurriedly replied. "We just wondered if you saw anything at the back of the barn that could explain it."

"I didn't even look at the back of the barn, and I sure didn't hit it. I may not have driven a lot in recent years, son, but I still know the difference between reverse and drive. But I forgot to tell you: I didn't have to use the combination you gave me, because the lock on the gate was undone when I drove out. I left it that way, 'cause I thought there mighta been a good reason it was unlocked."

"That's okay." He'd forgotten that he'd given his father the combination to the lock on the gate so he could let himself out. "How long did it take you to drive from Grace's place back to the salvage yard?"

There was a long silence. Then his father said, "You think I mighta knocked off a liquor store on the way back to work?"

"No, of course not." He realized now what a weird question he'd just asked his father. Some detective he was.

"I'm not like that anymore, son." His father sounded sad. "I'm an average joe now, a working man. Speaking of which, I gotta get back to it. I'll be home tonight if you change your mind and want to come back. I'll be there tomorrow night, too. And the next. And the next after that. I hope you feel better soon."

Jon slid his cell phone back into his pocket, feeling like he'd failed some sort of family loyalty test. It was the fault of that shithead Finn for planting rotten thoughts about his father in his head. Of course a detective would suspect Tony Zyrnek was involved in the break-in. Cops were like that. They'd never give an ex-con the benefit of the doubt.

His dad was so glad to be out of prison, so happy to have a regular job. It was a freaky thing to watch. The man was insanely happy. He talked forever about the glory of walking and driving where he wanted to. That was his father's word, *glory*. And *thrill*. It *thrilled* him to shop and cook and choose his own clothes. And he acted so proud of his son working with gorillas like a scientist.

Jon took a deep breath and relaxed his hands. He shook out his fingers and jiggled his shoulders to loosen them up. His father never meant to leave him the first time. He'd explained; it was all about needing money, Jon's junkie mom had run off with every cent they had. He made bad choices; he had been a desperate man. But he wasn't that man now.

Tony Zyrnek would never do that to his son. Not again.

"A what?" Brittany Morgan wrapped a strand of her long strawberry blond hair around a finger.

"Weimaraner," Finn repeated, "A big silver gray dog."

She shook her head. "I don't remember anything like that."

Grace leaned forward from her chair. "Did you see Gumu on Saturday?"

The teen's brow furrowed. "Sure. He was sleeping in the net. What does Gumu have to do with the dog?"

Finn touched Brittany's knee with a finger to bring her attention back to him. "Why don't you just tell me everything you did at the open house and maybe something will come back to you."

They sat in the family room of the Morgan house. In front of them, Ivy was banging a wooden spoon against a metal cooking pan, clearly delighted by the racket she was creating. The din made it hard to talk.

He leaned toward Brittany and raised his voice. "Where did you park?"

"In the front lot with all the guests. I figured the staff parking would be filled up."

So she'd be no help identifying vehicles in the back lot.

Ivy found a metal ladle. The banging got even louder. Finn couldn't take it any longer. "Ivy!"

The toddler looked up at him. Her chubby face burst into a gummy smile. She tottered over, whacked him in the knee with the ladle and chortled, "Papa!"

Grace faked a cough, covering up a snicker. Finn rubbed his knee. He should probably be grateful for anything that lessened the tension between two of them.

Brittany blushed. She hauled her daughter into her lap. "Sorry, Detective Finn." She pulled the ladle from Ivy's fist, and just as the toddler was about to begin bawling, Brittany put the ladle to her lips and pretended to take a sip. "Mmmm. Good soup."

Ivy grabbed for the ladle and pressed it to her own lips, made an uum-uum sound, and then held it up toward her mother's face. After another pretend sip, Brittany set Ivy back on the floor.

"Go feed soup to Blueboy." She pointed to a blue stuffed dog sitting in a nearby chair.

Turning to Finn, the teenager said, "Ivy calls my dad 'Papa.' That's her word for Grandpa."

Finn winced. He'd already been relegated to Grandpa status?

"Is Z okay?" Brittany asked.

"He's not too sick, but he still might be contagious," Grace told her. "He'll be fine."

Brittany fingered her hair again. "I mean, I'm not sure he has health insurance or anything like that. He's not a full-time student and his parents don't have him on a plan. Well, he doesn't really have parents with regular jobs, so I guess that's kinda impossible anyway."

"Sounds like you're close to him," Finn observed.

She shrugged. "That's one thing we all have in common— not enough money."

Which could be a good motive for stealing gorillas.

"At least Z has a job, sort of," the teen continued. Then her cheeks pinked as she probably realized that might be a criticism of Grace's pay scale. She rushed to say, "I can't work while I'm still in school, my parents say. Because of Ivy. But as soon as I graduate, I'm getting a job and a place of my own."

Finn suspected Brittany had a few painful reality checks waiting for her after graduation day. "Back to the open house," he reminded her. "Did you meet Jon's father, Tony Zyrnek?"

"Yeah. I've been to Z's place a couple of times, and his dad's staying there. He's nice, don't you think? Z's so happy to have him back. He was showing him all over Grace's place."

She hadn't seen where the Zyrneks had gone that day or what they'd done, and she hadn't noticed the time when Tony Zyrnek left.

Finn was running out of questions. "Did the gorillas seem upset to you?"

"Of course," Brittany said. "All those people. Gorillas are really very shy, you know. That's probably why Gumu moved to the barn, to hide out."

Grace stiffened. "You saw Gumu go into the barn?"

Brittany looked at Grace, then at Finn. "He was sleeping in the net, just like you told everyone. Then I saw him walk down the net toward the barn."

Grace asked, "What time was this?"

"When everyone was walking toward the art gallery to look at the paintings. Gumu came out of his blankets, and then he went down the net."

"That would have been around four-thirty," Grace told Finn.

Finn wrote it down. Gumu could have been responding to the noise of a break-in in the barn. Between the crowd and the music, the event had been loud. That might have been an ideal time to steal the gorilla that was not on public display.

The intruders might even have been hiding in the barn when Grace put Neema and Kanoni inside the enclosure. He was conscious of Grace tensing up beside him. She looked down at her lap and combed her fingers through her hair. Was she having the same thoughts?

He had volunteered to handle security. Why hadn't he checked the back parking lot and the perimeter of the barn? If anyone should feel guilty, it should be him.

Brittany was watching Grace. "What's wrong? Did something happen to Gumu?"

Finn shared a brief uh-oh glance with Grace. She quickly looked away and patted Brittany on the knee. "We're just trying to figure out where everyone was. It's this darn dog thing. I was thinking that maybe Gumu saw the Weimaraner and went to chase him away. You know he doesn't like dogs."

Finn's cell phone buzzed. He didn't recognize the number; it was a 360 area code used all over western Washington. "Thanks, Brittany. I've got to get to the station."

He briefly squeezed Grace's hand before standing up. She didn't squeeze back.

"I need to go soon, too," Grace said. "The college board wants to talk to me this afternoon."

He turned to look at her, eyebrow raised. In his hand, his phone continued to buzz.

She shrugged and rubbed at the back of her neck, her expression already strained.

Good luck, he mouthed at her. Then he answered the phone as he walked out the door. "Detective Finn."

"This is Officer Stremler, Tacoma PD. I checked on parolee Frank Keyes for you. He just arrived back at his apartment. Says he was camping on the Olympic Peninsula from Friday night to this morning. Alone. Paid his campsite fees in cash."

Great. The nutcase had no alibi. "You believe him?"

There was a brief pause. "No reason not to at this point. What is this about?"

"Do you know anything about Keyes's history? He killed a gorilla in Seattle."

"You mean an actual ape?"

How many different types of gorillas were there? "Yes, a real gorilla. The owner of the remaining gorillas has now relocated here outside of Evansburg. She has a no-contact order on Keyes. She thought she saw him on her property on Saturday." That made the second time he'd told that lie.

"I'll see what I can find out and get back to you," the officer promised.

Frustrated, Finn stuffed his phone back in his pocket. Time was flying by. Tony Zyrnek seemed the most likely culprit, but he couldn't yet rule out Frank Keyes. Zyrnek certainly had means and opportunity. But Keyes had the same crazy motive he'd always had; that teaching apes to communicate was sacrilegious and he was some kind of holy avenger.

Instead of his field of suspects getting narrower, it was growing larger. And this wasn't even an official case.

Chapter 8

At the station, Finn started his shift by swapping news with the early shift detective. Today that was Sarah Melendez. In the department's complex scheduling system, the shifts of the four detectives overlapped by an hour so the outgoing detective could pass off information to the incoming detective. Early morning hours were not covered by detectives at all. If a detective was needed in the wee hours of the morning, the dispatcher rousted one of them out of bed with the promise of comp time in a mythological future where funding existed again.

He'd left Melendez notes about his burglary case from yesterday, but Finn now filled her in on his dog case and the interviews with Tony Zyrnek and Grace's staff. A guy never knew who might talk in this town.

"What happened on your shift?" he asked.

"Another burglary." She pushed papers aside and sat on the edge of his desk. "I think we've each caught at least one now."

"Any thoughts on the perps?"

She hooked her chin-length brown hair with her index finger and tucked it behind her right ear. "I've got suspicions involving a circle of teenagers. And Sarge has me working that missing person."

"Yeah?" Finn had a vague memory of a missing person bulletin. He'd been a little preoccupied since Saturday.

She raised an eyebrow. "Get with the program, Finn. The case was opened three days ago by Kathryn Larson. Everything's online. Twenty-nine-year-old schizophrenic. The guy's been gone for nearly six weeks."

Finn made a face. "They're just now reporting him? Caring family."

"He's flown and returned before, so maybe they've got an excuse. Can't be easy to have a family member like that." She abruptly straightened and hissed, "Uh-oh. Speak of the devil."

Finn raised his head. A worried-looking older couple had walked into the office, accompanied by the desk sergeant.

"Ryan Connelly's parents," Melendez informed him.

"Connelly?"

"The missing schizo." She slid off his desk and quickly snatched her purse from her desk drawer. "I'm off duty. They're all yours."

He checked his watch. "I'm due in court in thirty minutes."

She waggled her fingers in the couple's direction as she passed them on the way out. Their weary eyes tracked her exit before they turned and followed the sergeant. Today it was the nicer one, Carlisle.

"Detective Finn will update you on the search for your son." Carlisle shoved an extra guest chair in front of Finn's desk.

Finn leaned across his desk to shake hands. Mr. Connelly's hand was callused and dry; the diminutive Mrs. Connelly's was soft and moist. Their faces were tense. They both looked like they hadn't had a good night's sleep in years.

"We've been talking to Detective Larson and Detective Melendez." Mrs. Connelly glanced sideways at the two female detectives' empty desks.

Finn assured her that all department detectives worked on every case. Which was sort of true. One detective was always the primary and worked most on any given case, but they shared information and were at least aware of all open cases.

He pulled up the Connelly case on his computer and quickly scanned Larson's and Melendez's notes. They had interviewed several associates about Ryan's possible location. The guesses of where the twenty-nine-year-old might be were all over the map.

"One friend said Ryan talked about joining a peace march in D.C.," he reported.

The parents looked at each other. "Yes," the father said, "Ryan is very opposed to U.S. intervention in other countries."

"Another said that Ryan wanted to go camping in the mountains, and his girlfriend told the detective Ryan said he was driving to the coast." Jeez, no wonder they couldn't locate the guy.

"Ryan is not allowed to drive," the mother said.

Finn checked the record. Ryan Connelly's driver's license had been revoked at the age of 23. There was no accompanying reason, but it was probably medical, either due to mental instability or his meds, or more likely his penchant for going off them. Or maybe for driving drunk; there were two DUIs listed. Apparently, like so many of the mentally ill, Ryan also had an alcohol problem.

Finn turned back to the parents. "I see that Ryan has several citations for driving without a license."

The father sighed heavily. "He didn't 'borrow'"—he used his fingers to put air quotes around the word—"one of our cars this time. And none of our friends has reported a missing car."

But Ryan might have taken a stranger's car. Or he might have hitchhiked to the mountains if the camping story was true. "Does he have camping gear?" Finn asked.

The father nodded. "He took his backpack, tent, and sleeping bag with him. We told all this to Detective Larson."

The mother rummaged through her purse and eventually pulled out a small envelope. "I brought these other pictures of Ryan so you could see what he sometimes looks like."

"I'll have them scanned into the record and returned to you." Inside the envelope was a photo of a clean-cut Ryan similar to the one in the record, a photo of the young man with long hair and an unkempt beard, and a photo of him with shoulder-length hair and a mustache. Finn looked up at the couple. "I'm sure these will help."

They didn't look as if *they* were sure of anything.

"I'm sorry that we have no definitive leads at this time," he told them. "But the appropriate bulletins have gone out and we all know what Ryan looks like, so all authorities are looking for him."

What he couldn't say was that unless Ryan committed a

crime, there wasn't much hope of the young man being found. There were simply too many crazy people walking city streets and too many homeless people living in the woods these days for law enforcement to deal with. And Ryan Connelly was of average height and average build, with brown hair and brown eyes. Even the pictures of him with long hair and a beard could have been any of thousands of men he passed on the street every month.

The three of them stared silently at each other for a long painful moment. Finn could feel their need for encouragement, for some shred of hope. The mother bit her lip, fighting tears. Mr. Connelly clutched the edge of his seat, his knuckles white with tension or anger, or probably both.

"I am due in court in a few minutes." Finn rose from his chair. "We'll be in touch if there are any new developments."

The Connellys stood up.

"We know our way out." The father turned toward the door.

"Please find our son," Mrs. Connelly pleaded before following her husband.

Finn sat down heavily. He'd rather work a murder any day than look for a missing person. Or a missing gorilla. Grace's expression at the Morgan house had been as anxious and stricken as the Connellys. At least with a murder, you knew the outcome for the victim from the beginning.

To Grace, finding the gorillas in the woods now seemed like a crazy wish, but at least searching for them felt like doing *something*. She let Jon borrow her van to drive down nearby logging roads in the faint hope that he'd spot a gorilla.

If the gorillas hadn't escaped, they'd either been killed or kidnapped. While Frank Keyes had already proven he was capable of killing a gorilla, Grace didn't know why he'd take the corpse of an ape. She didn't want to believe that some people might pay to have them stuffed as trophies. Steeling herself to focus on another more likely possibility—that the gorillas had been kidnapped for sale—she researched internet sites advertising sales of exotic animals. There were ads for monkeys, lions, cougars, bears, tigers, snakes, spiders, lizards, frogs—the list seemed endless. It hurt to see all the photos of these beautiful animals in cages.

But this was exactly the point that some outsiders made about her gorillas—they should be in the wild; they should be free. She wished Gumu and Neema and Kanoni had been able to live their lives that way. Sadly, her gorillas had no concept of how to survive in their native Africa, or in any wilderness setting. Neema had been born in a zoo to a disturbed mother that refused to care for her. Gumu had been captured by bush meat hunters when he was only a little older than Kanoni was today.

Not knowing the whereabouts of her three gorillas was agony. Visions of gorilla corpses, maimed gorillas stuffed into tiny cages, and gorillas tortured and dying of cold and starvation constantly paraded through her brain. She felt simultaneously paralyzed and frenzied.

She stared at the computer screen. Two chimpanzees were for sale. One orangutan. No gorillas. But this was a site for legal sales, and there were no doubt sites that only illegal traders knew about.

She closed down the legal site and typed "gorilla for sale" in her browser search box. Twelve hits. Six were toys, one was a Halloween costume, and one was a YouTube video cartoon. But then—oh God—the ninth was a gorilla skull on an auction site, the bones laid out on a backdrop of black velvet. The current bid was three hundred and twenty dollars.

The tenth link displayed a set of stuffed gorilla hands and feet, allegedly from Africa.

Her heart ached. If Africans only knew how smart gorillas were, they'd understand that eating one was akin to cannibalism.

The remaining two links were to articles about baby gorillas found for sale in markets in Africa, with prices as high as forty thousand dollars.

She sat back in her chair. *Forty thousand dollars?* Good

Lord. She'd thought the prices she'd paid for Gumu and Neema were high. That much money could ignite a reverse wildlife trade of captive animals shipped to Africa.

Could her gorillas be en route to Africa? That would be ironic. And so tragic.

After his court testimony, Finn returned to the station and found a message from Grace on his personal cell phone informing him that a captive gorilla might be worth as much as forty thousand dollars. That certainly upped the ante for wanting to steal one. Apparently even gorilla bones were worth money.

The fingerprints he'd submitted for the fictional Weimaraner case came back with matches for Sierra Sakson, Jonathan Zyrnek, and Grace McKenna; at some point they'd all touched the hasp of the barn door lock. Grace's fingerprints were no surprise. Jon and Sierra might have been merely doing their jobs, closing the back door or checking to be sure the lock was secure. So he was still at square one on the gorilla case.

He finished reading Melendez's notes from her earlier shift. She'd checked the local pawn shops and eBay and Craigslist for the stolen items, including the guns from his case last night. The victims had all been interviewed; they hadn't provided any leads. He couldn't think of anything more to do for the moment on the burglary cases. None of the prints recovered so far matched any in the system, and she hadn't left him any notes about the suspected involvement of local teens. So he was still at square one on the burglary case, too.

He studied the photos of the missing Ryan Connelly, trying to memorize the young man's appearance. Unfortunately, no matter the length of his hair or his whiskers, the guy had no distinctive features. Brown hair, brown eyes, five foot ten, 165 pounds. In other words, average in every way except for the voices in the poor guy's head.

Finn turned his thoughts back to the missing gorillas. No,

the fictional Weimaraner, he told himself. Now *he* was hearing voices in his own head. He called the phone company and requested last month's records for the Zyrneks' landline as well as Jon Zyrnek's cell phone. Then he ran the license plate number of Tony Zyrnek's pickup through the DMV database. The patchwork pickup was registered to Evansburg Auto Salvage.

According to licensing records, Evansburg Auto Salvage had been in operation for six years. It was the perfect sort of business for Zyrnek to meet other ex-cons; they often ended up in jobs that required physical labor rather than education. He ran a quick check on Grant Redd, the owner of the yard. Yep, Redd had stayed off the law enforcement radar in recent years, but he had spent nearly five years in a state prison for drug possession and assault more than a decade back.

The rain and wind had stopped for the time being. He drove to Redd's address outside of town with the windows down, enjoying the warm spring evening.

The Redd house was a manufactured home, too, like the Zyrneks', but a relatively new one in a tidy subdivision, with sweeping cedar decks surrounding the outside of the house.

A plump teen girl in rolled-down sweatpants and a T-shirt answered the door. When Finn asked for Grant Redd, she bellowed over her shoulder, "Dad!" and then walked away, leaving the door open a few inches. The electronic sounds of a video game bounced around inside the house.

After a minute, Redd appeared. He was at least fifty pounds overweight, and his muttonchop sideburns were a fashion statement from decades ago. "Yeah?"

Finn flashed his badge. "I'm here to ask about your employee, Anthony Zyrnek."

Stepping outside in his stocking feet, Redd closed the door behind him, then motioned Finn to a chair on the deck. "Zyrnek do something? He seems on the straight and narrow to me."

"He probably is." Finn pulled out his notepad and pen. "The department likes to check up on recent parolees."

"He's a good employee. Works hard, reports on time."

"What's his pay?"

Redd raised a bushy eyebrow. "Not that it's police business, but I pay a buck more than minimum wage."

"He work forty hours a week?"

"The schedule's variable. Kinda depends on intake and customer requests and such."

Convenient for a criminal to have a flexible schedule, Finn thought. "He drives a truck that's registered to you."

Redd squinted at him for a second. "Damn, I need to fix that. But the truck's his, mostly. He built the thing out of spare parts he matched up from my yard. It's only got my name on it because he's making payments, but I need to fill out the sales thingamabob so he'll be the registered driver. I'll fix that right away, Officer."

"Do that." The guy seemed to think he was there about the truck, which was a good lead-in for his next question. "The truck has a canopy over the back?"

"I think Tony found one somewhere, yeah."

"That truck was seen at the open house event held last Saturday by Dr. Grace McKenna."

Redd nodded. "Tony really wanted to meet The Gorilla Lady and see those gorillas. He talks about them all the time; he's real proud of his boy that works there. I drove him out there on his lunch hour 'cause he loaned the truck to his kid to pick something up."

"When did he drive it back?"

Redd stared at his blue-jeaned knees for a few seconds. "Can't say that I noticed. I was out of the office the rest of the day, delivering parts."

"How many other employees work there?"

"I have a gal who works nine till two six days a week in the office and then another guy who works Monday through Thursday out in the yard."

Finn wrote down the other employees' names, although neither of them had been there on late Saturday afternoon.

"Your salvage yard is a big place. How often do you take inventory?"

"We don't. We keep the cars in sections by type and we list everything in a database. We need a certain part that's still on a wreck, we hike out to that section and locate it for the customer."

In other words, there could be a herd of buffalos living in the back corner and Grant Redd might not have noticed. "Can Zyrnek get into the salvage yard after hours?"

Redd shrugged. "He has the key code to the front gate. But why would he want to?"

Finn shrugged back.

"Hell, I'll give you the key code if you want to check. I don't want any trouble."

Finn held out his notepad and pen. After scribbling down the numbers, Redd handed it back. He rubbed at a frown line on his forehead. "Let me know if you find anything that's not right. I mean, I think I'm doing a public service giving these guys a job, but I can't lose my business, you know? I've had to kick a few of their butts out over the years. Zyrnek doesn't seem like that type, but—"

"You probably have nothing to worry about. Like I said, we just check up on recent parolees in our jurisdiction. Err on the side of caution." Finn stood up and extended his hand. "Thanks for your cooperation."

He walked down the steps to his car. With the crappy pay and the knowledge that a gorilla might command a big price as an exotic pet, Tony Zyrnek had motive. He also had opportunity. At the salvage yard, he had a loose schedule and access to any tool he needed for a challenging task like cutting through a padlock. Plus, he had the perfect vehicle for transporting unconscious gorillas, and the perfect place to store them temporarily. And nobody could vouch for his whereabouts on Saturday afternoon.

Finn called the evidence tech on duty and told him to meet him at Zyrnek's.

* * * * *

When he rolled up to Zyrnek's lot, darkness was descending on Brigadoom and the yard light was on. Tony Zyrnek was outside, grilling over a little hibachi stove set on top of stacked cement blocks. The burgers smelled enticing.

"Detective!" Zyrnek waved his barbecue tongs in Finn's direction. "Nice evening, isn't it? Right now, I only got two burgers on the grill here." He winked and tilted his head toward the small grass plot that surrounded the trailer. A round cafe table was set up with a tablecloth and a glowing candle centerpiece, place settings for two, and accompanied by two folding chairs. "I can throw on another if you're staying for dinner."

A woman stepped out of the doublewide's door. Her long black hair was thick and glossy. Her dark eyes had an Asian slant to them, and her skin was either tanned or naturally olive. The overall effect was Polynesian, although she wore the jeans and long-sleeved tee typical of the Evansburg area. Her eyelashes were clumped wetly together, and she carried a wadded tissue in one hand. Pausing on the bottom step, she glanced uncertainly at Finn.

"Detective Finn, this is Heather Clayton. Heather, meet Detective Finn. He usually stops by to watch *Jeopardy* and have a bite, but tonight he's here to observe my excellent grill work."

Finn snorted at Zyrnek's description, and then nodded in Heather's direction. How did an ex-con rate a woman like that? Did she know who she was dealing with?

"Hello." She smiled and took the last step down onto the ground.

He turned back to Tony, who was grinning. "Hey, Finn, bring Grace over sometime; we'll have a double date."

"I'm here on the job, Zyrnek."

"I guessed that. Can I get you a beer? A soda?"

Smooth. A lot of women fell for that sort of con man charm.

"Say, Finn, have you seen Jon today? He called to say he

was doin' okay, but it seemed like he was afraid to tell me something."

Finn was thankful to see Rodrigo pull in behind his car. "We need to look at your truck," he told Zyrnek.

"I didn't hit a barn or anything else with it."

What? "That's an odd comment."

Zyrnek rubbed the back of his neck with his free hand. "Jon said something about damage to the back of the barn. That's not what you're here about?"

Damn, what else had Jon told his father? Finn said, "I only know about the dog. What did Jon tell you?"

"Nothing. So this is just more Weimaraner business?" Zyrnek stroked his moustache as if deep in thought. "I guess a dog could have jumped in yesterday without me knowing about it."

Finn didn't respond. Zyrnek wasn't a dim bulb; he knew that as a parolee, his vehicle and living quarters could be searched pretty much any time law enforcement felt like it, no warrant needed.

Zyrnek clacked his tongs together like castanets. "Knock yourself out. I hauled some compost in the truck after work"— he pointed at a heap in the corner of the yard—"but I hosed it out just about an hour ago down at the car wash, so you shouldn't get too dirty. C'mon, Heather, the burgers are done and our beer's getting flat."

The gorgeous woman joined Tony Zyrnek at the table and they talked about their jobs and about someone named Jenny. It seemed odd that Heather didn't ask any questions about what was going on. Most women would be curious if a couple of cops showed up during dinner. He needed to look into Heather Clayton's background and interview her later.

"Cheerful guy," Rodrigo murmured.

"Way too cheerful," Finn whispered back.

"I'd be cheerful too, having dinner with a woman like that." Rodrigo squinted and bent over, sighting down the length of the pickup bed. "What am I looking for?"

Finn raised his voice to be sure Zyrnek would hear. "Check

for hairs, blood." He straightened and nearly whacked his forehead on the corner of an awning protruding from the doublewide. Recovering, he pointed his flashlight at the pickup canopy tilted sideways up against the trailer a short distance away. "There, too."

Rodrigo pulled on a headlamp, snapped on gloves, and asked in a normal tone, "Still looking for that Weimaraner?"

"Sounds like a country western song," Zyrnek commented from the table. Then he sang in an off-key twang, "That's my story and I ain't lyin', there'd be no use in denyin', you wonder how I got this shiner? I was looking for a Weimaraner."

Heather burst out laughing, and a snicker escaped from Rodrigo before he stifled it. Finn grimaced. Had Jon Zyrnek told his father about the missing gorillas, or did they both already know where the apes were? Finn suspected that Zyrnek knew exactly what was going on. The man was playing him.

An ad for a baby monkey on the local Craigslist site caught Grace's eye. She clicked the link. The blurry photo showed a shadowy black creature in a cage; huge terrified eyes ringed by white looked out from behind bars. She couldn't tell for sure what type of simian those haunted eyes belonged to. Kanoni?

The timing was right; the ad had been posted yesterday. Damn, there was no phone number, just an anonymous email address. She saved a screenshot of the photo and then sent a message using her JaneAfrica gmail address. *When can I see this baby monkey? I've always wanted one!* She included her cell number.

Finally feeling like she might be on the trail of something important, she ran more general searches on the net, including the words *gorilla*, *ape*, and *monkey*. The term *gorilla* resulted in a long list of annoying links to articles about marketing strategies and videos of wild sex.

She found articles about dwindling ape populations in Africa, and new studies on the reasoning capabilities of apes, which reminded her that she should write more articles about her gorillas' language skills. Which reminded her that she no longer had her gorillas.

Swallowing painfully around a sudden constriction in her throat, she moved on to articles about monkeys, and clicked on a newspaper article from Spokane titled *More Than a Missing Pet*.

> Ten-year-old Maria Constello misses her best friend Pepito every moment of every day. Pepito is a pygmy marmoset that Maria's father brought for her from Brazil. Maria was born with spina bifida and is confined to a wheelchair. Pepito disappeared from his cage when the Constello house was burglarized on April 17. The family is offering a reward for information leading to Pepito's recovery. 509-555-5201.

An accompanying picture showed the tiny marmoset clinging to a child's hand and chewing on an apricot that was as big as it was. The creature had an odd vertical white stripe like an exclamation point above its left eye. The mark gave his little face a quizzical expression.

When Jon Zyrnek knocked on her door, she was surprised to see the sun had already set. Unable to absorb any more sad photos and stories, Grace shut down her computer. She picked up her cell phone and found a text from Finn saying prints hadn't panned out but he was working on some leads. She hoped he was making more progress than she was. She went outside to confer with Jon, painfully aware that this was the third night the gorillas were gone.

The cab of Zyrnek's pickup yielded no blood traces, and only a few hairs. From the crevices of the pickup bed, Rodrigo plucked out a few more. Finn wondered how easy it was to distinguish animal hairs of different types. He couldn't exactly ask if they came from a gorilla, could he? Or maybe he could—

Jon worked at Grace's compound, and he could tell the techs that gorilla hairs might be transferred into the pickup, but they were especially looking for dog hairs.

But if gorilla hairs were found in the bed of the pickup, he was going to haul both Zyrneks in for questioning, no matter what Grace said.

Dispatch called him on the way back to the station. Another burglary. Rodrigo duplicated his U-turn, and they both swung by a house shared by four college students. The place looked like something from the *Hoarders* television show. The only items the students could definitely say were missing were an I-Pad, an MP3 player, around two hundred dollars in cash, and a bottle of tequila. A couple of the students were squirmy; Finn guessed there were some illegal substances on the list of stolen items, too.

So now Evansburg had burglars out there who were probably drunk and high and had at least two guns. The college kids had no clue who might be responsible, but they'd all been away at the same party when the break-in happened, so maybe the party was a place to start. Finn wrote it down and left it for Sarah Melendez to pick up the next day.

He was washing his hands in the men's room when Scoletti emerged from a stall. The rookie looked at him in the mirror. "How come you haven't asked me about this Weimaraner?"

Finn was sick of that dog. He reached for a paper towel. "I was getting around to it. Did you see the dog?"

"Nope." Scoletti turned on the water.

"Notice anything suspicious going on?"

"Couple of near misses in the parking lot. Some old coots can't park worth a darn." He turned off the water and shook out his hands, drying them on the thighs of his jeans. Then he grinned. "And a couple of Gorilla Woman's volunteers are hot."

"I hope you're talking about the *female* volunteers," Finn quipped. "Because I'm pretty sure Jon Zyrnek is straight."

He dodged the balled-up paper towel Scoletti threw as he backed out the door.

At his desk, Finn reviewed the arrests and stops the

uniforms had made for the evening, keeping his eyes open for Melendez's missing Ryan Connelly. A drunk with no ID seemed like a possible, so he strolled down to the jail. No, the guy snoring in the cell looked older and had an old scar streaking through the growth of whiskers on the underside of his chin. The parents had told him their son had no notable scars.

Grace hadn't called with any updates, which meant there was no news. At one a.m., he texted her. *Thinking of you, sweetheart. Call if you're still up.* When his cell phone didn't buzz with a response, Finn drove home, feeling like he was on a slow road to nowhere.

Chapter 9

Just after dawn, Grace woke from a horrible nightmare in which the apes grew increasingly tinier and fainter as they became more and more distant. She stared at the ceiling fan above her bed, trying to get that spooky vision out of her head. She felt guilty for sleeping.

Thirteen years ago at the beginning of her graduate studies, she had adopted year-old Neema as a research project and created the gorilla sign language study. She had managed the project all of her professional life, teaching only a few seminars now and then, writing a few papers about her work.

Without the gorillas, she didn't have a project. She wasn't a professor or a researcher. Without the gorillas, she wasn't even an animal keeper. She was only the renter of a questionable property owned by the University of Washington. She was no longer on their faculty. If she didn't get the gorillas back, she wouldn't be associated with any educational institution, so the UW would soon boot her out and she'd be homeless, too.

Her parents and colleagues had often criticized her for letting her life revolve around the gorillas. That criticism had been right on target. Without the gorillas, she was, apparently, nothing.

It had been hard to sit through the college board meeting yesterday. Just as she suspected, her comment about Gumu's sad history and his ability to kill had been noted and were roundly criticized. There was a brief debate about whether the college deserved part of the proceeds from art sales. But overall, the board deemed the open house a success. She nearly broke down in tears at that point, and excused herself by claiming a migraine was coming on.

She'd given herself four days to focus on finding the gorillas before announcing the disaster to the world. Tomorrow would be day four. If they weren't home by then, she'd have to face her staff, then the community, and then the world. And admit that she was a total failure.

Snow mewed outside her window. She was the vocal cat. Nest was probably sitting beside her silently, but just as upset by all the changes in routine. Their sea-green eyes held secrets. If only she could converse with Snow and Nest like she could with Neema. The cats often hunted for mice in the barn; they often slept there. Had they seen what happened on Saturday evening? If only she could just take their small fuzzy heads in her hands, press her forehead to theirs, and read their thoughts.

These were probably not thoughts that passed through the minds of people with normal lives.

She had never thought of her gorillas as her babies. But now she felt a kinship with mothers everywhere, because this had to be how mothers of lost children felt. One moment you thought your life was under control, you knew your children were safe. And then your loved ones were simply erased from your world and you weren't a mother anymore and you couldn't stop imagining all the horrible tortures that they might be suffering while you were lying in bed, powerless.

Like Brittany Morgan had done when Ivy was lost, Grace wanted to get in her van and endlessly cruise the roads of the county, on the off chance of spotting a gorilla careening through the pastures or woods. She wanted to question everyone she met. "Seen any odd sights lately? Bigfoot? Funny looking bears? Any large black creature?" She wanted to post questions on Facebook and Google Plus, put an ad on Craigslist, make a plea to the public on the news.

Right. That would definitely alarm the locals. She'd nearly lost her right to keep Neema and Gumu last time they'd escaped.

The ceiling fan had no advice for her. Snow was getting louder by the minute. Grace made herself climb out of bed and, dress, and feed the cats. She didn't even want to face Jon

Zyrnek. She checked her email—nothing from Craigslist—then put on her boots, and went to search the grounds and the nearby woods again.

Reminders of the gorillas were everywhere. That broken branch under the alder had snapped when Gumu swung on it. Kanoni had dropped those pine cones when she found a fuzzy caterpillar more interesting. Grace picked up a twig with a splintered end and leaned against a tree for a moment, letting her eyes fill with tears. That fuzzed-out, flattened end had been chewed by Neema.

Her cell phone chimed just as she came out of the woods. She grabbed it eagerly, hoping for the Craigslist baby monkey seller. *McKenna, Maureen.*

Shit. She'd totally forgotten to make her regular phone call to her parents in California yesterday. She pressed TALK. "Hi, Mom."

"Is something wrong?"

Conflicting emotions raced through Grace's mind. She wanted to share her fears, but she knew confiding in her mother would most likely lead to advice to call the police, as well as an unspoken *I told you so.*

"Grace?"

She finally elected to be vague. "There's a new problem with the research project."

"Funding?"

"That's nothing new, Mom. That's *always* a concern."

"Yes, well." The atmosphere gathered density between them for a few seconds before her mother said, "How are you, dear? You sound anxious."

Grace took a breath. "I'm okay. How are you?"

"Your father and I have taken up ballroom dancing. We had our second lesson last night, and my feet hurt. Other than that, we're doing well. How are the gorillas?"

Tears welled up in Grace's eyes as she found herself on the verge of saying the words *probably dead.*

"What's happening, Grace?"

Finally she gave in to her emotions. She told her mother

everything that was happening, and ended up sobbing like a five-year-old.

"That's terrible, darling." Her mother was surprisingly sympathetic. "I'm so sorry you're going through all that. But I know you're strong."

Grace took a shuddering breath and blotted her tears with her shirt sleeve. "Thanks, Mom."

"I know this is a hard time for you, but it could be a turning point."

Turning point? "The End" was more like it.

"Maybe you should let it go."

Pulling the phone away from her ear, Grace stared at it in horror. *Let it go?* Was her mother suggesting she simply stop looking for Gumu, Neema, and Kanoni? Let whatever was happening to them simply *happen?* The blurry image of the sad-eyed little ape from Craigslist popped into her imagination.

Her mother's voice continued, more distant now. "Without the gorillas, you could do other things. Richard asks about you all the time. Did I tell you he's head of the Psychology Department now?"

About forty-seven times, she wanted to scream.

"It's not too late to have a normal life, Gracie."

Suddenly she was seething. She pulled the phone close to her mouth. "I've got another call coming in, Mom. Gotta go."

She punched END and stood there fuming. *Let it go?* And bringing up Richard? Richard Riverton had been her lover in grad school. A smart, good-looking man. A political man. He'd slept with two female professors to work his way up the academic ladder, always insisting to her that the affairs meant nothing to him. All that seemed to matter to her parents was that he had achieved tenure and now was head of a major university department. Richard had accomplished everything they'd expected from their daughter.

Then she saw it on the phone—a text message from the Craigslist ad. It was an address less than forty minutes away. Come by at 3pm.

She texted back that she'd be there. She debated calling Matt, but it wasn't even eight a.m. After working the late shift, he'd still be asleep.

Then she decided not to tell him at all. He was working at three. He had other priorities. He'd either tell her to leave this for the police, or he'd want her to wait until he could come with her. He looked like a cop; he acted like a cop. If the baby monkey seller was spooky, he might not even open the door if Matt was standing outside. And she had to see that little ape.

Before he'd even had his first cup of coffee, Lok and Kee reminded Finn that he'd run out of proper cat food by taking twin dumps on the plastic mat next to their food dishes. Just in case his human was slow to grasp the depth of his dissatisfaction, Kee also peed on Finn's dirty clothes, which incited Cargo to roll around in them. And now Lok was hell bent on shredding one arm of the couch.

Finn rushed to swat the clawing cat with a dishtowel. Lok easily stayed a yard out of reach, bouncing around the room from one piece of furniture to the next. Finn could have sworn the cat was grinning.

While Cargo was content to eat whatever Finn pulled out of the refrigerator, the cats had gone on strike against leftover mashed potatoes and eggs and bacon bits. Clearly he had to attend to some home fires. Feeling slightly guilty, he sent a text to Grace, asking her if she could finish gathering the information on her staff and their cars on her own while he went to the grocery store, washed his pissed-on hairy clothes, and mowed his lawn before reporting to work that afternoon. He tried to soften the message by promising he'd connect with her later.

Grace spent hours driving from one volunteer's house to another, snapping pictures of their license plates and tire treads to help Finn rule out the staff cars and tread marks from the intruder's. She knew he had his own life and home to take care of; she knew he had to work. But it still felt like he'd already given up on finding the gorillas.

At precisely three p.m., she arrived at the address sent by the Craigslist seller. It was a single-story house off the highway down a long gravel driveway. Behind the house was a huge field planted in corn, and beyond that she could see the tops of a few willows and alders that probably grew next to a stream. The house she was visiting was separated from its neighbors by straight windbreak rows of tall evergreens and newly plowed fields on either side. The general lack of forest and hills gave the area a chilly feel, emphasized by the brisk wind that blew across the flats. Several old cars nosed up to an outbuilding that looked like a workshop of some kind. The painful screech of metal on metal blared from within.

Someone interested in primates might have seen or heard a description of Dr. Grace McKenna, so she'd gathered her long hair into a ponytail and pulled it through the opening on the back of a Seattle Mariners ball cap, then added dangly plastic fish earrings that a friend had given her as a joke.

She stuck a wad of gum in her mouth and double-checked her appearance in the rear view mirror. Satisfied that the woman there looked different than Grace McKenna usually did, she tucked her wallet under the seat, left her keys in the ignition, and went to knock on the front door.

A graying woman with wild hair answered. She had an oven mitt over her right hand.

"I'm here to see the baby monkey?" *Please let it be Kanoni.*

The woman checked the driveway behind Grace. "Just you?"

"Yeah," Grace said. "My boyfriend wanted to come, but he had to work." She popped her gum for effect. "We always wanted a monkey. They're so sweet."

"Huh. They can be a handful, too. Monkeys are out there." She pointed to the outbuilding with her uncovered hand. "My husband Tim will show you." She shut the door.

As Grace approached the other building, the shriek of a

power tool cut through the air. When she paused in the doorway, she saw a man using a grinder to remove rust from a car fender. The chill wind blew through torn plastic strips tacked over the windows. Surely the woman hadn't meant that the animals were inside with all the racket and cold.

She waited for the noise to die down. When the man finally lifted the sander from the metal surface and the whining slowed, she shouted, "Tim?"

He startled, leaping back from the car.

"Sorry." She stepped forward. "I'm Jane? I came about the baby monkey? Your wife said to come out here."

"You scared about ten years off me." He set the sander down on the hood of the car, then yanked foam earplugs out of his ears and stuck them in his jeans pockets.

"C'mon, they're back here." He motioned her to follow him to the rear of the building.

Flicking aside a plastic shower curtain tacked to an overhead beam, he revealed two wire cages atop an old wooden table. How could anyone keep animals in these conditions? The noise alone would be terrifying and painful to any animal's sensitive ears; the cold might lead to bronchitis or pneumonia. The leftmost cage held straw and an old coffee can. The right one held the black ape. Placing a hand on the cold metal mesh, she bent down and leaned close to get a good look.

Finn had barely started going through Melendez's notes from the early shift when the Sergeant Carlisle walked into the squad room and handed him a slip of paper.

Finn scanned it and then looked up. "One-car accident?"

In his old job in Chicago, the department didn't send detectives when drunks drove off bridges or wrapped their cars around telephone poles.

Carlisle hooked his thumbs in his belt. "Covering the bases. Forest Service says it's at least a couple days old."

Finn did not look forward to viewing a decomposing corpse. And this wasn't even within the city limits. "Forest Service?"

The sergeant said, "It's off a Forest Service road, in Shadow Canyon. And before you start whining, I know it should be the feebs or County, but you're the only dick on deck right now."

Mason, the department's technical wizard, snickered over his keyboard at the next desk.

The sergeant's face turned the shade of a ripe tomato. He waved a hand in the air. "You know what I meant. Mutual aid and all that. Daylight's burning. Take a four-wheel drive and get out there. Coroner's on his way." After a glance at Mason, who stared intently at his monitor with his lips pressed into a tight line, Carlisle padded out of the room.

Finn told Mason, "Maybe you're too young to know that 'dick' is an old-fashioned term for detective."

The technician leaned back in his chair and grinned. "If you say so."

Mason was the worst gossip in the department. Both Finn and the Sarge would hear that "dick on deck" comment for weeks. Finn pushed himself up from his desk and grabbed his jacket. At least Carlisle had given him the opportunity to get out of the office.

It was a good thing the sergeant had suggested the four-wheel drive SUV. Shadow Canyon turned out to be a twenty-minute drive from Evansburg and then fifteen more up a potholed dirt track. The beauty of the surrounding country partially made up for the ugliness of the road. Tall evergreens guarded the bluffs. Chartreuse and sienna lichens dotted black and gray rock formations, and thick ferns bordered the spring creeks shimmering down deep slashes in the mountainsides. He'd love to paint those waterfalls. Maybe after all this was over, he could put together a picnic and bring Grace here, make a real date out of it.

When he saw the climbing ropes tied to the bumpers of the Forest Service trucks, he knew the scene was going to be bad. The county coroner stood near the cliff edge, his thumbs hooked in his belt under his substantial belly, watching the action below. Typical of Dave Severn to be observing instead of helping.

Finn shrugged on his jacket, pushed his camera into his pocket, and joined him. "Severn," he said with a nod.

Severn had been elected last year, due mostly to the large crony contingent he'd acquired while running the biggest car dealership in Evansburg. Finn had been astounded to learn that a man with no medical training was in charge of determining which bodies were sent for autopsies and which were declared accidental or natural deaths. Coincidentally, Severn's sister and brother-in-law ran the original Severn family business, East Valley Funeral Services. Which probably explained Severn's ability to dispassionately view dead bodies.

Severn returned the nod. "Finn."

Below them, down a steep rocky slope, a battered Ford Mustang had come to rest with its nose plowed into a large boulder. The car looked to be from the seventies, which would have made it vintage if it had been cared for instead of pocked with rust and dents. Now the left front wheel was splayed out and the roof was bashed in, as well as the side door, which hung open. The car had rolled at least once.

A man and a woman in USFS uniform jackets sat on rocks near the wreck. Between them was a collapsible stretcher with a rolled body bag on top. The man spotted Finn. "We're waiting," he yelled.

The female ranger looked at her watch. "We've only got a couple hours of daylight," she hollered, curling her arm in a come-on-down motion.

Finn glanced at Severn, who frowned back. "Don't look at me. I'm too old to be climbing up and down mountains."

Too lazy was more like it. Sighing, Finn grabbed hold of a climbing rope and stepped off the road bank. His shoes were crepe-soled, not the best for scrambling over rocks. He skidded on the mossy surface and fell onto his outstretched arm, tweaking his shoulder but saving his teeth and nose from bashing against the rock. He slipped a couple more times, giving his hands friction burns and tweaking a knee to match his shoulder.

The rangers stood up when he reached the bottom.

"Bill Adams." The man held out his hand.

The woman ranger introduced herself as Charlotte Nagel.

"One vic?" he asked.

"Over here." Nagel walked him around the Mustang. The hood was crumpled against the boulder, and Finn noticed the typical spiderweb cracking in the windshield where the driver's head had hit the safety glass. On the other side of the car, the driver's door was open.

"Brace yourself," Nagel said. "Animals found him before we did."

The body lay half in and half out of the car, one foot wedged under the dashboard. The head, or what remained of it, lay on the ground. Longish brown hair, matted with dirt and blood. One ear, the right one. The neck vertebrae were exposed, but the lower jawbone was gone, as was the dead guy's throat and the top part of his chest. A few flies buzzed half-heartedly around the putrefying flesh exposed to the breeze.

Adams shook his head. "Poor bastard."

The guy's shirt was shredded. Above his leather belt, his abdomen had been ripped open. Intestines swollen with decomposition gas extruded from the ragged hole. Finn jerked his gaze away and swallowed hard a couple of times, grateful the air was cool and they were out in the open. The smell was foul but bearable.

Brown hair, average size and weight, as far as he could discern. Hard to discern the age in the current condition. Could the corpse be the missing mental case, Ryan Connelly? Finn looked at the rangers. "ID?"

Adams gestured at the body. "We didn't look. We didn't want to muck anything up."

Finn didn't want to touch the corpse either, but someone had to. He snapped on a pair of latex gloves. Holding his breath, he gingerly slid his fingers into the dead guy's jean pockets in front, trying not to gag at the cold dampness he felt through his gloves. Then he patted down the back pockets, but found only a gunk-slimed quarter and a torn piece of red paper. "No ID."

"Maybe it was in his shirt pocket?" Adams suggested.

"You mean the pocket that's missing, along with part of his chest?"

"That would be the one." Adams looked up the valley off to the left. "We walked around a little, but didn't see anything that looked important."

After wiping his fingers on his handkerchief, Finn leaned into the car, opened the glove compartment, and pulled out the registration. "Allen Whitehead, Renton. Where's that?"

"Suburb of Seattle," Nagel said. "Sorta."

Finn folded the registration into a plastic bag from his pocket. "Good to know I can pass the joy of notification to the Renton PD."

He was relieved that the corpse was most likely Whitehead. He didn't want to be the bearer of sad news to Connelly's mournful parents.

Nagel nodded. They all studied the corpse for a few more seconds. Finn had seen bodies that had been smashed, burned, and cut up, but never one in this condition. "What could do that?"

The rangers took turns offering a variety of scavengers.

"Coyotes."

"Cougar. Bobcat."

"Bear."

"Raccoons."

Raccoons? He was going to keep a closer eye on the masked bandits that visited his deck each evening.

"Weasels. Rats."

Finn held up his hands. "I get it. Lots of possibilities."

"Lots of tracks." Adams pointed.

The ranger was right; there were dozens of prints in the patches of dirt between the rocks. Many looked like dog tracks to him, but then he was no animal expert. He snapped a few pictures of the wildlife footprints.

Wings flapped overhead as something big landed on the branch of the fir towering above them. "Forgot the birds," Adams said.

"Yes," the female ranger nodded. "Crows. Ravens. Eagles. Maybe even a hawk or an owl."

Adams sighed. "They'll be back as soon as we're gone. It's getting dark." He peered at the sky. "And it's clouding up again. Can we bag him now?"

"In a minute," Finn responded. He quickly snapped photos of the car, the body, and the general surroundings, wishing the Sarge had sent a certified tech with him. Maybe he didn't know the rangers weren't prepared. Or maybe he just assumed this was a tragic accident.

Grace's heart sank. The baby monkey was not Kanoni. It wasn't a gorilla, or a monkey, or even a baby. The thin black-furred creature was an adolescent bonobo, the smallest of the great apes. The cage was barely big enough for the creature to sit upright, but the animal was huddled into the corner with its arms over its head. Tim used earplugs—why wasn't he humane enough to realize that the poor little ape was in pain from the excruciating screech of the grinder?

"Oh, sweet baby." She poked her fingers through the wire mesh.

"Watch out, he bites," Tim said. "But once he gets used to you, he'll make a fine pet. Monkeys are real smart, you know. You can teach them almost anything." He picked up a wooden dowel lying beside the cage and poked the cowering animal. The bonobo squeaked and glanced at them over its shoulder, the whites of its eyes gleaming. Then it covered its head and pressed even further into the corner.

"Isn't it a little cold and noisy for him back here?"

Tim narrowed his eyes. "He doesn't mind."

She doubted that, but the man's expression didn't encourage further criticism. "How long have you had him?"

"He's not really mine," Tim answered. "I'm selling him for a friend."

"How much?"

"Seven thousand."

She sucked in air through her teeth. "That's a lot. Can I hold him?"

Tim shook his head. "No way, not right now. Like I said, he bites." Then he realized he was ruining his sales pitch and added, "After he settles into a new home, he'll let you hold him all you want. He'll be real sweet then."

She fingered a plastic fish earring. "Was he born in the U.S.?" Otherwise, the bonobo had been smuggled in illegally.

Tim studied her face for a minute, his reptilian gaze sending a chill through her. Maybe a typical exotic pet buyer wouldn't have asked about an ape's birthplace. She popped her gum and asked, "I mean, does he have an American name? Does he understand English?"

Tim relaxed. "Yeah, sure. His name's Blackie. Zoo didn't want him anymore; said they had too many. I got papers here somewhere." He turned his back to her and slid a bag of dog chow off a file folder, then sorted through the papers inside and held one out.

The form was a bad copy that practically screamed forgery. Blackie was listed as a "Large Monkey." As she studied the piece of paper, she caught a movement from the other cage in her peripheral vision. An animal was inside the coffee can.

She pointed. "What's in there?"

"Ah," he said. "You might like this baby even better." He opened the door of the cage and reached into the coffee can. "And I'm only asking four thousand for it."

He pulled out the tiniest monkey she'd ever seen, as small as a newborn kitten. "Hold out your hand."

He placed the animal into her outstretched left hand.

"Hold on tight. It can jump a long way."

She cupped her right hand over the little body and then peered between her fingers at the miniature creature. A pygmy marmoset, the first she'd ever touched, stared back, its eyes huge and liquid. A thin white exclamation mark decorated its forehead.

"It's adorable," she cooed. "What's its name?"

"Tinkerbell."

Pygmy marmosets were rare, and individuals with white exclamation marks even rarer. She'd bet ten thousand dollars the marmoset's name was Pepito, and a little girl was crying for it in Spokane. Its heart beat wildly against the palm of her hand.

Her own heart was hammering, too. No way could she leave this defenseless little beast here. Who knew how long the police would take to come? When the grinder started up again, the marmoset's heart might give out from sheer terror. "Would you take three thousand five hundred?" she asked, stalling for time to think.

He squinted. "Three seven fifty. Can't go lower than that."

"Does that include the cage?" Could she do it? Just take him?

"Nope, I need the cage. Just wrap the monkey in your jacket and then stick it in the trunk of your car. Or you could put it in the glove box or something."

"My wallet's in my van." She clutched the marmoset to her chest. "Come on, Tinkerbell, let's get the man his money and go home."

She hated to leave the bonobo there, but she had no choice. Walking rapidly toward the door, she said over her shoulder, "My boyfriend's going to be so excited!"

Tim trailed her toward her van; she could hear his booted steps behind her. She pushed the monkey under her jean jacket. Holding his miniscule warm body against her chest, she abruptly bolted, running for all she was worth. Leaping into the driver's seat, she managed to click the door lock button an instant before Tim grabbed for the handle.

"Hey!" He slammed a hand against the window. "What the fuck are you doing?"

She started the engine.

"Give me my money, bitch!" he yelled. "You owe me four thousand dollars!"

"Call the cops." She moved her hand to the gearshift.

His next blow shattered the window next to her head. She instinctively turned away from the flying glass as she slammed the van into reverse.

His nails gouged her neck as Tim latched onto her jacket collar. "Fucking bitch!"

Grace jammed her foot hard on the gas pedal. Her erratic steering made the van violently fishtail backward as she dragged Tim, his boots plowing through the driveway gravel. His hold on her jacket pulled her toward the open window. Only her grip on the steering wheel kept her in the driver's seat. She couldn't let go of the wheel to fasten her seat belt. She couldn't let go, period. Her foot was sliding off the gas pedal. In another second, Tim would yank her out the window.

Ducking her chin, she sank her teeth into his hand. The taste of grease and blood flooded her mouth.

"Bitch!" he shrieked. "Fuck! Fuck you!"

The back wheels of the van bumped violently up onto the asphalt highway, finally jarring Tim loose. He fell to the ground, cursing. Out of the corner of her eye, Grace saw the graying woman run out of the house. She'd traded her oven mitt for a rifle.

Grace yanked the wheels around as a loud blast slammed into the side of the van. She shoved the van's gearshift into drive and laid down rubber as she peeled out, watching the rear view mirror and praying her gas tank had not been hit.

Fifteen miles down the road after she had caught her breath, she removed one hand from her death grip on the steering wheel, and slid her shaking fingers gently inside her jacket. Yep, the marmoset was there, now sitting in her lap, nestled against her abdomen. She felt fingers as tiny as bird claws curl around her index finger.

"Hang in there, Pepito," she whispered, staring at the rearview mirror, watching for a vehicle racing after her. The highway was empty.

She'd stolen a marmoset. It was so rash, so unlike her. But it felt good. She had saved this monkey.

Oh, Kanoni, why couldn't it have been you? Or Neema. Or Gumu. Were her gorillas imprisoned in torturous conditions like that? She dialed 9-1-1 and told the operator to dispatch

some officers to rescue the poor bonobo. The operator asked
what that was.

"It's an animal?" the operator clarified. "Then it's a job for
animal control, not the police."

"It's being abused. It's a victim," Grace argued, then
realized that might not mean much to the operator. "That little
ape is most likely stolen property or imported illegally."

"Most likely?"

Grace clenched her teeth in exasperation. "Watch out, they
have weapons in that house." She hung up.

A few aspects of the accident scene bugged Finn. He'd never
seen a body half-in, half-out of a door before, especially on a
rollover. How often did that happen? Seemed like the car had
gone over the embankment, and the driver hit the windshield
on the first impact against rock, then flopped around inside as
the Mustang rolled. Why did driving like a maniac always go
together with not wearing a seatbelt?

Then the door popped open and the body would have been
flung out, except for the foot caught under the dashboard. It
seemed odd that the vic had no ID or money or anything in his
pants pockets. But Finn had known a few guys that carried
their wallets or money clips in different spots, so maybe the
ranger was right about animals carrying it off. Dusk was
already setting in here in the shadows between the hills. With
daylight tomorrow morning, they might find more items
scattered throughout the woods.

Had the guy been still alive when the animals attacked?
Finn shuddered, considering. Probably not. There didn't seem
to be much blood except for some streaks in the windshield
webbing. But then again, most of the vic's face and throat had
been eaten. And there'd be even less of him left tomorrow if
they didn't move the corpse now. Finally, he pocketed his
camera. "Go ahead and bag him."

It took all three of them to extract the body from the car and
stuff the stinking corpse into the body bag. Adams slipped on a

loop of intestines, which popped underfoot, releasing an indescribable stench. The ranger abruptly dropped the legs he held, and quickly turned aside to vomit.

Finn nearly lost his grip on the limp arms, and the corpse's head banged the rocky ground. The neck vertebrae snapped and the vic's skull separated from the body. Finn joined Adams in hugging a tree and giving up his lunch to the slugs.

"Weenies," Nagel commented, holding open the body bag when Finn and Adams finally arrived to slide the headless body inside.

Finn and Adams glanced at each other and then looked back at the jawless head on the forest floor. Adams swallowed. "I'll flip you for it."

Nagel snorted. "Oh, for Pete's sake." Letting go of the body bag, she trotted to the head, knotted her fingers in the hair and carried it back. Adams opened the bag and she dropped it inside. She looked a little green, but proud of herself.

Over the years, Finn had noticed that most women dealt with disgusting messes better than most men. Probably something to do with babies and diapers. Nagel probably had a couple of rug-rats at home. He wondered if she'd share this gruesome experience with them. *Guess what? Mommy carried a man's head around today!*

Nah, probably not. Although most kids would think that was a pretty sweet story for show and tell.

They strapped the body bag onto the portable stretcher. While Adams climbed the slope, Finn pulled a tiny flashlight out of his pocket and searched the car. Candy bar wrappers, paper fast food sacks, plastic straws and drink cups, receipts, a couple of empty beer bottles, but no owner info or insurance card that he could find. He had just finished copying down the VIN number from inside the door well when Adams shouted from above.

The male ranger attached a come-along to the haul rope, ratcheting it to help Finn and Nagel haul the dead weight up over the rocks. Everyone except for Severn was sweating by the time the stretcher slid over the embankment onto the road.

Severn unzipped the bag and studied the contents for a long minute, fingering aside the fabric sides to find the head. "Yikes."

Then he zipped it back up, stood and wiped his hands on his shirt front. He waddled to his Chevy Tahoe, opened the tailgate and motioned the rangers to slide the body inside. Finn helped them unstrap the corpse from the stretcher and flop the body bag inside the tailgate. He was glad the corpse would not be riding with him. Severn extracted a clipboard from his front seat and sat in the driver's seat, writing notes.

Finn asked, "Where are you taking the body?"

Severn answered without looking up. "Funeral home."

"No autopsy?"

Severn's chin rose and he frowned. "What's the point? He obviously crashed over the embankment, rolled, killed himself, and then got eaten to boot."

"But we don't know if he was drunk, or high, or what he was doing out here. We don't even know for sure if he's the owner of the car."

"What does it matter now?"

Good point. But the Sarge was concerned about covering bases, and in Finn's experience, leaving I's undotted and T's uncrossed often came back to bite a detective in the butt. He was damned if it was going to be his butt that got chewed. "You'll have to wait until next of kin is identified."

Severn rubbed a hand across his forehead. "Yeah, guess that would be a good idea. Otherwise the poor sucker won't get a service of any kind."

And the funeral home would get only the minimum payment for body disposal. Finn guessed that was the foremost thought in Severn's mind. "Can you shove him in a cooler for a couple of days?"

"He's not looking so good." Severn grimaced. "And his condition is not likely to improve." He laughed and slapped his thigh.

"Well, keep him for a couple of days, anyway. I'll send someone to get his prints and take a DNA sample, and I'll alert the police in Renton to contact next of kin."

Severn sighed heavily. "All right. You got forty-eight hours. Evansburg Hospital; the morgue's in the basement."

"I know the place." Finn turned to the rangers. "Where will you tow the car?"

They blinked at each other for a few seconds before Nagel answered. "We have 'em towed wherever the owner wants 'em to go. We don't have a budget for stuff like this."

Few government agencies did these days. "I'll contact the Renton PD and let you know what I come up with," Finn told them.

"It'll stay down there until we hear from you."

"Fair enough."

Severn honked the horn of his Tahoe and flashed his lights at them. He was blocked in by Finn's SUV and clearly in a hurry to leave.

"Can't wait to shower," Nagel commented.

"I second that," Adams said.

"Amen," added Finn. He slid into his SUV. The reek of decomposing flesh was stronger with the door closed. Shit, was that dead guy goo on his shoes?

Chapter 10

Neema stood upright and roared in frustration, banging her hands and feet against the metal sides. *Loud loud noise.* Kanoni ran away screeching, and climbed to the lowest limb of a tree. The baby didn't come back until after Neema had curled up near the grid, signing to herself. *Scared. Grace come. Sad.*

Kanoni tried to bite the wire between them. Neema whimpered and poked her fingers through the wire to touch her baby. Kanoni cried herself to sleep in a ball on the other side of the door while Neema stroked her foot with a finger.

Then Neema licked all the syrup from the pot, bit into the net around the bread to get the hard bread. Then the food was gone and she was thirsty. She wanted out. She needed out. She signed *Grace come. Neema good. Good Kanoni. Come now.*

Getting dark. Thirsty. Noise in the bushes. Then she smelled a new smell. Neema rushed to the other end of the tunnel to look. There. Not Grace. Animal. Black fur came out of the woods, nose first, swinging its head. Smelling her. Smelling Kanoni. Not gorilla. Big. Bad.

Neema grunted loud to scare it away. It stopped. She pounded on the metal sides of the tunnel. It stood up on hind legs, smelling the air. Long yellow claws. It looked at her with tiny brown eyes, down its long nose. Big big. It opened its mouth. Sharp teeth. Then it dropped to all four feet and began to trot toward her cage. Toward her baby.

She ran back to the stuck door where her baby whimpered, clinging to the wire. Neema shrieked. Run! Run now! Find Grace!

Kanoni dropped to the ground and, after a last look over her shoulder, loped hard on all fours, disappearing through the trees. Neema smelled Teeth-Claws as he rushed by. Close. Too close. Teeth-Claws crashed through the bushes along the side of the tunnel.

No! Neema shrieked, banging on the metal. *Stay away!* She cut her fingers pulling the metal grid. She couldn't see Teeth-Claws.

She slammed her fists against the metal sides of her cage and roared as loud as she could.

Then she saw him. Grunting with excitement, Teeth-Claws loped into the woods after her baby.

Chapter 11

Jon, his eyes glued to his cell phone, caught up with Grace as she opened the door to her personal trailer.

"Caryn and Sierra and Brittany and the others have all been calling. I have to tell them something. This is the third day we've put them off." He looked up at her. "Jesus!" he yelped. "What happened to your lip? And your neck?"

She wiped her mouth with the back of her free hand. It came away with a red smear. Tim's blood. Ugh. "That blood's not mine."

She spat on the ground and wiped her mouth on her jacket sleeve. Then she pressed her fingers to her neck, felt the burn of the long scratches there, pulled her hand away to see more blood. Hers, this time.

"What attacked you?" He studied her more closely, noticed the way she cradled her arm against her chest. "Something wrong with your arm?"

She pushed open the door with her free hand. "Come in. I'll tell you what I've been up to."

When she'd finished the story and settled the marmoset in a cat carrier with food and water, Jon held up his hand for a high-five. "Way to go, boss! Now you're one of us."

He was right; she'd joined the animal liberators. The criminal animal liberators. She didn't clap hands. "Keep that under your hat."

His face fell. "Are you kidding? That was *heroic*; it should be on YouTube. We should go get that bonobo. Caryn and Sierra could help."

"I alerted the local police. Let's wait and see what they do."

"Oh, right." He waved a hand in a gesture that dismissed the idea the police would do anything.

She sometimes forgot what a kid Jon could still be. "The gorillas are out there somewhere," she reminded him. "We don't want word to get around that there could be commando raids on exotic animal keepers."

He inhaled deeply. "I get it," he said. "They'll tunnel even deeper underground. Later, then, after the gorillas are back; we can go into action then."

She had to ask. "Z, is there any chance that ARU could have taken the gorillas?"

"No way." He looked stricken, as if she'd slapped him, and let his hands drop down to his sides with an audible slapping sound against his jeans. "We work here. And you always stand up for animal rights."

"I know it wasn't you, Z. But maybe it was something you told someone else, something that Caryn or Sierra—"

"No." He shook his head. "I'd know if ARU had the gorillas. But I could send out a message to watch for gorillas for sale."

"That would defeat the purpose of keeping this quiet, wouldn't it? But maybe you could send a message asking members to be on the lookout for exotic animal dealers. Maybe ARU could compile a list of people to check on. That would help."

He looked relieved. "Done."

"Can you keep the staff away for at least one more day? Tell Caryn and Sierra I'll pay their regular wages." Although that would make a sizeable a dent in her miniscule checking account.

"I'll try." He stuck his phone in the back pocket of his jeans.

"If nothing breaks in the next two days, I'll go to the police and tell them that the gorillas were stolen." She searched his eyes. She didn't want to mention his father, but could he suspect something he wasn't telling her? "Jon, if you have any ideas about where to look—"

His head jerked up. "Believe me, I'm trying to think of some way to find them, some hint of what might have happened, but so far..." He swallowed hard. "I'm gonna go walk the fence line, okay? I'll yell for Neema and Gumu while I do it."

"Thanks. I'll take a quick tour through the woods before dark." She also needed to call Finn and let him know what was going on, find out if the bonobo had been rescued. She picked up her cell phone and headed for the trees while Jon strode off down the back driveway, his shoulders sagging.

Jon Zyrnek shoved his hands in his jeans pockets and scuffed his running shoes on the road, sending gravel flying. So cool that Grace was out there rescuing monkeys; he'd love to do that. But where would he take them when he had them? You couldn't just set tropical monkeys free in the Cascade foothills. Grace could get away with this; but he wasn't a big name scientist with connections. He'd get arrested again.

He had to find the gorillas. If only it wasn't some big secret. He'd send emails to ARU asking them to keep tabs on exotic animal sellers—that was a righteous mission. Some would help, but some might dismiss it because he worked here. Caryn and Sierra had lost clout in the organization, too, just because they worked with captive animals. *Could* ARU have stolen the gorillas? They didn't always claim responsibility for their commando activities, especially if something went wrong.

And all that blood certainly proved that something had gone wrong. How could he find out? He didn't even know how to ask without causing a stink.

Why couldn't he think of something more useful to do than walking the fence line? How lame could you get? Why did this have to happen on the only job he really cared about? For once, he'd seen a decent future looking like a possibility; he was becoming an ape whisperer of sorts. He could teach apes to sign, and teach other people how to talk to them. He could write a book or maybe even make a movie. He'd be like Roger Fouts or Penny Patterson, but more public, on Facebook and Google Plus and Twitter and stuff. He'd make a difference in the world. People would finally respect animals. And they'd finally respect him.

Grace believed in him. Correction: she *had* believed in him.

Now, she'd probably dump him. Even if she didn't want to fire him, there was no job if there were no gorillas. He reached the end of the back driveway, checked the gate. Locked. The padlock was secure. He started a clockwise route inside the fence line, checking the electrical wire and the barbed strands beneath.

Why now, just when his Dad was finally back home, when both of them had decent jobs, when the world was looking like a hopeful place, had everything turned to shit? He tugged on his hair until it hurt. Why hadn't he gone out and checked on Gumu before sacking out on the night of the party? There had obviously been a struggle in the barn; why hadn't he heard it? Why hadn't he known something was wrong? Some ape whisperer he was.

He walked on, studying the fence, looking for breaks, for fallen branches that might disrupt the flow of electricity, for some way intruders could have come in.

The fence bordered the road and the front driveway; the other two sides of the property were guarded by thick woods that belonged to the national forest service. He walked along the border of the trees and back to the front side to finish his circuit.

As he was strolling up the back driveway, he saw the glint of metal in the weeds alongside the gravel road. He nudged the fronds of a fern aside with the toe of his boot. A padlock. It had to be the lock missing from the back of the barn. He turned in place, searching the surroundings. A few feet away, he found the bolt cutter. He felt a surge of excitement—maybe there'd be fingerprints. Maybe he *could* help bring the gorillas back.

Then he noticed the lettering etched into the handle of the bolt cutter. *Evansburg Auto Salvage.*

Inside her personal trailer, Grace looked in on the marmoset huddled into her sweatshirt in the corner of the cat carrier. She could see a tiny bit of dark fur rising and falling. He'd eaten a couple of grapes and maybe had a few sips of water from the shallow bowl she'd left there.

She checked her messages, hoping Finn had called or texted with news. There was nothing. While touring the woods looking for signs of her gorillas, she couldn't stop thinking about the imprisoned bonobo. About the other animals that might be at that farmhouse. And about what might happen to her. What would the couple say she'd done? Was a thief robbing a thief still a crime?

With some trepidation, she turned on the local news. There were no stories about gorillas rampaging through the countryside or about psycho women stealing monkeys. But apparently the problem bear had been caught yesterday evening.

The television screen showed wildlife officers sneaking toward a black bear snuffling through the woods. With its nose to the ground, the bear zigzagged as if it were trying to pick up the scent of another animal. It jerked up its head to gaze in the camera's direction a fraction of a second before the dart hit its side. Bawling in surprise and pain, the bear then loped a few yards before collapsing and plowing his nose into the dirt.

The scene then flashed to three Fish and Wildlife officers loading the tranquilized bear into a cage in the back of a pickup, while another commented to a reporter holding out a microphone. "This bear is a young male, approximately three years old. He's been sighted numerous times along properties in the Cheyenne Creek area. He will be relocated to a forest area thirty miles away where he can't cause any more trouble. Along with the capture of his brother yesterday, this should solve our marauding bear problem in the Evansburg area. Homeowners can feel safer tonight." After a brief tug on his cap toward the camera, the officer walked away.

In the background, a muffled voice asked something about traps that she couldn't quite decipher, which was followed by the barely audible response: "No need. We got our bear."

Then the field reporter signed off and the scene returned to the television studio and a story about a drug smuggler caught at the Canadian border.

As Finn drove out of the mountains past the migrant worker huts and Vista Village, his cell phone chimed. There was a breathless message from Grace about a seller of stolen animals and a 9-1-1 call she'd made to the police.

The following message was from Sergeant Greer.

"Rein in your damn girlfriend," he said. "Monkey Woman's got a lot of nerve, trespassing and complaining about *other* folks keeping wacked-out animals. Tim and Terri Smith have lived in this county for decades. And what the hell do you think you're doing asking *my* uniforms to search the salvage yard? Maybe it worked for you in Chicago, Finn, but you can't pull these prima donna stunts in Evansburg."

Finn tightened his grip on the steering wheel. Greer and his damned turf. So he'd asked a couple of uniforms to do a walk-through of Grant Redd's yard, looking for stolen items or anything else unusual. It was a legitimate request for the burglary case, given that ex-cons worked there, but apparently he'd bypassed the Evansburg chain of command by going directly to the patrol officers. Which probably would have been fine if they'd found anything of interest. But unfortunately the officers hadn't spotted the missing guns or any other suspicious items. Naturally, Finn hadn't mentioned gorillas, but surely even the dimmest rookie would have reported an ape if he'd noticed one there.

Could he mollify the sergeant with a bottle of whiskey or a six-pack of beer? With his luck, the grouch would turn out to be a born-again reformed alcoholic. He'd have to ask the other detectives for advice.

He spotted a slowdown ahead from a semi-trailer overturned on the highway. Flashing lights everywhere. Finn pulled over to talk to Grace and wait out the traffic.

The details of her escapade horrified him. "What were you

thinking? You should never have gone out there alone."

"The hag only nailed the side of the van. Oh, and her thug of a husband broke the driver's window. Thank God summer's coming on so I don't have to replace it right away."

"Grace!"

"Did your guys rescue the poor bonobo?"

He repeated the sergeant's report. "No sign of exotic animals. The Smiths didn't have a clue what your complaint was about."

"Fuck that," she snapped, shocking him. "They're lying. How'd the cops know it was me, anyway?"

"We can trace cell phone numbers, Grace."

"Oh. How long did it take the cops show up at that place? Your brothers in blue probably gave those numskulls plenty of time to hide the evidence and work on their innocent act."

"I'd have to check the log to see what the response time was."

"I have evidence. There was a Craigslist ad; I have the email on my phone. And maybe Mrs. Smith's bullet is still in the van. And Tim's DNA is probably all over the window glass and my jacket collar, too."

"He had *hold* of you?" Maybe Greer was right; he needed to rein Grace in for her own safety.

"I was dragging him until I hit the highway."

Finn shook his head, trying to clear that vision from his imagination. "Drive your van to the station and get them to check. I'll call ahead."

"No, Matt. Don't you think they'd ask a few questions about what I was doing there? And they'd probably impound the van. I don't have any other transportation."

He suspected there was more to her story. "Is there anything else I need to know, Grace?"

"They probably have that poor bonobo locked up in a cabinet somewhere," she wailed. "Or worse—they butchered him and buried the body parts in the corn field. What if monsters like them have my gorillas?"

"Please don't do anything like that again. You could be

killed."

"Neema. Kanoni. Gumu. They're all still out there."

She was obviously frustrated with his efforts. "I'm working on finding them as best I can while keeping this secret, Grace."

"So am I, Matt."

At the station, Finn stuffed his shoes into a plastic bag in his locker and walked in his socks to his desk to type up his report of the accident and body recovery in the woods. He made notes that the area needed to be thoroughly searched for more evidence, like the vic's jawbone and ID. After uploading his gruesome photos to a computer folder, he ran Allen Whitehead's name through the department database. Thirty seven years old, according to his driver's license data. The photo showed a generic white male who looked reasonably similar to the body in the woods. Hard to match faces when the dead guy was missing the bottom half of his head. He pitied the relative who would have to view the corpse.

Allen Whitehead had racked up a couple of speeding tickets; nothing more serious. Unless the guy had applied for a government job somewhere along the way, his fingerprints were unlikely to be in the system. Still, Finn sent email instructing the evidence tech to go to the morgue and collect fingerprints and DNA samples from the body.

A message popped up to signal that phone records for the Zyrnek household had just arrived via email attachment. He ran his finger down the enclosed list. Interesting. The call to which Zyrnek had responded "Not now" came from Monroe Correctional Complex. There had been one call per week from the prison, stretching back for the entire six months of records.

Months back, the calls probably came from Tony's efforts to maintain a relationship with his son. But now? Which old prison buddy was calling the Zyrneks these days? Finn wrote himself a note to call the prison tomorrow.

His email notification popped up again. Grace sent him a message—SUBJECT: THE BONOBO—with an attached photo

Grace had captured from Craigslist. The little ape was huddled in a cage that was far too small, fingers clasped tightly around the bars, looking thoroughly terrified. The picture definitely tugged at the heartstrings. But unless he could get a subpoena to make Craiglist hand over their records, there was no way he could prove it had come from the Smiths. No judge was likely to believe Grace's word over Greer's, and she'd certainly be questioned about what she was doing there. How could he make her understand there was no case?

After midnight, he padded to his locker to reclaim his reeking shoes, mentally apologizing to Grace for not working more on the case of her missing gorillas. He knew she was desperate. But he was only human. And tonight he was an exhausted human who stank of decomp.

At home, his shoe cleaning dilemma was quickly resolved. As soon as he took them off, Cargo rolled around on his shoes, moaning in canine ecstasy. And then the dog stood up, lifted his leg and unleashed a stream of hot urine all over the loafers. He beamed happily at Finn with his brown and blue eyes, black tongue lolling from one side of his mouth, proud of himself. Finn tossed both the mutt and the shoes out into the back yard.

Chapter 12

Let it go. Grace woke with her mother's words bouncing around in her brain. She pulled the sheet over her face to shield it from the brightness of dawn lighting the open window. It was not yet even six a.m., too early for her automatic coffeemaker to turn on. The goldfinches and thrushes were already singing their avian hearts out with the beginning of mating season.

Day four of the gorillas missing.

It's not too late to have a normal life.

She hated to admit it, but normal was a tempting concept. She tried to envision herself with a quiet job teaching psychology and linguistics in a college in a picturesque coastal town. She'd live in a small cottage filled with books and surrounded by flowers that would not be picked and eaten by gorillas. She'd dine out in trendy cafés and go for long walks with ... a husband? She tried to fill in that shadowy image. Did he look like Matt?

Would Matt ever trust women again after what Wendy had done to him? Would *she* ever trust men again after what Richard had done to her?

Her mattress registered a gentle thud. When she pulled the sheet from her eyes, Snow burrowed into the pillow beside her, one paw kneading her shoulder as he swiped his head across her cheek, purring.

A scene abruptly flashed through her memory: Neema responding to Grace's tears by handing her the white kitten, signing *Grace sad hold baby cat.* Neema comforting *her.*

And then she knew that she could never "let it go." Not as long as Neema might still be waiting for Grace to rescue her.

She pulled herself out of bed. In the cat carrier, Pepito sat on top of her sweatshirt, his expression now more curious than anxious. When she poked a finger in through an air hole, he grabbed it with his teensy fairy fingers and nibbled on her fingernail. She shared her breakfast, feeding him a piece of banana and a few cashews. It was always magical to commune with another species, and she felt lucky to have the experience of interacting with the marmoset. But she also felt a familiar pang of guilt, the same conflict she felt every time she visited a zoo. It wasn't right to capture wild animals and imprison them just for human gratification.

But would humans appreciate just how precious wild animals were if they never looked into their eyes, never felt the flutter of a bird's wings or the butterfly touch of a tiny monkey's fingers on theirs, if they never heard a lion roar or an elephant trumpet? She was a zookeeper of sorts, too. She thought about all the visitors who had attended her open house. Would they realize how smart and imaginative gorillas were if they hadn't seen Neema express her thoughts in sign language?

After the clock rolled past the reasonable hour of eight a.m., Grace tried the Spokane number for the Constellos for the third time. Still no answer. Pepito watched her from the cat carrier as she put the phone down. Making a chirping noise, he extended one doll-like arm through the hole, his paw open as if he hoped she would drop something into his palm. She gave him another piece of cashew. After a quick sniff, he dropped the nut and thrust out his paw again. His black eyes were bright and he seemed calm enough, so she opened the cage and carefully took him out. The tiny marmoset was as light as a sparrow.

"You can stay here as long as you like, Pepito," she whispered, sitting down with him at the computer. He was such a gorgeous jewel of a creature. It would be so amazing to see a tree filled with dozens of these miniscule monkeys.

She cuddled him against her chest for a minute. Then the marmoset wiggled free and climbed to her shoulder, where he sat clutching her ear, his fingers tickling like butterfly feet. He seemed at home there; it must have been his typical perch with Maria Constello. Grace decided to leave him on her shoulder while she did her research.

She checked the Craigslist ads; the Baby Monkey ad was gone. The only pet ads were for dogs and cats and one ferret. What had happened to the bonobo? She tried to persuade herself that the young ape had been moved to a better place. That it was still alive and would end up healthy and happy.

If only she could believe the same things about her gorillas. But the blood pool in the barn haunted her. Was Neema dead? Gumu? Little Kanoni?

According to Matt, the whereabouts of that maniac Frank Keyes at the time the gorillas disappeared were still unknown. She might be able to discover his address. And then what? Should she drive to Tacoma and confront him? She'd have to admit the gorillas were missing. If he wasn't involved, he'd certainly spread that news around. And supposedly, an officer in Tacoma was checking the guy's alibi.

But could Keyes have local cohorts? Was there another wacko determined enough to break in and stab a gorilla to death? Evansburg had its share of people who objected to her project—as made evident by the handful of protestors at the open house—but they hadn't been violent. Yet.

It seemed far more probable that the intruder was someone who wanted to steal gorillas. But why? Nobody in his right mind would want to keep a gorilla for a pet. But, she reminded herself, some wannabe owners *weren't* in their right minds; some wackos had cages full of rhinoceros vipers and some kept lions and leopards in their city apartments. A signing gorilla might seem like a fascinating animal companion to an animal lover who hadn't thought through the daily reality of living with a creature smart enough to turn on the stove and strong enough to hurl a human through a plate glass door.

So who knew about her gorillas and their capabilities? Unfortunately, that list was long, and mostly anonymous. She'd written dozens of articles about Neema and Gumu. She sold their artwork on eBay. To prove authenticity, each painting came with a video of the gorilla in the process of creating the painting. The paintings and associated videos typically sold for between eight hundred and two thousand dollars.

Most purchases had been single items, but a couple in San Francisco had purchased one each of Neema's and Gumu's paintings, a man in New York had the highest bid for three of Neema's pieces, and a gentleman in Boston had purchased five of Gumu's works. There were even a few international buyers. Four of Gumu's pieces had been shipped across the Caribbean to Caracas; a woman in Toronto, Canada had bought two of Gumu's and one of Neema's; and one of Gumu's had been shipped to France. Grace smiled to think that her big gruff male gorilla was winning the popularity contest as an artist.

Then she remembered that she might never see Gumu paint again. She might never see *him* again at all. Or Neema. Or Kanoni.

Unfortunately, anyone could peruse eBay. She had no way to get a list of users who had seen the videos or paintings. She didn't even have a list of people who had bid on the artwork. She knew only the final buyers, and that list was depressingly short and contained no local addresses. Still, she printed it to share with Matt.

A soft tail brushed her cheek. She reached up to stroke the little monkey. "Tell me it's not hopeless, Pepito."

She couldn't wait to reunite Maria Constello with her marmoset. If only someone, somewhere, felt the same way about Grace McKenna and her gorillas.

Finn sat in his recliner, sipping a cup of coffee, trying to wake up his brain enough to focus on the missing gorillas. He and his cat Lok were playing their usual game of fetch. Finn threw a green beetle wall-walker toy at the patio door. Lok followed the arc of the toy's flight, and then sat at the bottom of the glass door, watching intently as the sticky beetle slowly crawled down the glass on its sticky feet.

Through the sliding glass door, Finn watched Cargo romp enthusiastically through the flowerbeds as he chased an orange butterfly, trashing some lily-looking plants planted by his former in-laws. The plants had been growing buds, but they'd probably never bloom after his dog was through bouncing on them.

Rein in your girlfriend.

Who the hell was Greer to talk to him like that? The comment made him wonder if Greer beat his wife and kids to keep them in line. Besides, Grace wasn't exactly his girlfriend. Was she? Girlfriend. Why hadn't society ever come up with a less ridiculous word for adults?

And even if she *was* his girlfriend, he had even less control over Grace than he did over his pets. She'd sounded pretty snarly yesterday, implying that he wasn't doing enough. And then sending him the photo of the bonobo.

Lok leapt up and batted the beetle off the glass. He brought the toy back, jumping into Finn's lap. It was pretty cool to have a cat that fetched. He remembered how bad he felt when Lok had disappeared for a few days last year.

"I thought I'd find your guts strewn across the lawn by coyotes." He stroked Lok's orange head. "Or you might be dying in a ditch after you got hit by a car."

Memories flashed through his head: Neema asking Grace for a game of chase, Neema leaning her head against Grace's in sympathy, Neema and Gumu painting. Of course Grace was distressed. She'd lost three charges, three research subjects, three friends. But if she'd only been willing to sound the alarm right away, they might have been found by now. It was damn near impossible to mount a secret search for anything.

He scratched Lok under the chin. "How about you fetch me an idea on how to find three gorillas?"

He threw the toy again, and Lok launched himself from his lap. The plastic beetle landed with a satisfying smack on the patio door.

Since no ape corpses had shown up yet, the gorillas might

be still alive. It was painful to imagine the gorillas stuck in a cage. Especially if it was forever. Neema and Gumu and Kanoni might be animals, but they were very smart animals. In his mind's eye, he could see Neema signing *out out out*. Gumu throwing himself against the bars. Kanoni crying like the baby she was.

The image of the imprisoned bonobo loomed up in his imagination. Shit. No wonder Grace was on a campaign to confront exotic animal dealers. The whole idea pissed him off, too, but the trade was mostly legal. And he had no reason to believe the Smiths had taken the gorillas.

He was still betting on Tony Zyrnek's involvement. Picking up his phone from the end table, he looked up the number for Monroe Correctional Complex, and called to ask for the phone records he wanted.

"That'll take awhile," the clerk told him. "I've got a lot of requests in front of yours."

"How about just one call, then?" He rattled off the Zyrnek number, time, and date.

She hesitated. "I'm not supposed to do requests out of sequence."

"There's a box of chocolates in it for you," he wheedled.

She laughed. "All conversations are recorded here, Detective. You know I can't accept that."

"I'll find a way."

"Just this once, Detective Finn. And only because it's a reasonable request and you sound like a nice guy. Hang on." Elevator music started in mid-song as she placed him on hold. She was back in less than a minute. "Jarvis Pinder placed that call."

"Who would Pinder be to Tony or Jonathan Zyrnek?"

"Never met Jonathan, but Tony is a real sweetheart. He was released about twelve weeks ago. We still miss him around here. He used to keep us entertained with his stories and songs."

Yep, the guy was an entertainer, all right. Good at spinning yarns.

"Tony Zyrnek was Jarvis Pinder's cellmate for the last three and half years; my guess is that Pinder misses him, too. Tony isn't in any trouble, is he?"

"I don't know yet. I want to talk to Pinder."

"I'll put your name on his visitor's list. Your first opportunity is tomorrow."

"I'll be there." Monroe was nearly a three-hour drive from Evansburg, but tomorrow was his day off. "Can you tell me who else is on Pinder's visitor list?"

"Just a sec." He listened to a minute of a sappy instrumental tune before she was back. "Leon Shane, Heather Clayton, Mary Lou Pinder, Herbert Pinder, DeeDee Suarez."

Finn copied down the names. "Thanks. The chocolates are in the mail."

Heather Clayton, the gorgeous woman Tony Zyrnek introduced him to. Now wasn't that interesting? Finn moved to his office, set aside his paintings, and fired up his computer. Using his remote login, he accessed the department's database. Pinder, Jarvis Montane, 36, had been convicted of possession of several kilos of cocaine with clear intent to sell. The guy also had earlier selling convictions for a variety of drugs as well as a couple of more minor arrests for possession.

Zyrnek's association with Jarvis Pinder and Heather Clayton seemed suspicious—some kind of unholy trinity there. But he didn't see any immediate connection of Pinder and Clayton with the gorillas. He decided to drive to Grace's to brainstorm with her.

Without the gorillas, her compound seemed deserted. The white cat was the only life form in sight, sprawled across the picnic table in the sun. He knocked on the door of Grace's personal trailer. "It's Matt."

"Come in," she yelled.

She sat in front of her computer. The light from her workspace lamp reflected in her weary eyes. She wore a V-necked shirt, and her neck was swollen and red, with long deep scratches etched into puffy flesh.

"Oh, sweetheart. That looks like it hurts." He pulled the

collar of her shirt away from the wounds.

A black furry thing on the other side of her neck shrieked and leapt to the top of the bookshelf.

Finn stumbled back, hooked a toe under the desk leg, sat down hard on his ass and smacked backwards onto his spine. It hurt.

Grace burst into laughter, putting her face in her hands and bending over in her chair.

Finn pushed himself to a sitting position, glad he wasn't wearing his gun. Falling on that would have hurt a lot more. The creature stood on its hind feet on top of the bookshelf, black hair frizzed out in all directions, clasping its furry tail in its tiny hands, and fiercely displaying even tinier pointed teeth. It screeched at the top of its tiny little lungs like a psychotic squirrel. The noise was amazingly loud for an animal that could easily fit into his shirt pocket.

After a couple of minutes of uncontrolled giggling, Grace finally sat up and wiped her hands over her face, rubbing streaks of tears that trailed down her cheeks. "Are you okay, Matt?"

Still smiling, she stuck out a hand to help him up.

He took it and rose to his feet, rubbing his backside. "Just thought I'd stop by to amuse you. I suppose I should be used to this sort of thing by now."

He pointed at the screeching ball of fur and teeth. "What is *that*?"

She stood up and cupped her hands around the animal, then brought it gently to her chest. Its excited shrieks diminished to a nervous chatter. "This is Pepito. He's a pygmy marmoset."

"Where'd you get him?" Although *why* might be a better question.

"That animal dealer I mentioned. The 9-1-1 call."

"You bought him?" Why would anyone pay good money for a flea-sized screech toy?

She just sat there, cuddling the miniature monkey with one hand and stroking its tiny head with the other.

He abruptly realized what she hadn't told him. "You *stole* him, didn't you? *That's* why they were shooting at you."

"I *freed* him." She pushed the furball into a cat carrier on the corner of her desk, then pressed a few keys on her computer and pointed to a newspaper article on the screen. "And I'm going to return him to his rightful owner."

After scanning the article, he could understand how returning the marmoset to Maria Constello was a righteous move. He could understand how Grace identified with the girl. But the exotic animal trade was big business, full of dangerous animals and even more dangerous people. He looked at her. "Tell me you're not going to go around the country stealing animals now."

She didn't reply.

"Grace, there's already one wacko out there who hates your guts. And now you've made another enemy. Or two more, counting the wife. And by the way, I looked at your van. All you've got is holes. The bullet went through the other side. That evidence is somewhere along the highway." He held out his hands to show the futility he felt.

She continued to pet the tiny monkey. "What will happen to those scumbag Smiths?"

"You seem to be holding all the evidence." He sat down heavily in her guest chair. "It's your word against theirs. The Smiths have lived on that property for nineteen years without any trouble."

"Without getting caught, you mean." She leaned toward him, her eyes blazing. "They were keeping at least two animals in unbearable conditions, Matt. Pepito was stolen; I'm betting the bonobo was, too. They might know something about the gorillas. Put them under surveillance, or do a sting or something."

He clenched his jaw. What about *no evidence and no case* did she not understand? If there was going to be surveillance, it would be *him* sitting out there for hours. In his spare time. And the Smiths would now be on high alert for strangers loitering or asking about animals for sale.

"At least talk to them," Grace pleaded.

"I'll see what I can do." He switched subjects to fill her in on what he'd been doing to investigate Tony Zyrnek.

She started shaking her head before he'd finished. "I told you that it can't be him."

He sighed. "I know you like Jon. I know you trust Jon. I know Jon trusts Tony, or at least says he does. But *we* have no reason to trust Tony. The man's got a record, and he has motive, means, and opportunity."

When Finn reported for his shift, Miki was sliding a pink phone call slip into his IN box. "Just missed it," the young civilian tech told him. "An officer from Renton for you."

Finn returned the call.

"I went out to notify that Whitehead family about the car crash you reported," the officer told him. "Nobody was home, and it looks like nobody has been for awhile. The neighbors said Mr. Whitehead lived there alone, but they hadn't seen him for a week or more. The mailbox was full of mail."

"All of which fits with him lying out there dead in the woods."

"Looks like it. We'll try to locate some relatives, but I thought you should know."

"We'll keep the body on ice." Finn thanked him and hung up, then called the morgue. They weren't happy about keeping the corpse longer.

Detective Sarah Melendez rolled her chair from her desk to his, preparing to swap information before she left for the day.

"What's up?" he asked.

"Another burglary, a stolen car, and a couple of fake hundred dollar bills at the grocery store. The reports are in your email, along with the names of pawn shops I checked off the list." She pushed off his desk with a foot and rolled back to hers. "FYI, I saw your boy Zyrnek last night at the roadhouse."

"Jon Zyrnek?"

"Anthony. I remembered his name from your log sheet

because he's a fairly new parolee. Plus, I know his PO. Are you talking to Zyrnek about the burglaries?"

"Talked to him about several things," Finn said noncommittally, not wanting to bring the mythical Weimaraner into the conversation.

"He was with a young woman. Long dark hair, olive skin. Very pretty."

"I can guess who that is," Finn said. The luscious Miss Clayton, obviously a good friend of Tony Zyrnek, and the gal on convict Jarvis Pinder's visitor list.

Melendez looked at her watch. "I'm clocking out early today—dentist appointment."

"Have fun."

He booted up his computer and ran Heather Clayton's name through the database. Heather Lynn Clayton, born Heather Lynn Pinder. So Heather was a relative of Jarvis Pinder, the convict, Tony Zyrnek's cellmate. A sister?

She was thirty-two years old, divorced with no parenting plan or alimony agreement, nothing but a speeding ticket and a couple of parking violations. He called the work number listed on her records, reaching her at the counseling office of the local college. She agreed to meet him at her apartment after work. Finn thought it was odd that she didn't even ask why he wanted to interview her.

Heather Clayton lived in a tidy condo complex across the street from the rundown apartments where Sierra Sakson and Caryn Brown rented. When Heather answered the door at five-thirty, her expression was apprehensive, but she acted friendly enough as she invited him into the living room of her townhouse. She wore a beige skirt and silky blue blouse that hugged her curves.

After offering him coffee, she left him alone for a minute in her immaculate living room. The color scheme was deep blue and orange-gold. Even the candy in the bowl on the coffee table matched, wrapped butterscotch and blue mints and orange-red packs of gum. The complementary colors were much livelier than the browns and off-whites Wendy had left him with. He abruptly realized why his energy level sank the instant he walked in the front door of his own house. Crap, his home life was *beige*. What kind of an artist was he not to have noticed that before?

Heather returned and handed him a mug. "How can I help you?"

"How did you meet Tony Zyrnek?"

"You're asking about Tony?" She sat down opposite him on the couch, smoothing her skirt down with her hands. "I thought you might be here about my brother." She gave him a wary look. "Do you know who my brother is?"

"Jarvis Pinder." He took a sip of the coffee. It was strong and bitter. Probably reheated from this morning's pot.

"Okay, then." She folded her hands in her lap. "I used to see Tony sometimes on visiting days when I was talking to Jarvis. We'd all be in the visiting room together. At separate tables, you know, but you can see everyone. I always thought Tony looked like a nice guy. And Jarvis used to talk about him, too."

"So you know Tony from the prison."

She nodded. "Everyone deserves a second chance, don't you think? I hope Jarvis will get one, too. One of these days."

Personally, Finn thought the world would be a better place if Jarvis Pinder never saw the outside of prison again. "What did Jarvis tell you about Tony?"

She pursed her full lips as she thought for a minute. "Just day-to-day things, like how Tony loved to read and that he liked to play Scrabble or chess instead of poker, stuff like that. Jarvis thought Tony was a kind of an egghead, but a good roommate."

"Cellmate," Finn corrected.

She shrugged.

"How long have you and Tony been dating?"

"We're not dating." She pushed her hair back from her neck. "I didn't even know Tony lived here until I ran into him at the Roadside Tavern last Sunday. I was there drowning my sorrows because my boyfriend..." She worked her jaw around, swallowed, and then continued, "My boyfriend, Tyrone Linero, left me."

She sucked in a deep breath. "Tony was nice. Sympathetic, you know, not trying to hit on me like a lot of guys would. Since then, he fixed me dinner at his place two days ago." She met his gaze. "Well, you know that; you were there."

Finn's face grew hot at the memory of Zyrnek's smart-ass Weimaraner song.

Heather didn't seem to notice his discomfort. "And then Tony and I met again last night for drinks." She frowned prettily as she said, "Why are you asking all this? I know it's routine to hassle all parolees, but Tony's really a good guy."

Finn wanted to challenge her assertion that cops were in the habit of harassing parolees, but he couldn't imagine how that would shift the conversation in any useful direction. "Is it true that your brother once had an ocelot?"

She squinted at his abrupt change of topic. "An ossa-lot?" Then, a second later, "Oh, that's a kind of jungle cat, isn't it? That was a long time ago, but yes, he sent me pictures of it. Spotted, right? Pretty, but why would you want one? Wouldn't it shred your furniture?" She gazed at her pristine blue furnishings.

"Probably." Finn wondered what Lok and Kee were up to at the moment.

"Jarvis had snakes, too. I never understood why he liked those creepy animals. He had a tarantula when we were kids." She shuddered, somehow managing to make the movement appear graceful.

"Seems like your brother and Tony share an interest in exotic animals."

She brushed an orange-lacquered nail across her lower lip as she considered that for a minute. "Maybe; I never thought about it before. I know Tony is very proud of his son working with those talking gorillas. But Tony isn't crazy enough to keep one at home."

But maybe he was crazy enough to steal one. "What has he

told you about the gorillas?"

"Why are you asking about gorillas? I thought you were looking for a dog—that Weimaraner."

Finn had to restrain himself from rolling his eyes. "I am. But this could be relevant."

She shot him a dubious look, then crossed her arms and studied her lap. "Let's see. I've heard him talk about how the gorillas know sign language. And how they paint. And something about them having eighty-six percent the same DNA as us, which is a little hard to believe."

"I think it's ninety-six percent. Or maybe ninety-eight."

"Really?" She looked at him. "Do you believe that?"

It was his turn to shrug. He didn't want to get pulled into a debate about evolution or whatever she was concerned about. "Did Tony ever talk about anyone wanting a gorilla?"

"Like for a pet?" She made a face. "No. That's crazy. Who would want a gorilla?"

If Heather Clayton knew anything about stealing gorillas, she was doing a darn good job of hiding it.

So Tony Zyrnek knew Heather from his prison days. How many friends had he met through Jarvis Pinder? He switched topics to the other names on Pinder's visitor list. "Do you know Leon Shane?"

A shadow passed over her face. "I don't know Leon. I know his brother Leroy, although I wish I didn't. Leroy is a gang banger friend of Jarvis's. If there was any justice, he'd be behind bars right now."

Finn had checked all the visitors' records. Leon was squeaky clean, but now he would need to check this Leroy Shane's. Maybe he and Pinder were passing messages through his brother. "Does Tony Zyrnek know Leon or Leroy Shane?"

"I don't think so." She seemed perplexed. "I don't think either of them lives anywhere close to here."

That didn't mean the men weren't acquainted. Jailbirds often flocked together when they had a mutual goal. "Would your boyfriend Tyrone know the Shane brothers?"

"He might have met them sometime." Her face crumpled.

"And Ty is my *former* boyfriend." Her eyes welled with tears; she looked away. She inhaled deeply and then held her breath for a few seconds, pressing her lips together as she struggled to compose herself. Finally she said, "I still can't believe he left me like he did. But I'm done crying over him."

"I'm sorry; this must be a tough time for you." He folded his hands together to keep from patting her arm or thigh. "How did you meet Ty?"

She shook her head, dislodging a strand of wavy black hair that she pushed away from her forehead. "My family lived down the block from the Lineros in Spokane. I knew Ty in high school. Ty was the good Linero kid; I was the good Pinder kid. We got together a couple of years ago."

"So Ty knows Leroy Shane?"

She winced at the name. "We all went to the same high school, so they probably met. But they're not friends. What's Leroy done now?"

"We're just checking on a few things," Finn hedged. "Has Leroy been around here lately?"

Her gaze bounced around her apartment as if she were making sure all her possessions were still there. "God, I hope not. Now you're making me wonder what's going on."

Precisely, Finn thought, *wonder away. And then tell me.* "What kind of car does Ty drive?"

"Corolla, an old gun-metal gray one. And no, I don't know the license or have a copy of the registration or anything like that. I told Ty in the beginning I was not taking care of him."

"Do you know what kind of vehicle Leroy Shane drives?"

She fingered her hair. "Probably a stolen one."

"When did you last see Ty?"

Her face tightened. "Friday evening. I went to see my Mom in Spokane. Ty was gone when I came back Sunday afternoon."

"Do you know what Ty's plans were for the weekend?"

She twisted a strand of her hair between her fingers. "He said he was going to work on Saturday. He's been working part-time for UPS, but he told me he was going to pick up some more hours at another place. But now I know he had other plans, like packing up his car."

"I realize it's a personal question, Ms. Clayton, but can I ask why Ty left town?" *Could he have had a gorilla or three in his trunk when he peeled out?*

She looked down at her lap again, and wiped away a tear. Then she raised her eyes and gave him a hesitant smile. She was a stunning woman. Instead of bleary-eyed and blotchy, crying made Heather's face luminous. "You seem like a nice man, Detective Finn. If you'd ever like to go out and get a drink..."

This gorgeous woman was hitting on him? That was a first. He wanted to think it was admiration talking, but it was more likely to be desperation. Or else she was part of the same con game Zyrnek was running. Turning on the charm. He noticed he was leaning toward her and made himself sit up straight.

A wailing sound drifted faintly through the wall. Heather abruptly jumped up from the couch and disappeared down the hallway.

Her sudden exit was unnerving. Shit. He should have checked for other people in her townhouse. Finn unsnapped his holster and rested his hand on his pistol. But when she emerged cradling a baby with one arm and holding only a small piece of paper in her free hand, he slid his hand out from beneath his jacket and rested it on his thigh.

She handed him the paper and stood, shifting side to side, rocking the baby while he read.

> *It isn't working out, Heather. Sorry, I'm not cut out to be a family man. I need to live my own life. Good luck.*
>
> *—Ty*

Finn wasn't sure what to say. The standard 'I'm sorry for your loss' didn't seem appropriate, and anything else would be too personal. He thrust the note out toward her.

"*Good luck?*" Her expression turned angry. "We lived together for sixteen months! What kind of sorry loser leaves a note like that and then just disappears?"

"It does seem..."—Finn searched for the right word—"...callous."

"*Cold* is what I'd call it." She plopped down on the couch again and shifted the infant to her shoulder, where it rooted around against her neck.

He presumed the baby was Ty's. "You can get the state to go after him for child support." He placed the note on the coffee table in front of his knees.

Heather shook her head. "I have a decent job, and soon I'll have full benefits. If Ty's going to be like this, I don't even want him involved in Jenny's life." She patted the infant gently on the back.

He needed to get back to the interview he intended. "I have a few more questions."

"Fire away." She kissed the top of the baby's head.

"Did Ty share your brother's interest in exotic animals?"

She looked surprised. "No way. He didn't even want a dog."

But he might share an interest in money. "Do you have any idea where Ty would go?"

"Maybe back to Spokane?"

"I'd like to talk to him."

"I'll give you his cell number." She waited for him to pull out his notepad and pen, then rattled it off. "What are you going to ask him?"

"He left town right after this valuable dog disappeared, Heather. Do you think those two events could be connected in any way?"

"I guess anything's possible. Obviously, I have no idea what's been going on in Ty's head," she said bitterly. She pulled the infant's fist to her lips and kissed the tiny fingers. "Good riddance, right, Jenny?"

Then a strangled gasp escaped from her lips. Letting go of the baby's hand, she pressed her free hand over her eyes. "Jenny has a heart defect. She'll need surgery when she's older. More than one operation as she grows. Hundreds of thousands of dollars."

She squeezed the bridge of her nose, trying to pull herself together. "I know he was having a hard time finding work. But she's his daughter! How could he leave us like that?" she sobbed. "I loved him!" Tears slid from beneath her fingers and dripped down her face. "I thought he loved me."

Finn froze, seized with déjà vu, mortified to remember his own grief as he sat alone in his silent house with a similar note, shocked to discover that Wendy had ditched him. Should he pat Heather's shoulder? Tiptoe out the door?

Her sobs grew louder. The infant started to mewl. Finn awkwardly cleared his throat and stood up. "I'll let myself out. If you hear from Ty, could you let me know?" He slid his business card onto the coffee table. "Thank you for your help."

He was halfway to the door when he heard her murmur, "How did I help?"

He didn't really have an answer for that.

Back at the station, there was an email message from the Renton officer, telling Finn he was playing phone tag with Allen Whitehead's relatives, who lived somewhere in rural Virginia. The coroner, Severn, had left him a voicemail message saying the morgue was sending the family a form requesting body disposal instructions.

His desk phone buzzed. The operator said, "Finn, I have a real estate agent on the line who wants to talk to a detective."

"Tell him I already have a house."

"Tell *her* yourself."

He punched the button. "Detective Matthew Finn."

"Detective Finn, this is Darla Jacoby. I'm a realtor, and I just stopped by that foreclosed farmhouse at 103 Bell Road, and I think the police need to come see this."

"Squatters?" The whole state was having problems with people moving into vacant foreclosed homes.

"I don't think anyone is living here. Looks more like a warehouse. I see laptops and guns and jewelry—"

Sounded like a storage drop for burglars, which was why the

call had been referred to him. "Don't touch anything, Miss Jacoby. Please step out of the house and wait for me in your car. Lock the doors. I'll be there in twenty minutes."

The house looked forlorn even in bright sunlight. *Handyman Special*, the realtors would advertise. He snapped on a pair of latex gloves and preceded the realtor up the sagging wooden steps, holding the door open for her. "Was the door locked when you arrived?"

She shook her head. "But sometimes we leave the doors unlocked to these properties. Better than having all the windows broken out."

"If you say so." He copied down the sparse information she gave him—previous owner long gone, house vacant for five years, bank finally putting it on the market in two weeks.

"It'd make a nice place for a young family." She nodded eagerly. "Comes with ten acres. Lots of space to grow."

"I'll spread that around," he told her.

"Oh, *would* you?" She actually batted her eyelashes at him.

No, he thought. "Thank you for your help. You can go now." He held the door for her as she departed. Her car passed Guy Rodrigo's as he drove in.

A back room was piled high with items. Finn noticed several that were on his list of stolen objects, including the Duprees' Remington shotgun. Finally—a break in the burglary cases. The other detectives would be pissed that the call had come in during his shift.

Rodrigo joined him, a camera hanging around his neck and a fingerprint kit in his hand. His latex gloves were purple. "Aha. Steal it and store it. What's the plan?"

"Inventory, take photos, get fingerprints in here, and then get out ASAP."

"And leave all this here?"

"We will set up surveillance and catch the scumbags on their way in."

"Brilliant. What's first?"

Finn called the station and arranged for surveillance. Neither sergeant—it was Carlisle this time—was ever happy at that request because it took an officer or two out of the running to catch incoming calls. But since this incident involved several open cases, Carlisle assigned Scoletti to watch over the place until the end of the shift or the appearance of the burglars, whichever came first.

"Tell him to hide well back in the trees," Finn said. One of the problems with small police forces was that most everyone in the county knew the officers and their vehicles, even in plainclothes and driving unmarked cars.

"By the way," Rodrigo said after Finn had hung up, "I can't thank you enough for the headless horseman assignment."

It took Finn a few seconds to realize Rodrigo was talking about Allen Whitehead, the corpse the Forest Service rangers had found in the woods in the totaled Mustang. "Did you get fingerprints?"

"They're in the AFIS queue now, such as they are." Rodrigo grimaced. "Know what you have to do to get fingerprints from a decomposed corpse?"

"I took that course a while ago," Finn said. He didn't want to be reminded of the gory details.

"I collected tissue and hair, too."

Finn nodded. "Good. His home cops haven't located relatives yet and the morgue'll want to cremate him soon."

Rodrigo shuddered. "Couldn't be fast enough for me. I need that vision out of my head."

They set to work listing the goods stored in the bedroom. A sack of half-used drugs was particularly slow going. "Ketamine?" Rodrigo held up a dusty half-used vial between his gloved fingertips. "Haven't seen that in awhile."

"Some clinics still use it, and a lot of veterinarians do." Finn knew that ketamine was often used as an anesthetic for animals of all sizes. The drug of choice to knock out a gorilla? "Be sure to dust that vial," Finn told him.

"I'll get most of the prints in the system tonight. That dog case again?"

Finn nodded.

An hour later, Rodrigo complained, "It's getting too dark to see in here."

Finn's knees cracked as he stood up. He flipped the nearest light switch. Nothing happened. "Damn." They'd need floodlights to finish. "Let's load the laptops, the drugs, and the firearms. We'll send a crew for the rest tomorrow."

He drove back to the station, yawning, eager to hand off the processing and computer exploration to the incoming detective the next day.

Tomorrow was his day off, but he'd work if a fingerprint or the surveillance identified the burglars. The ketamine could be the key. With luck, he might nail a gorilla kidnapper and the burglary suspects at the same time.

Grace spent the afternoon researching the zoo trade. If a zoo wanted a gorilla for their collection, how much effort would it put into investigating whether it was legally owned and born in the United States? Documents could be forged, couldn't they?

She searched zoo websites for articles about the arrival of new gorillas. She reviewed hundreds of photos and film clips from zoos around the world. When her cell phone chimed, she noticed that the sun had set. She hadn't eaten dinner. Up to now, her schedule had always revolved around the needs of her gorillas.

The screen indicated only *Cell Phone WA*. Maybe the Constellos finally calling back? "Grace McKenna." She slid out of her chair and stretched her free arm toward the ceiling. Something in her neck popped.

"You have a hell of a nerve," a deep voice growled.

"Who is this?"

"I never deserved prison for doing God's work."

God's work? Who-? Oh, shit. "Keyes? Is this Frank Keyes?"

"You're not getting me in trouble again, bitch. You're the one who deserves to burn in hell."

She moved to the window, and stared out at the dark

courtyard. The moon was only a quarter full tonight. She could barely make out the picnic table in front of the staff trailer. "Where are you?"

The dial tone abruptly blared in her ear.

Grace pressed END and clutched the phone to her chest, trembling. Finn told her that Keyes was in Tacoma on Monday afternoon. But now it was Wednesday. She pressed her face close to the window. Was someone moving in the shadows?

She tapped in 9-1 before reason caught up with her. If the cops came, they'd want to know where the gorillas were; they'd want to search the barn and the other buildings. She set the phone down on the windowsill.

The staff trailer was dark. Jon must have already gone to bed. She couldn't ask him to get up and search if it might be dangerous; she was supposedly the responsible adult here.

She checked her watch. 10:21 pm. Finn was still on duty. She called anyway.

"Detective Finn." He sounded distracted.

"It's Grace. I think Frank Keyes just called me."

"I'm driving. Hold on while I pull over so I can take notes."

She felt guilty for calling him at work. "It's probably nothing."

After a brief pause, his calm voice was back. "What was the number?"

"Caller ID just said cell phone Washington; no number."

"Damn."

She recounted the few words Keyes had said. "Could he be *here*?"

"Don't go out; I'll call you back as soon as I get a check on his location back from Tacoma."

"Thank you." She ended the call.

A dark form scuttled across the yard and vanished into the shadow under the picnic table. Grace gasped. But the shape was way too small for a man.

Too big for a raccoon, unless it was a giant male. Too small to be a bear or a gorilla. Unless... The creature emerged from beneath the table, gripped the bench for an uncertain minute, and then barreled back to the trees.

She speed-dialed Zyrnek. "Jon, I need you outside. Now!"

It took Grace ten minutes to gather and place food on top of the picnic table, and then fifteen minutes more of silent lurking in the shadows between the trailers before a small shape scuttled through the darkness and leapt to the top of the table. Jon sprang out of his hiding spot, tossing the net into the air, and Grace launched herself at the same time. The net sailed over the creature. The animal shrieked in terror. Grace threw her arms around it, net and all.

The screeching was deafening. Something wet splashed down the front of her shirt and onto her jeans. "It's okay," she murmured, her soft tone nearly lost among the terrified bleats. "It's okay, it's okay, baby." She rocked the struggling bundle. "It's okay, Kanoni. It's me. It's Grace. You're safe, baby."

"I'm here, too, Kanoni." Jon rested a hand on the shivering baby gorilla. "Why is she alone?"

Grace shook her head; she didn't want to think about that right now. She wanted to be happy about the return of her smallest charge. Gradually the thrashing and screeches subsided to whimpers, and Grace loosened her grip enough to examine the gorilla bundle she clutched. Small black fingers and toes extended through the rope strands. A red-brown eye, ringed with white, stared at her. It was hard to read the emotion there—suspicion, fear, hope?

"Let's get her out of the net," Grace said. "Can you grab a foot?"

Jon lifted the net and circled his fingers around Kanoni's ankle. The baby gorilla squealed as he untangled the net from around her foot.

"Don't bite, Kanoni." Grace hugged the terrified baby harder, then she grasped the free foot while Jon worked to liberate the other one. It was an awkward process, but finally Kanoni and the net were separated. Grace pulled the baby gorilla into her arms, and Kanoni clung to her, quivering, as

Grace walked toward the study trailer. Jon trailed behind and followed them in.

Inside, Grace discovered that both she and the baby gorilla were covered with urine and spilled yogurt. When she tried to set the baby gorilla down on the table, Kanoni whimpered and climbed up Grace's belly, clutching her sweatshirt with both toes and fingers. "It's okay, baby, it's okay." She leaned forward and placed the little gorilla's rump on the table, but Kanoni wouldn't let go. Grace looked to Jon. "Help?"

Jon managed to peel Kanoni off despite the gorilla's alarm shrieks. "Kanoni, shush! We just want to clean you up."

He clasped the baby while Grace dampened a towel and wiped the worst of the wetness off the black fur. The little gorilla's lips and nose were bloody and raw. There was a long gash on her right leg, alongside the knee. Kanoni held up her arms, wanting to be picked up again.

"Hang onto her for a minute longer, please." Kanoni's whimpering grew louder as Grace rummaged in the supply closet for antibiotic cream and a work smock. She shucked her yogurt-and-urine-sodden sweatshirt and put on the smock. Then she returned to the table and smeared antibiotic cream on Kanoni's leg and face. The baby gorilla immediately used her tongue to lick it off her nose.

"Do we need to call the vet?" Jon asked.

"I don't think so; she's not bleeding. You can let go."

The baby immediately climbed onto Grace's chest. Kanoni's mahogany eyes were huge, and her lips were split into the uncertain grin of a frightened young ape. Her expression begged *Please don't hurt me.*

Had this baby seen something horrible happen to Neema? Was this the expression on Gumu's face after seeing his mother murdered by poachers? "You're okay, baby. You're home now."

Grace walked to the window and stared out at the yard. As far as she could detect, no creature was moving through the shadows, certainly nothing as big as a gorilla.

Why was Kanoni alone? The possibilities were terrifying.

The baby laid her head against her breast and Grace clutched the warm body tightly to her. "She's shivering, Jon. Can you fix her a warm bottle?"

He turned toward the kitchen cabinets. "Do we have baby stuff like that?"

Good question. Neema had nursed Kanoni, and Grace had long ago gotten rid of the baby bottles she used when Neema was this size. "Just mix some apple juice and milk, nuke it for a minute, and put it in a sippy cup."

Grace moved to the couch and examined Kanoni further, at least as much as she could with the baby clinging like a limpet. The little gorilla was very dirty, but other than her scraped face and the gash on her leg, she didn't have any injuries that Grace could feel with her fingers. She examined a small black foot. Did Kanoni's feet seem more wrinkled than usual?

Jon extended the sippy cup. "Is she okay?"

"Maybe dehydrated." She patted the baby on the back. "Here, Kanoni, milk. Juice." Kanoni leaned back from Grace's chest just enough to look. Her nostrils flared and then she eagerly grabbed the cup, pressing it to her lips with loud smacking noises.

"She's obviously hungry." Jon handed her the towel he held, then walked to the window and peered outside. After a minute, he turned, a worried expression on his young face. "Think Neema's out there?"

"I don't know what to think." Was Neema injured? Was she dead? Was she afraid or unable to come back? Could a gorilla as young as Kanoni have survived in the wild for four days on her own?

The baby squirmed in her lap, and Grace told Jon, "Let's put out more food in the barn. Just in case. Even if the raccoons get it."

He nodded. "I'll search the woods before I go back to bed. Just in case."

"If Neema's not back tonight, I'll drive around tomorrow morning, too." Kanoni turned in her lap to hold the sippy cup with both hands and feet. She upended it, sucking noisily, then popped off the top with her teeth and examined the interior with her long fingers.

"Empty." Grace wrapped her arms around the little gorilla to make the sign.

Kanoni sat up and met Grace's gaze, then raised her clenched fingers and tapped the tips against her rubbery lips.

"She knows the sign for food?" Jon was incredulous.

"Obviously. How about a banana?" Grace made the peeling sign for the little ape. Kanoni signed *food* again.

"She never did that before." Jon went to the kitchen.

Grace sighed. "Kanoni never needed to sign. Neema always did it for her."

All three of them jumped at the knock on the door. Then it flew open and Finn stepped in, his pistol held out before him. "Everyone okay?"

Jon turned, banana in hand. "Only if you're not going to shoot us."

Finn returned his pistol to his holster, then rounded the back of the couch to Grace. "Keyes wasn't at home. Why didn't you answer your phone? I was worried."

Kanoni abruptly leapt from Grace's lap into Finn's arms. His eyes rounded with surprise at suddenly finding a gorilla clinging to his chest, but he wrapped one arm under the baby's rump to support her, and, after carefully peeling her toes from the grip of his gun, put his other arm around Kanoni's furry back and patted her.

"Sorry, Matt." Grace smiled. "I forgot about all that when Kanoni showed up."

"Neema?" he asked. "Gumu?"

She shook her head sadly.

He peered at the black fuzzy head beneath his chin. "At least you've got *one* back."

His cell phone buzzed. He answered and listened for a second, thanked the caller and then hung up. "Keyes just arrived at his apartment," he reported.

Grace felt the tension slip down her spine a few inches.

"I'll report his call to the Tacoma PD. If they can prove it, that's a violation of the no-contact order, and could earn him more jail time."

It was some consolation.

He added, "We still don't know where he was this last weekend."

"Or if he took Gumu and Neema."

At the sound of Neema's name, Kanoni whimpered and leaned away from Finn's chest. Her little face was worried as she glanced around the room, searching for her mother.

Three raps sounded at the door. Finn glanced at Grace. She stood up, frowning and shaking her head, confirming that she was not expecting a visitor.

Shoving Kanoni into Jon Zyrnek's arms, he drew his gun. Would Tim Smith have the balls to knock on the door? The county had a murder like that just last year—knock, knock. Open, boom.

"Stand back." He pushed Grace away from the door frame, then flipped on the outside light and opened the door in one smooth motion, standing to one side.

An older couple stood on the small porch, blinking in the sudden brightness.

"Mom?" Grace stared in disbelief. "Dad?"

"Surprised?" Grace's mother raised her eyebrows. "Are we interrupting something?"

Well, crap. Way to meet the parents. Finn hurriedly tucked the pistol back in his holster.

Her father smiled tentatively, shielding his eyes from the overhead light with a hand against his forehead. "We came to support you."

Finn slid sideways into the doorway beside Grace. "Come on in."

He introduced himself and shook hands with Dr. Maureen and Dr. Charles McKenna. That's how Grace introduced them: Doctor Maureen and Doctor Charles, both professors at Stanford. He felt like he should have introduced himself as

Detective Matthew Finn to compete.

"Grace, darling," Maureen said, pulling a small package from her purse. "This is from Richard."

Grace's eyes darted to Finn and then back to her mother. The package was wrapped in green and white paper with a small tasteful silver bow. It looked the right size to contain a piece of jewelry.

"Okay." Grace quickly snatched the small box from her mother's hand and shoved it into the pocket of her smock, clearly uncomfortable.

Who the hell was Richard? Finn carefully watched Grace's face for a clue, but she didn't turn his way.

"This is where you live?" Maureen glanced around the interior. She held both hands against her chest as if she'd be contaminated by touching anything.

Finn recalled his first impression of the study trailer: the sagging couch, the overflowing toy box, the stained throw rugs on the scuffed tile floor, the barred cage that looked like a jail cell, and the tiny kitchen with padlocks on the cabinets and refrigerator. The place looked like a social worker's worst nightmare.

Charles McKenna shifted uncertainly on his feet, crossed and then uncrossed his arms, and finally settled on sliding his hands into his trouser pockets.

Grace sighed. "No, Mom, this is where I work with the gorillas. I live in that trailer." She pointed through the window at the singlewide across the lawn.

Finn tried to help. "It's much nicer inside. Compact, of course, but Grace has it fixed up beautifully. Blue and green color scheme. Very tranquil."

She shot him a look he couldn't decipher. Her finger moved, pointing to the other two trailers. "That one is for my staff members when they stay overnight, and that one is occupied by Josh LaDyne, my research associate and Ph.D. candidate. The barn is for the gorillas."

Jon stepped forward from behind the door, one hand extended. "I'm Jon Zyrnek, one of Grace's staff."

Kanoni slid down from Jon's arms. She waddled on her hind feet to Grace, holding her long arms up in the air.

Maureen stared. "Oh, my. So they're back?"

Finn couldn't tell whether Maureen was entranced or horrified.

"Just this one." Grace scooped Kanoni up. The baby gorilla curled her long limbs around her torso, then twisted her head to view the visitors. As usual, the long black hair on the top of her head was standing straight up. Her eyes were round with curiosity, or maybe anxiety; Finn was no expert.

The baby sniffed at Maureen, who extended a hand to gingerly pet her head. Kanoni clamped her fingers around the woman's forearm and then abruptly transferred her small body to Maureen, wrapping her legs around the older woman's waist, clamping her hands onto her shoulders, and nestling her fuzzy head against her bosom.

"Well, now..." Maureen's hands waved uncertainly the air for a second, and then she wrapped her arms around the baby gorilla.

"Mom, meet Kanoni," Grace said wearily. "She's eight months old."

Maureen stared down at the baby gorilla. Kanoni looked up, her liquid brown eyes asking for something. Permission to be there, Finn guessed.

"I always hoped there would be grandchildren," Maureen said, "But I never envisioned this."

After a few awkward open-mouthed seconds, they all burst into laughter. When it subsided, Charles turned to Finn. "Can you recommend a motel nearby?"

The choices were grim. Evansburg had three motels. The Overnite, a dilapidated noisy one-story alongside the highway; one ancient motor court close to the college where rooms were often rented by the hour; and the Convention Center, which he knew was currently booked up. He'd noted the sign *Welcome Bible Translators* out front along with the orange neon *No Vacancy* sign as he drove past, wondering what Bible translators would have to discuss.

"You can stay with me." He must have said it aloud, because all heads swiveled in his direction. He gulped and added, "I have a perfectly good guest room that never gets used." Then he remembered the beasts that ruled the house. "Unless you're allergic to animals. I have two cats and a dog the size of a Shetland pony."

Charles smiled. "We have a Persian, Chaucer, at home."

"We had a Doberman Pinscher until six months ago," Maureen volunteered, her voice melancholy as she stroked Kanoni's back. "We still miss Helen." She looked at Finn. "For Helen of Troy. That bitch was so beautiful."

For a minute, Finn wasn't quite sure if Maureen was referring to the historical character. He decided in favor of the dog. Professor Maureen McKenna seemed like the type who would use the correct term for a female canine and then set people straight if they questioned her terminology.

Chapter 13

Grace spent a sleepless night with a traumatized baby gorilla in her bed. At first light she carried Kanoni into the forest, moving in the general direction from which the baby gorilla had come. She alternated between shouting "Neema!" and asking the baby, "Where's Neema? Where's your mom?"

Kanoni clung to her with both hands and feet as she peered through the trees with terrified eyes. Grace made the sign for Neema over and over again, but the baby didn't sign back. Kanoni became more agitated as Grace walked deeper into the woods, her rapid breathing turning to whimpers and then finally to loud shrieks. When Grace let go of her back to make the Neema sign again, Kanoni screeched and crawled up Grace's chest and buried her face against Grace's neck.

Grace stopped walking, wrapped her arms around Kanoni again and patted the shivering animal on the back. "It's okay, baby. We'll go home."

Despondent, Grace turned back to her compound. What had she expected? Kanoni was an infant, and she was torturing her. Whatever the baby gorilla knew about Neema and Gumu, she was incapable of communicating.

Grace was happy to have Kanoni back safe, but the baby gorilla's return increased her fears for Neema and Gumu. She was certain now that Neema was either captive or dead; she would never have intentionally left her baby alone.

Thanks to Guy Rodrigo's 'headless horseman' remark, Finn dreamed about discovering a corpse face down in Grace's barn. When he turned the head to view the face, the head broke off in his hands. Heavy brow. Massive jaw. Gumu.

Finn woke up, his own jaw aching from grinding his teeth. His sheets were damp with sweat. And no wonder. His huge Newfie mix had his head flopped across Finn's thigh, snoring as he drooled on the blanket. Lok and Kee regarded Cargo with slit-eyed feline disdain from opposite corners of the bed.

Finn sat up and threw off the covers and the animals. He wasn't scheduled to work today, but as usual, he couldn't stop thinking about his open cases. The burglars had either gotten wind of the police discovery or spotted Scoletti in the woods; they hadn't returned to their storage depot. Today the department would clean out the old farmhouse, try to identify owners of the stolen merchandise, and route all the lifted fingerprints through AFIS. The fingerprint identification system generally reported back within minutes, showing the closest matches in the system, but then a human had to examine the candidates to determine if any were truly a match and the matching individual was a likely suspect for the crime. The whole process could take days.

The murmur of voices came from the kitchen. Grace's parents. Cargo barked and bounced out of the room to investigate, no doubt forgetting he'd met them the night before. Finn threw on some jeans and rushed to save the professors from his amnesiac mutt. But when he reached the kitchen, Cargo was eating calmly out of his bowl, the coffee was perked, and Maureen was making French toast. It was more domesticity than Finn had experienced in his home in two years.

They were all painfully polite with each other. The professors inquired about his past and he told them he'd been a senior detective in Chicago. They told him they were tenured professors at Stanford. They'd noticed his painting and asked him if he'd attended art school. He told them about his few watercolor lessons. What was next? Would they ask about the authors he read and want to know which was his favorite Shakespeare play? He quickly gulped down the French toast and took his dog and his coffee out to the deck with the excuse that he needed to keep an eye on Cargo.

The weather was sunny and windless and at any other time, he would have invited Grace for the drive he had in mind. But there was no way she'd leave her compound now unless she was hot on the trail of Neema or Gumu. Plus, he'd have to invite her parents, too. He gave the McKennas his spare key, told them to make themselves at home, and then left for Monroe Prison.

On the way, he called Grace. "No sign of Neema?"

"No. I'm watching the news and there's no mention of anything odd. Jon's out driving around now. She'd never leave Kanoni. If she could be here, she would be. I'm just so scared about what's happened to her."

He told her he was going to a prison to interview an inmate, and asked her what she had planned for the day. *Please tell me you're not going to steal any more animals.*

"Checking up on me, Detective?"

"I'm worried about you, Grace." He hoped that sounded concerned instead of condescending.

"I currently have a baby gorilla wrapped around my torso, Matt. Not to mention, my parents are on their way over. Pretty heavy impediments to going on animal raids, don't you think? But someone's got to take the illegal animal trade seriously. I've decided to send ARU instead."

What? He frowned at the Bluetooth readout on his car radio. The Sarge—and the Captain—would have a lot more to say than "Rein in your girlfriend" if Grace did that.

"I'm kidding, Matt."

He blew out the breath he'd been holding. "Thank God."

"But only because I haven't identified any more local animal seller sleazebags. If I find one and your brothers in blue choose not to do anything again, I'm not making any promises."

He thought about explaining reduced budgets and lack of manpower and priorities, but that would likely make Grace even more determined not to involve the police. "Can you at least tell me first?"

"Maybe. Depends on the situation."

"I see." Crap, he was driving twenty miles over the speed

limit. He removed his foot from the accelerator and flipped on cruise control.

"I thought I'd spend my day researching more zoo acquisitions. And return Pepito as soon as I can."

He wanted to solve at least one mystery. "Grace, who is Richard?"

For a long moment, he heard nothing but road noise. Maybe he shouldn't have asked. It was still early in their relationship. Grace had a right to her past; he certainly had baggage that he was still dragging around. It was just that he'd never heard her mention another man before. He expected her next words to be, "None of your business."

But instead, she finally said, "He's just someone I used to know. It's a long story, and it's not important."

"Why is he sending you presents?" He felt a trickle of fear in his gut. Maybe *he* was supposed to be giving Grace presents. Maybe that was the normal course of things these days. Damn, he was so out of practice with the whole dating scene.

"Matt, I don't want to get into that right ... Oh, joy, Mom and Dad are here. Have a nice day." She abruptly ended the call.

The weather was clear over Snoqualmie Pass, and for a little while Finn managed to push complicated women and missing gorillas out of his mind. The jagged peaks of the Cascades, still capped with heavy snow, stood crisply outlined against cerulean skies. These brilliant blues and whites were reflected in the shining surface of Keechelus Lake, a long reservoir bordering the highway that was straining at its banks with snowmelt. Firs and cedars wore chartreuse gloves of new growth on their long spiky branches. In three locations, Finn stopped to take pictures, longing for his watercolors and time to paint the scenes before him.

At the third stop, just as he was focusing on a shimmering waterfall streaming over lichen-dotted rocks, his phone buzzed. It was the Evansburg station operator. "I know it's your day off, Finn, but I thought you might want to talk to this officer from Renton. He says it's a follow-up call."

Renton. The body in the woods. "Put him through." A large black bird flapped past overhead. Crow? Raven?

The officer identified himself, then said bluntly, "Allen Whitehead is dead."

Finn was tempted to say "Duh!" like a teenager, but restrained himself. "Yes, I know. We have his corpse in the Evansburg morgue."

"Not possible. Allen Whitehead died in the Renton Hospital of complications from Hepatitis C a couple of days before you called. He's already been cremated."

"You sure?" Finn watched the bird circle and then land on a nearby branch.

"You need me to repeat what I just said, Detective?"

Crap. "Then we got an unidentified dead guy who was driving Whitehead's Mustang."

"Looks that way. I'll email you Whitehead's next of kin contact info; maybe they have some clue about who'd have the car. Ball's back in your court."

"Thanks." Finn shoved the phone back into his pocket. Why couldn't he close at least one case? He toyed with the idea of calling Melendez to tell her that the missing schizophrenic might be lying in pieces in the morgue, then decided to wait until he heard from Whitehead's relatives. They might have different information about the dead driver. He didn't want to put the Connellys through any unnecessary anguish.

Based on the odd clicking calls the black bird made, Finn decided it was a raven, supposedly a very smart bird with a sharp memory and a large vocabulary of sounds. He wondered what this one was trying to tell him. Get away from my waterfall? The winning Lotto numbers for the week? He'd never thought much about animal communications before meeting Grace and Neema.

He climbed back into his car and joined the traffic streaming down the west side of the mountains toward Puget Sound. Traffic was light, and even after stopping for lunch, he arrived at Monroe Correctional Complex in the early afternoon.

Jarvis Pinder was an average sized man with a wiry build. He had the same café au lait skin as his sister Heather, but he was definitely not the same pleasure to look at. Pinder's nose was askew from a break that hadn't been properly set and his left eye didn't open all the way, thanks to a scar running through the eyebrow above it.

His first question to Finn was understandably, "What's this about?"

"Tony Zyrnek."

Pinder raised both eyebrows. "Tony? What about him?"

"You call him every week."

The inmate squinted. "So? Since when is that illegal?"

"What do you two talk about?"

He shrugged. "What's happenin' in here. What's happenin' out there. Baseball."

"What did you talk about last Sunday?"

"We didn't. I called but he had somethin' else goin' on."

"What did you *want* to talk about?"

Pinder inspected his fingernails. "Can't remember. Those calls're recorded; you can get 'em if you want. Why we doin' this dance?"

He was right; it was a dance. This conversation would make a hell of a lot more sense if Finn could just admit that the gorillas were missing. But who knew where that would go? He decided to pretend he was enlisting Pinder's help. He lowered his voice and put his hands on the table. "Do you think Tony Zyrnek can be trusted?"

The chair squeaked as Pinder leaned forward and matched Finn's tone. "Is he in trouble?"

"Not yet, but I think he might be up to something. Did he ever talk to you about gorillas?"

Pinder's gaze fixed on Finn's face for a long minute. A smile played around his lips before he finally said, "Yeah. His kid worked with some apes; and Tony told me all about 'em. Pretty weird shit, signing gorillas. Hey man, gift a poor prisoner a twenty for some smokes?"

"Five," Finn said.

The convict made a face. "Every teensy bit helps."

Finn suspected that Pinder knew more than he was saying. "Did Zyrnek ever talk to you about stealing a gorilla?"

Pinder threw back his head and laughed, displaying several gold crowns on his back molars. Then he looked at Finn's face. "Oh man, you're serious? Who'd want to steal a gorilla?"

"I hear they're pretty valuable."

"No shit?" Pinder's eyes reminded Finn of Cargo's after the dog had stolen something off his plate and thought Finn hadn't noticed. Placing both elbows on the table top, the inmate leaned forward again and asked in a low murmur, "What's the going price?"

Finn shook his head. "What would you guess?"

The convict shrugged again. "Never tried to sell a gorilla. You think Tony stole a gorilla?" Pinder seemed pleased about the idea. "Man, I can't wait to see that on the news."

Shit. "I didn't say he stole a gorilla; I just wondered if he might be thinking about it."

Pinder smiled again. "Now why would you wonder that?" He sat back in his chair, crossed his arms and grinned as if he'd scored a point in a debate.

A muscle twitched between Finn's shoulder blades. This conversation was going nowhere. If only Grace had been willing to go public, he could ask questions that made more sense. "I've heard you and Zyrnek like exotic animals."

"Lotsa people like animals."

"I hear you used to have an ocelot and a couple of boa constrictors," Finn said.

The inmate perked up. "Yeah, they were gifts from a friend. That cat was a beautiful thing, man. Her name was Lupita. Her fur was like velvet, but she had claws an inch long." He held up a forefinger and thumb as a measure. "And FYI, one a them snakes was an anaconda, not a boa. Boas hang out in trees. Anacondas swim in *rios*, you know, like in the Amazon; they dig *agua*. They're water snakes." He waved a dismissive hand. "Sorta close though, I guess, if you don't know snakes."

"Which friend gave them to you?" Maybe Zyrnek had been

in contact with the same exotic animal enthusiasts.

"Let's see... It's been a while." Pinder looked at the ceiling for a minute as if trying to recall, then lowered his head to meet Finn's gaze. "Nope, can't remember. I got lots of friends and I had lots of animals. I've always been into wild things." He drawled the last two words, smirking.

Finn ignored the insinuating tone. "What happened to those animals?"

"Sold 'em to a dealer over in Idaho."

That figured. Idaho few regulations on any sort of business. But Pinder might have shared the dealer's name with Zyrnek. Finn pulled out his notepad. "The dealer's name?"

Pinder's expression turned wary. He rubbed at the scar that bisected his eyebrow. "I'd have to find it again on the internet. Not like I got my file cabinet here."

"Look it up."

The inmate gave him a cold stare. "What's in it for me?"

"Cooperation could get you a favorable vote next time you come up for parole."

"Yeah?" Pinder sneered. "You gonna come and testify for me, Detective?"

Finn didn't respond.

"That's what I thought."

"What is Leroy Shane up to these days?"

The unscarred eyebrow rose. "Why would I know what Leroy's up to?"

That sounded like yet another evasion. "His brother Leon's on your visitor list."

Pinder's mouth twitched. "So? Leon and me, we don't talk about Leroy—that bastard done me wrong."

"Who is DeeDee Suarez?"

The convict's head jerked back. After a moment, he snarled, "A damn fine looking woman, and a sweet friend of mine." Twisting in his seat, he signaled the guard. "I'm done talking to you. Say Hi to Tony for me. And whichever gorilla he's shacked up with."

"I don't think Heather would appreciate being called a gorilla."

Pinder faced him again. "Who?"

"Heather Clayton."

"Zyrnek's shacked up with my sister?"

"Looks like it."

"What happened to that fucker Ty?" A burly guard positioned himself behind Pinder and laid a hand on his shoulder.

"You'll have to ask her about that."

"I will. Remember that ten you promised for the smokes." The guard led Pinder away.

Finn clenched his jaw in frustration. He was pretty sure that Jarvis Pinder knew more than he was saying about Zyrnek and the gorillas, and the inmate had gotten downright hostile after he asked about Leroy and DeeDee. But he had no leverage here.

He dropped off a five dollar bill at the visitors' window, asking that it be added to Pinder's account. "Anyone else signed up to see Pinder today?"

The guard checked the list. "Nope."

"Who else has visited Pinder in the last couple of weeks?"

The guard pointed down the hall. "Superintendent's Office keeps those records."

The clerk in the office had the same voice as the gal he'd talked to on the phone. After asking for Pinder's recent visitor records, he pulled a bar of dark chocolate out of his pocket and laid it on the corner of her desk.

She eyed it. "That's not necessary, Detective Finn. This is my job."

"It fell out of my pocket."

She smiled and slipped it into her desk drawer before turning to her computer. Inside of a minute, she'd printed out the list of Pinder's visitors in the last month: Leon Shane, Mary Lou Pinder, DeeDee Suarez.

Mary Lou, Finn remembered, was the inmate's mother. "Do Leon Shane and DeeDee Suarez visit on a regular basis?" he asked.

The clerk swiveled her chair away from him again to search the files on her computer. After a few minutes, she said, "Shane was added three months ago; he's visited five times since then. DeeDee Suarez was added to Pinder's list only six weeks ago. She's been here three times. Before those two, Pinder didn't have any visitors except for family."

Interesting. Heather Clayton had named Leroy Shane as a bad guy, so maybe his brother Leon was not so "straight up," either. Criminal behavior tended to be contagious within families. She'd told him that Zyrnek didn't know Leon or Leroy, but maybe she'd been covering for her new boyfriend. DeeDee Suarez was a new name to investigate.

His visit to Monroe hadn't lasted as long as he'd allowed for. He decided to spend a couple of extra hours and drive to Tacoma to surprise Frank Keyes. He'd always wanted to lay eyes on the man who poisoned Spencer, Grace's first male gorilla.

After placing some calls, he determined that Keyes was at work. It took Finn a while to find the particular grocery warehouse within a maze of giant storage facilities, but he finally tracked it down. The manager handed Finn a hard hat and walked him to the loading dock where Keyes was using a forklift to shift pallets of canned goods to a waiting truck.

Frank Keyes didn't look like a murderer. He was a slight man with sloping shoulders and thinning hair. His jumpy manner combined with the overalls he wore made him look like more of a prison inmate than Jarvis Pinder.

"Why are you people harassing me?" he hissed in Finn's direction, his gaze fixed somewhere over Finn's left shoulder. "I haven't touched any of those stupid apes." His eyes darted nervously to his manager standing a few yards away. "You're trying to ruin me."

Finn pulled his notepad out of his pocket. "Where were you last Saturday?"

"I already told your other jackbooted thug. I was on the Olympic Peninsula, camping."

"Alone?"

Keyes's jaw clenched. "It's none of your business. I'll associate with anyone I want to. I don't have to tell you anything!"

"Do you still want to kill gorillas?"

"I have my rights! I can belong to any groups I want to. I can go where I want to."

"You called Dr. McKenna two nights ago."

Keyes's pale eyes rounded with alarm for a second before his face dropped back into a scowl. "You can't prove that."

"With cell phones and GPS these days, you might be surprised."

The other man didn't respond, just stared at the cement floor, his fingers tugging at the zipper pull on his overalls. Up, down, up, down, up.

"You cannot go anywhere near Dr. Grace McKenna's property," Finn reminded him.

"I haven't been near her or her damned apes!"

"Then give me an alibi I can believe. Give me someone who can corroborate your story."

"Corroborate? Alibi?" Keyes spat the words back at him. "I don't need an alibi! I'm not on parole any more, and you have no right to treat me like I am!" Keyes shook his fingers in Finn's direction as if he was hexing him. "I don't want to be within fifty miles of that witch. She says she talks to apes and they talk back! When the Rapture comes, she'll..." He glanced sideways at his boss again. Whatever he saw there made him leave the rest of that sentence unsaid. His hand dropped back to his side, and his voice dropped to a normal level. "I've got to get back to work, Detective. My parole was up more than a year ago. Please respect my rights and leave me alone."

Finn stepped close, backing Keyes up against his forklift. "If you ever contact Dr. McKenna again, I will find a way to put you back in jail. If you show up anywhere near her or her gorillas, you might end up with a bullet hole between the eyes. Do you understand?" He waited until Keyes's chin dipped slightly before he backed away.

Keyes climbed back on his forklift, maneuvered the tines into position and lifted the next pallet. As he turned the machine, Finn noticed a familiar sticker on the back: *I am NOT a monkey's uncle.*

Maybe there was a connection between Keyes and the events in Evansburg after all.

As he drove back over the mountain pass, Finn's Bluetooth system announced a call. He pressed a button on his steering wheel to answer.

"Yo, Finn," said a familiar female voice.

"Yo, Larson."

"I thought you might want to know this. Miki dropped your lab report in my IN basket by mistake."

Uh-oh. His fingers tightened around the steering wheel as he waited for a remark about ape blood. Instead, she read aloud, "Enclosed test results reveal that the blood sample submitted is human, not animal. Please advise if further testing is required."

Human?

"You working that llama case?" she asked. "I thought that was County's."

"Llama case?" Were animals being stolen all over the county? Was someone collecting for a private zoo?

"Yeesh, Finn, don't you read the reports? Black and white llama disappeared from the Bar T a week ago."

"Oh, yeah," he said, "Didn't the owners think it got out of the pasture? Isn't Fish and Wildlife looking for it in the mountains?"

"Yep. But we *all* still need to keep an eye out for it. So, what's *this* report about?"

The dog, he reminded himself. Pursuing one goal while pretending to be after something entirely different was a tricky business. No wonder criminals slipped up so often. "That visitor I told you about; the guy who claimed his purebred dog went missing after the open house at Dr. McKenna's. There was a patch of blood near his car, so we decided to test it."

"Looks like you got lucky. Maybe the dog bit the SOB. You can't match the dog with that sample, but now you can match the dognapper."

"We have to find him first. Anything else going on I should know about?"

"Possible lead on that missing schizo, but nothing definite yet. Ditto with our serial burglars—an anonymous tip reported two guys packing goods from an apartment into a gray Kia Soul in the middle of the night. Oh, and someone stole a body from the Sweet Song Nursing Home."

"Really?"

"Yep. Rosemary Benson. Ninety-five years old. The body disappeared from her room before the undertaker could pick it up."

"You're kidding."

"Who would kid about a thing like that? It's disgusting. Now a family can't lay great grandma to rest."

"You think it's a prank?"

"That would be pretty cruel. More likely some enterprising soul is going to chop her up and sell the bits and pieces. Body parts are big business. Right now on eBay, a complete human skeleton is going for nineteen hundred."

"Damn."

"You can say that again. You're lucky it's your day off." Her sharp exhale rasped through the speakers. "Why do *I* catch all the weird cases?"

If she only knew.

"Good luck. Thanks for letting me know about the lab report." He pressed the disconnect button on his steering wheel to end the call.

The blood sample came from a human? What the hell had happened in Grace's barn? Feeling slightly nauseous, he focused on the highway ahead. He might be able to explain covering up the death of a gorilla, but how was he going to defend not reporting a murder?

Chapter 14

Grace spent much of the day pacing around her compound with a baby gorilla glued to her hip while her mother graded papers and her father wrote on his notebook computer. How that was supposed to indicate their support for her, she couldn't figure out.

Uncertainty about everything was driving her crazy. There were too many questions. Had Kanoni escaped her captors somehow? Was Neema imprisoned somewhere nearby? Was she dead? How far had Kanoni traveled? Grace stared into the baby's mahogany eyes, wishing she had some way to get the answers that were locked into that little primate brain. Kanoni's response was to clamp her fingers around Grace's earring and try to pull it to her mouth, painfully reminding Grace that gorilla mothers should never wear jewelry.

She'd worked only with captive gorillas. She had no idea if a gorilla could normally find its way back home from a distance, especially a baby. Who could she ask? Only Dian Fossey's name came to mind, and that poor woman had been murdered long ago in Africa.

Finn had already nixed the idea of getting a police canine unit to trace the gorillas, but maybe she could hire a private dog tracker service just to trace Kanoni's path. She could pretend it was part of a scientific project. The only business she found online that sounded even remotely similar used bloodhounds to track wounded game, and that business was in Texas. She called Finn to ask for a recommendation but got only voicemail.

"He probably can't take cell phones into a prison, Grace," her mother reminded her. "He seems like a nice man. Are you and he an item?"

Why did her mother insist on talking like she'd been born in the Victorian era? Grace said, "Not in the way you mean. Not yet."

"Then you are friends with benefits?" Her mother gazed at her over her reading glasses.

"Mom! Matt and I are not teenagers. We are consenting adults." She'd hit forty next year—would this parental evaluation never stop?

"Where did he get his degree?"

Grace realized she had no idea whether Matthew Finn even had a college degree. "It doesn't matter to me."

"What was the gift that Richard sent to you?"

Grace hadn't even looked. She went to the closet and retrieved it from the pocket of her smock. Pulling the silver bow loose, she fingered off the top and set the little box on the desk in her mother's view.

Inside, on a nest of white cotton, was a silver chain and a pendant, the silhouette of a redwood emblazoned on top of a letter S inside a circle.

"Oh, how pretty!" Her mother picked the necklace up. "The Stanford symbol. What does the note say?"

Grace unfolded the tiny white slip of paper. "With fond memories," she read.

"I told you he misses you." Maureen carefully folded the chain and laid the necklace back in the box. "He wishes you were still there."

You wish I were there, Grace thought bitterly. Knowing Richard, he'd sent the pendant to remind her of the vast distance between her current life and his. She shoved the box into her desk drawer.

And so the morning went. When Maureen volunteered to feed Kanoni, Grace enthusiastically accepted and tried to lose herself in more computer research on the zoo trade. Most information available on the internet was cheerful news aimed to encourage donations; there was little public data about where animals came from or where they went when they left the zoos.

Her mother, unfortunately, chose to sit with Kanoni and her sippy cup in a rocking chair near Grace's desk. And she continued to talk.

"I'm sure that many zoos would be willing to take Cannoli." Maureen patted the gorilla's back as if she were burping a human infant.

"Not happening, Mom." Grace kept her gaze fixed on her computer screen. "And her name's Kanoni. It's Swahili. She's not a dessert."

"Isn't Swahili spoken in East Africa? I thought gorillas lived mainly in West Africa, in the mountains."

Grace made an effort to unclench her jaw. "Those are mountain gorillas. My gorillas are lowland gorillas. The Democratic Republic of Congo has lowland gorillas and Swahili is an official language there." Besides, Swahili was the only African language she had a dictionary for, but she wasn't about to say that.

"I see." Maureen sniffed. "Well, I guess I learned something today."

Grace sighed and switched her gaze from the computer screen to her mother. "Sorry I snapped at you, Mom."

Finishing her drink, Kanoni scampered from Maureen's lap to Grace's and slapped her hands against the keyboard. Grace grabbed the baby gorilla's hands in one of hers and used the other to switch the display to a cartoon jungle scene. Kanoni pointed to the colorful animated birds flying across the screen and chattered to herself. Grace looked around the room. "Where's Dad?"

"He's outside at that table you have in the yard. He said something about writing a press release for you."

"Crap!" Grace leapt up, dumping Kanoni into her mother's lap. "He doesn't have a phone with him, does he?"

She dragged her father into her personal trailer and then explained the entire embarrassing situation to both parents.

Her mother was shocked. "You mean you don't have the support of the community?"

"Think about it, Maureen," her father urged. "Would you be

thrilled if gorillas lived next door to us?"

Her mother's chin rose. "If it was a valuable research project and if they were under control, I'd be very supportive."

The operative phrase there was *under control*. Grace could hardly argue that her gorillas were. She didn't even try to defend herself. She sent her parents off to the local library to quiz the reference librarian about how zoos purchased and traded animals, and then to the grocery store to restock the kitchens in Grace's personal trailer and the staff trailer. Glad to have a defined mission, they departed in their rental car.

Shortly thereafter, Kanoni discovered Pepito in the cat carrier, and the two spent a half hour chirping and chattering at each other. When Kanoni decided to shake the marmoset out of the cat carrier—all the better to play with him, she supposed—Grace carried the baby gorilla into the study trailer and tried to settle her in a blanket nest in the cage area. "Nap time."

Kanoni was having none of it. She wrapped her arms and legs around Grace's torso as if she'd never let go and screeched each time Grace tried to detach her. Grace's head throbbed.

She returned to her trailer and her internet searches, her chin resting atop Kanoni's head, typing awkwardly around a gorilla in her lap, determined to track down at least one clue that might lead to Neema and Gumu. Kanoni slept against her chest, but woke when Grace's cell phone bleeped in the late afternoon. She picked it up without even looking at the caller ID.

"Dr. McKenna, are you missing a gorilla?"

Kanoni wrapped her long fingers around the phone and tried to pull it out of Grace's hand. Grace held on and pulled back. Hope and dread battled in her chest, preventing her from breathing. Then, recovering both the phone and her composure, she pressed the phone to her ear. "Who is this? Why do you ask?"

"This is Officer Ninen from Fish and Wildlife. Can I send a photo to this phone number?"

"Send it to my email address." She told him how to do it and in a few seconds, the picture came through. The dark eyes of a frightened gorilla were barely visible through heavy grillwork. Neema!

Relief and joy washed through her like a flash flood. For a second, she thought she might pass out. She'd been preparing herself for a tragic ending.

Tamping down her giddiness, Grace grabbed a pencil and jotted down the location Ninen gave her. "I'll be there with a half hour. Please don't do anything before I arrive. I'm on my way." She stuffed a bottle of water, a few apples, and some of Neema's favorite cookies in a pack, and then called Jon.

He was at her door in minutes.

"They've found Neema!" She peeled Kanoni from her front and wrapped the baby's arms around Zyrnek's neck. "She's alive!"

The youth's face lit up. "Who? Where?"

"I'll be back in an hour."

"Don't you want to take Kanoni?"

"I don't know what'll happen." She had no idea what sort of condition Neema was in, or how Fish and Wildlife might respond to catching a gorilla in their trap. She was afraid for the baby to see her mother injured or knocked unconscious with tranquilizers. She was afraid to be happy yet. "I'll be back as soon as I can."

Spots danced before her eyes as she drove, and she had to remind herself to breathe now and then. It took her twenty minutes to find the unmarked dirt road Ninen had mentioned. Then the van slipped and slithered through muddy ruts, moving deeper into the thick trees. When she spied the cab of a Fish and Wildlife truck among the trees, she slid to a stop. The truck had backed off the road into the forest to hook up to a culvert bear trap.

She introduced herself to Ninen and his colleague. At the sound of Grace's voice, Neema vocalized from inside the trap, hooting loudly. The gorilla was a pitiful sight. Breathing heavily, Neema pressed her face against the grillwork. She repeatedly signed *out Neema out* and pointed to her teeth and made a clawing motion. Teeth? Claws? Then *baby*. Stroking her fingers down the front of her throat, she signed *thirsty*. Then *eat eat* and then *out out* and *baby* again.

Kanoni is with Z, Grace signed. *I have water. I have food. Neema be good.*

Oblivious to the silent conversation taking place between Grace and Neema, the officers talked.

"You can imagine how surprised we were."

"This was the last critter we expected to catch."

"How long has this gorilla been on the loose?"

She wasn't about to answer that last question. Instead, she checked the forest around them for a black hulking shape. If Neema and Kanoni had both been loose in the woods, maybe Gumu—

Ninen stepped in front of her, blocking her view into the trees. "Are you missing more than one gorilla, Dr. McKenna?"

Offense seemed to be the best solution. She glared at him. "Did you leave any water in this trap? Let's get her out."

Out out out, Neema signed. The strange teeth and claw signs again. Then Neema twined her fingers and toes through the heavy mesh. The nails on her fingers were torn and bloody. She hooted mournfully, her voice unusually raspy. Had she been calling for help for days? She rattled the door, shaking the whole trap.

Officer Ninen grabbed the rifle at his side.

"You won't need that." Grace signed *Neema good quiet* in the gorilla's direction.

"It's loaded with tranquilizer darts," he said by way of explanation. "The dosage for bear should be about right."

"You won't need it," Grace repeated. "Just open the damned door!"

Ninen's eyes squeezed shut. He pushed his cap back and pinched the bridge of his nose, losing patience with this crazy woman.

Grace added, "Neema is signing that she's really thirsty and hungry. Look at her poor fingers and toes. And her face. She got separated from her baby; she's desperate to get out."

Ninen's colleague turned in a slow circle, scrutinizing the forest around them. "Where's the baby?"

"Back at my place." Grace motioned toward the door again. "Please. Just open the door and stand back."

Both men wore skeptical looks. "You sure? We can't be held responsible if—"

"She's mine. I know her. Just let her out."

It took both men to lift the heavy door on its track. As soon as she could fit, Neema squeezed through the opening and hurled herself into Grace's arms. Grace braced herself against the onslaught, hugging the gorilla and staggering backward to keep from falling down. Out of the corner of her eye, Grace saw Ninen raise his rifle.

"Don't shoot!" she yelped. "She just needs reassurance."

"Would you look at that!" Ninen's colleague pulled out a cell phone and took a photo.

When Neema had calmed down enough to put her feet back on the ground, Grace told her, "There's food and water in the van."

The gorilla turned in that direction, but stood staring at the surrounding woods, signing *teeth claws, teeth claws baby baby claws eat.*

"Oh, you poor thing, what did you see?" Teeth claws?

"Huh?" one the men said.

"Kanoni is at home." Grace signed while saying the words. "Your baby is safe. Your baby is with Z."

Neema huffed once as if she were skeptical.

Where's Gumu? Grace asked in sign language.

Neema huffed again and looked around uncertainly. Grace tried again with *Gumu here?*

Gone baby teeth claws thirsty thirsty baby gone. Neema raised herself up onto all fours, looking as if she were about to bolt into the woods again.

Grace pointed to the van. "Let's go home and see your baby. Let's get food and water."

Neema, abruptly deciding to trust Grace, beat her back to the van. She crouched beside the vehicle, signing *open open*

Neema thirsty food good open food.

Grace let her into the back of the van and gave her the bottle of water and the food, then shut the door and walked back to the officers. Both had their gaze glued to their cell phones. Ninen was typing with his thumbs, and the other was sliding his fingers across the screen.

"Thank you for calling me," she said, interrupting their internet moment. "You can see how gentle Neema is; she didn't do any harm." At least she hoped that was true. "I'd really appreciate it if you guys could keep this quiet."

"Uh." Ninen exchanged a guilty glance with his colleague.

Damn it. This would be all over the internet and the local news within minutes. If it wasn't already.

On the way back to the compound, she called Finn. "Two things. Fish and Wildlife found Neema."

"That's great news! Is she okay?"

"She will be."

"What about Gumu?"

"No sign of Gumu. Here's the second thing: The game wardens took photos with their cell phones."

He paused only a fraction of a second. "The shit storm is about to hit."

"Batten down the hatches."

His groan reverberated across the airwaves. "I just crossed over Snoqualmie pass. I'll get to your place as fast as I can."

Chapter 15

An unfamiliar beige SUV was parked in Grace's usual spot at her compound. Gad, the media tornado had touched down even faster than she expected. Then she saw the sign on the side door. Department of Agriculture. *Crap.* She'd completely forgotten about the inspector coming today.

Her shoulder muscles tightened with anxiety. The good news was that now she had two of her three gorillas back. What could she say about Gumu? *Think, McKenna, think.* agricultural inspectors were used to dealing with livestock. Would they believe that she'd loaned her male gorilla out as a stud? She quietly led Neema across the grass en route to the study trailer, hoping to settle the mother gorilla into the cage there with her baby before confronting the inspector.

Halfway across the courtyard, loud voices emerged from the barn behind her.

"That is a large volume of blood back there. Whose is it?" Grace didn't recognize the woman's voice.

"Dr. McKenna will have to tell you about that." Jon Zyrnek.

"The public has a right to know what goes on out here. Was a gorilla killed in that barn?"

"Talk to Dr. McKenna." Jon again.

Grace quickly pushed Neema into the study trailer ahead of her and yanked the door shut behind herself. Neema rushed to the refrigerator and pulled at the handles, then spied Kanoni in the cage. Spread-eagled as she clutched the bars with fingers and toes, Kanoni issued hopeful chirps, her eyes fixed on Neema. When Neema chuffed back at her, Kanoni bounced and shrieked to get out. Grace unlocked the door, and the baby rushed to her mother, leaping the last few feet to land on Neema's belly. Neema sniffed her and licked the baby's head as if to reassure herself that Kanoni was hers, and then sat down and signed to Grace around the bulk of the baby. *Yogurt milk red drink bread Neema hungry hurry.*

Grace smiled. If Neema had known the word for *anything*, she probably would have signed *I'll eat anything.* Kanoni dug her fingers into her mother's fur and sucked on Neema's left nipple like she'd never let go. Even Neema gazed down at her with concern, like Kanoni was a leech that had clamped onto her body.

Grace settled the gorillas in a corner of the cage, with a nest of blankets and toys and an array of food before them. Then, steeling herself for a confrontation, she walked outside to meet the inspector.

Four more strangers had joined the party. Three of them held out cell phones and snapped her photo as she walked toward them. The fourth had a video camera focused on her. Their eyes were too bright; their voices shrill and eager.

"Dr. McKenna!" one shouted. "Why was your gorilla found in a bear trap?"

The inspector, a woman in a tan shirt and blue jeans with a clipboard in her hands, swung around to face the reporter. "What? When? What's going on here? Dr. McKenna?"

Damn those wildlife officers. Damn cell phones. Grace took a deep breath.

"How long has a gorilla been missing?" the videocam operator wanted to know.

Grace evaded the question. "Neema is back with her baby now."

The agricultural inspector crossed her arms. "I need to see all three of your gorillas on this visit, Dr. McKenna."

"Come into my office." As she waved the woman toward the study trailer, Grace tried to marshal her thoughts.

The reporters surged forward in the inspector's wake. Grace thrust out a hand like a traffic cop. "Stop! Leave us alone."

She was amazed when they actually halted. "This is private property," she snapped. "You do not have my permission to be here."

"I'll make sure they leave," Jon told her. He turned to shepherd the foursome back to their cars.

Probably grateful to be left out of this *conversation*, Grace thought, following the inspector into the study trailer.

The story took a half hour to tell. In the cage, Neema signed *out out out*. When the gorilla began to hoot and rattle the cage bars, Grace escorted the inspector to her personal trailer to finish the conversation. She tried to defend herself as best she could, stressing the break-in and her shock at discovering her gorillas were missing.

The inspector was stony-faced. "How do you explain the pool of blood?"

Grace shook her head. "I can't, not yet. It must be Gumu's. I'm afraid someone killed him." She reminded the inspector of her history with Frank Keyes.

Finally, after taking copious notes, the agricultural inspector left. As Grace walked her to her van, she felt the gaze of someone watching her. On the front steps of the staff trailer sat Sierra Sakson and Caryn Brown, both wearing baggy camo pants, tank tops, and lace-up boots. Beside them, Brittany Morgan leaned against the railing, wearing white Capri pants and a ruffled rose-colored crop top. None of the three looked happy with her.

As soon as the dust swirled behind the inspector's departing van, the three young women surrounded her. Sierra and Caryn both stood with legs spread and arms crossed in a defensive stance. Brittany looked uncertain.

"You could have trusted us, you know." Caryn said in a low voice. Since Grace had last seen her, she'd colored her short blond hair a soft lavender shade. One of her eyebrow rings sported a small lavender stone as well.

Sierra added, "I knew it wasn't about a damn dog."

"Yeah," Brittany chimed in. "We were real worried."

"You're right. I should have trusted you from the beginning." Grace did her best to look properly chagrinned. "I'm glad you're here now. I could really use your help with Neema and Kanoni."

"You got it." Sierra uncrossed her arms. Purple must be the color of the day, Grace speculated, because the streaks in Sierra's long dark tresses were bright purple now, too, and so was her nose stud.

"Where's Jon?"

"Out front, guarding the gate," said Caryn. "The vultures are circling."

"Shit," Grace said under her breath.

"Yeah," Caryn said in sympathy. "Hey, I've been meaning to ask you, Grace, how does Finn know Heather Clayton?"

"Who?"

"She's a counselor at the college. Real pretty, long dark hair? She lives across the street from us. I saw Finn going into her apartment the other day."

Finn had never mentioned a Heather that she could recall. But then, she'd never mentioned Richard to him, either. "She's probably part of a case he's working on," she guessed.

Caryn gave her a look that implied Grace was clueless, but she said, "That's probably it."

Brittany brought the conversation back to the present problem. "What happens next?"

Grace had no idea what would happen next. Did the inspector have the authority to shut down her project? Would the woman sound the alarm about her missing male gorilla?

She got her answer after Finn drove in. He slid out of his car without saying a word, walked over and wrapped his arms around her. She pressed her ear to his chest, relishing his solid warmth, inhaling his scent, listening to the rhythm of his slow steady heartbeat.

He was a rock, and she was always causing him trouble. She rarely spent time alone with him; she rarely left the gorillas. How could she blame him if he was seeing this Heather woman? They hadn't made any promises to each other.

"We're going on patrol," Sierra announced quietly as she and Caryn passed.

In the trailer behind her, Neema's cries were growing more and more frantic. Two loud thumps issued from the thin walls.

"I'll go talk to Neema," Brittany murmured.

Finally, Grace leaned back to check Finn's expression. "Does everyone know?"

"Male gorilla reported missing in Evansburg area," he quoted. "Unpredictable wild animal. Approach with caution. Hit the airwaves just as I pulled through your gate."

"Is Jon still there?"

Finn nodded. "He let me in."

They walked to the study trailer. Neema was begging Brittany to release her from the cage.

Out out out, Neema signed. *Neema out.*

Out where? Grace signed back. *No trees.* She wasn't about to lose her gorilla in the forest again.

Out barn sleep barn, Neema signed.

Grace interpreted for Finn.

"What has Neema told you so far?" he asked.

"She's only signed *out* and *barn* to me," Brittany told them.

"Thanks, Brittany. Could you wait for me in the staff trailer? I might need your help with Kanoni."

"Sure." The girl turned to go. "But I've only got an hour."

As soon as Brittany left, Finn asked again, "What did Neema tell you?"

"Variations on *thirsty thirsty hungry*. I can't believe Fish and Wildlife would leave any animal in a trap for days with no water."

"They caught their problem bear," Finn reminded her.

"Still, they should have checked all the traps. There are more than two bears in the woods."

"Did you specifically ask Neema about Gumu?"

She sighed. "Several times. She hasn't given me a definite answer." Turning to the huddled gorillas, she signed as she spoke aloud. "Neema, where's Gumu?"

Neema signed *out barn out out.*

Kanoni, sitting in her mother's lap, reached up and patted Neema's face with a small black hand.

Out out out, Neema insisted.

Grace wasn't sure that going to the barn was a good idea.

"I'm worried that she's expecting Gumu to be there," she whispered.

"Maybe she'll re-enact what happened." Finn sounded hopeful.

Out. Neema grabbed the cage bars and screeched loudly, then thumped a fist against the wall. Alarmed, Kanoni stared wide-eyed at her mother.

Neema was going to continue pleading until she got her way. Grace opened a nearby cupboard and removed a collar and leash before turning back to the gorillas. It was impossible for a woman who weighed one hundred and thirty pounds to control an adult gorilla weighing in at two hundred and ten. The restraints were more of a reminder to behave than anything else.

"To the barn," Grace stressed aloud. She snapped the collar and leash onto Neema's neck, careful to avoid her chafed and bloody face. "Neema, be good."

Out out. Neema pushed Kanoni onto her back and stood eagerly behind the trailer's front door, rocking on all fours.

Once outside, Neema raced across the courtyard to the barn, dragging Grace. Finn jogged a few steps behind them.

Jon and Brittany caught up with them at the enclosure gate. "We'll make sure the back door is secure." They both disappeared around the back side of the barn.

Neema scraped Kanoni from her back and dropped her to the ground. Then she climbed into the netting and scaled the ropes to the top. After picking up the blankets that Gumu had left behind, she sniffed them and hooted mournfully.

Then Neema pulled the blankets over her shoulder and dragged them down the rope net, dropping onto the ground with a thud. Kanoni waddled to her mother, but Neema pushed her away and vanished into the barn.

Grace followed and switched on the lights, dispelling the evening gloom settling inside. She and Finn watched as Neema circled the interior, inspecting every inch.

Jon and Brittany joined them again.

Watching Neema's behavior, Jon groaned. "Oh God. She's

looking for him, isn't she?"

Grace felt her throat grow tight. "Neema lost Kanoni, and then she found her. Now maybe she thinks she might find Gumu."

"Could that mean she knows he's alive?" Finn said. "Can you ask her what happened?"

"I'll try."

Neema dropped the blankets in the sawdust and proceeded to climb methodically from one sleeping shelf to another, higher up the barn wall. Grace peered up at her and signed. "Neema, where's Gumu?"

Sitting on the highest shelf, Neema swiveled her head, looking all around. Then she sat back on her rump and emitted a long, mournful howl. On the ground eight feet below, Kanoni clutched the edge of the lowest sleep shelf with both hands and whimpered in response.

"Kanoni wants you, Neema." Brittany looked up at the mother gorilla. "Come get Kanoni."

Neema did not even glance down.

Grace asked, "Was Gumu with you, Neema? Gumu and Neema in the trees?" Neema wasn't watching her, but the gorilla understood far more words than she knew signs for.

Neema thumped down the sleeping shelves. Landing heavily on the ground with a grunt, she knuckle-walked to the blood stain. The humans followed.

"Oh my God!" Brittany pointed at the dark area, a look of horror on her face. "Is that...blood?"

Jon nodded briefly in her direction, then heaved a long slow sigh.

"Oh my God." Brittany put a hand over her mouth. Turning to Jon again, she whispered, "Gumu?"

Jon dipped his chin again. Affirmative.

Neema studied the stained sawdust with sad eyes, leaned over and sniffed, then finally pinched up a small amount and put it into her mouth. At her side, Kanoni watched and then copied her mother, tasting the bloody sawdust with a quizzical expression on her baby face.

Jon groaned. "This is killing me."

Brittany slid her hand into his.

"Neema," Grace kneeled beside the gorilla. She murmured softly, "Where's Gumu?"

Meat, Neema signed. She waddled back to the discarded blankets, carried them into the darkest corner, and pulled them over her head. Kanoni scuttled to her. Neema kicked the baby away. The little gorilla screeched.

Brittany scooped her up, and Kanoni buried her head against the girl's breasts.

Grace caught her lower lip between her teeth. Tears pricked at her eyes. She tried to will them away.

Frowning, Finn put his hands on his hips. "What does *that* mean?"

"I don't know, but it's not good."

Jon scuffed the toe of his shoe in the dirt. "Maybe she doesn't want to talk about what happened."

"Can't you give her candy or some other treat to make her talk?" Finn asked.

Grace walked to the corner, pulled the blankets away from Neema's head and took the gorilla's chin in her hands. The gorilla's red-brown eyes were haunted.

"Neema," Grace whispered. "Where's Gumu?"

The gorilla slowly unfolded her arms and briefly gestured. Then she abruptly shoved Grace away, pulled a blanket over her head, and curled up in the corner.

Squealing, Kanoni leapt from Brittany's arms, ran to her mother, and pulled at the blankets. Grace picked up the baby gorilla, walked to the lowest sleep shelf, and sat down heavily. A tear ran down her cheek as she patted Kanoni on the back. "Neema says Gumu's gone."

"She also signed *meat*." Brittany's brow wrinkled. "What does that mean?"

"That's what she called Spencer's dead body." Grace rubbed her fingers across her eyes, smearing tears into her lashes and blurring her vision. "It's the smell of blood, I guess. I think it means that Neema thinks Gumu is dead."

"Oh my God," Brittany said again.

"Grace, I have something I need to tell you," Finn murmured. His tone did not imply a happy story would be forthcoming.

Oh sweet Jesus, what now? She couldn't handle any more bad news. She rested her chin on the top of Kanoni's head.

From the gate outside, her father sang out, "Grace, we're back. Are you in there?"

She groaned, shaking her head. "I just can't..."

Finn put a hand on her arm. "I'll take them home with me."

Thank God. She crooked an arm around the back of his neck and pulled his face down for a kiss. He tasted like coffee. "Thank you."

She hefted the baby gorilla in her arms and stood up. "Let's all be happy that we have Neema and Kanoni back."

Turning to Jon and Brittany, she said, "I'll be staying out here tonight. I'll talk to you all tomorrow."

She crawled into the corner next to Neema in the blanket nest. The gorilla leaned toward her and laid her enormous head against Grace's bosom, whimpering. She gently stroked the fur on Neema's head. "I know, Neema. I know. But you're home now. Safe. Kanoni's here. I'm here. And we hope Gumu will come back, too."

How could she explain the concept of hope to a gorilla? Or did Neema already know there was no hope of ever seeing her mate again?

Chapter 16

The next morning, Finn asked his ex-in-laws, Dorothy and Scott Mankin, to come over for coffee. He needed backup. Somehow he'd managed to get through last evening with the professors, answering their questions about his favorite authors and television programs. He painted more than he read, and he didn't really have favorite books; he just picked up whatever appealed to him at the time. The McKennas suggested several titles, which he dutifully wrote down. For TV shows, he mentioned the Discovery Channel and Masterpiece Theatre, which seemed to score him a couple of points. But he was pretty sure he lost those when he couldn't remember the names of any NPR programs. It was pretty clear that the McKennas thought their daughter had not only chosen a career that was beneath her talents, but she'd also hooked up with a dolt.

He'd gotten up early to make coffee and thaw out some blueberry muffins he had stashed in the freezer. Now he gestured from the Mankins to the McKennas. "I thought you'd like to meet Grace's parents, Charles and Maureen McKenna."

"Well, this is just wonderful." Maureen McKenna stepped forward to take Dorothy's hand. "We're so pleased to meet Matt's parents."

"They're not *my* parents..." Finn started, then stopped. How to explain that these were his ex-wife's parents, but they were the closest thing to family he had in this town? He took the easy way out and finished with, "They're my friends."

Dorothy noticed the birth announcement on the table. "Oh, I see she sent you one, too."

"Sorry," Scott said.

"I'm happy for Wendy," Finn told them.

Dorothy tilted her head. "Really?"

"I'm trying to be," he admitted.

The McKennas politely waited for an explanation. Finn glanced at his watch. "Oh, no—look at that. I'm due in court this morning. I'll leave you all to get to know each other. Scotty, Dorothy, I thought you might like to show the McKennas around town."

Scott shot him a startled look. Turning his back to Grace's parents, Finn pressed his hands together in a begging motion and mouthed *please* to his ex-parents-in-law.

Dorothy recovered first, saying, "We'd love to. We can even take a drive up into the mountains."

Finn escaped. Except for the court appearance, it was technically his second day off. Maybe it was cowardly, but the police station seemed like a calmer place to hang out today than Grace's compound. As soon as he stepped out of his car, though, he had second thoughts. He was bushwhacked by the same two student reporters—one male, one female—who had been lying in wait last night when he exited Grace's gate. This time they had a camera jockey in tow. The trio barred his path to the station door.

He almost bonked his nose on the microphone the boy stuck in front of his nose. "Are you looking for the missing gorilla, Detective Finn?"

He shoved the microphone aside and shouldered the boy out of his way. The two took turns yelling as they trotted behind him.

"What about the blood in the barn?"

"Is there a killer gorilla on the loose?"

He pushed his way through the station doors and was thankful when his pursuers stopped outside. He passed through the lobby and into the detectives' area, sliding into his chair and tapping his computer's power button. The desk across from his was occupied by Perry Dawes, the other male detective. He took one look at Finn, sighed heavily, and said, "Oh, boy."

"I figured I was in for it," Finn told him.

Scoletti was pulling a report from the printer in the corner, and Finn waved him over. "Scoletti, you remember the guys carrying those protest signs at the open house?"

"Yeah?"

"The guy carrying the sign that said *I am NOT a monkey's uncle*—did you know him?"

"I can't remember who was carrying what. Let's see...there was Carl Lannereid and Eddie Melendez."

"Melendez? Any relation to Detective Sarah Melendez?"

"Uncle, I think."

Sergeant Carlisle rounded the corner, a sheaf of papers crumpled in his hand. "Finn! We've been trying to call you."

"I turned off my phone," Finn said mildly. "My court case got rescheduled to this afternoon. The hit and run from February. I'll be filing for comp time, by the way."

"Fish and Wildlife want to know if they should have hunters out looking for that gorilla."

He pondered that for a second. There was still a chance that Gumu was out in the forested hills around Evansburg. He told the sergeant that, then added, "But it's more likely that the gorilla was stolen or even killed, so mounting a big search could be a waste of taxpayer money."

He noticed a photocopy in his IN box and pulled it out. White-haired elderly woman. Rosemary Benson. The deceased lady whose body vanished from the nursing home. Melendez had written the date of death and her statistics at the bottom of the page. Rosemary was a tiny thing, only five feet tall.

Carlisle put a hand on Finn's desk and leaned close. "That dog tale was bullshit, wasn't it?"

From the next desk, Dawes laughed. "Good one, Sarge. Dog tale."

Carlisle's face reddened. Ignoring the jibe, he shook the papers in Finn's direction. "You knew that lab test was not for dog blood."

Finn held up two fingers, Boy Scout style. "I honestly didn't know *what* type of blood it was."

"But you knew that McKenna's gorillas were on the loose."

How to answer that one? "I knew that Dr. McKenna believed they were gone. But citizens around here don't typically report every animal that disappears for a few days, so I didn't feel that it was crucial." He ran out of words and left it at that. It sounded lame even to his ears.

"And when the lab report indicated the blood was *human*?" Carlisle bellowed.

Miki stopped digging in the file cabinet to stare. Mason pretended to scrutinize a laptop he was testing, but his posture told Finn he was completely tuned in, too. Two uniforms stood in the door of the break room, watching, and another swiveled around from the computer station where he was writing an incident report.

Then Mason abruptly turned up the volume on the laptop, and everyone heard the voice of Dr. Grace McKenna say, "Gumu could kill you." And then, "Male gorilla canines are particularly impressive—Gumu's are several inches long."

Oh sweet Jesus, some hot dog reporter had recorded Grace's talk at the open house and edited it for maximum impact. Finn tried to remember why he had stopped in. Oh yeah, to run DMV records for Shane and Linero, and to see if fingerprints had come back on the burglary items.

"Have you been sitting on a murder, Finn?" The sergeant tapped his fingers on Finn's desk. "Did a gorilla kill someone in McKenna's barn?"

Finn kept his voice reasonable. "Would that technically be murder, if an *animal* killed someone?" he asked. "Not that I'm saying that's what happened. Because there's just no way to know right now. But we don't charge sharks with murder when they swallow a swimmer, do we? And Kittling's stallion, last year, the one that stomped that kid to death, he's still standing at stud, isn't he?"

Carlisle looked as if his head might combust.

"It's my day off, Sarge." Leaning close to the man, he murmured, "I'm working on finding that gorilla."

"Get outa here, Finn," Carlisle growled.

He had no choice but to fight his way through the reporters

back to his car. He decided to check on Grace and make a few phone calls on his way.

He caught Sarah Melendez at home. He could hear what sounded like a party going on in the background. "It's Stacey's seventh birthday," she said. "We're having a family picnic."

He apologized and asked her about Eddie. Cousin, not uncle, she told him. "Yes, I can believe he was picketing the gorilla event. I think the label 'right-wing nutcase' was invented just for him. You should hear him shout at the Nature channel on TV."

She gave him her crazy cousin's phone number and wished him luck.

Grace's front gate barred the drive. A heavy chain and padlock hung ostentatiously from the top rail. Sierra Sakson sat on top of the heavy four-foot-tall post the chain was attached to. She stared pointedly into the far distance, swinging one booted foot idly and looking supremely annoyed. Two young males, no doubt student reporters, peppered her with questions, their faces level with her waist. When Finn drove up, she swung her foot out in a wide arc, and when the men stepped back, she jumped down and pulled out a key to let him in.

"Detective Finn! Detective Finn! Is it true that a gorilla murdered a man here?"

Finn didn't even bother to differentiate who yelled what. He thrust his head out the car window and looked from one to the other. "You two better be gone when I come out. You're trespassing on private property."

They stepped back onto the road.

"Not anymore," the shorter one said.

"Freedom of the press," the other one added.

Finn nodded at Sierra and pulled through the gate. On the way up the drive, he passed a Fish and Wildlife pickup on its way out. The two men in the front nodded curtly at him through the window.

When he stepped out of his car, he saw Neema sitting at the top of the net, in Gumu's usual position. She had Gumu's blanket wrapped around her like a cloak.

Grace answered the door of the study trailer with the baby gorilla wrapped around her back and shoulders like a shawl, her hair in disarray, and blue shadows under her eyes. Kanoni clutched a rag doll in one hand and a hank of Grace's tangled hair in the other. In the background, a cell phone chimed.

The trailer was unusually messy, too. A chopped banana lay on the tabletop, along with a handful of Cheerios and a sprinkling of broccoli and cauliflower. Grace's cell phone continued to chime. She grabbed it and switched off the ringer before tossing it back onto the table. "They never give up!"

"I saw Fish and Wildlife pulling out. Are they searching for Gumu?"

"No. Just alerting everyone for fifty miles around to be on the lookout for a gorilla. Fortunately the only hunting season open right now is for turkeys."

The cage area was empty.

"How's Neema?" he asked.

Kanoni made a chirping noise at the sound of her mother's name. Grace sighed and shifted the baby gorilla on her hip. "I'm worried about her. She wouldn't eat this morning and she won't nurse Kanoni."

"Sit down," Finn said. "You look exhausted."

"I *am* exhausted." Grace grabbed a handful of Cheerios and broccoli and they moved to the sagging couch, which was more than usually stained and hairy from all the baby gorilla activity it had hosted the past two days. She slung Kanoni around to her lap and then sagged back against the sofa cushion. "What did you do with Mom and Dad?"

"The Mankins have them."

"That should be interesting," she said. "Local Yokels take on the California Eggheads—who will prevail?"

Her meanness surprised him. "None of them is *that* bad."

She rubbed her forehead. "You're right. I'm just having a bad day. No," she said, "Make that a bad week. Two apes and one monkey found, one gorilla still to go."

"You still have the marmoset?"

"Pepito. He's in my personal trailer. I keep leaving messages for the owner."

Before he got into the big news, he had to ask the question that kept nagging at him. "Grace, who is Richard?"

She looked over his shoulder at the far wall. "He's not important. He's nobody, except in my parents' imaginations. I can't afford to waste time thinking about him now."

That wasn't really an answer, but he guessed it was as good as he was going to get at the moment.

She leaned toward him. "What did you want to tell me? Do you have any leads on Gumu?"

He gently laid a hand on Grace's knee. "I got the results back on the blood."

Kanoni leaned forward to place her small black hand on top of his as if she were encouraging him. The baby ape's fingers felt cool and leathery. He stared at her small fingernails, torn at the edges, pink toward the middle. So human-like. Or maybe humans were ape-like.

Grace held out a handful of Cheerios toward Kanoni. "Just say it, Matt. Neema had no serious injuries. So it has to be Gumu's blood."

"The blood was human."

A series of emotions flitted across Grace's face. Finally, her eyes brightened. "That's encouraging."

Not the reaction he expected. "Why?"

Kanoni peeled a Cheerio from her own lip and held it up to Grace's mouth. Grace pressed her lips together and shook her head, and the baby gorilla put it back into her own mouth.

Next, Kanoni picked up a piece of broccoli and shoved it toward Finn. Mimicking Grace, he pressed his lips together and shook his head. Kanoni squealed in disappointment, then jammed the broccoli into his chin. Finn snatched the broccoli out of the gorilla's hand. He leaned down and picked up the rag doll. Holding the doll in one hand, he pressed the broccoli to its embroidered lips. "Ummm. Good!"

Kanoni took back the doll and the broccoli and tried to force the toy to eat the vegetable. After a few attempts she settled for pushing the broccoli under the doll's dress and then pulling it out with her lips and eating it.

Grace rolled her eyes.

"Why did you say that human blood was encouraging?" Finn asked.

"It means that Gumu might still be alive." Setting Kanoni on the floor, she handed the gorilla the last Cheerios in her hand.

He hated to dampen Grace's enthusiasm, but he had to say it. "The volume of blood we found means that someone probably died in your barn."

She grimaced. "I hope so. The bastard deserved it."

A prosecutor was unlikely to see it that way. And while it was easy to dismiss the passing of a faceless criminal, knowing that a real person had bled to death on your property might be a little harder to explain. When they found out who had been injured in the barn, there would be a name, a history, and family members to deal with. His thoughts flashed briefly to the haunted faces of Ryan Connelly's parents.

"If Gumu bit an attacker, it was self-defense." Grace's green eyes bore into his. "What happens now?"

He thought about that for a minute. He checked his watch; he was due to testify in less than an hour, and it was a twelve-mile drive back to town. "The blood trail led to the parking lot; it's *possible* that the person didn't die, or at least not right away. No one has reported finding a body. I'll look into that, but I need to get to court soon."

"I'll call the hospitals."

He shook his head. "They won't tell you anything. But they have to talk to a cop. I'll see if anyone came in with heavy bleeding."

"And you'll continue to check where Keyes was over the weekend?"

Oh yeah. Keyes. "And continue to check on Keyes's whereabouts over the weekend." And check to see if Keyes had a connection with Eddie Melendez.

"Would be nice if it was Keyes's blood," Grace said bitterly. Her face took on a cunning look. "That gives me an idea."

The muscles between his shoulder blades tensed. "What sort of idea?"

She smiled faintly. "Probably best not to tell you."

"Not more animal stealing, I hope. Grace, have you seen the news?"

She groaned. "Yes. McKenna loses gorilla. Again."

"There was a blowup at the police station about the lab report." He smoothed his palms against the thighs of his pant legs. "Everyone in the place heard that the blood found in your barn was human."

She blinked and reached for the remote, then clicked on her tiny television.

"—missing from Dr. McKenna's research facility outside of Evansburg. And new evidence shows a large amount of human blood was spilled in the gorilla cage." The female reporter turned to her male companion on the news desk.

Catching her cue, the young man asked, "Does that mean what I think it does?"

The female faced the camera. "It means we may have a man-killing gorilla prowling through our neighborhoods."

"Please take precautions out there," the male said. "Safeguard your loved ones."

Then the screen went to what passed for a commercial break on the public access channel, showing a tour of a local restaurant that had recently been remodeled.

"What?" Grace yelped. "They can't leave it there! What about the break-in, what about someone attacking Gumu?" She reached for the phone. "I've got to set the record straight."

Finn knew the media storm was only going to get worse. He was more worried about how the county council might respond. The only way he could help was to find whoever had broken into the barn. At least with the real story out there, he could finally talk openly about the break-in and the missing gorilla, even if he wasn't welcome at the station right now.

When he left the study trailer, Kanoni was twirling in circles around the table and Grace was arguing for air time with a scheduler at the television studio. Before getting into his car, he took the time to call Grace's staff into the courtyard for a brief talk.

As he listened to Detective Finn describe the case, Jonathan Zyrnek watched an ant crawl across a plank in the picnic table. The tiny black insect was carrying a chunk of something bigger than he was. Brittany sat next to him, her hand on his thigh like she thought he was her boyfriend. She was nice enough, but he knew she was looking for a father for Ivy, and he wasn't ready for that. He'd spent most of his life living with families that weren't his own. When he was ready to have a family, he wanted his own kids.

Caryn and Sierra perched on the bench on other side of the table, both still smoldering for shutting them out of the secret.

"Here's the scenario as I see it," Finn explained. "Around four-thirty last Saturday, Brittany saw Gumu crawl out of his nest, climb down the net, and go into the barn." He dipped his chin, nodding in Brittany's direction. She beamed like she'd won a prize.

"That's likely when Gumu heard someone breaking into the barn," Finn continued. "There was a fight. Gumu was probably tranquilized, but not before one of the intruders was injured, possibly even killed."

"So the blood in the barn was *human*?" Jon asked.

Finn gave them all a stern look. "Yes."

"Good for Gumu!" Brittany's ponytail bobbed as she nodded. "He got him good."

Finn said intruders—plural—and it made sense that there had to be several. No single person could control Gumu. Jon asked, "How many intruders?"

Finn shook his head. "We don't know. But if one was injured, there had to be at least two others to get the injured man and Gumu to a vehicle. I would guess at least three or four people were involved." He continued, counting on his fingers. "So the first question is, who did Gumu injure? It looks now as if Gumu was taken after the fight, and Neema and Kanoni escaped later through the same door. So the second question is, where is Gumu now? And the third one—who else was in on this?"

Dropping his hands, he looked around their little group. "Concentrate on the facts: at approximately four-thirty, someone broke into the barn. There was a fight and someone was severely injured. Then Gumu was stolen and all participants drove away down the back driveway."

"The odds are that one or more of you saw something or heard something. Think about where you were between four-thirty and five o'clock last Saturday. Did you see a strange car? Did you notice activity on the back road or at the back of the barn? Do you know someone who was recently injured, or have you heard about someone who died unexpectedly? Do you know anyone who would want to take Gumu?"

Grace joined them, holding Kanoni. Upon spotting Brittany, the baby gorilla promptly transferred herself to the redhead's arms. Grace positioned herself next to Finn like they were two drill sergeants addressing the troops.

"Please," she pleaded. "If any of you know anything that could help Gumu, if any of you has heard anything, please tell us. The tiniest clue might save his life."

Jon looked at the others. He hoped his expression was as blank as theirs were. When he'd finally gone home last night, he saw that his dad had a bandage on his hand. And then there was the lock and the bolt cutter. He'd left those in place by the road but covered them up with dirt. *Evansburg Auto Salvage.*

What the hell had his father done? Could he find a way to save Gumu without sending his dad back to prison?

After his court appearance, Finn retired to his home office to make his calls.

The emergency room clerk at Evansburg Hospital told Finn they had an injury in the right time frame. Maybe he was finally going to get a useful lead. "I need all the patient's information."

"I can't do that," she said. "HIPAA rules."

Finn gritted his teeth. "Do you know that you can be charged with obstruction for preventing a police officer from investigating a case?"

"You sure?"

"Check the court rulings." Why didn't they teach this to medical personnel?

"Just a minute." The clerk apparently put the phone down on the desk, because he could hear voices and various office noises in the background.

His unfinished painting sat on the corner of his desk. The poppies still needed shadows, he noted. It *was* still technically his day off, after all. He rummaged through his tubes of paint and found a tube of Prussian blue, then searched for raw sienna. And a light yellow; he'd need that, too.

The clerk picked up the phone. She read him the case information.

"What's the patient's blood type?"

Unfortunately, the blood type didn't match the sample from the barn. He thanked her and hung up. He checked the surrounding counties, but came up with no likely victims. Either Gumu's victim had survived long enough to travel far away, or some unlucky hiker would eventually find a body in a shallow grave.

Thinking about the possible intruders brought Jarvis Pinder's smirking face to mind. The blood in the barn was likely to belong to an associate of his.

Finn logged in to the department's databases, relieved to find his login code still worked. The bosses might be considering giving him a reprimand, but at least they hadn't locked him out. He brought up the most recent court transcript for Jarvis Pinder and scanned through the pages of trial information and testimony. The prosecution accused Pinder of being a conduit for a well-known cocaine cartel centered in Venezuela. And just as Heather Clayton and Jarvis himself had intimated, Leroy Shane had been another major drug dealer who'd somehow managed a sweet plea deal by testifying against Pinder. It seemed odd that any member of the Shane family would still contact Pinder after that.

Finn discovered that Leon Shane owned an oil lube franchise in Spokane, which made his visits even more curious—it was one hell of a long drive from Spokane to Monroe. Finn called the business number and asked to speak to the owner. As he waited, he filled a glass with water from the kitchen and listened to the zrrrip zrrrip of a pneumatic wrench punctuating the background static on the phone line.

"Shane."

Finn identified himself. "I need to ask about your recent conversations with Jarvis Pinder."

"Who?"

"Jarvis Pinder. You visited him in Monroe twice in the last month."

"You've got the wrong guy."

"Don't waste my time playing dumb, Mr. Shane. You're on the visitors record there."

"What? I never heard of the guy." There was a hiccup of hesitation, and then Shane growled, "Shit. This is Leroy's crap again; I know it."

"Tell me more."

"Look, I've never been to Monroe prison, and I don't know any Marvin Pinder. But I'm betting Leroy does. My name is Leon Michael Shane. My worthless brother is Leroy Daniel Shane. Damn it, I'm going to kill Leroy! I haven't seen the idiot for years, but if he's using my ID again—"

"Do you look a lot like your brother?"

"It's the curse of my life." Shane groaned. "We're identical twins."

Finn gave Leon the prison superintendent's number so he could straighten out the visitor situation.

Although it needed further investigation, Leon's story sounded plausible. As a felon, Leroy Shane couldn't visit a prisoner, but posing as his brother Leon, he could. Now it seemed even more likely that Jarvis and Leroy were up to *something*. Could they be in cahoots with Tony Zyrnek and

Heather Clayton? Heather could be playing the sad role of the woman left behind, stalling for time to make sure her boyfriend, Ty Linero, could finalize the sale of Gumu.

Next, Finn researched the other mysterious woman: DeeDee Suarez, the unknown name on Jarvis Pinder's visitor list. He found a Washington State driver's license, with a full name of Delfina Delicia Suarez. The birth date indicating she was 33 years old, only five feet one inch tall, and weighed all of 105 pounds. She had no record beyond a few parking tickets and one traffic infraction. DeeDee's birthplace was listed as Seattle, so she was a U.S. citizen. Her mother's address was listed in Seattle, but beside the listing for her father, Roberto Suarez, was a note: Colombian national, deported 1997. Interesting, but not an uncommon history for many young Hispanic Americans.

DeeDee wasn't listed in any phone directory he could find. The number the prison had for her was no longer in service. Was that was significant in some way, or merely an oversight in recordkeeping?

Finn saw no obvious role for DeeDee other than the "damn fine looking woman and sweet friend" described by Jarvis Pinder. He pulled his half-finished painting close, mixed paints with water on his palette, and began to stroke dark shadows into the centers of the poppies and the creases of the leaves. Somehow mixing paints and moving the brush across the paper gave his mind time to make the connections, fill in the details to see the big picture.

Someone had broken into Grace's barn and been injured or killed. A gorilla was missing. Those were the basic facts. Now for the coincidences. This event had happened since Tony Zyrnek had been released from prison to live with his son, who worked with that gorilla. Tony's cellmate, Jarvis Pinder, called while Finn was present, and Tony had covered it up. He hadn't mentioned that Heather Clayton was his old cellmate's sister, and he hadn't said anything about driving his pickup from the barn down Grace's back driveway. Zyrnek had access to tools that would allow him to easily break a lock, he had a nasty wound on his hand that could have come from a fight with a gorilla, and nobody could verify where he was at the time of the incident. That was a lot of evidence in Tony's *Probably Guilty* column.

Jarvis Pinder and Leroy Shane had to be planning something with those fake ID visits.

Finn washed out his brush in the water, mixed yellow and raw umber, and began to paint highlights.

The gorgeous Heather Clayton was Pinder's sister and lived in the county where the crime had taken place. She had a baby by Ty Linero, who left the area at approximately the same time the gorillas had disappeared. Heather immediately took up with Tony Zyrnek, who had motive—he knew all about the gorillas and how much they were worth; means—he had a truck and easy access to bolt cutting tools; and opportunity—he knew the schedule of the open house, had access to the back of the barn, and most likely knew Pinder's other scumbag friends, no matter what he said.

Tony Zyrnek. No matter where Finn started, all connections led back to Tony.

He dipped the tip of his brush in paint and added a few streaks of pure bright yellow here and there, then stood up to get perspective on the painting. The sky was a wash of cerulean, with pale yellow and pink undertones to the clouds. The field of orange-red poppies was nearly finished. The blossoms had depth and detail now.

The woman wandering through the flowers remained a phantom figure. He still hadn't decided whether she should be moving away from or toward the viewer. A few quick strokes could make the decision. He wished Grace were here to give him her opinion. He called to tell her that.

"I can't talk now," she told him in a breathless voice. "I'm rushing out the door to do an interview at the TV station."

The recording of Grace saying "Gumu could kill you" leapt into his imagination. "You really want to do that? It could go badly."

"I have to, Matt. People have to know the truth. And

whether he's alive or dead, we've got to find out what happened to Gumu." She ended the call.

Finn decided to pay his most likely suspect a surprise visit.

Tony Zyrnek didn't seem surprised to see him pull up in front of the double-wide. He pulled the door open as Finn was on the first step. He held a cleaning rag in his unbandaged hand. "C'mon in, Detective. Is it true? Did Gumu attack someone? Is the big guy really missing?"

"Don't you already know the answer to that?" Finn stepped in. The place smelled like lemon furniture polish.

Zyrnek's brow wrinkled. "Jon didn't..." His quizzical look changed to a frown. "Oh Christ, *that's* what you were really looking for, wasn't it? You thought I was in on it."

Zyrnek tossed the rag onto the table beside the door alongside a bottle of lemon oil. "I guess I can see why you might think that. But I'd never do anything to hurt Grace or the gorillas, because that would hurt my kid, too. Can't you see that?"

"You hurt your kid before to get money."

"That was a long time ago, back when I had spaghetti for brains." He gestured with his chin toward the couch. "I have a steady job now. I'm done with all that."

Finn walked into the living area. "Jon has stolen animals before. Maybe he had a little help this time?"

The other man shook his head. "Look, I know that the Animal Rights Union is probably classified as an eco-terrorist group, or whatever you cops call it these days. But none of those ARU kids are terrorists. They're just animal lovers. They wouldn't steal a gorilla unless they thought it was being abused. Jon's not part of this. I'm not either." He fixed his gaze on Finn. "Not him. Not me. Really."

They both sat down simultaneously, Finn in the chair and Zyrnek on the couch. The place looked different somehow, but maybe that was only because the TV was off and the cowboy boots were on Tony Zyrnek's feet instead of under the coffee table.

"Does Jon believe I'm in this?" Zyrnek rubbed his moustache, thinking. "That could explain a lot of what's been going on with him."

Finn zeroed in on the differences in the house. A bowl of fruit was prominently centered on the counter dividing off the kitchen, and an array of artwork adorned the wall next to the entry door. Those hadn't been there before.

Zyrnek noticed him studying the framed pictures. "I hear you like to paint. I'm an artist, too." He stood up, walked to the wall, and took down a small framed drawing at the right edge of the collection. He walked back and handed it to Finn. "I finished this one yesterday."

The frame was plain fir with staples in the corners, probably from Goodwill. The scene inside portrayed the sun glowing through a maze of red maple leaves. The perspective, looking up through the tree branches toward the sky, was interesting.

"What do you think?" Zyrnek asked. "The shadows and shapes were hard to get right. Heather said she likes it. Ever worked in pastels?"

"Never tried them," Finn grunted. "Nice job. Great contrast."

"Thanks." Zyrnek returned the painting to its place on the wall. Zyrnek pointed to two small paintings that flanked it. They were of a totally different impressionist style. "I'm sure you recognize these."

Bold and messy splashes of color. "Gorillas?" he guessed.

"Neema." Zyrnek indicated a framed whirl of lilac and yellow splashes on top. "Gumu." He moved his finger to the bolder red and blue painting near the bottom of the array. He studied them for a long minute before turning back to Finn. "Amazing, aren't they?"

"Good use of color," Finn agreed. "But no depth perception."

Zyrnek laughed and slapped his leg. "You're right!" He slid into his seat on the couch. "We got a lot in common, you and me."

"I doubt that." Finn sat back in his chair. "Did Jon give you those paintings?"

"Yep. Having 'em on the cell wall reminded me that there was another world outside, one filled with interesting things like painting gorillas and my son who worked with them."

"You had them on your wall in prison?"

"Yeah." Zyrnek cast a glance back to the paintings. "They weren't framed then, of course, just taped to the wall, but they were nice to look at every day."

So Jarvis Pinder knew about painting gorillas long before Gumu disappeared. "Tell me about Jarvis Pinder," Finn said.

"Ah, Jarvis." The other man rubbed his palms over his blue-jeaned thighs. "Most everyone goes to prison for stupid decisions. Some of us learn our lessons, but others—like Jarvis—have never made a good decision in their whole wasted lives. He's a professional criminal."

"Why do you say that?"

"'Cause even though he's inside, Jarvis is always trying to start something up on the outside."

"What would be in it for him right now?"

"Jarvis likes to win." Zyrnek made a wry face. "And money, of course. He's up for parole in a few years. He'll get it; he hasn't been convicted of killing anyone."

Finn looked at him. "Why would anyone on the outside listen to him or share profits with him?"

"Because he'd find a way to get revenge if they didn't. Rumor is, he's had a few guys killed."

Finn scrutinized Zyrnek's face. Was the guy trying to tell him he'd been pressured into committing a crime? Was he trying to prove how smart he was by pretending to be an advisor?

Finn decided to play along. "Interesting. How would you advise us to find out what Pinder is up to?"

"Find out who he's talking to, besides me. Who visits him."

"I know who visits him. Leroy Shane. DeeDee Suarez. Those names mean anything to you?"

"I don't know him, but I've heard Jarvis talk about how

much he hates Leroy. DeeDee, I've seen on visiting days. She's kinda hard for a man to forget." He smoothed down his moustache with his index finger.

"How so?"

Zyrnek smiled. "She's a really hot little Latina. We all wondered why she was wasting her time with Jarvis. He already had Heather; that's understandable, her being his sister. But DeeDee? Me, I was lucky if the chaplain stopped by." He nodded again. "I'll ask Jarvis about DeeDee when he calls."

"How would Heather fit into Pinder's schemes?" Finn asked.

"Heather?" Zyrnek's brow folded into a frown. "She'd never have anything to do with any crime. She knows how that ends up."

But as a kid growing up in a family of criminals, Heather would have occasion to know when crime paid as well as when it didn't. Maybe the fiancé was the good guy; maybe Ty Linero ditched her after he discovered Heather was involved in a criminal enterprise with Zyrnek and her brother. "Do you know why Linero left her?"

"She showed you the note, right?" Tony Zyrnek grimaced. "I know they had money problems and things might be tight in the future, but Jenny's such a sweet little thing. You can't just toss a kid into the trash." He dug his fingers into his legs. "When I think about what Jon went through growing up..."

His voice trailed off and he stared at the far wall. Then Zyrnek shook his head as if to clear his thoughts and ran his fingers through his close-cropped hair. "Like I said, I learned my lesson. And Heather's a prize; she'd never be involved in anything like that. No, trust me, Linero's the loser in that relationship, not Heather."

"Trust you?"

Zyrnek held up both hands. "Well, okay, I know you don't really have any reason to trust me, but you can. I'm gonna think hard about all this. I'll let you know if I come up with any ideas."

"Thank you so much." Finn could hear his own sarcasm practically dripping onto the floor.

Frustration stiffened Tony Zyrnek's face. "I really want to help find Gumu. I'm one hundred percent on your side."

Finn stood up from the couch. "I'm not your buddy, Zyrnek."

Zyrnek's gaze met his. "I get that. But you could be."

"I'll be in touch," Finn told him.

"Good, I'll look forward to it." Zyrnek pulled the door open for him. "Stop by anytime."

"Thanks." He hadn't meant to say that. It was just automatic. He thumped down the steps.

"Maybe next weekend, if this is all settled, you and Grace could come over? I'd invite Heather; I could barbeque. I'm working on a killer hot sauce."

Finn didn't respond, although his mouth and stomach immediately warmed to the idea of barbeque. Zyrnek was a typical con man who couldn't stop rolling out the charm. Finn slid into his car. Pulling out his phone, he called Grace's landline. The call went immediately to voicemail, and there he got a terse machine-voice message telling him that the voice mailbox was full and to try again later. The call disconnected. He got through on her cell phone, but only to another voicemail message.

"Just wanted to see how your interview went," he said to the phone. "I'm working on a list of characters that might have taken Gumu. Call me when you get the chance."

He went home to his cats and dog and a message on his home phone from the McKennas informing him that they were taking the Mankins out to dinner and not to wait up. He went for a quick jog around the roads of his rural neighborhood. His heavy breathing and aching feet reminded him that he was getting out of shape. After a shower, he fixed himself an omelet for dinner and threw a ball for Cargo out in the yard until it was too dark to keep track of the black mutt.

Grace didn't call or text him, but she had two traumatized apes to care for again, plus an army of wannabe reporters to fend off. He called Jon Zyrnek's cell phone. Voicemail again. He left a message asking about the situation at Grace's compound. A minute after he hung up, a text message from the kid appeared on his phone: UNDER CONTROL.

It felt like there was an untyped GET LOST or FU after those two words. He replied TAKE CARE OF HER and then signed off.

He logged into the department's system once more and checked DMV for registrations under the names of Ty Linero and Leroy Shane. He needed to talk to both those men. Leroy Shane had gone to some trouble to impersonate his brother to visit the prison, there had to be a good reason for that. Ty Linero was either involved or at least might know what Zyrnek and Heather had planned.

He found the old Corolla license and VIN for Ty Linero. Every record listed for Leroy had expired long ago. He entered Ty's car data in the watch list that went out to all law enforcement agencies, stating that Linero was wanted for questioning in a theft case.

There were hundreds of cars on that list. Which meant that unless the car was cited for a ticket or involved in an accident, odds were pretty slim that anyone would notice it. Still, it was better than doing nothing.

He brushed his teeth and went to bed early, wondering if Grace was sleeping in her own bed or spending another night in the barn with Neema.

Chapter 17

Finn was awakened the next morning by persistent buzzing. Shoving a cat out of the way, he grabbed his cell phone from its charger on the nightstand. *Cell phone, VA.* Didn't they know it was only six a.m. on the west coast? He yawned.

Cargo sat up eagerly, plopping his front feet onto the bed. One sharp-nailed paw landed on Finn's balls, and he only half-stifled a yelp as he answered. "Finn."

"Detective Finn?"

"Yeah?" He glared at the dog and rubbed his genitals through the sheets.

"You left a message asking about Allen Whitehead?"

It took him a second to orient himself. Whitehead. The owner of the crashed car in the woods. Deceased, but not the corpse in the car. "Yes?"

"Allen was my brother. We haven't been close for a long time. I haven't—hadn't—even seen him for almost five years."

Finn pushed himself up in bed and rearranged the pillows between his back and the headboard. "Were you aware that he had a 1965 Mustang?"

"Allen always collected vintage cars. They could have been nice if he'd ever restored them, but he didn't take care of them. He emailed me to say he gave three of them away a couple of weeks before he died. He must have had a premonition or something. I hear another one is still up on blocks in the garage; you have any interest in a decrepit Camaro?"

"Uh, no."

"Well, in case you change your mind, I'm flying to Seattle to clear out the place next week. I could give you a great deal. Otherwise, it's probably going to end up getting donated somewhere."

He yawned again. He needed to buy one of those coffeemakers with a timer so the caffeine would be hot and ready when he woke up. "Any idea who your brother gave the Mustang to?"

"I have a note—sort of a will, I guess—that a doctor sent me. He wrote it in the hospital before he died. Hang on a minute."

While Finn waited, he rummaged in his bedside drawer for a notepad and pen.

"Mustang ... Mustang... Here it is. Looks like Kevin ... Norton? No, I think it might be North, Kevin North? Hard to make out Al's handwriting."

Who the hell was Kevin North? "Do you know the connection between Allen and Kevin?"

"Not a clue. Like I said, we haven't been close for a while."

"Thanks for your time. Sorry for your loss." He laid the phone down, then pulled himself out of bed and padded to the kitchen to put the coffee on and feed his menagerie. The guest room door was closed. Maureen and Charles were still asleep.

As the coffee perked, Finn booted up his computer to pull up North's driver's license on the DMV database. Turned out to be a fairly common name, but he did a more refined search and finally settled on the Kevin David North that had a past address in Renton—that had to be the Whitehead connection— and a more recent one on the outskirts of Evansburg. The license photo didn't look much like the dead guy, but then, having your throat and half your face ripped off could really change a guy's appearance.

North had a few traffic citations and a drug conviction for possession, so his prints were in the system. Finn called the fingerprint expert's voicemail and left a message for him to check the dead guy's prints against Kevin David North's as well as Ryan Connelly's. He hoped the corpse would turn out to be this parolee instead of Connelly.

His phone buzzed again. He didn't recognize the number. He hit the TALK button and identified himself.

"This is Kennewick PD Officer Lila Jones." Her voice had a Southern lilt. "I've got the Corolla you listed pulled over here for reckless driving."

Finn's uncaffeinated brain took a beat to catch up with this next zig of information. *The gorilla case. Corolla. Ty Linero's car.* That was lightning fast; he'd posted the information only last night. "Is Tyrone Linero driving?"

"That's the rub, Detective. The driver's license says Leon Shane, although oddly enough, he has another one that says *Leroy* Shane. Face matches the photo and description on both licenses. He also says the Leroy license was a mistake; he's Leon. He says he has permission to drive his friend's car. What do you want me to do with him?"

Why was Shane driving Linero's car? This might be the break he'd been looking for.

"Detective? You still there?"

"Does Mister Shane seem nervous?"

"Sweating bullets. And it's not actually that warm out here."

"Can you detain him a while? He might be the key to a big case I'm working on. I'm an hour and a half away."

"I'll think of something."

"I'm on my way."

He called the station to let the dispatcher know where he was before he pulled on his clothes. Then he trotted to his car and slapped his flasher onto the hood.

Grace's dictionary defined *hope* as "to wish, to expect and desire." It had been a week, but she still held out hope that they would find Gumu alive and bring him home. Could she communicate that to Neema? Should she try?

Her sad gorilla sat alone at the top of the rope net, in the spot Gumu usually dominated as he surveyed his domain. Neema had wrapped herself in the old quilt that Gumu had used before he disappeared. She insisted on wearing it everywhere, draped like Red Riding Hood's cloak over her head and shoulders. The blanket was caked with dirt, but

Neema refused to be separated from it.

From her position on the ground, Grace could hear Neema's soft whimpers as the female gorilla stared at the distant horizon. Kanoni, plastered to Grace's midsection, whined in response to her mother's sounds of distress. Neema had kicked Kanoni away so often that the baby gorilla was now afraid to approach her. Instead, Kanoni's eyes fixed on Grace's face, looking for reassurance.

"It's okay." Grace stroked the baby's head, smoothing Kanoni's wild hair. "I'll take care of you." But baby gorillas usually nursed two to three years, sometimes as long as five. She'd had her mother buy some baby bottles, but bottle feeding was a poor substitute for the comfort of a real mother's breast. "Pretty soon, your mom will be back to her old self, too."

She wasn't at all sure of the last statement. Neema seemed even more depressed this morning, eating nothing and refusing to even look at Kanoni. Had she expected to find Gumu back at the compound? Could that mean she thought he might be alive, or was it some child-like expectation that he might come back from the dead?

After Spencer, the other male gorilla Neema had been paired with, had been poisoned, his body had been taken away and Neema never saw him again. Did Neema assume that the same thing had happened to Gumu? Should she try to convince Neema there was hope?

If she promised Neema that Gumu would come and then he never did, would Neema ever trust her again?

If the gorilla had been a child, Grace could take her to a funeral, show her the dead body, describe how wonderful heaven was, say that Gumu was looking down from that celestial paradise. But as far as she knew, gorillas had no concept of heaven or afterlife. Religion would make no sense to an ape, unless perhaps it was tied in with food. She could envision Neema worshipping a god who dispensed food on a regular basis. Or maybe not even that, since the gorilla was not eating now.

Flies buzzed around the fruit and yogurt Grace left for Neema on the food shelf. Neema was oblivious even to the eager crows squawking overhead, waiting their chance to snatch a free meal.

This morning Neema had signed only *Gumu gone wet meat red*, repeating those words in a variety of sequences. Although Grace couldn't be sure, it seemed unlikely that Neema had witnessed an attack. Neema knew signs for *man, hit, knife, stick*, and various other words that she might use to tell the story. What was clear was that Neema believed Gumu was gone for good. Huddling under her blanket with her head down, the female gorilla was the epitome of mourning.

"Grace, honey," her mother called from outside the fence.

When had her parents arrived?

"It looks like Neema wants some private time," her father suggested. "How about a cup of coffee?"

Her mother added, "And your father insisted on bringing muffins. You have to eat."

After a last glance at the blanket-shrouded lump that was Neema, Grace reluctantly exited the enclosure, carrying Kanoni. Maybe her mother was right; maybe she just needed to leave the gorilla alone for awhile.

When she opened the door to her personal trailer, Grace found she'd left the television on. Big mistake. As they entered, a clip of her interview was playing at the worst possible spot.

"...knew that Gumu could kill someone, didn't you?"

"That's why we don't let most people get near him," she responded.

"But someone did get near him, didn't they? And he killed that person, didn't he?"

On screen, Dr. Grace McKenna visibly recoiled. "That person was an intruder. He broke in without permission. And we don't know for sure that person is dead."

"But you knew you had a violent gorilla. And now—where is Gumu, Dr. McKenna?"

She snapped off the television and sat down at the table with her mother and father. Her parents tried to overcome the awkwardness with polite chitchat about Finn's ex-in-laws, Scott and Dorothy, and the places they'd visited yesterday—the county historical museum, the Cascade foothills, the sprawling farms. Grace shared a muffin with the baby gorilla in her lap.

"It's a nice area," her father summed up.

Then they sat in silence for several minutes. Finally, her mother cleared her throat and then began, "Grace, your father and I have a question. We're curious about your project here."

Kanoni twisted in her lap, eyeing the rest of the muffins. Grace grabbed both the gorilla's hands to keep the baby from sweeping the lot of them to the floor. "Yes?"

"It's a scientific question," her father said.

They were tag-teaming her. Grace sensed this would not be a question she wanted to hear. "Yes?"

Maureen took her turn. "We don't quite understand the goals."

Grace swallowed. "What do you mean?"

Her mother continued, "Well, we know that apes can acquire sign language, thanks to your work and some of your colleagues."

Her father added, "And we know that they use sign language creatively, and that they even teach it to each other."

Grace selected a blueberry muffin from the basket. "Yes. They are thinking beings just like we are. Right now, I'm trying to figure out how to explain the idea of hope to Neema."

"Really?" Her father's brow crinkled. "That does seem like a difficult concept to get across. There's nothing to point to, nothing to act out."

Her mother put a hand on his leg and scowled briefly in his direction before turning back to Grace. "But, honey, now that we know they can do all that, what is the possible scientific purpose of your project here? What benefit is there?"

Grace's anger was instantaneous. She'd heard this before, from every institution she'd ever been associated with. Most recently from the local college. *Why should we fund your project?* She pulverized the blueberry muffin in her fist to keep from pitching it at her mother.

"Why did Anne Sullivan continue to teach Helen Keller, Mom?" Dumping the crumbs on the table, she wrapped her arms around Kanoni and abruptly stood up. The chair fell over behind her with a clunk.

Her mother squirmed. "Oh, Gracie, we just thought ending the project might be easier if you considered—"

"After Helen Keller made the initial connection of a sign with an object, Anne Sullivan had proved that a blind deaf child could learn sign language. So what could possibly be the point of teaching her anything more?" Grace slammed the door behind her as she left the trailer.

Apes were so much easier to understand than people.

Leroy Shane had the demeanor of an abused dog, and the skin of a teenager who had never learned to wash his face. His cheeks were pebbled with acne scars and uneven beard stubble. He sat in the interview room, his right wrist handcuffed to the table, a half-empty plastic glass of water in front of him. In the few minutes Finn watched from the observation room, Shane picked his nose with his free hand, wiped the results on his pants leg, scratched his balls, and then coughed twice and spat on the floor.

As soon as Finn sat down at the table across from him, Shane said, "I didn't steal that car. My friend said I could take it."

"Then we can clear that up fast, *Leroy*." Finn held out his cell phone. "Call him."

Leroy's eyes skated across the phone, landed on Finn's face for a minute, then bounced off the walls.

"You high, Leroy?" Finn asked.

"Not me." Leroy sat up straighter in the chair and managed to look Finn in the eye for a full ten seconds before glancing down at his own lap. "And it's Leon. Lee-on."

"That's not what your brother says."

Leroy made a face and rolled his eyes. "He's always trying to get me in trouble."

"Where's Linero?"

Leroy briefly looked perplexed, then chewed the inside of his cheek for a minute, then finally said, "Haven't seen Ro for a while."

"Ro?" Heather had called him Ty. Ro sounded more like a street nickname. "You mean Tyrone?"

"Ty-rone?" Leroy's brow crinkled and he mashed his lips together as if thinking gave him a headache. Maybe he hadn't ever heard Tyrone's full name. He went back to studying his crotch, but his mouth twitched as he said, "Yeah, if you say so. Tyrone."

"Where's the gorilla?"

The pale eyes jerked back up for a second. "What kinda crazy question is that?"

"I know you stole a gorilla."

Leroy muttered something that sounded suspiciously like 'lawyer.'

A spark of excitement ignited in Finn's belly. Leroy definitely reacted to his mention of a gorilla. "Where's the gorilla? Who's paying you? How does Pinder figure into this?"

A little louder this time, Leroy said, "Lawyer."

"Why are you driving Tyrone Linero's car? Where were you going?"

Leroy faced the mirror on the wall and yelled, "Lawyer! Lawyer!"

The door opened and Officer Jones poked her head in. "Detective," she said, "Can I see you for a minute?"

Gritting his teeth, Finn picked up his notepad and pen and joined her in the hallway. The car Leroy Shane was driving had not been reported as stolen, and although Shane had quite a history of drug possession and one burglary, he had no current warrants and he'd passed the field sobriety test. They couldn't hold him.

"Get the data from his cell phone?" Finn asked.

"Copied his contact list and his recent call list," she told him. "It's not a smart phone. No GPS. Does Leon want to press charges about the stolen ID?"

"I haven't been able to get hold of him."

"How about the owner of the car?"

Finn shook his head. The number Heather had given him for Tyrone Linero also went straight to voicemail, which told him the phone was most likely turned off for the moment. He had left yet another message there.

With no complaints from the possible 'victims' and Finn's flimsy evidence about the relationship of Leroy to Pinder and Heather Clayton and thus to the missing gorilla, there was no way any judge would give him a warrant to put a GPS tracker on the car. The best they could do was charge Leroy Shane with reckless driving and let him go on his way, but leave the car on the list and hope to get further reports. While the local officers processed Shane out of custody, Finn checked Leroy's cell phone information.

A number of calls listed were to "Ro." The number was different from the one Heather had given him. Looked like Tyrone had ditched his previous cell phone along with his life with Heather and Jenny. He tapped in the number for Ro.

A deep voice answered. "Talk."

Finn tried his best to sound like a street tough. "Shit, man, where are you?"

There was a short pause. "Fuck you."

The line went dead.

So much for impersonating a slimeball. He began the ninety minute drive back to Evansburg.

Chapter 18

On the outskirts of town, as Finn's thoughts wavered between a sandwich from the sub place and a full takeout meal from The Home Plate, he spotted a distinctive box-shaped car waiting to exit the parking lot of the Overnite motel. Hadn't Kathryn Larson reported that someone called in a suspicious dark gray Kia Soul in one of the burglarized neighborhoods?

The car made a right onto the street, two cars ahead of him. The light ahead turned green, and Finn slipped into the left lane and pulled up to get a better look at the Soul. The vehicle was an evergreen shade, not gray as Larson had reported, but the two colors would look the same at night. Through the back window he saw splotchy, light-colored fabric. Flowered pillow cases. Sitting on end, lumpy, filled with hard-cornered items. Two young men up front. The driver had dreadlocks and wore rainbow colored sunglasses. He turned his head, saw Finn looking at him, shifted his gaze back to the road in a hurry. Had Finn been dressed in uniform, he would have thought nothing about that; police officers made even the most law-abiding citizens nervous. But he was wearing plainclothes and driving an unmarked car.

Finn slowed and signaled right, ignoring the blaring horn of the following car, and pulled in behind the Soul. Dreadlocks, watching in the rear view mirror, held up his right hand, middle finger extended. Finn grabbed his mike, reported his location and described the Soul, and requested a patrol car to assist in a traffic stop. Then he rolled down the window. As he was slapping his light on top, Dreadlocks slammed down the gas pedal. The Soul roared ahead through a red light, barely dodging a pickup that had started across the road. Finn hit his siren and crept through the intersection.

Not one, but two patrol cars closed on the Kia, one coming from each way, sirens blaring. Apparently it was a slow day on patrol in Evansburg; multiple uniforms had responded. They forced the Soul to the shoulder as Finn pulled up and threw open his door, swiveling his feet to the ground and pulling his pistol out of the holster. Scoletti was exiting his patrol unit when the doors on the Soul burst open. Both occupants decided to make a run for it in different directions. Scoletti took off in foot pursuit of Dreadlocks. The officer from the other unit was talking on the radio, then slid back in his seat to follow in his car. The other suspect dashed toward a vacant lot.

Finn sighed—he wasn't dressed for a run, but then neither was the typical police officer in Kevlar and service belt. He yelled, "Stop! Police!" and then, when the suspect inevitably didn't slow down, he kicked into high gear after the fleeing kid, who zigzagged across the lot between tufts of overgrown grass and abandoned junk. Finn stuck to a straight line, leaping over obstacles and closing the gap, until his foot came down on a piece of pipe that rolled his shin straight into the edge of a rusted-out engine block. Cursing, he staggered on like Frankenstein, sticking behind the kid as he galloped to a barbed wire fence and tried to slip between the strands. He apparently was not a farm kid, because first he caught the back of his shirt and then the lower leg of his jeans and ended up wriggling like a fly caught in a web.

He was a scrawny kid, probably no more than eighteen. Close cropped brown hair, innocent Boy Scout looks. But not an innocent mouth.

"Fuck!" he yelled as Finn grabbed him by the waistband and hauled him back through the wire. "Fuck, fuck, fuck!"

The Boy Scout clawed at the front of his jeans, whirled like a dervish, landed on one knee. Then he burst up out of the crouch jabbing something toward Finn. A stiletto abruptly sprang from the silver cylinder in his hand. Finn leapt back as the kid slashed the right side of his jaw with a switchblade.

"Now you're pissing me off," Finn growled.

The kid slashed wildly again, snicking Finn's shirt front this time, and as the back of his hand passed, Finn gave the kid a swift kick in the side. The knife flew from his hand, sailing into the bushes. The violence felt alarmingly satisfying; and Finn realized he had been wanting to hit someone for quite a while now.

"Fuck you," the Boy Scout managed to yelp as he dropped to his knees, holding his side and gasping in pain. He stared at Finn and then pursed his lips, working up saliva.

No. This lousy day was not going to end that way. Finn popped him in the nose before he got a face full of spit from the little twerp, and then shoved the Boy Scout face down in the dirt. Straddling him, he bent the kid's arms back, pulling his handcuffs from the back of his belt. "Get a thesaurus, kid. Learn some new vocabulary."

He hauled the Scout to his feet by an elbow and marched him back to the cars. Scoletti was stuffing Dreadlocks into his patrol car. The other officer—his nametag said Barton—approached to take possession of the Boy Scout. Stopping in his tracks, the officer said, "Whoa."

Barton's eyes wandered over the kid's bloody face, then took in the slashes on Finn's jaw and chest, and finally rested on Finn's right leg. "Want me to call an ambulance?"

Finn looked down. The bottom of his pants leg was drenched with blood that was still pouring out of a gash in his calf. Must have been the collision with the engine block. And damn, now that he saw the extent of the damage, his leg started to throb. "Just let me borrow your first aid kit."

"Sure thing." Barton grabbed the Boy Scout by the arm. "What's the charge, Detective?"

"Burglary, for starters," Finn said. "Resisting arrest. Assaulting a police officer."

"Fuck you," said the Boy Scout.

"Add the usual foul language penalty," Finn joked. "And demerits for lack of imagination."

It felt so good to finally catch some bad guys. He followed the patrol cars to the station, where the Sarge insisted that a uniform take him to the hospital.

After twelve stitches in his calf and six on his jawline, Finn returned to the station, spotted with bandages and lugging two ice packs, to interview the suspects.

Kathryn Larson had thoughtfully held off so that they could grill the kids at the same time. Larson took Dreadlocks to the break room, flipping the sign on the window to indicate it was in use. In Finn's absence, she'd identified the Boy Scout—20-year old Elijah James Winter—and had an EMT examine the kid's nose. Elijah was handcuffed to a chair in the interview room when Finn limped in and sat down, pressing the ice pack against his burning jaw.

The Boy Scout held a matching ice pack to his nose with his free hand. Without prelude, he whined, "It was all Octo's idea. He said I had to do it or he'd pound my ass."

"Octo?"

"That's what he calls himself." The kid squinted at him. "The hair. Like octopus arms. His real name's probably Wilbur," the kid sniggered. "Or Stanley.'"

"If you say so, Elijah."

The kid's eyes narrowed. "I go by Lie."

"Good choice. Descriptive."

The blue eyes looking back at him over the ice bag sobered. "Octo's the iceman, dude. Everyone knows he friendly-fired a whole platoon in Iraq."

"Yeah?" Finn didn't think either of them looked old enough to join the military. "No wonder you're scared of him."

"You gotta protect me from him."

"Then give me the whole story so I can lock him up."

"He made me steal those things."

"Where'd you get the ketamine?" Finn asked.

"Ketamine?"

"The little drug vials." Those were probably the least valuable items the kids had stolen, but they might lead him to Gumu.

The kid rolled his eyes. "That stuff. I didn't even want to take it. Pills are easier to sell. Not many freaks want to stick themselves, you know?"

"Where did you get the ketamine?"

"I didn't steal it. Someone dumped it."

"Where?"

"You know those shacks across from Vista Village? I found it on the ground there."

"When?"

"Saturday night." He set the ice bag down on the table and used his thumb and forefinger to feel the swollen bridge of nose. "Around six thirty?"

"You live in Vista Village?"

"Nah. But I work there a lot, cleaning carpets and drapes."

So Elijah had been the carpet cleaner working next door to the Duprees. "Why would you stop at the shacks across the street?"

"I seen one car drive in and three cars peel out." He glanced warily at Finn. "They seemed in kind of a hurry, so I thought they mighta dropped something, left something important behind. You know, like something valuable that someone would miss."

"Or that they were stashing stolen goods in empty buildings just like you were."

The kid ignored that. "Only one of them little vials had anything in it." He pressed the ice bag to his face again. "There was a fuckin' dart there, too." He tried to hold up his left hand, but the cuff clanked against the table. "I stuck my finger on that fuckin' thing. Hope I don't get some sicko freak disease. Blow darts? Like some fuckin' Indiana Jones movie or somethin'."

"What did you do with that dart?" It might contain important evidence—human or gorilla blood or human prints.

"Tossed it in the weeds."

Finn wondered if it was worth sending an evidence tech or a uniform out to look for it. "What can you tell me about the vehicles you saw over there?"

"Three guys came in a white utility van, you know, like Comcast has, but a lot more beat up. Said Rent-a-Wreck on the side. They unloaded something from the van; I couldn't see what. Then one got into this really old car—it was like from way back in the eighties or something, and one of 'em took off in that, and one of 'em followed in a piece of junk old Toyota."

It was the same story the Duprees' neighbor told. Had the Toyota been Ty Linero's car? Had the utility van had a gorilla in it? "What time did you come back to rob the Dupree home?"

The kid licked his lips nervously. "Did Octo get a lawyer? You think I should get a lawyer?"

Finn stood up.

Elijah plopped the ice bag on the table and held out his free hand. "Hey, no hard feelings, right? I popped you; you got me back. I'm not yelling police brutality or nothing."

"We'll be sure to keep that in mind, Elijah." As the door closed behind him, Finn heard the Boy Scout say "Fuck" again.

He met Kathryn Larson in the hallway. She held up her right hand; he matched it with a high-five. "Now to sort out the loot," she said. "Returning all that stuff will get us a lot of gold stars. Maybe even enough to outweigh your demerits, Finn."

Finn snorted and rubbed a hand over his head. He was exhausted.

The other detective studied him. "You know your shift was over two hours ago, right? I'll mop up here."

"I still have to find a gorilla."

"And I have to find great grandma's corpse," she sighed. "And Ryan Connelly."

"Lots of finding to do," he agreed.

"Kind of like being a detective, isn't it? Any apes appear on the radar tonight, I'll let you know."

"And any shriveled DBs and lunatics I stumble across are all yours." They bumped fists and parted ways.

As he limped back to his desk, he heard a familiar voice emanating from the Captain's office.

"How long are we going to allow that woman to terrorize our county and make us the laughingstock of the whole damn country? The Council's revoking her permit to keep those apes."

Travis Fielding, County Commissioner. The last voice Finn

wanted to hear right now. He couldn't make out the Captain's quieter reply.

"We're doing our jobs. You do yours, if you expect to keep it!" Fielding bellowed.

Because he had investigated his son Charlie last year and outed the Fielding family's embarrassing financial difficulties, Finn was still high on the Commissioner's hit list. He quickly retreated to his car, where he tried Grace's landline number. When he held the phone to his ear, he inadvertently brushed his wounded jaw. Wincing, he shifted the phone to the other ear.

"The voicemail box you have reached is full. Please try again later."

Crap. He tried her cell phone with the same results. Double crap. Grace was no doubt still besieged with calls from reporters.

He slid the seat back and tried to stretch his legs. A jolt of pain from his injured calf made his vision go white for a second. Damnation, whatever the doc used to deaden the gash before suturing was wearing off fast.

After the fog in front of his eyes drifted away, he turned his thoughts back to what he'd learned from Elijah. He called Rent-a-Wreck and asked about white vans that had been rented recently. The clerk said they only had one. And it had been rented for the weekend to Tyrone Linero.

Aha! Ty, boyfriend of Heather, conveniently gone missing at the same time as a valuable gorilla. Finn gingerly shifted to a more comfortable position in his seat. "Where is that van now?"

"Let me see." Finn heard keystrokes in the background. "It came back on Sunday, and now it's rented to Linda Swartzski ... Schwarzaki ... something like that. Man, what a name, huh?"

"Who dropped it off on Sunday?"

"We don't keep that. The record just says returned 10:17 a.m. Sunday, with 195 miles added to the odometer. It has a checkmark under 'Good condition' and there's a note that says "Washed inside and out."

"What do you do to your vehicles after you get them back?"

"Run 'em through the car wash, vacuum the interior, and since this is a utility van, they mighta hosed the inside out if it still needed it. We don't exactly detail them, if that's what you're asking. This is Rent-a-Wreck, not Rent-a-Rolls-Royce." He chuckled at his own joke.

After the first washing, there was little chance of recovering meaningful trace evidence. The second left faint hope of finding anything at all. But Finn took down the current renter's contact information and passed it along to the Sarge with a request to assign an evidence tech to try to lift prints and check for blood and hair inside the van.

"Human blood and hair?" Greer asked. "Or gorilla?"

As if an evidence tech could tell on sight. "Either. Both."

He tried the two numbers he had for "Ty" and "Ro" Linero. Voicemail in both places again. Tomorrow he'd call from a spoofed number, see if that would net him better luck.

Ty was the good Linero kid, Heather had told him.

Hardly.

Three guys at the migrant camp; three vehicles. Ty Linero, obviously—he'd rented the van, and the Toyota sounded like his, too. Leroy Shane was a good bet, too. He was driving Ty's car, so there was obviously a connection. But who was the third man? Tony Zyrnek?

Had Gumu been in the back of the van? Alive? Or dead? The van had taken off in the direction of town and the highway. He suddenly remembered the fresh heap of compost in Zyrnek's yard.

His shift was long over and the sun had already set as he drove to Brigadoom. His headlights showed that the compost heap was gone. It was too dark to see much, but white tags fluttered at the edges of a dark square. Looked like Zyrnek had planted his garden.

Tony Zyrnek opened the door. The bandage on his hand sported multicolored stains. He took one look at Finn and drawled, "You look like you been rode hard and put away wet."

"Long day." Finn cautiously touched the bandage on his jaw

as he limped into the mobile home.

No enticing cooking aromas lingered in the air this time. Clearly he was too late for dinner. The television was off. A multicolored array of crayons and a drawing pad were laid out under a harsh light over the tiny dining room table. Centered on the table top was a purple bearded iris in a blue-green glass vase. A half-finished representation of the flower lay on the surface of the table in front of a pulled-out chair.

"Where's Jon?" Finn asked.

"Guard duty, he said." Zyrnek sat down in the chair he had vacated and gestured to the one across the table. "He feels so guilty about Gumu. He figures the least he can do for Dr. McKenna is to keep the reporters out of her hair. Caryn and Sierra are keeping him company."

Remorse set in along with fatigue as Finn plopped down heavily in the wooden chair. He should have thought of the security angle himself; the press had probably surrounded Grace's compound by now. "Damn reporters."

"That's the other thing Jon said." Zyrnek ripped a sheet of cold press paper from the pad and shoved it toward Finn, along with the plastic tray of crayons. "Help yourself. These are what they call student grade, but they're still pretty decent."

On closer inspection, Finn saw they weren't crayons, but pastel sticks. He picked up a blue-green stick labeled Peacock. It felt heavy and thick, more like chalk than a colored pencil. "I'm not here to draw with you, Zyrnek."

"Sorry; I don't have paints. Only pastels. They didn't let us have the brushes in prison."

Finn supposed it would be a quick job to hone a plastic or wooden brush handle into a nasty shiv. The stitches on his jaw burned with the reminder of a sharp blade. "What do you know about Rent-a-Wreck?"

The question seemed to surprise Zyrnek. "They rent old cars?" He hovered his hand over the box and then selected a pastel stick.

The guy lobbed answers back so quickly, Finn felt like he was in a tennis match. He lobbed one back at him. "You were seen out at the migrant shacks across from Vista Village."

Zyrnek tilted his head. "Has to be a mistake. I don't even know where that is. What was I supposedly doing out there, and when? I got a curfew, you know."

"I see you planted your garden."

"Yep. Greens, squash, tomatoes, herbs. Some ought to be up a few days."

"How deep did you dig?"

"Six feet down." Zyrnek waited a beat as he made strokes on the paper. Then he looked up and grinned. "Actually, the rototiller digs down about eight inches, I think. Maybe ten. Feel free to stick a ruler in. Or bring one of those X-ray gizmos that can see through dirt. Could be buried treasure down there."

"I might do that." Finn frowned. "Did you talk to Pinder?"

"You probably know I did." Zyrnek gave him a sly look. "And I'll bet you already know what we talked about, so you know Jarvis wouldn't say anything very interesting."

"Did he say anything about Leroy Shane?"

Zyrnek shook his head. "Didn't mention him. The only thing Jarvis ever says about Leroy is that Leroy 'done him wrong' and is 'gonna pay up what he owes or else he's gonna die.'"

If Zyrnek was telling the truth about Pinder's influence outside of the prison, that sounded like motive for Shane to do whatever Pinder asked. But that was a big if. It seemed much more likely that all the ex-cons on the outside had concocted some gorilla kidnapping scheme. "Tell me the truth about Ty Linero."

"Ty?" Zyrnek's gaze flicked between the flower and his paper as he stroked his flower's edges in a deep rose. "All I know is what Heather's told me."

"What did she say?" Finn touched the tip of his pastel stick to the paper, drew a tentative stroke for the left side of the vase.

"That he was a good guy." Zyrnek made a scoffing noise as he rummaged in the box, trading his rose pastel for a blue purple hue. "How good could he be, taking off on a woman and baby like that?"

The trail left by the pastel stick did not feel like a wax crayon, as Finn had expected. The texture was somewhere between chalk and grease. Finn smeared it with his index finger to see how the pastel worked on the rough paper, transitioning the color from a dark sharp edge to a pale center to represent the translucent glass vase. "Did Pinder ever talk about Linero?"

"Yeah, sometimes." Zyrnek twirled his stick, tracing the curly edges of the iris. "The families grew up on the same block. Sometimes Jarvis would talk about how this Linero was a bad ass and other times he'd talk about how that Linero was a goody two shoes."

"What did *you* think of Tyrone?"

"Never met the guy. I've just heard Heather and Jarvis talk about him."

So Zyrnek was sticking to that story. Finn added a streak of dark green to the vase on his paper. "Did Pinder call Linero 'Ty' or 'Ro'?"

"He mostly said just Linero." Zyrnek stopped drawing and looked at Finn. "Heather said Ty was always the good one."

"It seems like Linero has a Jekyll and Hyde thing going."

"Guess Ty does, what with taking off like that. But Jarvis said that Ro was always the bad ass."

Finn paused, his pastel stick dangling from his fingers. Ty and Ro were different people?

Zyrnek focused his gaze on the flower and started working on his picture again. "I've been thinking about Jarvis, and I got to wondering where he met DeeDee. But he wouldn't say, and it's not smart to ask Jarvis too many questions. I've heard them talking in Spanish, and Jarvis dealt drugs from South America. So maybe they met down there?"

Finn's leg throbbed. He was having a hard time focusing on Zyrnek's zigzags. "So what if they did?"

Zyrnek shrugged. "I just thought it might be important somehow. Plus, Jarvis keeps talking about all the expensive toys he's gonna have when he gets out."

"How could he manage that?"

"Jarvis has, uh, excellent entrepreneurial skills. He's working on something, I guarantee it."

Zyrnek was suspiciously eager to rat on his cellmate. Finn raised an eyebrow. "I thought Jarvis Pinder was your friend."

Zyrnek laid down his pastel and used the tip of his middle finger to blend the colors on the paper. "I bet living with Jarvis is a little like living with gorillas. You could enjoy their company, but you better never forget they can turn on you any second. I never forget Jarvis's true nature."

"Good for you." Tony Zyrnek was probably trying to transfer suspicion. But he'd inadvertently given Finn some potentially useful information. Ty. Ro. Different people. He'd also reminded him of a possible South American drug connection between DeeDee Suarez and Jarvis Pinder.

Finn put his pastel stick back in the box and stood up. The wound on his leg cramped, sending a sharp reminder through his nervous system. The pain bent him over. He flattened both palms on the table.

Zyrnek rose, too. "You okay?"

Between clenched teeth, Finn said, "I need to go."

"Bathroom or door?"

Finn scowled. "Door."

"You just got here."

"Duty," Finn muttered, pushing himself erect.

Zyrnek thrust a paper towel at him. "Might want to clean off. Wouldn't do for a detective to leave colored fingerprints everywhere, would it?"

Sucking in a breath, Finn wiped the smears from his fingers, then tossed the paper towel onto the table. "We found gorilla hairs in your pickup, Zyrnek."

He actually hadn't gotten the lab report back yet, but he wanted to see the guy's reaction.

Zyrnek nodded. "I'm not surprised. Jon's been in there a bunch of times after work. And you already know that sometimes I let him borrow it for work, too. Maybe sometimes he had Gumu riding shotgun." He laughed, then sobered.

"Man, it would be tragic if Jon never saw Gumu again."

Damn, the guy was cool under pressure. He had an answer for everything. Finn limped to the door.

"I'll save your picture for you." Zyrnek jerked his chin toward the vase Finn had drawn on his page. "You can finish it later."

Finn wondered if he could safely drive. He was totally exhausted. His leg had a heartbeat of its own. His jaw throbbed, too.

He hadn't seen Grace in two days, and he'd only barely crossed paths with her parents. Life had to be hell for her right now. Just like she'd predicted, the media and county were both out to get her. She wasn't answering her phones. He should go over there. But at least she had her parents and the ARU kids looking out for her.

Gumu was still missing and his to-do list kept getting longer. He needed to research Ro Linero. He needed to arrange for a spoof phone and call Ty, Ro, and even Leroy. The only way he could stop this freight train of disaster was to find Gumu and the scumbags who'd taken him.

In fifteen minutes, it would be midnight. Sane people would be asleep, or at least on their way to bed. He decided to pretend he was one of them and drove home.

Chapter 19

After the first food binge on her return, Neema had not eaten again. Grace wondered how long her hunger strike could continue. She continued to push Kanoni away, too. The baby was losing weight. Both gorillas' hair was dull and brittle. Kanoni's gaze radiated anxiety; Neema's was completely vacant. Each day, the mother gorilla sank further into depression and lethargy.

Grace had to work hard to keep herself from slipping down that black hole, too. Every day brought reporters as thick and annoying as horseflies and a new tirade from the County Council and more questions from the sheriff's department. She hadn't heard anything from Matt in a long time. Her parents said he'd been gone most of the time.

She didn't blame him for avoiding her. She'd gotten him in trouble at work; she was an embarrassment to him. She'd avoid herself, too, if she could.

Trying to pull them both out of their funk, Grace dragged Neema into the study trailer to watch a video.

"Which one?" Grace signed as she asked aloud, pointing to the shelf of Neema's favorite videos. "You choose."

The gorilla idly fingered a few boxes, but she seemed disinterested.

"*Babe*?" Grace suggested. "*Romancing the Stone*?" Neema was a fan of talking pigs and romantic adventures.

Neema pivoted to face a locked file cabinet behind her. *Open Gumu,* she signed.

Grace hesitated. The cabinet was full of video recordings she'd made of Neema and Gumu and Kanoni. Would watching videos of Gumu help Neema get over her grief, or would it deepen her sorrow?

Gumu open see, Neema signed. *Open open see Gumu.* Frustrated with Grace's reluctance, the gorilla gave the cabinet a hard slap that left a dent in the metal top.

"Neema! Bad gorilla!" Grace pointed to the carpet in front of the television. "You sit. Be good."

She waited until Neema parked her rump there before she pulled the key from her chain and opened the cabinet. She selected a video of Neema and Gumu filmed shortly after Kanoni was born, pushed it into the DVD slot, and turned on the television. Maybe it would inspire Neema to begin caring for Kanoni again.

The instant Gumu came into view on the screen, Neema huffed and signed *Gumu come Gumu.*

Was this magical thinking on Neema's part, that she could wish Gumu back home? Neema had an active imagination and often asked for things she couldn't see, most notably candy. Grace had used the sign for *maybe* with her, usually in conjunction with *if*. *Maybe* candy, *if* you're good. It was clear that Neema understood cause and effect for behavior and rewards or punishments, but she'd never made the *maybe* sign on her own. Grace wasn't sure the gorilla grasped the sign's meaning.

Gumu now come Gumu, Neema signed to the television screen.

What the heck. Grace paused the video. What did she have to lose by trying to teach Neema to hope? She stepped in front of the television. *Maybe Gumu come tomorrow*, she signed. *I hope.*

Gumu now, Neema signed. *Now.* She ended her plea with an emphatic snort.

"Maybe tomorrow," Grace signed as she spoke. Then she made the new sign again, pointing to her head and clutching her fingers together. "I hope."

Neema stared, her expression unreadable. Grace repeated the signs in a new order. "I hope Gumu comes tomorrow. Maybe."

Neema looked over her shoulder at the cabinet of DVDs on the wall behind her. Then she lifted both hands and flipped them up and down in an awkward imitation of Grace. *Maybe.*

Grace's mouth fell open. Was Neema only copying or did she really understand the meaning of "maybe"? Her studies required that Neema make every sign in context without prompting. That was the only way she could be sure that the gorilla had mastered the sign's meaning.

Next, Neema pulled on her own ear.

Grace froze. She hadn't seen Neema use that gesture for years. The ear tug was Neema's sign for Spencer, the gorilla murdered by Keyes. Neema's first mate had a split ear and Neema had invented that sign for him.

The gorilla signed *Spencer come* again.

Oh God. Grace's heart thumped painfully in her chest. Was Neema saying that if Gumu could come back, Spencer should, too? Or was she trying to tell her that Gumu was as dead as Spencer? It was incredible that Neema would remember Spencer at all in this moment. She wished there was a video camera rolling, because if she repeated this story, odds were that nobody in the academic community would believe her.

No, Grace signed sadly. *Spencer gone, Spencer dead.* She flipped her hands over in the air.

Neema huffed, grabbed a handful of Grace's tee shirt, and tried to drag her out of the way of the television screen. Then she signed *see Gumu* again.

Maybe, Grace signed, digging in her heels. *Hope.* She stepped out of the way and restarted the video. Neema settled to watch. On the screen, Gumu investigated a week-old Kanoni, sniffing the tiny baby that nursed at Neema's breast.

Grace strode to the cage and retrieved a sleeping Kanoni from her nest of blankets. She hurriedly carried the baby to Neema, signing *Kanoni here now. Feed baby.*

Neema shook her head violently and pushed both of them away. She scooted closer to the television. Sitting only inches away, her lips almost touching the screen, she signed *Gumu Gumu Gumu.*

The front door opened, and Grace's mother peeked in. "Oh, here you are. You're not answering either of your phones."

"I turned them both off because every ten minutes another reporter calls."

"Oh. Well, yes, I suppose so." Her mother stepped into the trailer. She patted Kanoni on the head. "That employee of yours with all the piercings was arguing with someone when we drove in."

Sierra? Caryn? Grace had to remember to do something special for the three ARU kids. Her other volunteers weren't half as tough, but Jon, Sierra, and Caryn gave back as good as they got. She shifted Kanoni to her other hip.

"Did you know your voicemail box is full?"

"What? No." She didn't even know that was possible. How could she fix that? Did she *want* to fix that?

"Your father and I and Scott and Dorothy are going out to lunch in town. Why don't you come with us?"

Grace was surprised. "You like Scott and Dorothy? You enjoy their company?"

Maureen smiled. "They are gracious people, and very interesting, in a homespun kind of way. We find them a pleasant change from the set we usually associate with. Sort of like you and Matt, I guess. You enjoy Matt's company, although you have more in common with Richard."

Grace grimaced. The only thing she had in common with Richard was a Ph.D., and he'd probably say his was worth more than hers any day. Her parents might very well agree.

Maureen glanced at Neema in front of the television set. "Neema?"

The gorilla twisted her head to gaze back over her shoulder, surprised to hear someone other than Grace say her name.

Maureen made a motion with her hand. "That's too close to the television, dear. Back up. You'll hurt your eyes. And you need to take care of your baby. Right away."

Neema snorted. Then she signed *Gumu come* again and pressed her lips to his image on the screen.

Grace laughed.

"Well, you said she understands a lot more spoken English than signs," Maureen complained.

"She does, but she's not exactly a human child." Although Neema certainly was acting like a stubborn three-year-old right now.

"Maybe you don't give her enough credit. She knows how to take advantage of you. So, lunch?"

Grace shook her head and hefted Kanoni higher on her hip. "Thanks, but I need to take care of Kanoni."

Not to mention that she was persona non grata in the whole county right now. The locals might throw rotten tomatoes. Or lynch her. Talk about blaming the victim.

"Can't Finn help you?"

"He's got a full-time job of his own. He helps me in other ways. He's not responsible for the gorillas."

"Is this how he normally treats you? He wasn't home when we went to bed last night, and his door was closed when we left this morning. Surely he's not working all the time. Is he avoiding us? Is he avoiding you?"

Good questions. She knew he was in trouble at work, and that was her fault. Maybe he *was* avoiding her. Maybe he'd given up on finding Gumu. Maybe he'd moved on to Heather. She really couldn't blame him.

She sighed. "I don't know, Mom."

There was no record in any database for Ro Linero. Finn found a Horatio Orrin Linero and a Ricardo Juan Linero. There was no mention of a Ro Linero in Tyrone Linero's record, either. He had to get into juvie records to find a conviction for attempted robbery of a convenience store when Ty was fifteen.

Under the desk, Lok rubbed against his leg, purring. Finn gasped, his eyes watering with the pain. He shoved the cat away with his good foot. He'd stayed home this morning, cursing and popping antibiotics and pain pills the hospital doc had given him. They didn't seem to help much. His calf had swollen so badly, he couldn't pull his pants up over the bandage. He was sorely tempted to swill down a couple of beers although it was only ten in the morning. He'd gotten up late, missing Maureen and Charles, which was probably a good thing. Each time he tried to call Grace, the phone went straight to voicemail and he got the 'full mailbox' message again. Rejection by voicemail was starting to feel like the story of his life.

The cat jumped onto the desk and plopped down next to the computer. Finn focused on the screen again, checking the DMV records. There was no registration for any vehicle under Ro Linero. Damn.

He'd caught a lucky break on the burglary case yesterday. He relished that victory in his imagination for a moment, reliving his fist bump with Kathryn Larson. They should have gone out for a beer or something. He needed to celebrate something good.

"I nailed a burglary ring yesterday," he told the cat.

Lok slitted his eyes and switched his tail.

Cargo heard Finn's voice and whacked his tail against the door to announce himself as he trotted into the office. He parked his butt beside Finn's chair, an expectant look on his face.

"I was injured in the line of duty," he told the dog.

Cargo tilted his head—blue eye down, brown eye up—as if this were a fascinating detail.

"I fought off a knife attack," Finn added. "And I think I'm getting closer to finding out what happened to the gorilla."

The dog abruptly emitted a sharp bark.

"Attaboy, Finn," he translated, patting himself on the shoulder. Then he pointed toward the doorway and told Cargo, "Go lay down. Don't eat any more of my recliner."

The black behemoth sank to the floor beside him and did his best imitation of a bear rug.

Finn rested his head in his hands for a minute, trying to think of what should come next. Charles and Maureen were probably lobbying for Grace to move back to Stanford and take up with this Richard guy. If Finn failed to find Gumu and rectify the situation with the county, Grace might have to move on. Without him.

Heather Clayton seemed his best bet for getting more information, and he hadn't yet called to tell her about Leroy driving Ty's car. It was Sunday, so unless Heather was an avid church-goer, odds were good she'd be home with the baby. He limped to his bedroom and found a pair of old sweatpants that stretched over his swollen calf. His normal button-down work shirts looked ridiculous with sweats, so he finally decided on an open-necked golf shirt he could pull down to hide his back holster.

When Heather opened her door, she was dressed in blue capris and a white blouse. In her hand she held a small towel and tiny spoon.

"Detective?" Her gaze skated over his face.

He'd forgotten about the bandage on his jaw. He raised a hand to cover it. "I have a few more questions. I need your help."

"Come in."

He followed her into the kitchen, trying not to lurch like Frankenstein's monster. The red-orange color she'd used as an accent in the living area dominated the wall tile here, as well as the artwork and even a tea kettle on the stovetop. A spring-green towel and oven mitt hung from hooks under the cupboards. Heather definitely had an eye for color.

The baby was harnessed into a padded seat strapped to a wooden chair, her chubby cheeks smeared with green goo. A cup of coffee and an open bottle of strained peas sat on the table. Something in the oven smelled wonderful.

"Sorry to interrupt." He pulled out a chair and sat down heavily, straightening his bad leg out before him.

"No worries," Heather slid the tiny spoon into the jar and held out a mouthful of peas to the baby. "We're going on a picnic at noon, but we're not too busy right now, are we, Jenny?" After poking the mush into the baby's mouth, she glanced at him. "What do you need to know?"

He told her about locating Tyrone's car in Leroy Shane's

possession.

"Oh, crap," she said. "Ty said he was going to get some money. But why sell the car to Leroy? He'll use it in a stick-up or something, and then the police will be knocking at the door." She smiled ruefully at him. "I guess the police are already knocking at my door."

Shaking her head, she said, "I cannot believe Ty's been talking to Leroy. But then, I wouldn't have believed he did what he did."

"If Ty sold the car, what would he use for transportation?"

"He bought a motorcycle about two months ago."

"I didn't see any registration for that."

She made a face. "He probably hasn't filed it. He always worries that he'll get tagged for sales tax."

"I know you call Tyrone 'Ty.' Does anyone ever call him 'Ro'?"

"No." Her posture stiffened. She laid the spoon down and turned to face him. "Who mentioned Ro?"

"Leroy Shane. Plus, there's a Ro on Ty's list of phone calls. Who is Ro?"

"He's Ty's cousin." She shivered. "He's also a slimy lowlife."

"Are they close?"

"They lived in the same house for years. Ty's parents died in a car accident when he was fourteen, and Ty and his sister moved in with their aunt and uncle in Spokane. Ro's the one who got Ty in trouble when he was a teenager. Ty did four months in juvie. Ro did two years."

"What's Ro's real name?"

"Harold?" she suggested. "Something like that. And his middle name starts with O."

"Horatio Orrin."

"Really? That sucks. I remember that kids called him Ho for a while, but then he somehow managed to change it to Ro." She chafed her hands together. "This could explain a lot. If Ty's been talking to Ro, that's probably why he took off. Ro talked him into one of his little money-making projects."

Her eyes glittered with gathering tears. "This is probably all my fault. I was haranguing Ty about money for Jenny, and now he's going to end up in jail and Jenny's going to end up without a father."

"Has he called you?"

She shook her head. "I've tried him a bunch of times, but all I get is voicemail." A tear spilled down her cheek and she pressed the towel to her face. "Damn him."

Finn's cell buzzed. Finally, it was Grace. "Sorry," he said. "I need to take this."

Heather nodded. He held the phone to his ear.

"Hi, Matt. I called to find out what you've been up to. You've been sort of out of touch lately." Grace sounded worried.

"I'm sorry. Your voicemail box wouldn't take any more messages, and I've been a little busy. Where should I start..." As Heather pulled the towel from her face, she left a smear of green under her eye. He tapped his own cheek and then pointed to hers.

She looked at the towel, folded it carefully to expose a clean spot, and then wiped the peas from her face. "You're so nice to me," she said.

The temperature of Grace's voice took a sudden nose dive. "Where are you? Who are you with?"

"Um." Had he explained to Grace anything having to do with Tony Zyrnek and Heather and Leroy and Pinder? What could he say in front of Heather?

A timer on the oven dinged. Heather stood up. "Apple cinnamon muffins coming right up!"

"It's this case—" Finn began.

"It's alright, Finn. We made no promises to each other. I know I've been nothing but trouble to you."

"Grace—"

"It's okay, I understand." She hung up.

Shit. Now he'd have to drive out there and explain everything to her.

* * * * *

By evening, Grace was unable to stand sharing the close quarters of her trailer with her parents any longer. The sky was predicted to remain clear for a few hours and the winds had died down, so she moved them all to the courtyard table outdoors for a picnic dinner of takeout chicken, potato salad, and iced tea. Kanoni amused herself with somersaults on the sparse lawn and attempts to steal food from the table. Neema was again alone in the barn enclosure, sulking as she watched the sunset from the top of the net. Grace was tempted to climb up there with her.

"Did you know that Richard Riverton is head of the Psych Department at Stanford now?"

Grace clenched her jaw. The intimation always seemed to be that she should have followed his successful route through academia. "Yes, Mother. You've told me that several times."

"Richard asks about you all the time," her father told her.

"And you've told me that."

Matt Finn drove up, parked beside the barn, and pulled himself slowly out of the driver seat. Grace couldn't decide whether she was happy to see him or not. His clothing was a strange combination and he had a bandage on his jaw. As he crossed her yard, he was noticeably limping.

She tamped down a surge of initial sympathy. He'd obviously been working on something other than trying to find Gumu in the last few days. And he'd sounded normal enough this morning as he was exchanging sweet nothings with some other woman.

Her father waved a hand in Matt's direction, then turned back to Grace.

"I got this email from Richard yesterday." Her mother thrust a piece of paper toward her. When Grace refused to take it, Maureen pulled it back. "I'll read it to you."

When did her mother have time to print out an email message, and where? At the library? Or did Matt let her parents use his computer at home?

"Dear Maureen," her mother read. "I would be thrilled to

welcome Grace to my staff. We could find an opening for her to teach psycholinguistics, neurolinguistics, semiotics, and perhaps experimental psychology. I'm sure the Modern Language Department would also welcome her expertise in general linguistics and sign language acquisition. Have her contact me to discuss."

"He signs it 'Fondly, Richard,'" her father finished.

Thrilled to welcome her? It had been a long time since anyone in academia had been even mildly interested in her. The reluctance of most educational institutions had to do with the cost and complexity of the gorillas' upkeep and, as both her parents had so painfully noted, the somewhat questionable ongoing scientific goals of her sign language project.

Yes, she was sought after as an occasional lecturer. But no institution wanted to take on Dr. Grace McKenna *and* her gorillas. Richard's offer would have strings attached, too, strings pulled by her mother, and possibly her father, too. She pictured herself as a wooden puppet prancing across a cardboard stage.

"You see, you do have alternatives, Grace," her mother summarized. "You don't have to accept..."—her gesture included the barn enclosure and the surrounding trailers— "...the status quo."

Her father chimed in. "You can make a change. You do have a place to go." He tapped the piece of paper with an index finger. "Richard says you will be *welcome* on his staff."

It did sound tempting. She could almost see the white light beckoning at the end of the black tunnel, the exit from this nerve-racking media storm, an end to the ongoing money and public relations program. The monkey—well, the apes, to be correct—lifted off her back. A different life. A serene and well-respected career.

She gazed up at Neema's hunched form silhouetted against the sunset. Sadness and guilt warred with a painful longing in her brain, and she almost hated her parents for inflicting this torture on her.

Her mother touched her forearm. "You know Richard

always loved you, Grace."

* * * * *

As Finn lurched slowly toward the picnic table, trying not to put too much weight on his bad leg, he heard the McKennas talking about how Grace didn't have to accept the current state of affairs. It sounded like her parents were urging her to take a position elsewhere. Did they think he couldn't hear them? Did they think he wouldn't care?

Given the current political climate in Evansburg, Finn couldn't blame her if she wanted to move to greener, more accepting pastures. But who the hell was this Richard, who had "always loved" Grace?

Damn, he didn't want her to go. Why were women always leaving him? God, his leg was throbbing again. And his face felt like he had a third-degree burn.

When he finally arrived at the picnic table, Grace said only, "Where have you been?"

Charles's greeting was only slightly more welcoming. "Good God, man. What happened to you?"

"I tackled a burglar last night." Finn wiped a hand across his sweaty brow.

Grace made a face. "Right. A burglar. And then what happened after that?"

Maureen squinted at her daughter. "Gracie?"

Grace was clearly stressed out. Finn realized he'd never told her about connection between the ketamine and the burglary ring. He looked at her. "I'm making progress on finding Gumu."

Grace looked down at her plate. "The County Council is making progress on throwing me under a bus. The college called me twice in the last two days."

She sounded like she thought he should have been able to prevent that. Squeezing onto the picnic bench beside her, he wrapped his arm around her. Her shoulders stiffened under his arm. Clearly she was in a bad mood after misunderstanding his conversation with Heather. How could he set things right?

He faced Maureen and Charles. "No matter what happens," he told them, "With or without gorillas, Grace will always have a place right here in Evansburg. With me."

Grace turned to look at him, her lips open in surprise. He winked at her, then reached for a chicken leg from the platter on the table.

He'd surprised everyone, including himself. Was he inviting her to move in with him? Was he offering to marry her?

"I'm not your job, Detective Finn. You don't have to rescue me. Did it ever occur to you," Grace said in a low, gruff tone, "that maybe I don't need your pity? That I might not want to stay in Evansburg with you?"

He didn't have a snappy comeback for that.

Chapter 20

The next morning, Sierra and Caryn intercepted Grace when she emerged from her personal trailer. The two young women were way too chirpy for the early hour. She usually appreciated their enthusiasm, but sometimes the exuberance of youth was simply exhausting to be around. The aftereffects of the three glasses of wine she'd swilled down last night didn't help, either.

Before she could ask, Sierra reported, "Jon and Brittany are watching the front gate, we fed Kanoni, and we put food and fresh water out for Neema."

"Did she eat anything?"

They both shook their heads.

Damn. Neema hadn't eaten for days. Were there anti-depressants for gorillas? Would Neema have to be sedated and force-fed? Grace wanted to collapse onto the ground and cry.

"We have a present for you, Boss." Caryn pointed to a large wire-mesh pen sitting on the grass in the courtyard. It was approximately six feet long and four feet wide and maybe two feet tall. Two ends of the wooden frame sported handles, and one also had wheels.

"It's a portable chicken pen," Sierra informed her. "See, you can flip down the wheels." She pulled up on the handle and then flicked one down beneath the box. "And then you can pull it to a new spot. It's designed for sustainable poultry grazing."

She flipped the wheel back into its upraised position and set the pen back down on the ground, then looked expectantly at Grace.

They thought she wanted to raise chickens? Weren't a suicidal mother gorilla and a neglected baby and a traumatized marmoset enough to handle for now?

Maybe the two young women simply wanted to distract her from her troubles. She roused herself to say, "Thanks. I'm sure poultry would really like it."

The ARU girls shot perplexed glances at each other. Then Caryn told Grace, "We borrowed it for Pepito. Let the poor little guy outside for a change, since he seems to be stuck here for now."

"Ah," she said, finally understanding. "It's perfect! Go get him."

They eagerly slipped into her trailer and emerged a minute later, Sierra clutching the marmoset against her chest with both hands. When released into the portable poultry pen, Pepito eagerly scampered around, exploring the grass and springing from one side of the enclosure to the other, chattering with excitement.

The ARU girls were right, she'd kept Pepito cooped up in a cat carrier inside her personal trailer for far too long. Neema and Kanoni had been taking up all her time. Kanoni had also been overly enthusiastic about playing with the miniature monkey, so she'd separated them before Pepito bit the baby gorilla and Kanoni flattened the marmoset like a bug.

She'd left eight voicemail messages, but Pepito's owners, the Constellos, still hadn't responded. What the heck was she going to do with a marmoset if they never did? Maybe she could get Matt to locate them. As if she felt like asking Matt a favor now.

She was mortified about the way she'd treated him last night. He didn't deserve that. He was in trouble at work because of her. She was the stinking albatross around his neck. She'd been dragging him down since she met him. He deserved a better life. He deserved to be happy. Maybe that other woman could make him happy. She'd tell him that.

Caryn barred her way. "We have another surprise for you."

Grace allowed herself to be led into the staff trailer. The kitchen and living area were cluttered, but she saw nothing unusual. Sierra and Caryn looked at each other, their eyes shining, bursting with eagerness. Caryn was somehow telepathically elected to deliver the news.

She said, "We got him, Grace."

Gumu? Her heartbeat doubled. They had Gumu?

No, she realized with a pang of disappointment, that couldn't be true. It was too quiet. If Gumu had been back, the whole staff would have woken her up to tell her. They'd be celebrating big time.

Sierra took her hand and towed her through the small living area toward the closed bedroom door. "Careful," she said, her hand on the knob. "He's shy."

They stepped into the dark room. Caryn turned on a small clip-on lamp attached to the top bunk bed frame. And there he was, huddled into a blanket wadded into the corner on the lower bunk—the bonobo she'd left behind in the Smiths' workshop. His arms and legs were drawn up to make himself as small as possible; his eyes were large and wary. A shiny stream of mucous dripped down his lip from his nostril.

"They had him locked in an outhouse in the wheat field," Sierra said from the doorway. "We might not have ever found him, except for this crazy guy camping in the woods who told us there was an alien in there."

"An outhouse!" Caryn echoed, her voice outraged.

"Did anyone see you?" Grace asked. It felt like a question one criminal would ask another.

"Only the crazy guy, and he was ... well, bonkers." Caryn made the traditional spiraling motion near her temple. "He thought we were with the government."

"The three of us wore black and crawled through the wheat," Sierra explained.

Three of them. That meant that Jon had been in on it, too. ARU strikes again.

"How'd you know the bonobo was still there?" Grace asked. The police certainly hadn't bothered to check.

Sierra lifted a shoulder. "He's valuable. We figured it was a good bet. Took us a while to search all the buildings, though."

She envisioned them slipping in through open windows in

the dead of night.

"I didn't hear that," Grace told them.

Both girls grinned, and they all turned to gaze at the bonobo.

From a cold, dark, ear-splitting auto repair shop to a cold, dark, smelly outhouse. Grace wondered what the poor creature had endured before ending up at the Smiths. "It looks like he might be sick."

"The vet says it's just a cold, but he got a shot of antibiotics just in case," Sierra contributed.

"Which vet?" Grace asked.

Sierra looked to Caryn, who chewed her lip. Neither was willing to say the vet's name. So it was a veterinarian loyal to the ARU cause.

"We'll be super careful to wash before going anywhere near Neema or Kanoni," Caryn said.

Sierra sat gingerly on the bottom bunk, at the opposite end from the little ape. Pulling an apricot from her sweatshirt pocket, she held it out toward the bonobo. "We knew you'd understand, Boss."

Various threads of thought tangled themselves in Grace's head. She was happy to see the bonobo saved from Tim Smiths' Palace of Animal Torture. She wasn't sure that she was glad to see the poor creature on her property.

The timid ape's gaze flashed from the fruit to Sierra's face several times. Finally, he sprang forward, snatched the apricot from her fingers, and leapt back to his corner to eat.

"We're calling him Bo," Sierra said.

"What do you plan to do with Bo?" Grace asked with some trepidation. The tiny marmoset was easy enough to hide, and she knew where it rightfully belonged. Keeping a rambunctious bonobo was a lot more problematic. Her gorillas might very well consider this smaller cousin a territorial threat. The County and the Department of Agriculture were already on her case, and they didn't even know she had two stolen simians on her property.

"You don't need to worry about that," Caryn quickly

reassured her. "We'll make sure he ends up in a good home."

Sierra rested gentle fingers on Grace's forearm. "We wanted you to see that he got out. Thanks to you."

"I never saw a bonobo here." Grace backed out of the room. "I didn't hear any of this."

They followed her out, closing the door quietly behind them. When she turned, they were smiling. It wasn't appropriate or boss-like, but Grace couldn't help smiling back.

An hour later, Grace carried Kanoni into the barn enclosure, determined to give Neema another chance to start eating and care for her baby. Leaning against the fence, she watched Kanoni try to play with her mother, scampering and rolling in the dust and then leaping and rebounding from Neema's back. In the past, Kanoni's behavior would have inspired either a game of chase or a gruff rebuke. Today, Neema sat hunched over, absorbing the blows of her baby's feet with no reaction. After a few minutes of this one-sided diversion, Kanoni gave up on gaining Neema's attention. She found a short twig in the dirt, and began to poke it at every object she found like a little boy with a pretend sword. When she poked it at Nest, the calico cat swiped a paw at the twig, and the two animals played together for a few minutes until Kanoni decided it would be more fun to whack Nest with the stick. The cat dodged around Neema to hide.

Neema disconsolately sat on her rump a few feet away from the food shelf, where flies buzzed around the uneaten fruit and bread. The gorilla slumped, round-shouldered. She seemed to be studying her toes. Overhead, perched on the roof mesh, a crow eyed the scene, squawking and trying to judge his chances of stealing a snack. Nest rubbed against Neema's foot, and the gorilla pulled the calico cat into her lap and then cradled her against her chest. The crow dove through the roof mesh and hopped closer. Perching on the edge of the rope net, it turned its head sideways to study the gorilla and cat with a beady eye.

Neema rubbed her cheek against Nest's velvety head, and for a moment, Grace had a spark of hope. Maybe the gorilla was returning to her former self. But then Neema set the cat on the ground and pushed her gently but firmly away. The cat leaned against Neema's foot, rubbing and purring, but when it got no further response from the gorilla, it strolled to the food shelf to investigate its contents.

The crow, apparently deciding his snack was in danger, dive-bombed the cat with a raucous squawk. Nest cowered, flattening herself to the ground.

Neema pounced. One second the gorilla was collapsed in near catatonia, and the next she had crumpled the crow's wingtip in her right fist. The bird flapped its free wing, screeching as it pecked at the gorilla's hand, its feet clawing for purchase against Neema's arm and leathery chest. The thick fingers of the gorilla's left hand closed around the bird's head. Its cries changed to higher-pitched, more desperate shrieks of terror. Then there was a snap, followed by silence as the crow went limp.

Horror froze Grace in place. She stood with one hand clamped over her open mouth, and the fingers of the other twisted into her T-shirt.

Neema wasn't done. Moving her hand from the bird's neck to its other wing, she stretched the dead crow out in front of her face, sniffed its breast, and then yanked, ripping a wing from the bird's body. Dropping the pieces in the dust, she jammed a finger into the bird's breast, then stepped in the feathers and blood as she ambled to the rope net and pulled herself up onto it.

Grace watched, revolted, her heart sinking as the big gorilla slowly climbed the rope webbing. Neema had always hated crows, but she'd never hurt another animal before. Did she believe she was protecting Nest? Or did she simply want to kill something?

Kanoni approached the bloody corpse with halting steps. After studying it for a few seconds, she thrust her stick forward to nudge the bird's beak. Stepping over the mess of feathers and blood, Grace snatched up Kanoni with one arm and Nest with the other and carried them outside the enclosure.

Jon Zyrnek stood just outside the gate. His expression was grim.

"You saw?" she asked.

"Nobody else did." He put his hand on the gate, just above hers. "I'm going to clean that up. And then I'm going to get rid of all the blood in the barn, all right?"

Grace nodded. She rested her chin on top of Kanoni's head as she kept an eye on Neema at the top of the net.

Neema's eyes had been devoid of emotion while she ripped the bird apart. In her relatively short lifetime, the female gorilla had lost two mates, the only other members of her species she'd known before Kanoni was born. Unlike a gorilla in the wild, Neema didn't have an extended family to comfort and support her.

Humans scarred by tragedies could turn into monsters, but people might understand why. Mentally ill people sometimes got help. Mentally ill animals were usually exterminated.

Was the gentle gorilla she loved gone forever?

Chapter 21

Finn woke up burning with fever. He called in to tell the desk sergeant he was going to be late.

"It's just as well, Finn, you're not exactly the Captain's favorite person right now. The reporters are driving us all bonkers."

Wonderful. He wasn't anyone's favorite person right now. Grace had certainly made it clear he wasn't hers. Why had his offer of a sanctuary made her furious? He'd never understand women. He swilled down three aspirins and fell back into bed.

When he regained consciousness three hours later, a cat was curled up on his chest, and another one was draped across his head. He found the dog in the living room chewing on a leather shoe, a woman's slip-on. The McKennas had made the mistake of leaving the guest room door ajar. Now Grace's mother would hate him, too, as well as thinking he was an uneducated hick.

He limped to the guest room to return the shoe. The bed was made and the room was empty, except for the mate to the chewed shoe, which sat on a neatly written note in the middle of the dresser.

> *We're on our way home. I'm not sure we helped Grace, but surely she realizes we only want the best for her. And for you as well. We know you have been affected by our daughter's troubles, too.*
>
> *Hope you're feeling better. Do you know a one-legged woman who might use this shoe? We'd suggest giving it to Cargo, too, but you shouldn't reward bad habits.*

Thank you for your hospitality, Matt, and please extend our gratitude to Scott and Dorothy for their kind company in this trying time.

—Charles and Maureen McKenna

He crumpled the note. Well, at least that one complication removed from his life. Now for the others. Pulling himself together, he drove to the police station and limped through a small cluster of shouting wannabe reporters. Wading through that human barricade was starting to feel routine.

On his computer, he found an emailed report saying that the corpse in the woods was definitely not Kevin David North. Damn.

But, the report noted, the corpse did have the same blood type as Ryan Connelly, so further DNA testing was being done. Remembering the exhausted expressions of the parents, Finn wondered if Ryan's death would be a mercy to the Connelly family. They'd grieve, but the anxiety of constant worry about their son would finally be over.

That reflection, of course, shifted his thought to Grace and Gumu. What would her reaction be if Gumu was found dead? Or if the male gorilla was never found at all? There were support groups for parents of missing children, and for spouses of the deceased. But having a gorilla stolen or killed wasn't an issue that a person could find a support group for.

Ty Linero's car had been reported abandoned beside the road between Kennewick and Moses Lake. There were no reports of other cars stolen nearby, leaving Finn to wonder if Leroy Shane had hitchhiked or been picked up by one of his buddies.

Burglars Elijah and Octo hadn't been able to raise bail and were in jail awaiting trial. Detective Finn would be notified when the trial date was set. He needed to work at matching the list of stolen items with their owners. In his current condition, comparing paperwork and doing notifications seemed easy and welcome tasks. At least those two criminals had been located and captured; he was tired of looking for missing people and animals. He was beginning to hate that word, missing. Usually people were not truly missing, but intentional runaways. Or simply absent, no-shows.

Which reminded him, the truck driver at Grace's had mentioned that a worker hadn't shown up on Sunday morning to help remove the portable toilets after the open house event. He called the office of Samuels Sanitation. The dispatcher had to contact Nate via radio, but he called Finn within a few minutes.

"Do you remember the name of the guy who didn't show up for the McKenna job?" Finn asked.

"Remember him, but his name? I'm bad at names, but I'll have it here, hang on..."

Leroy Shane. Tony Zyrnek. Finn was betting on Nate's next words naming one of these. Instead, the man said, "Here it is. Ty Linero."

Ty? He swallowed. It fit. Ty had told Heather he was picking up a job to get more money. He hadn't lied about that, anyway. "Was he the guy who was supposed to lock the gate when you drove out?"

After a brief hesitation, Nate said, "Yeah. That's right."

Finn thanked him and hung up. So both Ty Linero and Tony Zyrnek had access in the right time frame. Both knew their way up the back road to the parking lot in the rear of the barn. It seemed probable that Zyrnek had lied to him about knowing Linero.

Mason hailed him from the other side of the room. As was so often the case, the tech had been surfing the internet. He pointed to a video clip on the screen. "Weren't you looking for this guy?"

The news clip showed Frank Keyes at the door of his apartment. At first he looked surprised to find a reporter and camera operator standing on his doorstep. He smoothed down his hair with his fingers as the reporter said, "Mr. Keyes, years ago you were convicted of killing a gorilla named Spencer who belonged to Dr. Grace McKenna."

"A gorilla is not a who," Keyes snarled on the screen. "Animals are not people."

"Do you have any knowledge about Dr. McKenna's current missing gorilla, Gumu?"

The reporters looked like the usual college kids out for a scoop. This had to have been what Grace meant when she said she had an idea about Keyes.

In the video, Keyes's eyes gleamed with anger. He was practically frothing at the mouth as he said, "You are harassing me."

"Did you kill Gumu, Mr. Keyes?"

Keyes took a step toward the camera operator, who backed up, jarring the camera, which briefly showed a close-up of the reporter's hair and then the apartment building wall before focusing again on Keyes's face.

"*I* am not the criminal!" he yelled. "People who believe in talking gorillas are the criminals. They are the sinners! Satan rules the earth and tries to persuade good people that we are descendants of monkeys." He turned toward the camera. "Armageddon is coming, people. Are you ready to face Judgment Day?"

The video ended.

"Think he had something to do with all this?" Mason asked.

"I'm going to find out. Thanks for showing me." He returned to his desk and called Melendez's cousin, weird Eddie who used the same sign maker as Frank Keyes. *I am NOT a monkey's uncle.* Unfortunately, Eddie was out running errands, but his wife seemed willing to talk. "Yep, I've seen him carrying that monkey's uncle sign. He and all the others are so proud of that slogan."

"The others?"

"The Repentance Angels. Eddie was like a mangy bear that weekend, he was so mad because they said he needed to stay here and protest when they were all having fun camping out somewhere. But he's a good soldier."

He thanked her, hung up, and dialed the officer who had

checked on Keyes's whereabouts. "Know anything about a group called Repentance Angels?"

"Repentance Angels. They are a group of religious extremists who believe they'll get extra credit in heaven for doing all sorts of wacko stuff. They are pretty much anti-anything that could be considered liberal or progressive or scientific. They write a lot of wacko letters to the editor. They like to break windows and spray paint "Repent!" all over the place. Their members have trashed businesses and thrown paint and manure at various people."

"Think they'd steal a gorilla?"

"I don't know why they would, but anything's possible with these nuts. They're not exactly rational."

"Great," Finn groaned. "Can you check on the members on the weekend that Keyes was missing?"

"I don't have to. They had a big convention over close to Forks, on the Olympic Peninsula. I got a friend who's a ranger over there, and he told me about a clash over the size of their bonfire. If Keyes was with them, it's no wonder he didn't want to admit it."

Finn thanked him for the information and hung up. So it looked like maybe Keyes did have an alibi after all. At least that was one door closed.

His brain felt as swollen as his leg. All he had was circumstantial evidence, and he hadn't located anyone. How could he get more information out of Zyrnek? Would it do any good to try Leroy or Ro or Ty's phone again, using a different spoofed number? While he was pondering those questions, Miki strolled through with the mail cart. She delivered two faxed reports and a couple of stamped envelopes to his IN box and then slapped a *USA Today* down next to his keyboard. "Sarge wanted you to see this."

He unfolded the newspaper. *Gorillas and Tigers in the Back Yard: The Dangers of Exotic Pets in the U.S.* was the top news story. Crap.

Yes, the case of Dr. Grace McKenna's missing male gorilla was prominently featured, along with other instances in which a tiger was found walking down an Ohio road, a puff adder had killed a pest control technician, and a lion had mauled a trash collector to death after escaping from a private sanctuary. Apparently, Americans needed to watch out for wild animals from around the world even if they never left their own hometowns.

Jon Zyrnek watched his father's face as he looked up at Neema, perched high in the net. Tony's expression was worried. "And that's all she does?" he asked. "Sit up there wearing Gumu's blankets?"

"Pretty much," Jon told him. "She won't eat. She won't take care of Kanoni." He wasn't about to describe the crow killing.

Tony shook his head and made a tsk-tsk sound. "Will she get over it? Can't you distract her with candy or toys or something?"

"I think the only thing that would help is for Gumu to come back. Otherwise, she might just die of grief." He watched for his father's reaction.

Tony Zyrnek's expression didn't change much as he turned and put an arm around Jon's shoulders. "I'm sorry you've been going through this. I know it's hurting a lot of people. Detective Finn's been over to talk to me a bunch of times."

Jon shifted away from his father to study his face again.

"I know," his father said, meeting his gaze. "Finn thinks I might be in on this. Do you think that, too?"

He didn't know how to answer that, not yet. He swallowed and said, "I need you to take a walk with me, Dad."

He led his father down the back driveway. At the spot he'd marked with three rocks set in a triangle, he stepped off the road. Picking up a small windfall branch still bristling with pine needles, he used it as a brush to sweep away the dirt he'd kicked over the bolt cutter, revealing the words *Evansburg Auto Salvage* etched into the metal handle.

He watched carefully as his father squatted and bent close to look.

After staring at the bolt cutter for a long moment, his father said, "Oh, crap."

So it was true. He was going to lose his dad all over again. He was going to be the son of a jailbird for the rest of his life.

"There's this, too." Jon moved over another foot and swept the lock clean, too.

Tony Zyrnek stood up, frowning. He waved his bandaged hand over the tool and lock. "Did you take a photo of these?"

Jon's throat was so tight, he had to swallow again before he could answer. "Several." He hoped his father was not going to ask him to delete them.

His father nodded his head. "Okay." He studied the area for a minute longer, then said, "If I took the photos, they'd never believe me. They still might not." He held out his hand. "I need to borrow your cell phone, son."

Jon handed it over and waited as his father punched buttons. Of course Tony Zyrnek would make a call to warn the scumbag friends who had helped him kidnap Gumu. Next he'd ask Jon to hide the evidence again. Jon steeled himself to refuse.

But then he heard his father say, "Detective Finn? You need to get out here to Grace's back driveway as soon as possible. There's something you gotta see."

His dad hung up, patted him on the shoulder and said, "Good job, son."

The kind words made what was coming all the more painful. They spent the next twenty minutes talking about plans for the future. Hiking this summer. Road trips to places they'd always wanted to see. Rialto Beach. The San Juan Islands. Things that would never happen now. His dad was telling him about Palouse Falls when Finn roared up the drive.

Tony pointed him to the bolt cutter and lock, and Jon told Finn the story of when he found them. Finn transferred his angry gaze from son to father and back again as if trying to decide who to hit first. Finally he grunted in disgust, and then squatted to inspect the items carefully, taking photos with his phone.

"You need to look for a man named Keno," his father told Finn. "We worked together at the storage yard until he got fired."

Finn returned to his car, snapped on some latex gloves, and then pulled out a baggie of little orange flags and a marker. He wrote numbers on two flags and pushed them into the soil to mark the locations, then he bagged the bolt cutter and lock and moved them to his trunk.

"Am I going to find your fingerprints on these, Zyrnek?" he growled.

"You might," his father said. "'Cause of where they came from. But you need to look for Keno. Unless he was smart enough to wipe 'em, his prints will be there, too."

"Right." Finn slammed the trunk of his car. "And does this mysterious Keno have a last name?"

"I don't know it. Ask Grant Redd at the salvage yard; he'll know."

"I will." Finn aimed an index finger at Tony Zyrnek. "I better not find out you left town while I'm checking this." He pulled open the driver's door of the car.

"You won't. Hope your leg is better."

After Finn took off, his dad swatted him on the arm and smiled. "This is the first big break, and we owe it to you. We're going to get Gumu back."

It sounded plausible. He wanted to believe. But he couldn't forget that his dad was an excellent storyteller. And an even better con man.

Finn stopped at the salvage yard and sighted Grant Redd walking to his office from his shop, wiping grease from his hands with a rag.

"Uh-oh," said the owner on seeing him. "This can't be good. Zyrnek's not here. Monday's his day off."

"Does the name Keno mean anything to you?"

Redd twisted the rag in his hands. "Yep. That's the guy I canned a couple of months back."

Finn pulled out his notepad. "Last name?"

"North."

North? That was the name of the guy Whitehead had given the Mustang to. "*Kevin* North?"

"Yeah. But he went by Keno."

"Kevin David North?"

Grant put his hands on his hips. "Don't know about the David part, but Kevin North is right."

"Why'd you fire him?"

"I could never trust him to show up on time, and I saw him in town a couple of times talking to a pretty rough-looking dude. The two of them looked like they were cooking up something."

"Wait here." Finn walked back to his car and pulled out his case file. As he walked back, he leafed through the pages and then held out Leroy Shane's mug shot to Redd.

The owner nodded. "Yep—that's the mutt Keno was friendly with. He just looked like trouble, and you know ex-cons aren't supposed to associate, so I just figured, you know, nip this situation in the bud before it comes back to bite my ass."

"You have good instincts," Finn told him.

"Another thing about Keno," Redd added, "Seemed like a lot of things went missing when he worked here."

"Tools?"

Redd squinted. "How'd you know? I lost a couple of pry bars, a blow torch, a bolt cutter, and probably some other stuff I didn't notice. Each thing's not worth so much, but it adds up, you know?"

Finn flipped through the case file on the dead guy in the Mustang, and held out a copy of Kevin David North's driver's license photo.

"That's Keno," Redd confirmed. "But that's got to be a really old photo, or else he was wearing a rug when he had it taken. He was bald as an ostrich egg when he worked here. I think he shaved his head, but there wasn't much there to shave to begin with."

"Did Keno and Zyrnek get along?" Finn asked.

Redd shrugged. "Far as I know. But then Tony's real easy to get along with."

Finn knew that better than most. For good measure, he showed Grant Redd photos of Ty Linero, Allen Whitehead, and Ryan Connelly. He was beginning to wonder if they were all linked in some way. Redd didn't recognize any of those three.

"Tony's not in trouble, is he? He'll be back at work tomorrow?"

"Call me if he's not," Finn told him. *And I'll send everyone I can think of out to nail his ass.*

With an ache in her heart, Grace observed as Neema persisted in her restless search through the barn. At least Neema's pattern of activity was changing; maybe her violent acting out this morning had been cathartic. Neema hadn't eaten, but she had taken a drink of water and she was moving again. She often stopped to gaze at the area where the blood stain had been. Maybe this was a normal grieving process that the gorilla would eventually emerge from.

While Grace had been at local television station recording a plea for Gumu's return, Jon and his father had discovered an abandoned bolt cutter and lock out by the back road and reported it to Finn. *Please*, she prayed to whoever was listening, *let that be a break that leads us to Gumu.*

Near the back door, Neema bent over on all fours to examine an object on the floor. She flicked away sawdust, and then Grace saw a brief flash of red as Neema transferred a small object to her mouth.

Grace rushed to her. "Neema, what was that?"

The gorilla stared at her stubbornly, her eyes sullen.

"In your mouth. What did you put in your mouth?" She held out her hand. "Give it to me."

Neema obstinately transferred her gaze to the barn wall.

"Be good. Show me."

Finally Neema faced her and opened her mouth. What looked like a piece of red paper lay on her tongue.

"Give it to me, please."

Slowly, Neema extruded her tongue. Grace peeled off the object. It was a stick of gum, wrapped in foil and orange-red paper, now damp with saliva and dented with a couple of teeth marks. It was a stick of clove gum.

Grace's breath caught in her throat. Neither she nor Jon nor any of the volunteers chewed clove gum. Or any kind of gum, for that matter. She didn't allow gum in the presence of the gorillas. This had to have come from an intruder. She needed to call Matt. She turned and nearly collided with Caryn, who had walked up behind her.

"Boss?" The young woman held out Grace's cell phone. "I cleared your voicemail box," she said. "I know I should have asked, but I was worried that someone might be trying to call with information about Gumu."

Grace bit her lip. Why hadn't she thought of that? Had she subconsciously given up hope of locating the male gorilla alive? She held out her hand. "Thanks."

"Almost all messages were from reporters, but a few were from Detective Finn." Caryn's cheeks pinked on saying that, and Grace wondered what Matt's messages had contained. He had every right to be angry with her.

"It's okay, Caryn," she said.

The girl took a breath. "Anyway, there was this one other call that seemed important, so I called him back. I know you're going to want to talk to this guy." Caryn handed the phone to her.

"This is Grace McKenna," she said hesitantly.

"Dr. McKenna, this is Steven Constello—Maria's father. You truly believe you have Pepito?" His syntax was more formal than most Americans, and his voice held a trace of an accent—Hispanic? Brazilian? In the background Grace could hear the excited chatter of a girl.

Grace assured them that she did have the pygmy marmoset. The girl came on the phone. "Does he have a little streak of white fur on his head?"

"Looks like an exclamation point."

Maria squealed at the top of her lungs, and Grace quickly yanked the phone away from her ear, smiling. It was wonderful to be able to share good news for a change.

The father came back on. "Thank you so much for this gift of happiness in a very sad time, Miss McKenna. When may we meet to get Pepito? We are happy to drive to you."

She couldn't invite them into the media circus surrounding her home. If any of the media saw the marmoset, she could be arrested. The Smiths had never reported the theft, which told her that the monkey was indeed stolen, but in the current climate of the county, she might be charged with having another exotic pet she hadn't reported.

She checked her watch. It was late. She arranged to meet the Constellos the next afternoon in a state park about a half hour's drive east along I-90. She'd miss the little marmoset, but she was delighted that Pepito would soon be back home.

Chapter 22

The next morning, Finn was impatiently waiting for initial fingerprint matches on the bolt cutter and lock. He hadn't been able to locate Kevin David North. The guy's cell phone had been disconnected, and he'd been evicted from his apartment six weeks ago. No news on either Ty or Ro Linero or Leroy Shane. It had been more than a week since Gumu had disappeared, and although he felt like he was getting a handle on who might be involved, he still didn't have a clue what had happened to the gorilla.

His cell phone buzzed as he was in the process of instructing Miki to search for online stories of apes for sale or new apes in zoos.

"Look for anything involving apes or ape products," he summed up as he fished for his cell in his shirt pocket.

The young technician scowled. "I'm not dense, Detective. I'll figure it out. I'm planning to be a detective, too."

The arrogance of youth. "You have to be a police officer first."

She tossed her head. "I'm going to the academy this fall."

"Good for you." She seemed to think that achieving detective status would be a fast climb for her. Maybe it would be. In Evansburg, Miki had the home town advantage.

After the girl walked away to her work station, he put the phone to his ear. "Finn."

"Hi, Matt. Sorry to bother you at work." Grace.

He was glad to hear that she didn't sound mad any longer. "I guess you know your parents left today?"

"Thank God. How's your leg? And your face?"

"They both hurt. But I'll live. How are Neema and Kanoni?"

"Not good." Grace's long pause told him the situation might be worse than he was imagining. He could feel her struggle for emotional control. "I don't want to talk about that now. That's not why I called. First of all, I need to say I'm sorry about how I behaved last night. I know I've caused you a lot of trouble, and I understand why you'd want to—"

"Grace, we need to talk." Miki appeared at his elbow again. The expression on the twenty-year-old's face told him she was intently eavesdropping. So was Mason at the next desk over. "But can we do this later?"

"Okay. Whenever it's convenient for you. But I need to tell you about something Neema found in the barn. I sent a photo to your work email."

As he listened, he refreshed his email list and pulled up the photo. Clove gum? That was unusual. The red-orange wrapper looked familiar. Red paper. The room suddenly felt like the air pressure had bottomed out as he realized where he'd seen that kind of gum before. He asked Grace to bring the stick of gum to the station.

After hanging up, he pulled up Tyrone Linero's DMV photo and studied it carefully.

Miki laid two printouts on top of his keyboard. A gorilla skeleton had appeared for sale on eBay. And a zoo in Mexico City had acquired a new male gorilla. He stared at them sadly and nodded at Miki.

This was going to be a bad day for a lot of people.

An hour later Finn was in the interview room at the police station, sitting across the table from Heather Clayton. "Heather, did Ty chew clove gum?"

She picked invisible pieces of lint from her skirt, crossed and then uncrossed her legs. Simply being in a police station made most people nervous, and apparently Heather was no exception. Her eyes widened. "How did you know?"

"I remembered you had some in your apartment."

She looked nervously at her watch. "I need to be back at the office in a few minutes for a counseling session."

"You might need to cancel that." He held out the scrap of cloth the morgue technician had saved from the remains of the corpse's shirt. "Do you recognize this?"

For a long moment, she stared at the fabric piece lying in the palm of his hand. Then she swallowed hard and reached for it, stretching it between her fingers. "This matches the shirt I gave him for his birthday in February."

When she looked up, her eyes were filled with tears.

He felt like he was torturing her. He moved his chair around the table to sit beside her. "Did Ty have a small round scar on his forehead, and a pierced hole in his right earlobe?" After the corpse had been washed, these small details had been revealed.

A frown creased her forehead. "Why are you asking me all these questions? Why are you using the past tense?" She splayed the fingers of her right hand on top of the table as if she needed the support.

Finn put his hand on top of hers. "Heather, Ty didn't leave you and Jenny."

"Go on," she whispered, not looking at him.

"I'm sorry to tell you that about a week ago, a body was discovered in a Mustang that crashed off of a forest service road."

"I read that in the paper." She shook her head violently. "But that can't be Ty. He doesn't have a Mustang."

"The Mustang was registered to Allen Whitehead in Renton."

"I've never heard of Allen Whitehead. I don't even know where Renton is."

"Do you know a guy named Kevin North?"

"No."

"He used the nickname Keno. He got out of jail thirteen months ago. He worked briefly at the auto salvage yard here. We think the Mustang came from him."

"Let me guess—this Kevin was one of Leroy's or Ro's lowlife friends." She shook her head again. When she spoke, her voice was a hoarse croak. "So maybe that dead guy you're talking about is Kevin. That can't be Ty."

He didn't want to show her the morgue photo. But it seemed he had to. He carefully placed his thumb across the area beneath the corpse's nose, hiding the missing jaw and protruding vertebrae, and then slid the picture in front of her downcast eyes.

"Oh God." She turned her head away and buried her face in her hands. "He didn't leave me," she moaned, leaning toward him.

He put his arms around her.

"He didn't leave Jenny." She sobbed the words into his shoulder.

"That's right." Finn patted Heather's back, glad he could at least give her that consolation. Tests remained to be concluded, but he was sure the blood in the barn would match Ty's. Either Gumu had killed Ty, or one of Ty's partners in crime had.

Over Heather's head, Finn glanced at the window of the interview room. He'd hadn't drawn the blinds tightly enough, and between the slats he saw Grace standing in the hallway watching, several pages of paper in one hand and a cup of coffee in the other, with Miki by her side. He'd asked Miki to photocopy the *USA Today* article on exotic pets for Grace. After spying him with Heather in his arms, Grace turned away and dumped the coffee into a nearby trash bin, then disappeared from sight.

Miki mouthed the word *Sorry* before she vanished, too.

"Why doesn't your article say that Gumu was stolen?" Grace argued with an assistant editor at *USA Today*. "You made it sound like he escaped."

"We didn't say anything of the sort. The article simply says the gorilla vanished and left behind a pool of human blood." The guy sounded irritated. "That's true, isn't it?"

"He vanished, yes," Grace snapped, "because someone *took*

him. And he did not 'leave behind a pool of human blood,' because he didn't leave voluntarily. Gumu is not a dangerous wild animal unless he's mistreated. And the poor gorilla has been mistreated by humans most of his life. It's a wonder Gumu's not a serial killer."

Her phone bleeped, and she pulled it away to see *Call Waiting – Matthew Finn.* Ignoring that, she put it back to her ear and heard the editor insist, "We have no reason to print a retraction."

"There's a complete male gorilla skeleton for sale on eBay today. Where did *that* come from? And a zoo in Mexico is advertising that they have a new gorilla. Where did *he* come from? Great apes are being slaughtered and sold illegally all around the world."

"Read the whole article, Dr. McKenna. It points out how animal trafficking is a multimillion-dollar criminal enterprise. And we did say the case was still under investigation. Thank you for calling *USA Today.*" He hung up.

She sat down in her desk chair, fuming, and checked the eBay site again. The bid was up to eighteen hundred and twenty dollars now for the gorilla skeleton, and there were still hours to go. The description said the bones were "historical," whatever that meant. That had to be how the seller was slipping under the CITES radar. Gorillas hadn't been classified as endangered until the late nineties. But in the photos, the bones looked fresh and white, not weathered and yellowed. Was she looking at all that remained of Gumu?

She pulled out the photocopied article about the new male gorilla in the Mexico zoo. Was the black ape in the photo Gumu? He was peeking out from behind vegetation; it was impossible to tell. How could she force both of these parties to give her a DNA sample? She needed an attorney, but with no funds and the rarity of the situation, finding one who would actually help was a tall order. She placed the photocopy down on top of the letter from Tacoma saying *You deserved it.* She covered those pages with the notice from the County Council that she had lost her permit and had ninety days to get rid of the gorillas. And then she topped off the stack with the official letter from the college board stating that they had decided not to renew her grant for the gorilla sign language project.

Excited shrieks penetrated her fog of despair. She went to the window. Sierra stood near the portable poultry pen as Pepito leapt around inside. They had only another couple of hours with the marmoset before she would take him back to his rightful owners.

Brittany was play-chasing Kanoni and her daughter Ivy around the yard. Neema had resumed her post at the top of the net.

On the desk, the phone buzzed. *Matthew Finn.* She didn't feel like talking to him right now. Dr. Grace McKenna was going down like the Titanic, and he didn't deserve to sink with her. She'd have to leave Evansburg. Matt belonged with that beautiful woman, Heather.

Was this the end of the road? Her mother had probably been right; a zoo would be glad to take Kanoni. But Neema, in her present condition, was more liability than asset. What institution wanted to take an unpredictable, suicidal gorilla?

For that matter, what institution would want Dr. Grace McKenna, who had now managed to lose two of the four gorillas in her care. And if Neema didn't start eating, the loss of a third one might be only days away. If Neema died, would Kanoni quickly follow? Gorillas might be the largest of the great apes, but they were also the most delicate. Seemingly healthy survivors of gorilla massacres in the wild had been known to die of sorrow and loneliness.

Maybe Neema would be better off with someone else. Grace didn't know how to save her.

She picked up the email printout her mother had left behind. Richard Riverton, her old college lover, now head of the Psych Department. Maybe it would be for the best, to leave this all behind, get a fresh start in academia. Swallowing her pride, she called.

Of course his secretary answered, emphasizing the difference in their status. She was put on hold for a full six minutes of soft jazz before Richard came on the line.

"Grace! How are you holding up?" he asked.

"So you know what's been happening?"

"*USA Today* is on my desk as we speak. It seems a bit unfair, given that the gorilla was stolen from you."

"Thank you for saying so, Richard. Congratulations on making department head."

"I've been here two and a half years." Another reminder of how far behind she'd fallen in recent years. She had a hard time remembering what she'd found attractive about him. He'd always been a bit of a stuffed shirt, far more ambitious and political than she was. Detective Matt Finn was more her type.

She shook her head to clear out that thought. Matt was gone.

"Richard, I wanted to ask you about the email you sent to my mother, saying you had a position for me."

There was a long moment of silence on the other end. Then, "Grace, I sent that email before all this news hit the national wire. I'm sure you understand that now..." He sighed. "You know how tight funding is these days, and the politicians have their fingers in everything."

She waited for more, but he didn't say anything. "Are you retracting your offer?"

"Actually, I never made a formal offer," he said stiffly. "But Grace, I truly wish you—"

She clicked the OFF button and set the phone down. It buzzed again almost immediately. *Matthew Finn.* She watched the cell phone vibrate around on the desk until it went silent.

Forming her hand into a big letter L, she tapped her forehead with it. Loser. She contemplated drinking the bottle of tequila she had stored in the cabinet over her refrigerator. Loser, loser, loser.

Then she straightened, furious. She didn't deserve any of this, and neither did the gorillas. If the newspapers wouldn't print the real story of her gorillas, she would post it on the internet herself. She opened her word processing program and wrote about how Neema had witnessed the murder of her previous mate Spencer and now had suffered the loss of her second partner. She described how Gumu had been captured as a baby after his whole family had been murdered around him. And now he'd been kidnapped again and taken to God only knew where.

Forty minutes later she wiped the tears of frustration from her cheeks and went outside, let herself into the barn enclosure, and climbed to the top of the net. Perched beside Neema, she just sat with her gorilla for a while, holding onto her massive ape hand.

Then she climbed down to drive Pepito to the park. She could do at least this one thing right.

Chapter 23

Finn left three messages for Grace before he finally gave up and went home in the afternoon, his head and leg throbbing like the bass track of a hip-hop recording. He was getting close to cracking the case, he could feel it, even if it was going to lead to that gorilla skeleton on eBay. If only he could convince her to collaborate. Her voicemail setup didn't leave him enough time to explain the connections between Ty Linero and Ro Linero and Heather, and Tony Zyrnek and Kevin North and Leroy Shane and Jarvis Pinder. He washed three aspirin down with a beer and a couple of antibiotic pills and settled into his easy chair. Both cats settled in with him.

He couldn't have been asleep for more than a few minutes when the doorbell rang. He trudged to the door fuzzy-mouthed, fuzzy-headed, and with the giant dog in tow.

Tony Zyrnek stood on his doorstep. "What the hell?" Finn growled.

Cargo wiped a wet nose on his sweat pants as he nudged around him to stick his nose in Zyrnek's crotch.

"Sorry, sorry," the man said, patting the dog's head and extending a commuter cup in Finn's direction. "I've been thinking about all this, and I just couldn't wait to talk to you, and they told me you'd already gone home." He tilted his head in the direction of the cup in Finn's hand. "I can't afford Starbucks or those places, but I made that with a good dark roast Colombian and a splash of real half and half. It might be a bit strong, but I figured you for a strong coffee type."

Finn took a sip. Might have used a larger splash of half and half, but it was good.

"How do you know where I live?"

"County assessor records. I figured you owned a house

around here. I made ham and cheese on onion bagels, too."
Zyrnek held up a paper bag.

The man was smart and resourceful. All con men were;
that's what made them dangerous. Finn stepped aside and
gestured Zyrnek in.

They sat at the dining room table. Cargo laid his head in
Zyrnek's lap, trying to romance a bagel out of him. Zyrnek
scratched him behind the ears. Cargo thumped his foot in
ecstasy on the floor.

"Heather called me last night," Zyrnek said. "I spent the
night over there."

He must have noticed the expression on Finn's face,
because he held out both hands in a stop motion and said, "It
wasn't like that. She's a wreck. I just held her and helped with
the baby. Her mom's coming today."

"I know you didn't tell her that the blood in the barn
belonged to Ty," he continued. Again he held up his hands.
"Jon told me about that, and there was the newspaper article,
too. I can add two and two. So Ty was there when Gumu
disappeared?"

"It looks that way," Finn agreed. He didn't think he could
prove what had happened in the barn, but when the DNA came
back, he'd be able to prove that Tyrone Linero had been there.

"Like I said, I've been thinking about all this, and I know
Jarvis is behind it. I know that sounds farfetched to you, but
believe me, Jarvis knows how to pull strings even when he is
behind bars. And when he called this week, he asked me how
you were doing on the case of the missing gorilla. Did you
record that?"

"Maybe." Finn took a bite of the bagel sandwich. It was
good. He made a "continue" motion with his hand.

"Well, if you did, you know he wouldn't say much and I
didn't tell him anything. Not that I know anything." Zyrnek
took a bite of his own sandwich. "Not bad, huh?"

Finn answered by taking another bite. After a swallow of
coffee, he said, "So what is Jarvis up to?"

"Well, you know how when you were over, we were looking

at the gorillas' paintings on the wall."

"Yeah." What was the guy hinting about?

Zyrnek dipped his head and ran his fingers through his hair. "I don't like to say it, but I can see how I'm in this mix, although I didn't do anything wrong. I hope you can see it that way."

"Go on."

"We had those paintings in our cell. Jarvis really liked Gumu's and he said he knew a guy named Elamo who would really like them, too, and pay good money. I didn't want to sell them, but I told him about how you could buy the paintings online and how that would support Jon's work with the gorillas. And then a while later, Jarvis said that his friend had bought some paintings and he thought the videos that came with them made them worth a whole lot more. I mean, gorillas that paint are pretty cool, right?"

"They're certainly different."

Zyrnek leaned forward. "So you said this Leroy has been visiting Jarvis. And you know that he'll be up to something outside; he owes Jarvis and he's gotta pay up."

"I figured that."

"And then all of a sudden the beautiful DeeDee Suarez starts coming, too."

"Lucky Jarvis," Finn commented.

"Got that right. And then I'm working with this Keno guy. And he's real interested in the gorillas, so I tell him all about them every chance I get. And then I hear he's planning to make a lot of money and he got canned because he's hanging around with some lowlife who sounds a lot like Leroy."

Finn had been thinking along the same lines of connections among the parties.

"And Leroy and Jarvis, they know the Lineros."

"So you figure they're all in this together," Finn summed up. "But what did they do with Gumu? And how does DeeDee fit into the mix?"

Zyrnek leaned back in his chair and looked at him. "You're the detective. But I figure that DeeDee, seeing as how her family's from South America, is linked up with the drug business and with Elamo."

Assuming that Zyrnek wasn't making this all up, it might be a new thread to follow. Finn walked Tony Zyrnek to the door.

After arriving at the station, Finn pulled up Jarvis Pinder's last court transcript on his computer. Pinder had been convicted of selling cocaine and suspected of being part of the infamous A.A. Reyes cartel from Venezuela. There was no mention of anyone named Elamo. Finn googled A.A. Reyes and found numerous articles in Spanish and English. The English versions were all about drug busts. The Spanish ones came with photos and looked more interesting.

He called Guy Rodrigo, the evidence technician he usually worked with. "Rodrigo? You speak Spanish, don't you?"

"Sorta," Rodrigo said. "I understand it better than I speak it. My dad always spoke it to us, but he's been gone a while now."

"Where are you now? Can I send you something to look at?"

He was in luck; Rodrigo was just down the hall in the evidence room logging in some new items. He showed up at Finn's desk within ten minutes.

"Can you read this?" Finn turned his monitor so Rodrigo could see it.

Rodrigo squinted at the screen for a minute. "It's about a major cocaine drug pin in Venezuela. Ariel Asimov Reyes—his mother must have been a very confused woman, to give him a name like that."

Grabbing Finn's mouse, he scrolled down. "It says he lives like a king. Built himself a palace with galleries that rival the Louvre. He has a private zoo. Even has an elephant." Rodrigo turned to Finn. "What does this have to do with anything?"

A zoo? Finn tried not to show his excitement, saying only, "I'm not sure yet. Have you ever heard of a drug boss named Elamo in South America?"

Rodrigo laughed. "I'd wager every drug boss is called 'El Amo.'" He pointed to the screen. "I'm sure this guy is usually called El Amo. Two words, not one. It means master or boss man."

Finn slapped him on the back and let him go back to work.

So Jarvis Pinder knew Ariel Asimov Reyes, drug lord from Venezuela. And Reyes had his own private zoo. He'd know the value of a gorilla. Reyes had to be El Amo, the man who'd bought several of Gumu's paintings.

He pulled up Grace's lists of buyers for the gorillas' paintings. Why hadn't he done anything with these before? There it was—Maravilla Enterprises, Caracas, Venezuela. He'd bet a million dollars that Maravilla Enterprises was a front for Ariel Asimov Reyes.

He had finally found the link. Now all he had to do was find the gorilla.

Grace had been in the park for about ten minutes when a black car pulled into the picnic ground. She watched from her position at a picnic table as the tall stranger unfolded a wheelchair from the trunk of the car and helped a girl shift from the passenger seat to the chair. Both of them were dressed in black. These had to be the Constellos. Grace grabbed the cat carrier by her side and went to meet them.

It was clear that Pepito had missed Maria. As soon as he sighted her, the marmoset began chattering with excitement. When he was let out of the cat carrier, the miniature monkey jumped to the girl's shoulder and began grooming her, moving his tiny paws through her curly black hair, his eyes bright and his jaws in constant motion as he prattled on, no doubt telling the girl how much he'd missed her. Giggling, Maria reached behind her head and stroked his back, pulling gently on his tail. He grabbed her index finger with both tiny hands and rubbed along it, twisting his head from side to side to slide his face along her skin. If he'd been a cat, Grace was sure the little monkey would be purring.

Both Constellos thanked her profusely. Steven tried to press money into her hands, but Grace refused. "Seeing all this joy is reward enough."

Steven and Maria insisted on hugging her, several times.

Which brought tears to her eyes. She walked them back to their car and waited while Steven settled Maria and Pepito into the front passenger seat.

Steven Constello pulled open the driver's door, then stopped and took her hand. "Thank you again."

"My pleasure."

"I know that you are the lady with the missing gorilla. Do you believe it's possible that the same man who had Pepito also took your gorilla?"

"I don't think so," Grace told him. "We will investigate, of course," she said, while thinking that would never happen, "but right now, we still have no clue where Gumu might be."

"Then it is still a sad time for you." He clucked his tongue sympathetically. "Maria and I have been through our own sad time; that's why finding Pepito is such a blessing."

Grace looked pointedly at the man's black shirt and pants. "I couldn't help but notice that you are in mourning."

"That's why we didn't receive your phone messages until yesterday. My wife passed away a week ago, and Maria and I accompanied her back to Peru, according to her wishes."

Oh God, the man had lost his wife and the little girl her mother. No wonder they hadn't answered her messages. "I'm so sorry," she said. "It's so painful to lose a loved one, and to ship a"—she thought quickly to come up with a substitute for 'body'—"...casket...to another country must be a hard thing to do."

He dipped his chin. "It was."

What a grim business. But likely a profitable one, considering the popularity of international travel these days. Probably involved a lot of paperwork, and possibly inspections, too. She wondered if it was easier to ship human remains than to transport live animals.

Suddenly she grabbed his arm. "How did you transport the body out of the country?"

He stared at her hand on his arm. Embarrassed at her rudeness, she let go. "Sorry."

He smiled uncertainly. "Fortunately, Miss McKenna, there

are companies that specialize in that process." Steven Constello slid behind the driver's wheel. "THR Shipping is one. There's a branch in Moses Lake."

Grace waved a hurried goodbye, then picked up her phone to call Finn and tell him that Gumu could have been shipped somewhere hidden in a casket.

The screen showed a text message from Finn. *Art buyer Maravilla Ent. kidnapped G? = A.A. Reyes, w private zoo*

She read Matt's text twice. Was it possible? Maravilla Enterprises, the buyer that had purchased all those paintings by Gumu, had a private zoo? She called THR Shipping in Moses Lake.

When a female voice answered, she said, "Hi, I'm Delilah Cooper from XTX Corporation. I have a rush package that needs to go to Maravilla Enterprises in Venezuela. Their rep told me that you ship to them? Do you have any flights leaving soon?" She was a little surprised how easily the lies just slipped from her lips. *Please God, let this be the key. Don't let Gumu already be in South America.*

The clerk checked the roster. "You're in luck. Normally the cargo for Caracas would have gone out a week ago, but we're backed up because we had to have our jet repaired. You probably heard about that crash."

"I hope nobody got hurt."

"The pilot was out of the hospital within a few days. The plane took over a week to fix. That's why we have only one shipment going that way this week. And unfortunately, that load is already pretty heavy because of the backup."

"You're shipping them a casket, right?"

"How did you know?"

"I was told there was a death in the family of an exec at Maravilla, a relative traveling in the U.S. So sad."

"There are actually two caskets going out on the flight today, along with a lot of other freight. So we're bumping up against the weight limit. How much does your package weigh?"

She thought fast. "It's less than two pounds. It's just a bunch of legal contracts that need signatures. All the export papers are already attached."

"The jet is scheduled to leave in about an hour and a half—any chance you could make it by then? That's your only option for four more days. Our office is at the airport. Terminal C."

"I'm on my way right now." She ended the call, started the engine, and backed out of the parking lot, raising a cloud of dust.

As soon as she was back on the highway, she picked up the phone again and called Matt.

"Grace! Did you get—"

"Matt," she interrupted breathlessly. "THR Shipping is transporting two caskets to Caracas from the Moses Lake airport. The jet is leaving in an hour and a half. I'm on my way there now."

Casket. Caracas. It might be exactly the combination Finn had been searching for. He'd felt stymied for the last week. Now everything was happening too fast.

"That's more than an hour from here. I'll try to have the plane stopped," he told Grace. "But I don't know if—"

"I'm forty-five minutes away right now. Gotta go." She apparently threw down the phone without ending the call, because the next sounds he heard were what sounded, oddly enough, like cows bawling, quickly drowned by the drawn-out blare of a horn. That was followed by a faint muttered "Same to you, buddy" from Grace, then by "C'mon, come on! Out of the way!"

He didn't want to think about how recklessly she might be driving and he knew her old van did not have a Bluetooth connection, so he ended the call himself and called information to find THR Shipping. After entering the number into his phone, he held it to his ear as he jogged from his desk to his car. A young man and woman were lounging on the hood of a silver Jetta across the lot, sipping coffee from paper cups. As he peeled out of his parking space with his flasher attached to his roof, they leapt to their feet, throwing their cups on the ground, then slid into their car and followed.

The gal who answered at THR quickly transferred him to her manager, who immediately told Finn that no way in hell was he going to stop that jet without a court order. He punched in the number of a magistrate he knew to be friendly—Judge Sobriski, but got a message saying the judge was away from his desk. And no wonder—it was 1:20 according to the clock on the dashboard, and the courthouse closed down from one to two each day for lunch. What crappy luck. He left a voicemail message for Sobriski and then focused on driving. Crappier luck—Moses Lake was a different county and neither he nor the judge had jurisdiction there. But maybe Sobriski could convince a colleague to cough up the appropriate form.

He checked his rearview mirror from time to time. Sure enough, the Jetta was sticking to him. He was doing eighty-five with his flasher and siren going; he hoped a state trooper would soon pull the reporters off his tail.

Chapter 24

Grace hadn't counted on the Moses Lake airport being so far out of town. It took her seventy minutes to get there, so she didn't even attempt to find the THR Shipping office. Instead, she screeched her van to a halt in the first space she found, and ran into the terminal building. Sure enough, out on the tarmac, a small jet painted with a THR logo was parked, its cargo doors open. Three uniformed employees were loading boxes up a moveable conveyor belt ramp. Two giant crates—no doubt the caskets—waited beside the conveyor belt.

It was a small, mostly commercial airport, so she wasn't surprised that the terminal was practically empty. Only a couple of beleaguered-looking women watched over small children running up and down the carpeted corridor.

She hailed the first uniform she saw, but he turned out to be a janitor. "Security?" she asked.

He pointed to the far end of the airport, where an overhead sign read GATES. She glanced out the window. At the bottom of the conveyor belt, a front-loader moved into position, lifted the first casket on its fork, and swiveled into position to load the crate onto the conveyor belt. Another minute and the casket would be on board. Another ten minutes, and both caskets might be on their way to Venezuela. She had no time to run all the way down to security and try to convince them to stop this flight.

The nearest door had a big NO EXIT sign plastered across the glass. She took a deep breath and then punched the handle. An alarm blared as soon as the door popped open. She raced out onto the tarmac, shouting and waving her arms and hoping she wouldn't be shot in the back. "Stop! Hold that casket!"

Behind her, the alarm shrieked continuously. Within

seconds, the din was joined by high-pitched shouts of "TSA! Stop! Security! Stop!"

Another voice joined the first. "Stop, lady! TSA! Security police! Stop!"

And then someone else was shouting "Security breach! Security breach! Tarmac Gate five!" Which must have been radio talk, because she heard a burst of static afterwards.

She didn't hear "...or I'll shoot" and could only pray they didn't have guns. It seemed like a marathon run, and she could see the first casket was already on board and the second was on the front-loader's tines when the whole crew stopped and turned in her direction. When she finally reached the jet's loading zone, she was so breathless she could hardly talk.

"What the hell?" the front-loader operator muttered.

The two employees loading the conveyor belt stared, their fists on their hips.

"Stop loading ... the caskets!" she gasped the words.

Footsteps thundered behind her, and then something heavy and solid slammed into her back. As she hit the tarmac, her breath was knocked out of her lungs. She found herself face down on the asphalt with a hand or an elbow or maybe a knee between her shoulder blades. Then an overweight man straddled her buttocks. He wrestled her hands behind her back, nearly dislocating her right shoulder. The cold metal of handcuffs encircled her wrists, and she felt a pinch as he ratcheted them down tight. In the distance, she heard the wail of a siren join the blaring security alarm.

Finally, two men—they both wore the black uniform of TSA officers—used her elbows as convenient handles to jerk her to her feet.

"What the fuck, lady?" puffed the younger one. He held one hand against his chest as he tried to catch his breath. She knew the feeling.

The older one patted her down from behind and reported, "No weapons." Stepping around to face her, he swiped at his gray moustache and said, "Wanna tell us what the heck you think you're doing?"

She licked her lower lip, tasting blood there. A piece of gravel was stuck to her cheek beneath her left eye. She tried to rub it off with her shoulder, but couldn't reach it.

"One of these caskets has a gorilla in it," she said.

All five men looked at each other, and then back at her. "And you know this how?" said the younger TSA agent.

The front-loader operator chuckled. "Gorilla probably called her on his cell phone."

The silver-haired TSA agent took her arm. "Lady, you violated about seven different laws running out here. What the hell is going on?"

The sirens slowed to a growl and then abruptly went silent as a Moses Lake police cruiser and a port authority SUV parked next to the jet.

The older TSA agent peered deeply into Grace's eyes. "Are you by any chance a psychiatric patient?"

"She probably should be," she heard a familiar voice say behind her.

"I hesitate to admit that she's with me." Finn strolled into the tense gathering. He flashed his badge around the little circle.

He stepped in front of Grace. A trickle of blood ran from her lower lip down her chin. "You okay?" Reaching up, he flicked a piece of gravel from her cheek.

"I am now," she said, licking her lower lip.

The alarm still shrieked from the terminal's outdoor speakers, making it hard to think rationally and speak calmly.

"Set the casket down," Finn shouted at the front-loader operator, pointing to the ground. He turned to the TSA officers and tilted his head toward the terminal. "Can you turn that blasted thing off?"

Another patrol car screeched into position near the jet, and two additional Moses Lake police officers warily approached, hands resting on their holstered guns.

"It's okay. I'm a police detective," Finn hollered, slowly panning his identification badge from one to the other.

The younger TSA officer turned to face the building and made a slashing motion against his throat. The alarm died, leaving only the sounds of the creaking conveyor belt and the front-loader motor, and a ringing that still lingered in Finn's ears.

The officer who had silenced the alarm inspected his badge. "You're out of your jurisdiction, Detective."

"I'm working an active case and I need to inspect the contents of these caskets." He hoped that would be enough. Usually the counties and city departments cooperated with each other. He wasn't so sure about the feds.

He nodded toward Grace. "She's the crime victim. Uncuff her."

"Are you sure that's a good idea? She...uh...said that she believes there's a gorilla in that casket." The officer tapped his finger on his temple and gave Finn a meaningful look.

He nearly laughed at the absurdity of the situation, but he managed to maintain a sober expression and said, "I'll take responsibility. Just uncuff her."

The older TSA officer complied. Grace rubbed her wrists and gave him a shaky smile.

Finn turned to the casket on the front loader's tines and bent over to read the papers attached to the crating.

"Velasquez family," he muttered. He avoided looking at Grace as he straightened. If she was wrong about this, they'd both be in deep manure here.

He looked up at the worker standing in the jet's cargo bay. "What's the destination of the other one?"

"Just a sec." He disappeared from view, but was back in a few seconds. "Says Maravilla Enterprises, Caracas."

"Yes!" Grace pumped a fist in the air. They all turned to look at her with curiosity. She lowered the hand back to her side.

"I need to inspect that one," Finn told the worker. "Get it back down here, please."

"Crap," the guy said. "I just got it set."

One of the workers on the ground hopped onto the belt and walked up. "I'll help."

As the two THR workers wrestled with the crate, Finn nervously watched the security officers who still gazed at Grace, their hands resting on their weapons. Would she be arrested for this? The charges could be federal, and serious. If Grace's hunch didn't pan out, he'd be visiting her in jail for a while. Maybe she'd be charged even if her hunch *did* pan out.

But she'd say it was worth it if she saved Gumu. Because saving Gumu would mean saving Neema, too.

Finally the first crate was back on the ground. He confirmed that the papers were addressed to Maravilla Enterprises.

"I need to borrow a crowbar," Finn said. "Let's open it up."

The other men's faces twisted into expressions of disgust. "You do know there's a corpse in there," said the front-loader operator.

One of the security officers bent to read the form taped to the crate. "The export docs say it's the remains of Marisela Antonio Benitez, 95 years old, going back home to Caracas."

"I have good reason to believe this is a shipment organized by a drug cartel leader," Finn told the cluster of uniforms.

The security officers studied Finn for a minute longer, then one waved the THR employees to move away from the area. "Take fifteen, guys."

The THR employees shut off the conveyor belt and front-loader and reluctantly walked away, casting glances backwards over their shoulders. With a crowbar and a couple of screwdrivers borrowed from the trunk of the police cruiser, Finn and the two TSA officers dismantled the crate around the coffin.

"Ready?" Finn asked everyone. Nods all around.

He held his breath as they pried open the heavy lid. He could tell that Grace was doing the same.

Then they all stared in silence at the waxy perfection of a very small corpse lying against a satin pillow.

The old woman's makeup was perfect and her hair was starched into sleek white waves. She looked utterly at peace, as if she'd simply fallen asleep in that elegant position, her tiny gnarled hands laid gently on top of a white leather Holy Bible, labeled in gold lettering.

"No," Grace moaned.

"Uh-huh," grunted the younger TSA agent. He pulled his handcuffs from his belt again and took a step toward Grace.

The port authority officer frowned. "Detective?"

Finn was absolutely mortified. He was never going to live this down. Worse than that, he was going to be jobless and then homeless.

"She's no bigger than a mosquito. Why'd they put her in such a big casket?" a security officer wanted to know.

"Plenty of room for drugs?" suggested a Moses Lake police officer.

"Who ships drugs *from* the U.S. *to* Venezuela?" the first argued.

"Money, then."

Then Grace surprised everyone by saying, "Take her out."

She stepped to the head of the casket and shoved her hands underneath the corpse's shoulders. Afraid that she might simply flip Great Grandma out of her satin bed if he didn't help, Finn moved to the corpse's feet.

After he carefully tucked the satin sheet around the little body, the two of them hefted her from the casket as the security officers glanced nervously at the terminal. The body was much lighter than he'd expected, but so limp they had a hard time not dropping her.

After laying the corpse gently on the tarmac, he leaned into the casket and pulled aside the satin quilt she'd lain on. He found a handhold in the corner of the bed board and yanked the board up and out.

The gathering gasped and stepped back, then quickly surged forward again to stare at the contents of the bottom compartment.

"It *is* a gorilla!" someone said.

Gumu's eyes were taped shut with adhesive tape, his hands and feet were bound together with cruel zip ties that cut into his flesh. A plastic mask was strapped over his mouth and nose. Finn wondered where the kidnappers had found one that big. A hose led from the mask to a tank beneath the gorilla's left arm, and Finn could hear a soft hissing sound.

Grace pulled off the mask, then curled the fingers of her left hand around the gorilla's broad throat. Was it possible to feel a pulse through all that thick muscle? She placed her right hand flat against the black leathery skin of the massive chest and leaned in.

"Gumu?" she said softly.

Nothing.

Shit. If Gumu was dead after all this, Finn didn't know what would happen. Grace might *become* a psychiatric patient after losing two gorillas to murder.

The massive chest finally rose and fell.

Grace stepped back, turned and threw her arms around Finn. "He's alive! Gumu is alive!" Then she turned back to her gorilla, leaning into the casket to rub her hands over his inert form.

One of the security officers threw his arms in the air. "Now I can retire. I've seen everything."

Looking back over Grace's head, Finn saw a crowd at the window of the terminal, and he suddenly realized what a macabre sight this was. A group of law enforcement officers ogling a casket, a corpse on the ground beside them.

He squinted. Among the faces at the window he identified Leroy Shane's mug. Close to him stood two other men, a tall thin one, and a man with a shiny bald head. Most likely Linero and North. It looked like all three wore blue coveralls; they must have dressed as janitors or maintenance workers. The three seemed to be arguing. When one glanced his direction, he quickly looked away.

"Three men in blue overalls at the window back there," he hissed to the airport security officers. "Detain them ASAP. They're my suspects."

The officer made a quick phone call. The three men disappeared from the window. They all waited impatiently for a few minutes before there was a radio message back that the three men had been stopped in the airport parking garage and were in custody.

Finn finally blew out the breath he'd been holding for what seemed like days. Bright flashes from the terminal window indicated that spectators were taking photos. Or maybe the student reporters had succeeded in trailing him all the way.

Either way, he knew he would forever be known as the Great Ape Detective from the modest town of Evansburg.

Chapter 25

Grace found it almost unbearable to leave Gumu at a Moses Lake large animal veterinary hospital, but she needed to get back to Neema. She had to show her a photo of Gumu, to tell her to hang on, her mate was going to come back.

Jon Zyrnek volunteered to come and stay with the male gorilla for as long as it took. Brittany would drop him off at the vet's, he said. When Grace left to return to Evansburg, Gumu was still unconscious, strapped to an operating table generally reserved for horses, his nose and mouth still covered with an oxygen mask, and his arms and legs punctured with multiple IV lines. His skin looked more gray than black and he was so limp and breathing so slowly that he seemed dead, but the vet assured her, "He's most likely only severely dehydrated and starved. And deeply sedated. There will probably be no brain damage.

"Only?" she asked. "Probably?"

Gumu had bruises and deep cuts on his hands and feet where he had been bound, as well as a gash on his head and several across his back. The vet couldn't make any predictions about psychological damage. She was anxious about the frame of mind the gorilla might be in when he regained consciousness. Would he wake up terrified? In a rage? Most likely both. She didn't want to think about what he might do.

After being reassured that Jon would watch over him every minute and that both the doctor and the vet tech had experience with animals as large and ferocious as bears and bulls, she finally let Finn drive her back to her compound. Jon could drive her van back.

Exhaustion overtook her. It was hard to put one foot in front of another. Finn might be used to the adrenaline rush of chasing down a suspect, but she wasn't. She was just so, so grateful that the THR jet had slammed into the tarmac last week. That probably wasn't a kind thought, but if that hadn't happened and Gumu had been shipped out, the odds of ever getting him back from Venezuela would be practically nil. In the midst of fretting about how he'd been kept prisoner during all this time and the drugs he'd been given, somehow she fell asleep on the drive back.

It was dark when they arrived at her compound. With the help of airport security, they'd managed to evade the reporters, so Gumu was safe and nobody knew where she and Finn had gone. Grace guessed the whole airport escapade was already on the news. At her gate, there was still one car with an expectant looking young person in the driver's seat, but Caryn was guarding the entrance and locked the gate after them.

The light was on in the barn. At the top of the net sat Sierra. The bonobo explored the rope web nearby, a leash stretched out between them. Caryn walked across the yard to greet them, Kanoni clinging to her back.

Matt looked hard at Caryn, then glanced up to Sierra, then back to Caryn. "If Caryn has Kanoni, then who is that up there?" He pointed skyward toward the dark silhouettes.

Grace smiled. He'd called the bonobo a 'who' instead of a 'what.' "You don't need to know everything, do you, Detective?"

He studied the caretaker and the little ape for another minute, then shook his head. "No, I don't. I never saw that creature. Just like I never saw that tiny monkey thing you have in your office."

She patted his arm. "Pepito is back home where he belongs. And that creature"—she tilted her head in the bonobo's direction—"will be gone soon, too."

Grace found Neema hunched down in a corner of the barn.

"Neema, I have wonderful news." She knelt in front of the gorilla and looked up into her eyes. "I found Gumu today. Gumu is coming back."

"Really?" Caryn murmured from behind her. "Really? So

Gumu really is okay? We were afraid to believe Jon when he told us. Wahoo!"

Her shout brought Sierra and the bonobo down the net. "Gumu's really coming back?"

"He's sleeping right now," Grace told them, signing for Neema. "He's sick. He's very tired. But he'll be back soon."

Neema showed little reaction, giving Grace only a dull-eyed look that told her the gorilla didn't believe her. Grace turned on her phone and showed Neema the photo of Gumu, unsure whether that would help. Gumu was unconscious in the photo; he looked as good as dead. "He's sick, Neema. Bad men put him in a cage. They gave him medicine to make him sleep. But he'll be home soon. Maybe tomorrow."

Neema pushed the phone away and hung her head.

"Tomorrow," Grace repeated, desperate to make Neema understand. "Gumu will be here tomorrow." *Please hold on that long.*

Matt was studying the bonobo on Sierra's hip.

"Found him at the Smiths," Sierra told him. "Out in the wheat field. In an outhouse! A crazy guy in the woods told us there was an alien locked in there."

"The Smiths never reported any thefts," Grace told Matt. "That should tell the police something."

He turned away, shaking his head. "I don't want to know. I never saw this animal."

After a minute, he turned back to Sierra. "Wait a minute—who was this crazy guy? Young, old? What did he look like?"

"Dirty, mostly. Dark hair, short beard. He hadn't shaved in a while. But you can tell he's not really old. And his camping gear looks pretty good and so do his clothes, so he hasn't been homeless for too long."

"Where was he?" Matt asked.

Sierra filled him in. "He was living in a tent in a little patch of trees behind the wheat field in back of the Smiths' house."

In a sarcastic tone, Caryn added, "You remember, Detective—that house with no illegal animals."

"Ryan Connelly," Matt muttered.

Grace had never heard the name. "Who is Ryan Connelly?"

"I have to go." He turned on his heel to leave. But after he'd gone a few steps, he trotted back to grab her and plant a smack on her mouth.

"Sorry." He touched his thumb gently to her split lower lip. "I couldn't resist. This is turning out to be a really good day."

Matt faced Neema. It seemed to Grace that the gorilla's eyes betrayed a small spark of curiosity about the excitement around her. Or was that only wishful thinking?

"Neema," he told the ape, "Tomorrow will be an even better day for gorillas."

Then he left without telling her what was going on. She sighed. Matt was such a cop. He was always going to be a cop. He was always going to feel responsible for righting everyone's wrongs, not just hers. He was always going to run off to follow some new clue. But somehow, even though they were both determined to follow their own paths, they made a pretty good team.

Chapter 26

Grace couldn't keep her promise of "tomorrow" to Neema. It took four days to get Gumu back on his feet. He was a confused angry giant, at first staggering as if he'd had a stroke, lurching around and throwing himself against the bars of his cage. If any of the veterinary staff came close, Gumu bared his teeth and beat his chest and screamed. Only Jon Zyrnek could touch him or feed him. He slept on a mat next to Gumu's cage. The vet was slowly weaning the gorilla from the heavy tranquilizers that had flooded his system for more than a week.

Jon documented the gorilla's progress each day, posting video clips on YouTube. Grace debated whether it might be better to bring Gumu back into familiar surroundings, but the videos of his tantrums terrified her. Neema had killed a crow out of frustration and anger. Gumu had killed a man, although nobody could be sure if he knew he'd done it. Jon told her the male gorilla had signed *bite bad man* several times. They both hoped he would never make those signs in front of anyone who could knew sign language.

Each day, Grace showed Neema the video clips of Gumu. On seeing her mate moving and making sounds, Neema hooted and signed *Gumu Gumu come* over and over again. She pressed her lips to the computer screen and repeatedly asked Grace *where Gumu?*

Gumu is sick, Grace told her. He'll be back when he's better. Neema understood what *sick* meant; she knew about taking medicine and getting better. She abandoned her post at the top of the net to sit in front of Grace's computer and demand to see Gumu over and over again. Although she was not an attentive mother, she tolerated Kanoni sucking on her nipples and clinging to her. Neema had little milk because although she ate a piece of fruit or a cup of yogurt each day, she refused to eat more. Both mother and baby gorilla were skin and bones. Grace worried that Neema didn't quite believe her and that she'd go back on her hunger strike if Gumu didn't completely recover.

Yesterday she'd been to Moses Lake to see Gumu, and she and the vet decided it was time to bring Gumu back. She'd spent the evening and night with Matt, trying to settle her nerves.

The next morning, he turned his television on to see if her gorillas had made the news again.

"Caretakers at the PeaceTree Ape Sanctuary in Oregon got a surprise today when they fed their troupe of bonobos, the smallest members of the ape family. Instead of the usual five bonobos that have lived at the sanctuary for the last eight years, this morning there were six. The newcomer is a young male that was apparently smuggled *into* the bonobo pen."

"Well, isn't the news this morning full of surprises." Grace handed Finn a cup of coffee and then, pushing Lok aside, sat down on the couch beside him with her own cup.

The screen flashed to a middle-aged woman with a rake in one hand and a long graying braid over her shoulder. "We're calling him Houdini," she told the reporter.

"A veterinary certificate of health and five hundred dollars in cash was also found outside the fence," the desk reporter said. "It's a new twist on animal smuggling, and it seems to be happening all over the country."

"That's right," chimed the reporter's teammate. "Two days ago, a pair of bushbabies appeared in an unused cage in a sanctuary, complete with appropriate vegetation and food. And the Cincinnati zoo had long wanted a mate for their lone female tiger, Mia, and presto, yesterday morning, a young male had materialized inside the cage with her. A Chicago resident claims the male tiger is his, that he raised him from a cub in his city apartment."

"Good luck getting that cat back, you asshole," Grace mumbled. "Raising a tiger in an apartment?"

Finn asked, "We don't know anything about who might be behind this trend, do we?"

"Of course not."

He hoped nobody at the station was tracking this latest wildlife trend.

Grace checked her watch. "The vet's bringing Gumu back at five this afternoon. I've got a lot to do before then."

"We'll go back to your place soon," Matt agreed.

She strolled back to the bedroom to get dressed, stopping before his study door. "I love that painting, Matt."

He joined her in the doorway. The morning light made the poppies glow and backlit the woman strolling through the field of flowers. He'd finally finished the painting yesterday afternoon. The woman was moving toward the viewer, her face cast down but smiling, one hand out over the flowers, as if she was exactly where she wanted to be at that moment.

"I want to be that woman," she whispered.

"Grace, you *are* that woman." He leaned in for a kiss. "And I am the man who is waiting for her right here."

In the late afternoon, Neema sat high up in the net, still using Gumu's blanket as a cape. Now she looked more like a mummy than a gorilla. Outside the enclosure, Finn and Tony Zyrnek talked while Grace bounced Kanoni on her hip as waited for the van to arrive.

"I'm so glad you're coming to my barbeque tomorrow." Tony looked from one to the other of them. "I hope Heather and Jenny will come, too. I'm a good cook, and I need to pay you back. It's kind of ironic, in a pathetic sort of way, how this all turned out." He patted Kanoni's head. "I don't know if I can ever forgive myself."

Finn raised an eyebrow. "What the hell are you talking about?"

"You thought it was me all along," Tony told him. "And in a way, it was. I was the common denominator. If it wasn't for me talking about the gorillas nonstop, none of this would have happened."

"You don't know that," Grace said.

"I'm pretty darn sure. It's all kind of like dominos crashing into each other, but it all started with me. Jarvis got the idea to kidnap Gumu because his South American drug guy liked Gumu's paintings so much, and he would never have known about those if I'd kept my mouth shut and I didn't have those paintings in our cell. And then he roped in DeeDee to arrange the deal and then Leroy because Leroy didn't want to die, and Leroy got Ro and Keno, and Keno knew all about the open house because of me, and Ro got Ty involved. So Gumu would never have got kidnapped and Ty Linero would still be alive if it weren't for me." He stuck his hands in his jeans pockets and stared at the ground.

Ty Linero's cause of death was listed on the autopsy report only as exsanguination, and the staging of the car "accident" was just one more crime added to the long list for Ro Linero, Leroy Shane, and Kevin North. Not many people had figured out Gumu's connection to Ty's death. Finn hoped they never would. In a fairer world, animals would be able to claim self-defense just like people did.

Finn looked at Tony. "You're not responsible. Jarvis Pinder cooked the whole thing up."

"Will he do extra time for it?" Tony's expression was hopeful.

"I'd like to think so," Finn said. But the truth was, the case against Pinder wasn't strong. The convict hadn't made any of the arrangements. He hadn't done any of the dirty work. "Watch your back, Tony."

Tony rocked on his feet. "I am. I will."

"At least Ro Linero and Kevin North and Leroy Shane will go to prison," Grace said. "Although they should go for a hell of a lot longer. Sentences for crimes against animals are never long enough."

Finn nodded. Although Grace called the crime a kidnapping, according to the law, it was only theft and animal cruelty.

The van pulled in, and everyone got quiet.

Grace, holding Kanoni against her chest, opened the gate for Jon, who led Gumu in. The vet had assured her that Gumu had recovered from the anesthetic, but the big gorilla still seemed confused. Or maybe he was still in shock; suffering from a kind of post-traumatic stress disorder. After seeing Neema murder the crow, Grace was worried. Gumu had twice Neema's strength, and had never trusted humans much.

Humans had killed his family and captured and tortured him as a baby. Now he'd been captured and tortured as an adult. Being drugged and chained and locked up for a week was enough to make any creature psychotic.

Grace wasn't at all sure that gorillas possessed any concept of forgiveness. She could only hope that both Gumu and Neema could remember which humans had been kind to them.

At first, Gumu sat on the ground next to Grace, his muscles tense as he surveyed his surroundings in silence. Grace studied him with sideways glances, not wanting to confront him with direct eye contact. Gumu's gaze seemed jumpy, unfocused. Did he know where he was? Did he remember *who* he was? Did he remember who they all were?

After a minute, he raised his chin and sniffed at Kanoni's back, his nostrils flaring. Grace froze, anxious about what would come next. Gumu then clasped his massive fingers around the baby's leg and made a low rumbling sound deep in his chest. Grace's heart thumped. Gumu could easily pull the baby out of her arms. In the wild, silverback gorillas frequently killed babies they did not recognize. Did he remember that Kanoni was his offspring?

Then Kanoni raised her head, looked at Gumu, and chirped softly in response.

Above them, near the top of the net, the blanket slid down to reveal the top of Neema's head. Her dark eyes fixed on them. Grace held her breath for a long moment as both adult gorillas stared at each other. The silence felt as heavy as mud, lasting long enough for Grace to hear the crows calling as they settled into their evening roost in the nearby woods.

Neema hooted softly, as if testing the reality of the situation.

Gumu raised his head and flared his nostrils. He leaned forward on his knuckles and huffed back at her.

Another tense second of silence passed. No one—human or gorilla—moved.

Then Neema threw off the blanket. She barreled down the netting, doing a forward roll in her rush to the bottom. Gumu threw both arms out just as Neema leapt from the bottom of the net. Grace dodged out of the way as Neema tackled Gumu, landing on his massive chest.

Both gorillas rolled on the ground, hooting frantically and slapping each other over and over again. Kanoni screeched and bounced against Grace's chest, wanting to join in the reunion. Grace held tight to the primate's little body. It wasn't time yet to add a third member to the party. Jon opened the gate and joined his father on the other side of the fence. Grace followed him out of the enclosure and stood by Finn.

They all watched as Neema and Gumu rocketed around their enclosure, chasing each other up and down the netting, embracing and tickling each other over and over again. Their racket was deafening.

Grace couldn't stop grinning. She turned to Finn. "Isn't it amazing?"

He smiled back. "Amazing is the perfect description."

Kanoni transferred herself to Finn's arms, and although he stiffened for a second when the baby took hold of his ear, he grinned even wider.

"They are happiness in motion." Tony Zyrnek shouted to be heard over the gorillas' excited hoots. He held up a hand toward his son, and Jon high-fived with his father.

Finally the two adult gorillas quieted and sat in the netting, snuggling in each other's arms. Grace took Kanoni from Finn, opened the gate, entered, and pushed the little gorilla up onto the rope net. The baby climbed up to her parents and sat hesitantly beside Neema, one hand resting lightly on her mother's leg. After a moment, Neema pulled Kanoni onto her stomach between her and Gumu.

Neema peered over her baby to Grace, raised her arm and signed.

"Smile happy gorilla," Jon translated.

Neema crossed her arms briefly, wrapping her baby inside for a second, before she turned her back on the humans to face Gumu.

Grace translated the last sign. "Love."

"That pretty much says it all, doesn't it?" Tony Zyrnek drawled.

Chapter 27

Although he had never met the family of Rosemary Benson or visited the elderly woman at Sweet Song Nursing Home, Finn felt like it was only right that he and Grace should pay their last respects at her service a week later. The family had cremated her body, and so there was only a large urn among bouquets of roses up front, along with a huge photo of the elderly woman in a white silk robe heavily embroidered with stars and other symbols. Long carved jade earrings hung from her ears. A wreath of dried flowers was twined through her hair.

On the table next to the urn was a series of smaller photographs of Rosemary at all ages, dancing in a circle of folk dancers, painting designs on the cheeks of children, bending to touch noses with a tiny spotted fawn, posing in backpacking gear beneath a sign on a tree that read Pacific Crest Trail, standing in a prairie with hands out, covered in butterflies.

"Granny was a Wiccan," an attractive young woman told them. "She would have gotten such a hoot out of jet-setting with a gorilla. She would have loved being part of your detective story."

So much for anonymity. Finn wondered if he'd ever get used to the way that everyone knew everyone else's business in Evansburg.

The granddaughter turned to Grace. "How are the gorillas?"

"Neema's happy now that Gumu is back, and Kanoni is happy now that Neema's happy. Gumu is understandably even less trusting than he ever was, so we have to be extra careful with him."

"He'll recover over time," the granddaughter suggested.

Finn hoped so. It scared him to think about Grace living

and working with a killer. Even if Gumu had only killed in self-defense, the big gorilla was now aware that he could do it.

"Gumu has started painting again," Grace said. "I hope you don't think this is in bad taste"—she quickly glanced around the room—"but we thought you might like a small reproduction of his latest work."

Moving to the folding chair where she'd left her bag, Grace pulled out a small framed print. The painting was darker than Gumu's previous abstracts, with a background that was mostly cobalt swirls. In the foreground was a swipe of black and one of pink, and across both of those was a vivid splash of brilliant crimson.

"Fight." The deep voice came from a man at the granddaughter's elbow. He was staring intently at the painting. His freshly shaved cheeks and chin were lighter in color than the rest of his face, giving him an odd, otherworldly look.

"Ryan," the young woman said. She laid a hand on his arm. "I haven't seen you since the high school reunion! How are you?"

"Good." His light colored eyes flashed to quickly to Finn and back. "I'm fine now."

Back on his meds, Finn guessed. He glanced around the room, spotted Ryan's parents talking to another couple. Mrs. Connelly caught his eye and smiled. He dipped his chin in response. Evansburg was sometimes a very small town.

"How did you know Gumu called it *Fight*?" Grace asked Ryan.

He cast his gaze down to his dress shoes, embarrassed. "It's obvious."

Were gorillas and schizophrenics on the same otherworldly wavelength? Finn found the stark portrayal of a violent scene disturbing. How could a *gorilla* paint so suggestively? Oddly enough, the painting had saved Gumu's reputation and Grace's project before the county council. It was impossible to view that painting and not believe in the intelligence of the painter and the story behind it. Jon Zyrnek's videos of Gumu's recovery and Grace's heartfelt account of the gorillas' history appearing in *USA Today* hadn't hurt, either. The college had refused to renew their funding, but Gumu's paintings were selling for a premium and Grace had a book contract in the works, so she thought they might be okay for a while.

Neither of them knew what the future would bring for their careers or for their relationship, but then again, who really did? The best you could do was enjoy the ride.

The granddaughter studied the painting, a smile on her face. "Thank you so much."

She placed it with the photos of Rosemary. The splashes of pink and red in the painting echoed the red and pink roses surrounding the urn, making the painting look as if it belonged there. "We'll treasure it."

"Rest in peace, Rosemary," Grace whispered to the face in the photo.

"Oh, she will, I'm sure." The granddaughter folded her hands together. "May you walk in peace and beauty, as Gran would say."

Finn thought Rosemary Benson must have been a very wise woman. As they strolled out of the chapel into the sunshine, he noticed tears glistening on Grace's cheeks.

Happy cry? he signed.

Smile happy, she signed back.

A couple walking into the chapel gave them a strange look. When Finn's gaze connected with the man's, the stranger dipped his head and said, "Afternoon, Detective," then turned and nodded at Grace. "Dr. McKenna."

No doubt everyone at the station would have heard about this by the time he reported for work tomorrow.

The Great Ape Detective and The Gorilla Lady.

Finn decided to embrace it all.

Books by Pamela Beason

THE SUMMER WESTIN MYSTERIES
Endangered
Bear Bait
Undercurrents

ROMANTIC SUSPENSE
Call of the Jaguar
Shaken

NONFICTION
So You Want to Be a PI?
SAVE Your Money, Your Sanity,
and Our Planet

THE NEEMA MYSTERIES
The Only Witness
The Only Clue

THE RUN FOR YOUR LIFE YA ADVENTURE SERIES
Race with Danger
Race to Truth (coming)

There's always another book on the way. Keep up with
Pam by signing up for notifications on her author
website: http://pamelabeason.com

The following is an excerpt from SHAKEN,
a romantic suspense novel

SHAKEN
by
Pamela Beason

Chapter 1

When the first ripple of earth surged toward her, Elisa
Langston stood up and stared, not trusting her eyes. The field
around her was quiet; all she heard was the rasp of rubbing
branches overhead. Even after the wave had lifted her and set
her back down, then rolled on toward wherever it was going,
she didn't quite believe it. Was she hallucinating?

But then a second wave, this one more malevolent, roared
through the ground, driving her to her knees. Ridge after ridge
of earth rolled through her field like breakers surging toward
the beach. Car alarms sounded in distant parking lots.
Increasing in speed and size, undulations of soil rose and fell
around her, tearing landscape fabric, noisily tossing her neat
rows of potted plants into mangled piles. Overhead, branches
cracked and popped as the taller trees around her shimmied
and swayed like crazed hula dancers, showering her with red
and gold leaves.

A streak of black-and-white fur flashed past.

"Simon!" she shouted, but the panicked cat was gone. She
didn't blame him. If she had four legs, she'd be running, too.

This was the biggest earthquake she'd ever experienced.
And the weirdest. It felt as if the planet had suddenly returned
to its ocean origins, and the whole world was liquid again. A
large wave swelled up beneath her, toppling her backwards,
and she was nearly buried by a sudden deluge of rainbow-
colored foliage. A tremendous ripping sound came from the
north, followed by a thundering crash that reverberated

through the ground and rattled her teeth. The old homestead! Elisa dug her fingernails into the dirt, trying desperately to regain her feet and turn toward the noise. Snapping sounds erupted all around her. A sweet gum crash-landed a few feet away, its impact jolting every bone in her body. She flailed wildly, struggling to find purchase in the roiling soil. A rush of cold air blasted her face, and then she felt a crushing blow to her legs and chest. After a brief close-up of speckled bark, her world went black.

When Elisa opened her eyes again, it was dark. How long had she been lying here? Her eyes wouldn't focus on the numbers on her wristwatch. The first stars were out, weak pinpoints of light barely visible among scattered clouds. A gust of wind blew leaves and dirt into her face. Rain would follow soon.

The uneven soil beneath her was cold, and its dampness had soaked through her clothing and hair. Waves of shivering rippled through her. Her head pounded so badly that she would have sworn a freight train rumbled somewhere nearby.

The tree trunk pinning her to the ground was no more than eight inches thick. She was strong, even if she was small. If she could get proper leverage, she should be able to shift it off her body. When her shivering subsided for a few seconds, she tried to move her legs. A lightning bolt of pain shot through her, white hot, then icy, leaving her breathless.

Giving up for the moment on her lower limbs, she fingered the wetness at the back of her head. She'd landed on a rock. When she stretched her hand in front of her face, it was dark with sticky fluid. Groaning, she managed to squeeze her fingers into her front jeans pocket and slide out the penlight she habitually carried. Its tiny beam confirmed the blood on her hand.

She wrapped her arms around the trunk again, pressing the stinging heat of her scratched cheek against the cool bark of the American sweet gum that had nearly killed her. The tree was one of the Festival variety, prized for its brilliant foliage in an area dominated by evergreens.

"I'm never forgiving you," she hissed into a cluster of orange leaves. "I babied you for years. This is how you pay me back?"

A thin wail drifted on the breeze. A cat crying? "Simon?" she whimpered. "Go for help, buddy. Run to the office. Get Gerald."

Right. As if a cat could rescue her. Her business partner, Gerald, usually left the nursery promptly at five, and for all she knew, Simon needed to be rescued himself. It was an unbearable thought, that her pet might be lying nearby, in pain, waiting for *her* to make things right.

"Anyone! I'm out here!" She slashed her penlight through the air. "Hey!"

Sirens wailed, nearing, then receding. How bad was it out there? A fresh surge of shivers gripped her. She gritted her teeth, picturing buildings reduced to rubble, fires raging from broken gas lines, streets made impassable by wide crevasses and upthrust chunks of pavement.

Her stepmother worked thirty miles away, in Seattle. Had she been on the Evergreen Point floating bridge when the quake hit? Elisa shut her eyes, tried to blank out the sudden, unwanted vision of a giant wave sweeping Gail and hundreds of other hapless commuters into the frigid depths of Lake Washington.

"Hey!" Her shout sounded insignificant, even to her own ears. The sixty-five acres of Langston Green were hardly a wilderness, but they felt like one now. How many times had Gerald begged her to carry a cell phone? If she'd only given in, she could dial nine-one-one now. But instead, she lay here, trapped, only a fading penlight. Her pockets held nothing more than a pair of sharp-edged cutters and a small ball of twine. At best, she could snip twigs away from her face and entertain herself with string games until help arrived. *If* help arrived.

How long would it be before someone thought to look for her out here? They'd check her apartment first, then the office and greenhouse. When they didn't find her, they'd probably think she'd walked the few blocks to the coffee shop or grocery store as she often did in the evenings. Only Timo knew her plans. She chewed on her lower lip, fretting. Did anyone know where *he* was? Was he all right?

Two fat raindrops spattered her cheek, warning her of what was to come. The nighttime temperatures now dipped into the low fifties. Odds were good that she'd expire from hypothermia before dawn. "Anyone out there? Help!"

She wasn't prepared to die. What could anyone say about Elisa Maria Langston in an obituary? Hers was a pathetic life to review. Finding a lost kid on a mountain as a teenager had been her only accomplishment worth noting. She'd peaked at sixteen. How mortifying. No adventures. No great achievements.

Who would miss her? A stepmother and stepsister, an aunt, a handful of colleagues and friends. No Significant Other would cry at her graveside. She always imagined that by now she'd be married, have a child or two. What the heck had happened to that plan? Sure, she'd had dates and even a few torrid sexual liaisons. But embarrassingly few of them, now that she stopped to count. Most men were put off by an assertive Latina who drove a backhoe.

Over the years, she'd been proud of managing by herself. She was strong, self-reliant, and independent. But at the moment, she simply felt alone.

Clouds swirled in the dark skies overhead. Their movement made her nauseous. Closing her eyes, she clenched her jaw to silence her chattering teeth. She couldn't feel her left foot anymore.

Twelve miles away, Jake Street held up one hand to halt traffic in the lane behind the accident, then motioned for the vehicles on the other side to come through. The drivers slowed as they passed, taking in the tragic spectacle of a minivan flattened by a fallen tree. While two firefighters wielded the jaws of life on a van door, another held a woman screaming for her baby. Jake swallowed hard and turned his gaze back to the traffic. A trickle of rain slid down his neck.

A squad car pulled onto the shoulder behind the minivan, and an overweight officer climbed out. He extracted an orange safety vest and hand-held stop sign from the trunk, then approached Jake. "You look like you've done this a few times."

"Plenty." More times than Jake cared to think about. But at least he was just directing traffic this time. The smashed vehicle, the EMTs, and the flashing lights brought back memories of another night that ended with a lot of blood and death and guilt.

"I'll take it from here. Thank you, sir."

"No problem." Jake returned to his Land Rover. His cell rang just as he slid into the seat.

"Where are you, Jake? Are you okay?" It was the secretary at Atlas Security.

"I'm fine. I'm in Kirkland. I was on my way to Langston Green when the quake hit."

"Oh yeah, Langston. Our latest scammer."

Scammer? He flinched at the word, especially as applied to Elisa Langston. His heart had nearly stopped when he'd spotted her name on his list of possible fraud cases.

"Reports are coming in from all over," the secretary said. "I guess it's pretty bad down south. Bill's working on getting the helicopter up. He'll want you to ride along."

Like many insurance companies, Atlas Security had emergency procedures in place to check on their clients and speed recovery in any way possible. It was good for the customers and good for Atlas's bottom line. But if the situation in Seattle was as chaotic as it was here, it could take a while to get a chopper into the air.

"The floating bridges are closed, traffic lights are out all over, and trees are down everywhere. No way I can make it back to Seattle now," he told her. "I'm going to continue on to Langston Green; I can at least see how that client is doing. Call on my cell when you need me."

He stuck the phone in his pocket and pulled away from the accident scene, glad to be gone before the firemen extracted the infant. The only wails he'd heard came from the mother.

Elisa closed her eyes against the rain and tried to marshal her thoughts. She had to figure a way out of this. She was a problem solver. The tree that pinned her was simply the biggest obstacle she'd had to tackle so far. Not to mention the heaviest.

She moved her legs just to feel the pain, to bring back some focus. It was becoming harder and harder to think. Hypothermia was taking over. With numb fingers, she dug the penlight into the soft dirt at her side, angled the bulb toward the old homestead building in the faint hope that someone might spot the dim glow.

This was ridiculous. She had hidden out here to trap her vandal, her Gremlin; not to get trapped herself. She couldn't die shivering in the mud, pinned under one of her own trees. Shoving the heels of her hands into the dirt, she pushed hard. A black wash of pain rolled through her, so strong that for a few seconds she thought it was an aftershock from the earthquake. After catching her breath, she tried again. This time a dark fog surged up from the agony in her leg to wrap around her head. Her vision dissolved into a swarm of buzzing gnats.

After nearly an hour of detours on back roads, Jake Street finally pulled his Land Rover into the parking lot of the Langston Green nursery. The property was pitch black. He drove slowly toward the remodeled farmhouse that served as the nursery's headquarters. He stared in surprise as his headlights illuminated the enormous root ball of a Douglas fir. The tree's equally massive trunk lay in the crevice it had plowed into the upper story of the building. From a nearby pole, a snapped power line swung in the wind, showering comet-tails of glowing sparks.

Switching on the overhead light, he quickly flipped through the property description attached to his clipboard and found what he was looking for. Gas. The place used natural gas for heat. Crap. He thumbed through the pages, scanning the information for the location of the shut-off valve. Offices downstairs, a one-bedroom apartment on top. Oh God. *Resident: Elisa Langston.* He knew she was the nursery manager, but she lived here, too? He hastily retrieved his all-in-one tool from the glove box, switched on his flashlight, and stuck one leg out into the rain.

His cell phone chirped. He impatiently shook it out of his pocket. "Street here."

"The 'copter's warming up at Boeing Field," the secretary told him. "Bill wants you with them to document damage and secure the sites. They could pick you up at three locations on the east side." She rattled them off.

He chose the closest one. "Hayward Playfield. I'll be there in an hour."

"Bill said thirty minutes."

"Tell Bill to go without me if he needs to. I've got to deal with a situation here first." He disconnected before she could object, pulled up the hood of his windbreaker, and ran toward the ruins of Langston Green.

The front door of the old house was locked. The gate in the wooden fence was also locked, but thankfully it was only six feet high and had no barbed wire on top. He managed to climb over it with little difficulty. No guard dogs rushed him from the darkness beyond the sidewalk. He found the gas meter by the back door and turned off the flow.

The door was unlatched. He stepped in. "Hello? Anyone here? Elisa?"

He made a quick sweep through the first floor. Offices, a small kitchen and bath. This story was not too badly wrecked by the tree, but the floor was littered with debris. Rainwater steadily dripped in through the huge hole punched in the ceiling.

He played his flashlight beam on the steep, rain-slick stairs that rose to the second story. The groaning of the downed tree against the house's splintered timbers was ominous. He gritted his teeth. Stable or not, he had no choice but to go up. He grabbed the railing and climbed the steps.

He knocked on the door at the top of the stairs. No answer. He pushed it open. "Elisa?"

The apartment was tiny. And ruined. The tree had taken out most of the roof. He had to crawl under the dripping limbs to shine his light into the kitchen. He quickly scrambled out, avoiding the ragged hole ripped into the floor, and headed for the bedroom. "Elisa?"

His flashlight illuminated the emptiness of the place. She lived alone, judging by the lack of male paraphernalia in the rooms. Her taste was uncluttered: no doodads littered the bookshelves or the dresser, but the bright quilt on the bed and the flamboyant art on the walls spoke of a passion for the exotic. Her open closet door revealed jeans, flannel shirts, boots, coats of varying weights. He measured a small jacket against his six-foot frame. Tiny and tough, that's how he remembered her.

Where was she? He looked out her bedroom window. The wind gusted and tree limbs scraped the walls behind him, reminding him that he needed to get out of here. The file said Langston Green covered sixty-five acres. His gaze roamed the fields to the south. Pitch black out there, except for a dim yellow ember of light in a far corner. What the heck was that?

A voice penetrated the cold fog that claimed her. "Elisa?"

She opened her eyes to the harsh glare of the moon shining directly into her eyes. But then, in a startling maneuver, it retreated upward, its light forming a smoky halo around a man's silhouette. It had been a flashlight, then. But who-?

The Gremlin! Her heart leapt into flight mode. Her fingers dug trenches in the dirt. The pepper spray she'd carried for just this moment lay out of reach somewhere near her right foot. She was a trembling bug on a pin, completely at his mercy.

~ END OF EXCERPT ~